the MAZE

the Maze

a novel by

Gavin Hill

RoseHeart Publishing

IMPRINT

This book is a work of fiction. Names, characters, places and incidents are either a product of the author's imagination or are used fictitiously. Any resemblance to actual events, locales, persona, living or dead, is entirely coincidental.

THE MAZE

All Rights Reserved © 2009 by Gavin Hill

Cover Design by CH Creations
Interior Layout and Design by CH Creations

No part of this book may be reproduced or transmitted in any form or by any means, electronic or mechanical, including photocopying, recording, or by information storage and retrieval system except by a reviewer who may quote brief passages in a review to be printed in a magazine or newspaper without written permission from the author.

Published June 2009

FireFly
FireFly is an imprint of RoseHeart Publishing
www.roseheartbooks.com

ISBN 10: 0-9822337-8-7
ISBN 13: 978-0-9822337-8-8

Printed in the United States of America

Dedication

I think that being able to write a book is one percent power of the author and ninety-nine percent power of God. So first of all, I would like to thank God for giving me the added power to write The Maze and her sister books. Of course, a book without a publisher is little more than row upon row of black on white. Let me then thank the good people at RHP for their faith and support. To Peter Gustafson, Sandra Andrén, June Ribbfors, Roy and Lena Mueller, without the five of you I would not be the person I am today. You have taken care of my problems, listened to me, loaned me money and cooked me meals in times of hunger. And last but not least, you, my number three. You who inspire me today as you inspired me back then. You who brighten my life and strengthen my goals, there is a candle in my heart that eternally burns for you. There is a piece of you in this book, much more of you in part three. You will always be my number three.

I would like to dedicate this book though, to my son, Mick. Mick, you are a constant reminder to me that God is with us. You have come so close to death two times in your short life and yet still, God has spared you. I dedicate this book to you, my son. God bless.

Chapter 1
The Awakening

Eric woke with a loud yawn, and rolled over to look at his 'Forgotten World' digital clock, last year's Christmas present from the Adams family. Strange, the way in which they sent something each and every year without fail; never forgetting a single Christmas, Easter or birthday. Strange because of who they were—strange. They were not exactly flavor of the month—far from it. Since moving to Barrymoor Avenue just four years ago, they had done nothing but complain.

The Baker's dog, Sam. "Yap, yap, yap, that wretched little crossbreed. One fine day I'll silence it for good!"

George Adams hated it, hated all dogs, hated anything in fact, that made a mess or a noise. That included children. Children … now that was the remarkable thing. George and Annie—Fanny, as the youngsters whispered behind her back—hated children. The times that either George "Gorgon" Adams or Annie "Fanny" Adams had shouted at, or complained about the amount of football being played in the street, about bad language or lack of respect for elders were uncountable. Time and time again all over those months, all those long months put together made up four, long, long, years.

Eric had heard it all and had been accused of it all. His favorite trick was to sit on the fence, the dreaded, Adams family fence. To sit and to pry barking sessions from Sam, that wretched little crossbreed on the other side of the street. How he loved it, that howling chorus and excited yap …and oh, but how the Adams family hated him for it. And yet, yet for some reason the presents always came in just like clockwork of the tick-tock mice. Go figure.

The 'Forgotten World' digital clock was a particular favorite. It fit in well next to the miniature Triceratops figure, the three-horned battle tank in a silent, motionless struggle to the death with the mighty Tyrannosaurus Rex. On the wall was the poster that said it all. His size chart. There were as many dinosaurs as the imagination could ever desire, all clumsily crossing an invisible plain. The huge Diplodocus with its tree trunk neck and solid, snaking tail. Ankylosaurus with its armored shell, Stegosaurus, Dimetrodon, Sphenacodon and many more. Up in the prehistoric skies of cloudy black-upon-shaded-red flew the Pteranodon, Rhamporhynchus and Archaeopteryx.

Eric was dinosaur crazy and that clock, that clock from a world far gone by, was something else. That clock was dearly prized—one of a kind—a reminder of a forgotten world. The time read 09:15.

He clamored out of the warmth of his single, white-framed bed, thrusting the blue-patterned-on-white duvet away from himself, reached for his slightly faded blue dressing gown, and wrapped it around his semi-conscious frame before stepping into a pair of tatty, threadbare slippers. Stumbling sleepily from his room, he threw open the door, it creaking loudly in the stillness and stepped out onto the landing, an icy cold nipping at his young bones.

The house seemed strangely quiet as he descended the stairway, the boards moving slightly at each touch of a step. As he hurried to the kitchen, to the warmth of his mother's Aga (cook stove), which always kept him warm first thing in the mornings, he noticed no warmth, but a bitter cold seeping under the old oaken door. The whole house echoed its silence, so empty, so void of life. His footsteps pattered like dried peas, falling pitter-patter onto a sheepskin drum.

He easily pushed on the door, easily swinging it open.

Eyes, sleepy and dusted with the blur of night, his feet scraped across the powdered-cork, linoleum floor to the Aga, to its cold bulk that only yesterday was a warm and welcoming sight.

Upon entering through the room, he thought back to yesterday. Back to his mother's cheerful smile as she handed him a cup of hot tea and a plate of his grandmother's homemade, chunky strawberry jam to fill his hungry belly. His mother's morning song; the sound of water filling the large rectangular ceramic sink, the familiar clatter of dirty dishes being washed and placed neatly on the draining surface seeped through his memories. He stood in silence, deep in thought. But where were his parents, and why no note to explain the obvious?

His next thought was only to the icy cold tearing into his tender skin. Moving toward the Aga, he picked up a small box of matches from the sideboard and built a fire with coal, a few woodsticks and yesterday's newspaper, which he found in the corner of the room. In no time at all the Aga's dusty interior breathed a sigh of life, like a sleeping dragon awakened by a knight in shining armor. A bellow of smoke; dark and curling. A spark, a crackle, a roar; the fire-breathing dragon preparing to fight the battle that dreams and heroes are made of. The Aga was alive, a bulky, iron, fire-breathing dragon. It pulsated life. It was life itself, each flame twisting around the other in plumes of orange and yellow, dancing across the pages until yesterday's headlines became lost in a dusty gray.

A warmth began to fill the room to the crackle of dry, brittle wood sticks, a warmth filling him with renewed life and vitality. The knight slain, the dragon resting calmly, warming his lonely cave.

Eric lifted the large and cumbersome, black kettle from its warm plate, filled it with water then put it back to boil. With a skip and a jump, he hurried over to the bread bin, reaching for the bread. It felt damp and warm in its red and white wrapper. Three slices would be sufficient. Once done, he placed them under the grill, covering each slice with butter and a thick layer of his grandmother's tasty strawberry jam. In his eyes, his grandmother made the best strawberry jam in the whole world, easily the best he'd ever tasted and besides, with all that love and care, not to mention years of experience that had gone into making it, how could it possibly not taste good?

When the tea was done, he sat down to eat. Sounds filled his head, those homey sounds that help one feel at ease. The drip, drip, drip of the old metallic tap with the faulty valve, the Aga, fresh from slaying the knight of the great mountain fortress, the maiden still in distress, still locked up in the cave of the ferocious dragon, hissing and crackling, throwing its heat around the room like whispers in the wind. Then the best sound, the best sound of all, the sound of crunching crusts between his pearly white teeth. Ever since he'd been old enough to chew, he'd taken the edges away from his toast and saved them for last.

The dragon hissed contentedly in much the same way as it had done every morning of Eric's young life. It was almost a companion, a close friend. Always there, always ready to warm the soul of a sleepy young boy. That dragon, that lime green, dusty, iron bulk. That dragon that Eric's parents had argued about so much in the past.

"Sometimes you're just so selfish," his mother had often ranted. "It's me who must stand here starting this thing up. Me, who must dirty myself before I can cook." And her husband, Mr. E. Wilson, Sr, well, he just wasn't the type to throw out a perfectly good Aga, a potential gold mine, he'd often replied. Who needs a cheap-looking gas cooker? Who needs one?

Once he'd eaten and had cleared away the dishes, Eric slowly stretched, releasing the night from his body. Tying his faded blue dressing gown tightly around himself, he opened the door, dashed up the stairs and into his room. He snatched his clothes from a mangled, twisted pile on the cream and soft blue rug next to his bed, his starchy blue jeans cold, clinging to his legs as he yanked them up. Next was his Hell Riders T-shirt, his prize possession ever since the day Suzie Perkins had said those magic words. "You look really cute with Hell Riders written across your back." Whether it had been said in jest or for real didn't really matter. That fact, as far as he was concerned, was that she'd said it at all. Anything Suzie Perkins said sent his heart aflutter.

The Maze   11

Suzie Perkins. The schoolboy dream, a sweet little thirteen-year-old. Golden hair, cornflower blue eyes and a smile displaying the best set of pearly whites that one might ever come across. And he knew her, had actually spoken to her, had even walked with her to an English class. She had even let him carry her books. Mind you, he was only eleven and a half back then. Still, that day was a milestone in his life, a day to remember and never to forget, a day he felt sure he would cherish for the rest of his life. Every boy at Redmond Secondary had, at one time or another, the hots for Suzie.

The times Eric had watched her on the playground, he'd dreamed of life, of Suzie as his leading lady. Life with her though, was nothing more than a pipe dream, a simple pipe dream.

He reached down for his blue and gray, striped sweatshirt, thrusting his arms down into the sleeves, raised it to his head and yanked it down around his ears until, finally, it rested neatly across his slim shoulders. Pulling on a pair of black cotton socks, he shoved his feet into a pair of scruffy, grass-stained sneakers and strode out of the room, not forgetting his black woollen cap.

Although it was mid-June, Eric had bad ears and always kept them covered first thing in the mornings. He closed the door firmly behind him, jumping down the stairs two steps at a time, tripping on an upward pointing nail head. The front door was unlocked and slightly ajar. He stopped, listening for signs of activity before swinging it open and stepping outside. He stood sharply, breathing in a strange, unknown smell. A smell that seemed to grip him by the nostrils, a smell he'd never smelled before. A cold, evil, empty odor lingering in the air as if ready to pounce.

Across the garden he strolled to the old shed where his father grew tomato plants.

"Dad? Dad, you there? Mum, where are you?"

No reply reached his ears. The sun hung low in the sky, seeming sad and tired of living. No birds were singing in the high oak trees lining the end hedgerow and no strong winds were whipping up from the sea. Just a stillness that almost hurt.

Chapter 2

Andrew Smears, The Discovery

Andrew Smears lived in a big house on the corner of East Street. He was tall and athletic, a Mr. Popular. School was over, the summer holidays just beginning. Another year completed, another lousy year. His grades had been good, good enough for his mother and father at least. For them Andrew was a golden boy and, indeed he was. He was an only child and his parents adored him. His life was set, all on the rosy. That boy would go far. And for those who thought differently, Mr. and Mrs. Smears were always there to set the record straight.

School … now school was something else. He liked it, of course he did, but he could live without it. He never really knew if school was a place of learning or a place for meeting one's friends. He never had problems with certain subjects, not like some. He wasn't a homework freak. He didn't sit studying for tests revising word for word. He just showed up for class, completed his test sheets, walked away and came up trumps. What a wonderful boy—polite and well-mannered. A little cock sure of himself maybe, yes. The girls loved him though, oh they did, much to his friend's disgust. Andrew this and Andrew that. Yes, this was a golden boy. Indeed, he was.

His parents had taken him with them to Bournemouth for a

two-week holiday by the sea. Every year, they took their vacation there. His parents to enjoy the warm summer air and a stroll along the promenade in the cool evening breezes whipped up from the sea. A chance to feel young again, a chance to forget the years, a chance to feel free, to relish the memories of eighteen years of marriage. Andrew, on the other hand, went more for the sea front amusements; pretty girls sprawled out, tanned and brown on the golden-yellow sands, discos and beer, a chance to live a little.

The car ride to Bournemouth had been a long one, three hours of, "oh I do like to be beside the seaside, oh I do like to be beside the sea... Father's, "who needs them!"

Three hours of hearing reasons as to why Bournemouth was such a wonderful place. The remembrance in which his parents met eighteen glorious years ago. The same old story told over a thousand times, if not more. Eyes meeting in the light of a ghostly moon, fatal attractions, instant love.

Bournemouth—home of romance. Quaint little holiday inns, restaurants, the picturesque Pier Theater, the gardens and those tame little squirrels. Their inquisitive little faces, the way in which they came up without fear to take nuts straight from the hand. Oh Bournemouth, glorious Bournemouth. Ah, those glory days.

On this visit, however, things seemed strangely different. The sun shone with a misty ray on a quiet, shapeless beach. Waves rolled slowly in against a level shoreline before turning and mixing with the gray of the deep. Andrew had noticed it, even if his mother and father were too busy reminiscing. As if they had passed through some kind of crazy time warp back to their very first encounter, back in time to when they first met in that shimmer of a cloudless sky. A time before commitment, before the birth of their son. Before. Andrew had noticed it.

The Smears family booked into The Sunshine Guest House, which sat on the West Cliff. They always used the same guest house and knew the proprietors very well. Andrew breezed up the narrow, concrete path, holding the main door open for his mother and father then headed into the reception area, ringing the bell on the old oaken counter. Within a short time, Mrs. Wallis entered the room. She was a rather plump little old lady with arthritis and varicose veins, as well as a permanent smile. It had been a long time since Andrew had set eyes on her—a year in fact. An autumn, a winter, a spring and part of a summer. He could well have thought the same thing each year.

This lady, this sweet little old lady with a heart of solid gold, lit a candle deep down inside of him. In his younger days, not more than fifteen years ago, that's about as far back as he could remember, she had always greeted him with a stick of rock candy from the sweet shop down by the pier, or give him a few pounds to do with as he pleased. In later years, she'd shake his hand and tell him of things to come. Parades, fun fairs, carnivals or shows, all things that might be useful to a youngster on holiday. Later still, up to the present day, she'd just quite simply greet him with a few polite words, tell him just how much she had missed him, ask him if he had any plans to stop growing. In general, she'd let him know that he was at home, home away from home.

One couldn't be sad when Mrs. Wallis was around, couldn't be unhappy, down or depressed. It just wasn't the done thing. Besides, the slightest glimpse of those warming, speckled gray-green eyes was enough to turn the saddest face into a glow of light.

"Hello, Mr. Smears," she greeted with more grin than a Cheshire cat. "Oh, it is nice to see you again," She shook hands with Mr. Smears first then his wife. "And Andrew. My word, you get taller every time I see you. If you're not careful you're going to hit your head on the ceiling soon. What do they feed you at home? Now I remember when you were so small..." She lowered the flat of her flaky dry hand to knee level. "Lovely hair, oh you did have. Lovely long locks." She laughed aloud, raising both hands joyfully to her mouth. "You'll always be my golden boy!" Andrew blushed a beetroot red; the corners of his mouth curling slightly toward a somewhat embarrassed smile.

"Would it be possible for the wife and I to have the same room as last year, Mrs. Wallis?" Mr. Smears asked, nodding toward his son. "Only it's so nice to be able to wake up and see the sea through the window."

Mrs. Wallis laughed once more. "Oh yes, of course you can. Wasn't it number nineteen you had, and seventeen for you, Andrew, I believe?"

Mr. Wallis strolled lazily into the reception. He looked different, his usual smile, that twinkle in his eyes, the one that always made Andrew like him so much. That Popeye look, the great seafaring man with the love of spinach and his beloved, Olive Oyl. That twinkle was gone, that cheer and razor-sharp tongue.

Mr. Smears smiled, making his usual greetings before handing over his car keys and letting him fetch the luggage. Andrew glanced around the reception area, perplexed by Mr. Wallis' attitude. So strange the way in which he had acted. No smile, no hearty, "hello." Nothing. Not even a nod of recognition. There was an ad on the counter and Andrew read its silently, bold, welcoming letters. It read:

For the time of your life come on down to Rylie's Bar
Opening Saturday, June 24th
Be there...

The Smears family paid up and collected their key cards before leaving for their rooms. The corridor had been re-papered, out with the old and in with the new. Replaced was that sickly lime shade that annoyed Andrew so in his irritating, early teens. That carpet with the ugly flower pattern. Gone, all gone, thank goodness, he thought. The corridor was now a rather tasteful red and cream, the ceiling artexted and fresh-looking; somewhat like a lashing of whipped cream up above them. An improvement, a vast improvement.

"Okay, son!" Andrew's father said with a certain youthful chirp in his voice. He handed him a key card, plus a ten-pound note, opening up his own door, letting his wife slip through. "Peace, son. That's what I need. Just me, your mum and peace." He raised his left index finger to his thin, pale lips. "How about you take yourself off and have a good time?"

Andrew smirked an acute sarcasm. He turned to face his own door; the seven broken, making seventeen look more like eleven.

"Kids," Mr. Smears retorted. "Be back by eight thirty, if you want supper."

Andrew listened as his father disappeared, locking the door behind him, then walked with a contented smile along the corridor to his own room.

An easy sigh left his parted lips. "Wait till I get down town, I'll show them girls a good time."

On entering his room, an unease filled Andrew's heart. Inside, the room felt cold and damp, unlike previous years. A sour, musty odor lingered in the air, clinging to the soft marbled carpet and the off-white wallpaper and rose-cream bedspread. A smell not that much unlike the nose twitching acrid odor of soured milk. It played on his senses, not just tickling them but drawing on them. His thin, neat, slightly crooked nose, the crook of a rather unfortunate accident on the rugby field two years ago, sniffed curiously, unable to define the odor for what it was. It wasn't really disgusting, not the sort of smell that might send one running for the nearest exit, but then again, it wasn't the most inviting of smells either.

Placing his bag down on the floor at the end of his bed, he took a look around. Mr. Wallis, who had taken their luggage up for them, had opened the large lattice window in a possible attempt at freshening the room up a little, although most definitely, to no avail.

"Shit!" he muttered beneath his breath, leaving his room and locking the door securely behind him.

The whole house seemed strangely different, he noticed. Something was missing, some very important addition to a holiday by the sea. Descending the stairway, his mind drifted back to previous visits, to meeting the Giles family in the corridor. Mr. Jack, I'm-just-so-bloody-perfect, Giles. His stuck up wife with her phoney accent. "Done this, done that. Been here, been there." Blah, blah, blah. Who cares?

Their daughter, on the other hand. What a pair of legs she had. They began at her petite little feet and carried on all the way up until reaching her bikini clad, tight little butt, a butt to die for and he would if Jack, the schmuck, or his snob wife, ever found out his intentions.

The Stevens family. Now there was a family. They too, like the Giles family and the Smears family, came back to The Sunshine Guest House every year. Mr. Stevens was a real nice guy. Had the fashion police seen him, though, they'd surely put him away for life. He always strolled around in his over-sized Bermuda shorts, his fat belly hanging over the edge, just waiting to roll away. He was white as a ghost, except of course, after a day on the beach. Then he'd come back with the same shade of pink as a cooked lobster. His evenings were spent sitting in the bar with his wife. He was loud, as was she. But they were a fun couple. This was the first visit in as long as Andrew could remember that he hadn't seen them, or at least, heard them.

That summer feeling he usually felt in his bones just wasn't there this time around. That feeling of being away from it all, two whole weeks of fun, of girls sunning themselves, young and fresh, lazing about on the soft warm sands. Drinking in various bars downtown, chasing a few memories. This year was different, no sparkle, no razzmatazz. The house so quiet, like Christmas without presents.

He strolled through the reception room, the counter little more than a lifeless form. A moment to think, to run things over in his mind, he left the building and stepped out onto the dreary street. A small but pleasant hotel sat on the next corner, a spacious bar in the basement, and he headed toward it. He followed the pavement, searching out those familiar green and red rays of the illuminated, 'Welcome' sign, and he listened for the chatter of people in the courtyard beer garden. However, he heard and saw nothing. No young people sitting on curb edges sipping at ice cool beers and bragging of new found loves. No cars passing by down at the T-junction. Nothing but an empty, eerie silence.

On turning the corner he stopped, his heart dropping like a stone. The beer garden stood empty except for the odd, half-filled beer tankard resting aimlessly on a few dusty white, plastic tabletops. The sign that had shone for as long as Andrew had been coming to Bournemouth, and probably many more years before that, did not shine into the night sky. Instead, it slept, a grubby welcome covered in dust.

He paused for a long moment, wondering if maybe it

would have been better to just stay at The Sunshine Guest House, maybe it would have been better to have just taken a beer in the bar. A shiver edged its way, icy cold for a split second, down the length of his spine. His mind ticked over, a softly thoughtful purr before answering a burning curiosity.

Taking a deep breath, he slowly stepped forward and padded inside. Upon entering, he observed many faces, dull, sad, pathetic faces, nothing but objects of silent gloom. The unnerving walk across to the mahogany-panelled bar felt like an eternity, each footstep hitting the floor boards like thunder claps in a midnight sky. Finally he was there. Politely he called across to a tall, gray-haired man who was standing behind the glasses and pumps.

"Pint'a bitter please, mate." Bitter, golden brown. Nectar of the gods, his father had always said. Poison, his mother had always added. There came no reply. Cautiously Andrew leaned forwards. "Excuse me."

Just then he heard a noise. His heart pounded louder than a steaming train rushing up to meet his pale, dry lips before falling once more like a brick out of time. A loud thud sounded somewhere in back of him, and he uneasily turned to see what it might be. His eyes lit on an extremely fat man in the corner of the room, throwing darts at a photo of Sir Winston Churchill. The fat man gazed over, meeting Andrew's uncertain look, almost swallowing it up like a hungry beast of prey. He held his last dart loosely in his right hand, an impression of a smile on his chubby, rough-shaven face.

"Wanna drink, boy?" His sudden words echoed off the bar room walls.

"Umm, yes. Yes, I do."

The fat man threw his last dart, hitting Sir Winston Churchill squarely on the nose, before marching across to the bar. Leaning over, he reached for a beer tankard, filled it and then handed it over to a very uncomfortable Andrew.

"Thanks," he managed to utter. "Thanks a lot."

The fat man stood a while, so silent and still, almost like a waxwork dummy, an emptiness in his dusty brown eyes. Seconds passed, could have been minutes. Felt like years, nothing said. Andrew felt the urge to turn and run, run back to The Sunshine Guest House, to climb those stairs, fall into his room and leave the world behind. Could it be that in time he'd wake up, in time this nightmare would end? Could it be that in time he'd open his eyes and find himself wrapped up tight and warm in his own bed on East Street? Oh, dear God, please.

The fat man raised a hand to his face, scratching the end of his large nibbed nose. "Si'down, boy, I don't bite."

Andrew wasn't so sure; a gut feeling burned him inside out. Cautiously, he followed the fat man and seated himself on a well-varnished, oak wall bench, his back resting against the soft green-papered wall and placed his beer on the table.

A handful of people sat around on chairs and stools. Each held a full tankard of beer and yet, none of them appeared to be drinking. Vacant eyes stared out across the bar room, cutting into and passing through objects as if they weren't there before carrying on toward infinity. The nightmare wasn't about to end, he knew. This time, this nightmare was a wild one. If Andrew was on East Street; wrapped up tight and warm in his own bed, if this was just a nightmare, then the pinching of his knee wasn't going to wake him up.

"Why did you come?" the fat man asked suddenly. "Why did you come? Who sent you?"

Andrew nervously pondered the question. What kind of question was that? What kind of answer should one give to a question like that? He played with those two lines in his head as if this were a game of chess, the most important game of chess in his life. Could this be checkmate? Was this the end of the game?

"Sent me? Well, nobody sent me, mate. No, see, I'm just here for the holiday. That's all."

The fat man stared long and hard into Andrew's beer tankard. He looked thoughtful, somewhat afraid, as if the weight of the world was resting on his strapping shoulders. "Not yet, maybe not, but they will. Just you mark my words, they will." He paused, dragging his head back as if something had lodged itself in his eye. No longer fear, nothing. He gazed, just gazed straight ahead. Lost and tormented, the same as his fellow non-drinkers.

Andrew felt the urge to taste his beer, to raise that tankard and take a good sip. It sat on the table, dark and inviting, just waiting to be drunk and yet, for some reason, he just couldn't. His lips were dry and in need of refreshment, his mouth tasting sour, like a dirty ashtray he might have said on a more suitable occasion. Still he couldn't bring himself to raise the tankard to taste that nectar of the gods.

The fat man made a rather strange face, leaned forward and raised both hands to his head, brushing dirty, heavily chewed fingernails through fast-thinning, wispy light brown hair. He sighed heavily then looked up once more. Slowly he pushed to his feet and headed for the door. Another stood up and then another, and one more. It wasn't long before every sad face was up and on foot.

The atmosphere was thick and intense, suffocating the room. The tall, gray-haired man left his post behind the glasses and pumps, and followed silently behind. Andrew just sat, too unnerved to move from his wall perch. Shivers charged up and down his spine, skipping an ice cold, devil dance all the way down his back.

Suddenly, it hit him like a brick in the face. That was it. People, or no people, as the case appeared to be. The Sunshine Guest House. Mr. Wallis. He hadn't said a word, had just fetched the luggage and proceeded up the stairs with it. Mrs. Wallis, so cheerful and yet, maybe a little too cheerful. The hand she had lowered when comparing to the childhood Andrew. A hand that looked flaky and dry, almost like death itself.

A mother, a father, himself and Mr. and Mrs. Wallis. That was it, there were no more. No extra noises sounding in adjacent rooms, no children in the corridor. No families entering or leaving the premises. Nothing.

Jack, I'm-just-so-bloody-perfect, Giles and that stuck up witch of a wife, the curse of society. Two misfits, whom without fail, managed to disrupt a good Smears family holiday. Their daughter, Maria, a ray of sunlight on the horizon. A reason for putting up with the rest of her family. They were always there during the last two weeks of June.

He jumped to his feet, lunging for the door, the group marching slowly, almost mechanically away in a funeral-like procession. They turned in single file down a side road and disappeared from sight. Andrew raised a shaky hand, steadily dragging it through a crop of short, spiky brown hair. He thought of his mother and father slacking off the years only minutes away. The tall, gray-haired man with eyes of steel. Those lost faces in a motionless bar room. The fat man with the strange questions. He wasn't the same as the others. He showed expression. Expression, yes that's what made him different. He showed expression. He *was* different. He spoke as if trying to give some kind of warning, as if trying to help in some unnatural kind of way. And yet, still he was one of them, one of that strange group. Seconds of normality then without apparent reason, he'd stood up and headed the procession. He, who had stood out from the others, the camouflage so convincing that even the wisest of men could have been fooled.

Andrew's parents were probably fine. After all, he had heard his father lock the door. A curiosity wandered in, an urge to know where these people were going. His head buzzed a crazy, unexplainable excitement, strange and unpredictable, an excitement that almost lifted him off the ground. Who were these people and where could they possibly be going in such a strange manner? He had to find out, just had to know. This would be a great one for the boys back home, worth a few laughs over a pint down at The Naiv's Tavern, not that his parents knew of his nights out.

He gathered courage, inhaled and exhaled through his nose, then set off at a safe distance. An intense loneliness filled his fast beating heart, a feeling of being hungry and yet, at the same time, of being full.

The group turned once more, heading up the weed-infested path to a shabby-looking, white-washed building. They moved blindly through the large open door space and up the stairway. Just then footsteps sounded behind him. Not a second to waste, he dived over a hedge, the divide to the next garden. Holding his breath in the still of the greenery, he noted another group stepping up the path and entering the building. Men, women and children, heads hung low, arms swinging limply at their sides. Then silence.

Andrew waited a short while, his head spinning in a frightening daze. His life passed him by. All those far-off distant memories rushing up to meet him. Bournemouth in years gone by. Last year, the warmth of a summer holiday by the sea. Getting up early, leaving his parents to wake up to a new day at their leisure. A trip down to The Horse & Plough for a fried special. Off to the beach full and contented, bathing trunks and towel in hand. Evenings spent sitting in bars, drinking and chatting to holiday girls.

He tried to wish it all back, wish back the good times. Times of safety, times of ease. Tried to wish away his present predicament. Wish it could leave him and return to the way things once were, but there it was. There like an angry tiger about to pounce. There, closing in on him, breathing daggers of icy steel down his back. He felt lost in his fearful confusion.

"Damn it," he whispered to himself. "Damn it and damn it again. Come on, get yer ass up."

After composing himself, he climbed back over the hedge and onto the path, edging his way into the building with a tiptoe, his heart thumping without mercy. Inside, the box hallway was damp and dirty. Mold clung to loose sheets of wallpaper that had at one time, at a guess, been a pale blue. A brutally frayed soaking-wet rug covered the rotted wooden floors.

On reaching the top stair to rest, he listened, chewing on his lower lip. There wasn't a sound. The room to his left was full of old potting tubs and a pile of copper tubing. The next room had at one time obviously been a bathroom. Old lead pipes poked out from moldy plasterboards, a rusty old bathtub rested in one corner, the remnants of a sink in the other. A sickly odor filled his nostrils, a stench of mold and mildew.

Checking each room in turn and finding nothing but the odd relic from the past resting on rotted wooden floors and in damp, unliveable corners, he began to wonder what it was that he was actually doing there, began to wonder if the people he'd seen and what had just happened, had just been some kind of wacky imagination trip.

There was one more room at the far end of the hallway and he moved toward it. The doorknob was old and rusty beyond belief, and it took a forcible effort to turn it. With a long awaited creak the knob turned and the door was free.

Andrew waited a moment, feeling the time had come. This had to be the room, even if the doorknob looked as if it had never been touched. The other upstairs rooms had all been checked, so this was it. He peered into the room through the split gap in the space, swore to himself, cursed his frayed nerves, and hurriedly pushed the door fully open before he lost his nerve. In an instant, it was cold—a bone-chilling bitter cold. He tried to pull his eyes away, but something held them at bay.

The room was empty, except for a broken rocking chair in the near, right-hand corner. Its left leg and rocker was smashed in two, one piece resting on a damp newspaper. A shiver tickled its way down Andrew's spine, tearing into him like sheets of jagged ice. He tugged on his T-shirt before stepping in.

The far wall beckoned and pulled at him. It was the same as any other wall in the derelict old building—dirty, moldy and damp. Strange though, this wall seemed to be staring back at him, watching him with dark, invisible eyes. This wall was almost alive. He tried again to pull himself away, to escape the glare of that room, to be free of all that he didn't understand.

"What the…? What the hell are you?" He felt himself being drawn closer by the second, transfixed by its demonical being.

A slight sound reached his ears. A faint, distant murmur of a child. It seemed to come from nowhere and yet at the same time, from everywhere, growing louder and louder, far off chuckles and playful giggles. Then came an added sound. The sound of little girls jumping rope, the slap, slap, slap of tender young feet avoiding the skipping rope's constant sweep. The familiar song that went along with such a school playground activity. He'd heard it before, a thousand times before, had even skipped to it as a child.

> *"Ring a round a rosy/a pocket full of posies,*
> *ashes, ashes/we all fall down."*

Around and around the song echoed in his head. Around and around and...

Suddenly he was there, a little snip of a lad in gray shorts, white shirt and emblemed blazer. There he was jumping the rope, up and down in time to its swing. Danny Baker held one end, little Mike "Fag Ash" Fletcher, the other. Mike Fletcher was a weak child, a child from Andrew's early school days. He had a serious illness and his body was so thin that he wasn't allowed to jump the rope for fear of him falling and hurting himself.

Andrew smiled, sitting back, remotely surprised to find himself no longer there with his friends. He was watching himself, was sitting back in a soft red velvet chair. A mighty screen ahead of him, a cinema screen, a projector ray behind him cutting through the darkness. He was a star. Slowly the memory of that day came into focus.

Yes, he remembered it all now. Must have been 1999. He was seven years old, just one week away from the summer holidays, almost time for another holiday in glorious Bournemouth and he had just survived an English lesson with the dreaded Mr. Cleeson. That's right, now it was all coming back.

Just then the rope bit. He broke out in a cold sweat, drops mounting across his brow.

"No!" he yelled. "No, go away. No!" It was too late. It was Joe Curuthers, the school bully. Andrew tried to fight it off, turning his head from the screen only to find the pictures moving in his head. He found himself screaming at the top of his angry, hateful voice. "Piss off, Curuthers, leave 'im alone! Curuthers!"

"Make me!" The rope stopped turning, thrown to the ground. "Make me, Smears, make me!"

"Fag Ash, you little creep!"

Suddenly Mike Fletcher was down, his head bleeding a crimson flow, forming thick, fast congealing pools on the ground. He was still. He was dead. Those tears of anger that swept Andrew's cheek gave way to roaring punches, Andrew's first ever, real fight.

"You killed 'im, you bastard! You killed 'im!"

Joe Curuthers went down under Andrew's weight. Fist after fist after fist rained down, the school bully cowering like a scolded child. Moments later, Andrew found himself lifted into the air, caught by the dreaded Cleeson grip. Such words as, "stop!" had meant nothing as he'd kicked and struggled to free himself. Finally calm, he'd faced the carnage around him before being dragged off.

Andrew ground his teeth, shaking uncontrollably, the horror of his childhood now fresh in his mind.

"No, no more!" he screamed, throwing himself up from his seat. The projector stopped, the cinema showing, over. A fierce wind whipped up, buffeting him to the ground, voices, screaming, and calling out his name.

"Andrew, Andrew, come to us."

"No, leave me alone!"

The cinema was gone.

He found himself back in the grime of the room, the voices twisting about him in blazes of fury. He struggled against a raging, unholy wind as he edged his way back toward the door. His body throbbed, pounded, felt as if it might explode into a billion fleshy particles at any moment. Those screams so close now, surrounding him, on him, within him with suffocating blows. He strained, forcing himself to go on, desperately willing some inner strength to rise up and defeat the devil within.

"Andrew! Andrew, come back, don't go!" It was Mike Fletcher, his faint cry, his whimper unmistakable, so weak and wasted. "Andrew, don't go, I need you! It's Curuthers, make him stop. Andrew!"

"You're dead! Leave me alone!"

At last he was there, fingers reaching awkwardly, grabbing for the doorframe to ease his way through. Silence. His head cleared, mind returning to a nerve-racked normality. His heartbeat, like life's train easing into the station of all things good, slowed down, relaxed and he eased himself up onto one knee, raising a nervous hand to his face.

The voices were gone, washed away in the wind. Peace at last, the nightmare was over. He stood and headed off like a thunderbolt down the corridor, gathering strength as he ran. Turning to face the stairway, a second to think, he stared down.

Suddenly the main door space was blotted out by a mass of

human rush. A group of nearly thirty people fell in, pushing their way up the stairway toward him. He turned to avoid the rush, falling hard against the stair boards, forced down by sheer human weight. Footsteps rained upon him, as they surged blindly up to the second floor. He let out a muffled cry, a murmur of severe pain, when foot after clumsy foot dug into his already badly battered frame. Head throbbing, he prayed for an end, prayed to die right there and then within the darkness of eyes, closed tightly.

The last foot dug its way over his petrified body and then he was alone once more. With a pained groan, he opened his eyes, tearful and red, and fell outside.

Something lay on the ground. Something curled in a human ball. A boy. His sweatshirt was grubby and torn at the sleeve and his starchy blue jeans were ripped at the left knee.

Andrew bent down shaking him slightly. "Come on, what are you doing here?"

The boy sobbed uncontrollably, tears riding down his dusty cheeks. "Mom," he whispered.

"She ain't here, kid. Look, don't cry Just don't cry, okay?"

The boy rubbed his eyes, drying a sore, tear-stained damp face. "We can talk later. You don't wanna be here. I'll help you find your mom, it'll be okay."

He took the boy by the hand, helped him up and headed off toward The Sunshine Guest House.

A cold and repulsive wind prowled each lonely street, nested an invisible second in tree or dusty porch space before taking off once more. The sky was the dullest, darkest gray with clouds swooning in masses, growing, swelling, roaring in the heavens above.

As soon as they reached The Sunshine Guest House, Andrew pulled the rather antique mahogany door open, letting his new-found friend pass through. The reception area was empty, void of life.

"Come on then," Andrew said softly, tugging lightly on the boy's sweatshirt. They climbed the stairway, continuing along the newly-decorated corridor and into Andrew's room.

"I only got here today, so I haven't even had time to un-

The Maze   27

pack yet, as you can see." He studied the boy, brushed him up and down from the expression on his dusty, bruised face to the untied laces of his scruffy, grass-stained sneakers. His eyes were tear-stained and bloodshot, washed in rainfalls of intense worry and fear. And yet they shone like two flickering candles in a Christmas window. "I'll just go fetch the ole lady. Won't be but a jif." Andrew left the room, leaving the boy to settle down.

He moved swiftly along the corridor to his parent's room, knocking firmly on the door.

"Mom, Dad, you in? Open up, it's important!" There came no reply.

Knocking one more time, he turned the leafy-patterned, knob-like handle, twisting it to gain access to the room. He pushed the door open and stepped inside. The room was empty, no sign of his parents, the bedspread not even creased. The large, fake crocodile skin suitcase, the Smears family, members of WWF, The World Wildlife Fund, didn't believe in killing any kind of animals for the sake of a case or flashy pair of shoes, was placed neatly in the far left hand corner next to a splendid old oak lamp stand, its tassels dangling a good two and a half inches in a circular parade. Glancing quickly about the room; eyes dusting the fine decor, he turned around then left for his own.

On entering, he noticed the boy holding a dirty old black cap in his equally dirty, right hand.

"Where d'ya get that from?"

The boy looked up, his eyes swelling like ocean tides. Tears danced gently down across his well-proportioned cheekbones, followed his jaw line then petered out, lost in the grime of the day. He looked so sad, so lost and distraught.

"My mom," he whimpered, choking on his words. "She made it for me."

Andrew searched his mind for something to say. "Okay, listen. Just relax." He knelt down before the boy, resting a gentle, comforting hand on his knee. "Just take it from the beginning."

The boy gazed down at the floor, dragging the cap through desperate fingers. He stared deep into its blackness, almost as if analyzing it for a biology project. Slowly he began.

"Well, I was in the old shed looking for my mom and dad and... And, well, I saw these people walking past the house. I, um, I followed them, then saw my dad. I saw him slap my mom across the face. I mean, really slap her, you know." He raised a hand, impersonating his father's anger. "He was shouting at her, really shouting. I've never seen 'im so angry."

Once again the boy's eyes clouded over, swelling up into transparent pools. "It didn't faze her. She just kept right on walking, like she didn't know 'im, like she didn't care. I thought they'd had a fight maybe, that's all."

Andrew listened; his mind focused one hundred percent. Ghostly tingles danced up and down his spine, shivers of fear taking him by the shoulders with dagger claws of ice. "Go on, I'm here."

"I was scared cause I thought he might hit me too, but I just wanted to know where they were going." Andrew raised to sit on the bed by the boy. "And, and then I followed them to this old house."

"Go on, you went to this old house. Take it slowly." The word, 'old house', burned itself into Andrew's very being, fearful unease dragging at his very soul.

"Dad saw me. He was really mad at me. He hit me, pushed me to the ground. Said he'd be back for me, then... Then, then I don't remember anymore."

Andrew jumped to his feet, hit by the sudden realization of the past few hours. He had desperately tried to block out the horror in his head; the young boy's words bringing them back with boiling, bubbling, burning fury.

"Oh, no. Mom, Dad, they're gone!" He lunged for the door, swinging it open and charged down the corridor. On turning to descend the stairway, he stopped, his mother traipsing up the steps toward him. Her shoulder length, drab brown hair hung loosely in all directions. She looked a mess. She passed him by, walking awkwardly toward her door.

Andrew easily swung himself around, raising both eyebrows with a slight shake of the head. "Mom, what's up?"

She quite simply hadn't noticed him, her own son, his call

going unheard. He frowned, brushing thin, well-looked after fingers wearily through his hair before climbing the stairway once more and hesitantly crossing the floor to her door.

Raising a trembling hand to the doorknob, he suddenly froze, a terrorized scream coming from inside. He shoved the door open, almost catapulting himself into the room.

"What happened? You okay?"

His mother was resting squarely on the bed; her confused mind noticeably a thousand miles away. She was wearing a thin white cardigan over a soft pink pinafore dress, typical summer wear for her. Andrew moved over to where she lay, crouched down and rested at her feet. She turned an empty gaze to stare at him, her face strained and gaunt.

"Where am I? What happened?"

Her loyal son rested both hands on her shaking, soft pink-coated knees, smiled weakly and comforted her a while before replying, "Bournemouth, Mom, we're in Bournemouth. Where's Dad?"

Her eyes flickered rapidly. She was afraid, searching without end the depths of her tormented mind. "I don't know," she mumbled. "We were walking down through the Lower Gardens, thought we'd go up to the Pavilion and buy some tickets for the show tonight, and then..." She stopped dead for what felt like a decade, bit on her lower lip, almost to the point of drawing blood, and sighed deeply. "I really don't know."

Andrew stood up with a loud groan, moving into the center of the room. His tongue slid smoothly across the serrated edges of his teeth. "What the hell's going on, Mom? I mean, come on. Jesus, I don't have a damn clue what you're talking about. I need some answers, help me out a little here."

Just then a figure entered the room. The young boy stood before them, a beam of light sliding across his thin, dirty face as it travelled through the window, silently dancing on his brow.

Mrs. Smears jumped, her body rigid with fear. She flung herself around her son, screaming fearfully. "Get out! Go, go, get out of here, get out!"

Andrew grabbed her firmly by the shoulders but comfortingly, holding her, feeling her loosen her grip. "Easy, Mom, what's got into you? He's a friend, a friend, okay?" He turned to the boy. "Come on, kid, come on in and sit down."

Mrs Smears faked a smile. "I'm sorry, what's your name?"

"Eric," came the reply.

Shakily, she looked about the room before heading slowly for the door. "I'm going to go and find your father. Stay here with Eric, I'll be back soon."

Andrew listened to the sound of her footsteps descending the stairway. Bewildered and uncertain, he sat in silence. Part of him screamed with rage. A part of him he might at one time in his life called pride. You can't let her go, can't just let her leave. Who the hell do you think you are? That part of him that was brave and strong, the born leader in him screamed the words through his head. The part of him that had, in the past, stood up and said, "We do it my way!" The part that had taken him to new heights back home had helped him to become the liked and well-respected person he was.

Yet there was another part to him. The child deep down inside, the uncertain, almost pathetic little boy, chanted incessantly. Mother's right, Mother's always right. Mother always knows best. You be good and do just as Mother says, and she'll reward you for being such a good little boy. Yes that was Mother.

Just then a sound, a muffled sound came from the reception area just under the bedroom.

"Jesus! What the hell was that?" His voice was severely harsh. "Stay here Eric, just stay here!"

He flung himself toward the door, threw it open and ran along the corridor until he reached the stairway. The silence was nearly deafening. He tiptoed down the staircase one step at a time, stopping with a sudden jolt, staring in disbelief at the gruesome sight ahead of him. His eyes were fixed, unable to move as a decapitated head rolled before him, the head of his mother.

Thick, fast congealing blood seeped from a torn neck into a beige carpet. Her mouth hung open, silently screaming her pain to the world, eyes bulging, blood red, staring straight at her son.

Chapter 3

Terror At The Campsite

Edward Davier had taken his scout group on a camping expedition to Dartmoor. The children; all aged between twelve and sixteen were laughing and singing all the way to the campsite. On arrival Davier climbed out of the driving seat, stepping out into the fresh summer air. The sun shone warmly, caressing his aging face. He moved away from the mini-bus, a rather dirty old, ex-postal rust bucket he'd managed to purchase cheap, and admired the view, inhaling deeply, filling his lungs with the smells of the country. Memories of past visits to the same spot, and there had been many, ran through his head. Years gone by, years of camping experience, of living with nature and of understanding its ways. Years gone by, those were good memories. It didn't need a camera to revive the beauty of all these things. Didn't need a photo to remind him of all those years, all that had been seen out on those moors. Returning was enough. Back to the wild, back to all those ways. He was home, he had returned.

After completing a trip down memory lane, he turned to look at the boys smiling and chatting in the back of the mini-bus.

"Okay lads, out you go. Come on, let's get those tents up," he called out with great excitement. The boys piled out of the mini-bus, a tangled twisted mass of kits and limbs. Poles and canvas were thrown out into the field and the boys proceeded with the task of setting them up. Clueless … bulls in a china shop, maniacs on the loose with the spoils of war. Children, always full of life, always out for fun. Tender youth left to run wild. Any training taught back home was quickly forgotten. Tent poles, inventions, new ideas. Lightweight silver sabers, a futuristic swordsman's trusty friend. Knights in shining, nuclear bomb and acid rain, protective armor, battling it out for the love of Princess Zania of the seventh moon of Kraiton. Canvas, perfect for rolling in, for hiding in, for generally messing about in. Perfect in fact for almost any boyish act. Turning into tents on the other hand, well, that was a different matter.

After much todo, Davier came over to lend a helping hand, as well as to calm the tent pole riot down. He'd already quite successfully set up the food tent and had started to prepare a meal. He tutted loudly, shaking his head with slight amusement before wading in and getting on with the job. He hadn't really expected a bed of roses on this particular camping trip. These children were special, not just average children. They were special and besides, even the best of children will be children until the day adult hood comes along.

Once they were all set up, the boys moved their belongings inside. Edward returned to the food tent to continue cooking for what seemed more like five thousand hungry mouths as each noisy second ticked on by. After a further half an hour, he beat on a large, black cast iron frying pan with a wooden spoon. It was time.

"Grub up, come and get it!"

The boys collected their knives, forks, spoons, mugs and plates before rushing over to the food tent. Each filled his mug with hot tea, adding milk and sugar if they wanted. Then they formed a line, a line that looked more like a rabble of drunks fighting to get to the bar at a sleazy down town strip joint. The line filed away, each child taking a healthy helping of baked beans, mashed potatoes and a big fat sausage. They sat down on the ground to eat, each making jokes about cold baked beans, lumpy mashed potatoes and burned sausages.

Davier's face shone a rosy red, a smile stretching from ear to ear. All ready he felt ten years younger, felt he really was home. His first ever camping trip had been ten years ago. His first ever camping trip as the scout leader, in preference to Edward Davier, the scout. He was a leader, and what a leader he was. The things he'd taught his children over the years—well, they just couldn't be counted. And those children, the first. The people they had become. Great things, businessmen and teachers. One had even become the lead singer of a very well-known rock band. Yes, those children, the people they had become, made him proud and he felt as if he were part of it. He'd shared in their youth, had been the one to help them out in times of need. He was a well-respected man, a leader.

Seven days. He was facing seven days. Seven days of baking potatoes on a late evening camp-fire. Seven days of living with nature, of seeing rabbits and deer camouflaged in the greenery about him. Seven days of hearing the morning bird chorus, of walking in the long grass. Seven days of heaven.

The sound of cheerful banter filled his ears, the scrape of cutlery on plates, slurping of tea along with many other boyish sounds. An after dinner song broke out:

> *"Baked beans, bad for your heart,*
> *the more you eat, the more you fart,*
> *the more you fart, the better you feel,*
> *so eat baked beans for every meal."*

"Okay boys, that's enough now. Tommy, David! Can you two wash and wipe up today?" A polite way of saying, 'you will clean up today' "The rest of you can go outside."

After dirty plates, mugs and eating utensils had been untidily stacked in one corner, the others charged off into the fields leaving Tommy and David to the task of cleaning up.

Tommy rushed for the cloth. "I'll dry, you wash!" he instructed.

David rolled up his shirt sleeves with a reluctant smile before reaching for the heavily-dented kettle. He raised it from its resting place on the calor gas stove and poured its contents into a rather stained, white plastic dish pan. Although they were twins, David was much quieter than his brother, preferring to avoid trouble.

Tommy was a wild one, big for his age. He had bullied David, almost from birth without mercy. On numerous occasions, he'd made David take the blame even though he was innocent, had made him look the fool, even though he was within the top two percent of his class. He had in fact, done everything to put him down, and all in the name of brotherly love.

Once everything had been cleared away, plates and cutlery gleaming in the beams of sunlight that twinkle-danced through the canvas door flaps, they left.

"Come on, follow me!" Tommy called back as he charged out into the next field. David trailed silently behind. Within a short while Tommy had spotted the others crouching down low in the greenery. They were staring out across waves of breeze-whipped yellowish-green to another group of tents scattered like canvas seeds across the far end of the next field. They crept up to their fellow scout companions, gliding stealthily through daisy and buttercup heads until they were no more than a stone's throw away. Suddenly Tommy jumped to his feet, waving outstretched hands into the air.

"Hi guys, what's happening?" he yelled as he dived into the group like a hungry tiger pouncing on its prey. Peter, the eldest in the group turned and grabbed him, one hand around his throat, the other across his mouth.

"Shut your mouth, why don't ya! What's the matter with you, you stupid little shit!" he growled in tight, toothy anger.

"Yeah, sure, Pete. Take it easy, okay? My God," a stunned Tommy answered. "What's happening anyway?"

David silently crept over, joining his group. He had the greatest respect for Peter. Their friendship went back a long way. Peter wasn't a bully. He was a sixteen-year old hard nut, damn he was. David had met him through a school friend and within a comparatively short time, they had become best of pals. It was just a shame Peter disliked Tommy so much, not that David could blame him really. Tommy had an intense need to be at the center of everything, had to be in the lime light. He just had to be in the center, had to at least try. Peter, however, *was* the lime light, at least for his young friends anyway. He was never pushy, convincing, but never really pushy. With age came respect, and he had both. Everybody on camp knew Tommy was treading on thin ice and Peter knew only too well that one day he'd have no choice but to do something about it.

Peter cleared his throat before motioning to the twins. "See those tents over there? Well, girls, need I say more?" Tommy beamed and chuckled into cupped hands.

Peter started again. "Listen up, right. See that old building over there to the left of the big bell tent? Well, that's the shower rooms." The others gazed, wide eyed ahead as two girls left the shabby red brick building, each holding a towel and a washing kit.

"Okay guys, let's go take a closer look. And Tommy, keep your mouth shut for a change, understand?"

Off they set, crawling through the long grass, cutting through its thickness, the blades falling away, leaving a trail. They soon reached a good vantage point behind a clump of bushes. The building rose from the ground no more than ten meters or so away like an angry, lava-spewing volcano. They were on the edge of no man's land. This was it, operation, 'check it out'. Yes, this was a plan that just had to work. The volcano had to be scaled, had to be capped, the future of mankind depended on it.

"Okay, David. You come with me. You others just wait here."

Peter and David pushed on toward their ultimate goal, their bodies hugging the ground. Peter's mind filled with thoughts of victory, he and his faithful side-kick. They were on a mission, a *secret* mission. They were spies in the Secret Service. And, this was it. Years of training completed. Now they were alone, alone against all odds. This was a matter of life and death, and both would come back as heroes. The building was on them, the mighty fortress walls stretching up high above them.

The boys sat behind their clump of bushes with their hearts beating furiously in their throats. Boyish excitement exploded from each and every face. Peter was almost there, standing on David's shoulders. Fingers lunged upwards, clasping and gripping at the rusty guttering. One last heave and he was up and on the roof. He took a quick second to scan his surroundings then reached down for David's hand. Hands touched, gripped and held on. Up, up and away, the rocket leaving Planet Earth, distant, alien civilizations just waiting to be discovered. Stars and comets passing by, black holes and far off galaxies. Space suits on, ray guns at the ready, the spaceship landing on Planet Neacon. Down, down, down. Thump, boosters off, 'a successful landing, sir.' "Thank you lieutenant!" They had made it, they were there.

Peter beamed proudly before edging his way across to the sky light, David in tow. It was quite small and covered in the dust of years gone by, although one could nearly see inside. The group waited with cheerful, silent smiles. Peter and David were there, had landed and were ready to investigate. They had completed the first part of their mission. Now it was time to move on to phase two.

While the boys explored, Edward Davier lay on his sleeping bag, the door flaps of his one-man ridge tent riding in a light summer breeze. A beautiful, swallowtail butterfly fluttered within canvas confinement, its dainty wings like angels of God. He studied it curiously, wondering what it might be like to be able to take off and leave the pollution of mankind's doing behind. He was thinking, and spent many an hour questioning the meaning of life. Not that he had a quarrel with it—he just possessed a mind that screamed out for information.

In his youth he had been somewhat the quiet type, preferring to avoid the hustle and bustle of everyday life. His fondest memories were of his many fishing trips with his father, God rest his soul.

His other great passion had been the scouts. He was born to be a scout, fast to learn and eager to please. His first job, after leaving school had been as a gardener at Bell Mead Manor. He held a vast knowledge of plant and bird species, and somewhat like a computer, could give the Latin name as well as a detailed description of almost any living thing. Not just the perfect scout, but thought himself to be the perfect scout leader as well. And indeed he was.

While Davier slept, the mission proceeded as planned. The boys looked on as Peter and David's waiting drew to a close. Three young girls strolled over, entering the building, hot and sweaty after a day in the summer sun. The two boys gazed down as tight denim jeans and training shorts were peeled off, as T-shirts fell to the rustic red stone tiled floor. Peter's eyes grew wide with excitement, bras and panties coming away to reveal soft bodies of virginal silk.

"Oh boy," he whispered, hardly able to contain himself. David never said a word. He was stunned, amazed, at a loss for words. He'd never seen anything like this before. It wasn't really his scene. Being there felt good, looking down felt good. That buzz it gave felt good, too, but still something felt wrong. Maybe it was the way in which Peter had chosen him, as if he were trying to get at Tommy. Maybe it was the adrenaline rush tearing through his bones. No. More than likely it was just wrong. He felt like a pervert, felt lower than low. A dirty dog, a nobody. A part of him wanted to jump down to run back to Davier, to leave it all behind, to get away. Yet all the same, that feeling felt good. Females, three beautiful females, naked and blind to his sight.

The girls moved in toward the rusty shower pipes, turning them on, a crystal cascade falling transparent rain drops over pure, tender clear skin, following each curve of their well-shaped breasts. Down past smooth, tantalizing thighs and onward, ever onward to teenage, ivory feet.

Peter licked his lips lustfully, leaning forward for a better view just as one of the girls, a breath-taking fifteen or sixteen year old blonde beauty with a much more alluring figure than the others, swung her head back to pour shampoo over her long wavy mane. She screamed when she caught a glimpse of somebody looming above her.

"There's someone up there!" she screamed, running for her clothes and throwing them back on. She speedily left the building just ahead of her two young female companions. The two peeping Toms' scrambled across to the roof edge, jumping down into the tall grass.

Their cover was blown. There must have been a mole in

the system, and now they were alone on Neacon, the Neacon army closing in on them. Every network was out to get them. They had to get away, just had to, the very future of Planet Earth depended on it. Mission aborted, mission aborted...

Like lightning bolts, they fled up the field along with their fellow, potential Secret Service agents, closely followed by a rather fat old lady, Sergeant Nait of the 'Neacon Android Task Force', shouting at the top of her voice, "Yes run, you better run, you little perverts. If I catch you, you'll be in for it!"

Peter and his merry band of ruffians ran on ahead provokingly toying with her. She soon stopped, too old and too fat to keep up with their teenage spirits. On arrival at their own campsite they all fell on the ground in fits of laughter.

"All right, boys?" Davier called out from inside his tent.

"Yes sir, we've just been out in the fields," Peter replied loudly. "Yeah, just doin' us a bit'a bird spottin'," he whispered under his breath. A slight, boyish chuckle filled the air, followed by a curious chatter.

The time was ten minutes past eight, the evening in full swing. Since arriving at the campsite laden with canvases and poles, rucksacks full of clothing and boxes of food little more than six hours before, so much had happened and if the last six hours were anything to go by, then the next seven days were bound to be seven days to remember.

"Fifteen minutes, boys, then you can come and find me," Davier called across to them as he left his tent and headed off into a sloping bed of brackens. After much searching he found himself an adequate spot, a rough area surrounded on two sides by a one and a half foot high ridge of granite rock. A forest stood proudly by, canopies of greens and browns no more than three hundred feet in the other direction. This was it, this was the place.

He set about the task of building a well-sized, but easily controllable fire, placing neat bundles of sticks in an upright position, and then covering his skeleton-like structure with an assortment of dried brackens and ferns. Once done, he marched briskly back to the food tent, returning a few minutes later with a small sack of potatoes and a large, brown cardboard box. He took out a cigarette lighter from inside the box, lighting the structure with a crackle, it was an old pink, disposable lighter, used but one week of the year. He was not a smoker and didn't believe in burning money only to pave the way to an early coffin.

Flames grew in size, angry and ferocious, tearing across the brackens, relentlessly twisting over lengths of dry, brittle branch, biting away at its interior until dying down into a glowing mass. He wrapped twelve large potatoes in tin foil then tossed them down into the campfire heat.

Within a short time, Davier and his scout group were sitting around a campfire, the evening sun sinking into the horizon, lighting up the clouds like peach candy floss. The boys chatted amongst themselves about all manner of subjects, hearts young and alive, full of excitement and wild thoughts of days to come. Edward gazed up into a fast darkening sky, twilight fading into a dusty black.

"When I was your ages," he began as he cleared his throat in his usual, 'okay, stop what you're doing and pay attention', manner. "When I was your ages, all I ever wanted was the chance to take a holiday in the country. It's just so nice to be able to sit on fresh grass and watch the sun go down." He reached for a long, thin twig and poked at the glowing cinders, rolling each potato in turn. "My parents were poor people, much too poor to be able to afford to take my sister and myself on holiday. Of course, I was brought up in the city during the great depression. You really don't know how lucky you are. Boy, youth is wasted on the young."

Peter quietly sniggered to himself, knowing that the dreaded Davier speech was over. This was an Edward Davier special. He gave the same speech every year, give or take a sentence or two. Maybe it was just his way of playing the father figure. Man of the world, been there, done that, seen it, know all about it. You're all very safe with me. Maybe he was just a silly old fool, forgetting his conversational chit-chat from year to year. It didn't really matter, nobody ever listened.

Once the potatoes were done, their jackets a crisp golden brown under the charred foil, he gave one to each of the boys along with a paper plate, a plastic knife and fork and a red serviette. Then he handed around a family-sized tub of margarine. Crickets sounded in the shrubbery, the odd hoot of an owl searching out a tasty meal. Within the group childish chatter danced on a cool, fresh breeze. Silly jokes and ghost stories, songs and laughter filled Davier with a warmth of the heart, a feeling that tingled contentment from the top of his fast-balding head to the bottom of his size ten feet.

As time drove on, young heads growing sleepy, the boys stood up a few at a time, made their excuses and retired to warm sleeping bags until Davier was alone, a solitary figure under a starry night sky. He smiled to himself, happy in the knowledge that although he had never fulfilled his childhood dream, a holiday in the country, just his mother, his father, his sister and himself, he had in fact shown his young group the benefits of getting away from the city.

The children of his group were special children, very special children. They all had problems of one kind or another. Be it a problem making friends or quite simply, problems getting on in life. He, a practising Christian, believed with all his heart that with a little friendly persuasion or appetizer they could be given that little push in life. All they needed was that little knock, the one that might help them along their merry little way.

Peter had been in the group the longest, following on six previous visits. He was a youngster with a determined attitude and an awful lot of excess energy. He had a certain way of getting his point across, a certain way of getting his friends to see things his way, to do as he said, and not always for the best. He came from a rather rough background, his father leaving him with his alcoholic mother when he was just a child. A time in his little life when he needed a father the most. Unfortunately, in later years this had been his downfall. The local police knew his name very well and had taken him home on numerous occasions after finding him drunk or worse still, high on substances unknown. The lads in the group, on the other hand, loved him. He was fun to be with, always had a trick up his sleeve, always had a smile. It was just a shame that at sixteen years of age he'd seen so much hardship, hardship that in many ways had scarred him for life. Edward Davier had on numerous occasions been forced to take him aside, had been forced to sit him down with a firm hand. And oh, how difficult he had found it saying the things that had needed to be said. Peter was a child, just a child, a child who screamed out for attention. A child who screamed out for the love of a father he never really knew. Screamed out for the love of a mother who couldn't stop her selfish, un-motherly ways and get down to the serious business of straightening herself out. How hard it had been to turn and tell that child he had to stop or risk being forced to leave the group. Nevertheless, he had done it.

Only once had he used such words as, "to leave" the group—only once. Two years ago, as a fourteen year old camping at Dartmoor under his supervision, Edward found Peter alone one evening in his tent stoned out of his mind.

It was a heart-breaking time, a time of deep concern. Edward had told that child that very evening, had told him that this was the final straw. He'd said it and had meant it, meant it then. In time, he'd thought things through, had changed his mind. That was it, the one warning. There were to be no more.

Peter was clean now, said so at least. Said it was all behind him and, maybe it was. Maybe it was all behind him back on those dirty London streets, or maybe it was back there awaiting his return. When out camping with Davier and the rest of the group, he was clean anyways. When attending the scout group meetings, he was clean. What happened on those streets afterwards was sadly, very sadly, his affair.

Well, there were to be no hearing of police cars, no busy engine roars, no getting into trouble after school and no hanging around on street corners. This week, just one week in fifty-two, would be spent living with nature, following the various tracks and trails of Dartmoor, listening to the song of the breeze chanting its way through the trees and wild grasses. This week would be one week to remember. He kicked dust over the glowing hot cinders, then left for his own tent.

Peter and David crawled into their sleeping bags, turning their flashlights onto Tommy's empty sack.

"I wonder where Tommy is," David yawned.

"Who cares?"

"He hardly spoke all evening. I think you hurt his feelings a bit today, Peter."

Peter sniggered, lying back and making himself comfortable. "Yeah, well he's just too bloody much sometimes. Any how, you should try standin' up for yourself once in a while. You let him get away with murder. I'm buggered if I would!"

David sighed, brushing a hand through a crop of short, dark hair. "What d'ya think'll happen about them girls?"

"What about 'em?"

"Well, you know!"

Now Peter was sighing, he was bored. The worst game ever invented was, without fail, the 'guessing game' and this, this was it. "What about the bloody girls, Dave? Don't worry 'bout it. We ain't got caught yet, now have we? And we copped us a good eye full, didn't we? Now go ta sleep." He switched off his flashlight, placing it down by his side.

"Dave, turn yours off now, okay? He'll be back when he's done sulkin'."

"Yeah, well I think I'll leave the door undone anyway. That'll be all right, won't it?"

"Anything, Dave, any bloody thing. Just let me get to bloody sleep!" His words were long and drawn, each syllable flying like the venom of an angry serpent. Now he was mad, how easy it was to start him up.

David didn't say anything else, experience told him it was better to just let Peter fall into the land of dreams without further interruptions. He, however, couldn't sleep, not straight away at least, his mind elsewhere. Two fields away elsewhere, in fact. What a day, what a fantastic, even if a bit weird, day. Tired, his eyes slowly closed, body resting. Sweet thoughts of camp-fire chit-chat and pretty girls in shower changing rooms filling his head.

Morning came to the shrill cry of a rooster from the nearby farmhouse. Everybody began to roll over in their sleeping bags, looking somewhat like butterflies fighting to free themselves of multi-colored cocoons, yawning and stretching, thinking of the new day ahead.

"He never came back last night," David groaned wearily. "Unless he got up real early this morning."

Peter jumped up, climbing into his jeans and slinging on a sweatshirt. Once David was dressed and Peter had slipped into his, reasonably new sneakers, they headed for the scoutmaster's tent.

Just then two lads charged past shouting at the tops of their voices.

"Mr. Davier, Steven and Paul. They're gone!"

With a loud yawn, Davier climbed out of his tent, rubbing his sleepy, gray-speckled green eyes. Strands of fast graying hair stood at awkward angles like tinsel town streamers exploding from his head. He glanced at his watch, sniffing loudly.

"It's twenty-to-six, twenty minutes to six o'clock in the morning. Why are you all up so early?"

"Mr. Davier, Steven and Paul are gone. They're missing, they're missing."

What did you say?" he mumbled, pulling his jacket tightly around his thin, although quite muscular, frame.

"Sir, they're gone, Steven and Paul. They were in our tent last night and now they're gone. We've looked everywhere."

Peter awaited his chance to speak, staring deep and hard into the scoutmaster's eyes. Davier tutted loudly, raising a hand to his face and gliding it firmly across his left cheek in a twisting motion, bringing it down past a neat, well-pointed nose and finally over thin dry, thirsty lips.

"You boys'll be the death of me!"

David moved forward, nervously stumbling over his words. "Sir, um, well... It's just that..."

"Tommy's gone too, sir," Peter cut in boldly, stepping in for his friend.

There was a moment's silence as Davier assessed this new problem. For a split second his mind drifted back to previous years, previous mishaps, previous solutions. Each and every year, something new, some new dilemma, a new course of action. There was the time three years ago when two of the boys decided to go on up to the farmhouse and throw stones at the chickens, two chickens and one prize rooster had died of fright that day. The year before a dead mouse, minus its head and tail, had been neatly placed in another boy's sleeping bag, to last year when a youngster had set fire to the food tent after playing with a box of matches. Luckily it wasn't a serious fire. The tricks that had been pulled, the games that had been played, the stories that had been told. Was this now a game, another boyish prank?

"Okay, Peter," he began. "Can you, David and Jason go off into the next field and take a good look? John, Darren and Mike, you three can take the top field, but don't go too close to the farmhouse. Jamie and Brad, follow me."

The three groups split up, Jamie and Brad waiting a good five minutes whilst Davier dressed himself properly.

The ground was damp with an early morning dew. The odd cotton wool clouds, fluffy and white floated in a summer blue sky. Davier set off across the field, Jamie and Brad in tow.

"Never five minutes," he complained. "All I do for you boys and this is how you pay me back. If this is just another hoax, there will be no trip to Exmouth today."

There was no sign of the missing boys and the Davier search party split up, the scoutmaster heading off toward a grassy hill, Jamie and Brad trying the next field. Peter had his own suspicions, marching off into the long grass.

"Little bastard," he swore half aloud.

"Who?" David asked curiously.

"Your brother. We all know where he is."

"No, we don't."

"Well, makes sense, don't it? He's down at the girls tents, ain't he?"

David didn't reply, just turned his head toward Jason, shrugging his shoulders.

On seeing the girls' tents, they crouched down low. A little canvas ghost town. Not a sign of life. The girls were asleep and Tommy was no where to be seen. David smiled to himself, almost happy in the knowledge that Peter had been so wrong. Tommy could be stupid, very stupid. But not that stupid. No sir, not that stupid at all. John, Darren and Mike sat down. They were bored; an hour-long search had gotten them nowhere.

The Maze   45

"I'm hungry," Mike growled.

"You're always hungry," Darren cut in. "Hungry cause you're so bloody fat and slobbery."

"Pack it in, now," John demanded. "Why don't you just leave 'im alone?"

"Make me."

"It doesn't matter, John. I'll just tell Davier when I see him."

"Yeah, sounds like you, fat boy. You dirty little snitch."

"I'm warning you, Darren, shut your mouth."

Suddenly Darren was up and on foot. He flew at John like a stray bullet, sending him back on the damp, grassy earth. Two bodies rolled and tumbled, two pairs of fists clashed with painful blows as Mike screamed for them to stop.

Davier made it back to the campsite. He hadn't had any luck at all. He entered the food tent and began to prepare a meal. Slowly, the other boys filtered back. Jamie and Brad were first, they had had no luck either. Then Peter, David and Jason and after a good fifteen minutes, Mike.

He bent down, hands resting on his knees, panting like a thirsty dog. Two minutes later Darren and John arrived, Darren a good few steps behind. The youngsters chatted among themselves like a gabble of geese after an unwelcome visit by 'Freddie Fox.' Neither Darren nor John looked too worse for wear and it wasn't long before they were happily gabbling with the other geese.

"Listen up," Davier cut in. "Has anybody seen them?" The replies were all negative. "Okay, then. Peter, can you help me out here? I've started breakfast, so really all that needs to be done, is the serving. Can you do that for me?"

"Sure, no problem."

"I mean it though, Peter, I'm trusting you. Don't waste that trust."

"Trust me," Peter beamed as if butter wouldn't melt in his mouth.

"Where are you going?" Jason asked Davier.

"To the farm house. They might be there. I won't be long. The rest of you get washed up, and no goofing off while I'm gone." He strolled across to the door flaps, pulling them apart then turned, eyes sternly cutting into Peter. "Remember now, Peter. Trust is an acquired thing. Now you have it, don't throw it away." With that he left, pacing up a dew-coated track, leading into the upper field.

Peter glanced over at his friends and making the most of his new found authority, said in a loud voice, " Okay, you heard the man, now get your dirty selves cleaned up. Then get your asses back here, ASAP."

The boys galloped over to their tents, a mighty herd of wildebeest fleeing Peter, the hungry lion. The fleeing wasn't over, the herd separating, gathering in small groups on white canvas plains. Then, like flashes of lightning, they moved on once more—towels, flannels, toothbrushes and toothpastes, soaps and clean changes of clothing in hand. Joyfully they entered the rather small, totally inadequate washing facility, which basically consisted of seven upright poles, six canvas sides and several buckets of near-freezing water.

"How come we don't get real showers like the girls?" one asked, receiving a swift slap on the back of the head.

"Shut up, Mike, you stupid, fat sod. We aren't supposed to know." John didn't say a word; his glare was enough to put the cork in Darren's vindictive mouth.

Peter set about the task of finishing the breakfasts, whistling some old tune while setting everything out neatly on serving trays. He felt good, as if he had the edge. This was his intended position in life, being in charge and boy, what a good feeling it was. After fifteen or so minutes, seven reasonably clean and presentable boys stepped out to a breath of bacon and eggs. Once washing kits had been carelessly thrown onto respective sleeping bags, they charged off to eat, each collecting their particular plates, mugs, and cutlery before forming a rabble-like queue. Peter stood behind a large serving table, two deep saucepans, a frying pan and a large black, rectangular tray of toast in front of him. He wore an over-sized white apron and in his best, fine English countryman's accent, said, "One slice of toast or two, kind sir?"

David smiled. "Two please, one egg, a small spoonful of

your wonderfully burned baked beans and... " He paused to gaze down on a pile of black and charred bacon lying half cremated at the bottom of the pan. "And um, no bacon, thank you." Then he took his breakfast and sat down to eat.

Peter pulled in his chest, breathing in exaggeratingly through the nose. A rather impressive impersonation of Edward Davier. "You really don't know how lucky you are, boy. My mother and father couldn't afford to buy food for my sister and myself. We had to live on bubble and squeak, you know, the old cabbage and potato dish, but never once did we complain."

"Come on, mate, I'm starving here." Jason giggled, tapping his fingers on the table.

"Very well, sir." The tent filled with laughter, all topics of conversation.

A fresh morning breeze brushed through the loose, canvas door flaps, whisking a pungent manure odor into the throng. The sky outside was a pale blue. Birds flew in its heavenly arms, swooping down on unsuspecting insects. A blue and green, tinted red and purple dragonfly hovered above the boys' heads, oblivious to the attention it was receiving.

"Look!" Mike said loudly, amazed by the flying creature's gracious beauty. "Wow, just look at those colors." He eased himself up, leaving his breakfast. "My dad says they carry the souls of the dead."

"Your dad's a jobless bum." Darren hated Mike. There wasn't a reason for it, he just did. "What does he know about life? He can't even get one."

With that he jumped up, swatting the dragonfly. It fell silently to the ground, landing on its back. Its legs twitched slightly, reaching for life. The almost fluorescent flying machine finally grounded for good, its life force fading, an out of order soul carrier. It was still. It was dead.

"You bastard!" Mike swore softly, although with a certain decisive anger the others had never heard escape him before, as he gazed down at the dead dragonfly. "You bastard, you stupid bastard!" His face was red, his eyes suddenly dark with vengeance. For the first time in his life, he was angry, out of control.

Without warning he flung himself sideways, a forceful

shove sending Darren hurtling to the ground. Nobody said a word, least of all Darren. The sleeping, once thought to be a non-existent volcano, had erupted then and there for all to see. Years of victimization bottled up inside. Now, the flip of the coin, the turning of the worm. No longer the victim, he was the victor. He sat astride his tormentor, raising a fist in the air, holding it without motion. Darren pleaded under his cowardly breath. The bullying battleship was sunk.

"I could do it, y'know, I really could! I could kill you now, you bully." He held his breath a split second, scrunching his face up like a discarded paper bag. A split second, a glimpse into the past. Years of being the stupid fat kid on the block, years of being the butt of cruel, back-stabbing jokes. When there had been a fool to be made or an evil, bitter, twisted story to be told, Darren had always been there. Always been ready to take the glory and ride off victorious, leaving the broken remains of his victim.

Actions speak louder than words, and Darren was a coward. Words for him were actions. Words for him were power.

"Mike, get off 'im now, okay?" Peter said with a certain cheer. "You've proven your point, now get the hell off."

Peter looked somewhat contented, his day complete. The sight of Darren weak and defenseless under Mike's impressive weight. Not that he particularly liked Mike. Darren was right to a point, Mike was fat. Stupid, too. No, it was quite simply the idea of seeing Darren on the ground. Darren was Peter's competition, the only person within the group, except maybe for John, who in the past had stood a chance of making him feel less than the man he thought he was. His only real threat was laying under Mike, the fat kid. How perfect, how truly perfect.

Just then Davier arrived. He pulled the door flaps wide apart, sun beams avalanching in. Mike jumped up, standing back and leaving Darren to lift himself from the ground.

"What's going on?" the scoutmaster demanded suspiciously, not that he wouldn't have asked anyway. Everything was back to normal, children happily eating and chatting among themselves. Edward made a mental note of this; he was too old and far too wise to be fooled by such goings on. There's nothing

The Maze

wrong with being suspicious. Nothing at all, especially concerning his scout group.

He glanced across the tent's interior to Peter holding a plate of bacon and eggs.

"Now, I've been up to the farmhouse and, so far it all sounds very negative. You can all go out into the fields, I'll clear up here then I'll contact the police. When you're done, just leave your things on the serving table, and don't go getting into trouble out there." He smiled, almost unwillingly and moved across to the serving table, eyes catching a dark mass, the charred remains of once-lean rashers of bacon.

The serious business of eating was over, finished long ago, somewhere between a near brawl and the sudden if not, inevitable, Davier entrance. The group almost simultaneously stood up and filed outside.

"Wait up a minute," Peter yelled back at the others as he ran on ahead. "Just gonna get some other clothes on."

Davier poked his head out. "Say thank you to Peter for me." As Peter stepped out onto a thick green, buttercup spangled field, a chorus met his ears.

"Hip, hip hooray. Hip, hip hooray. Hip, hip hooray." Peter blushed a beetroot red. "And one more for luck. Hip, hip hooray." They cheered eagerly, slapping him on the back, their heads full of summer spirits.

The group moved on. Final destination: there could only be one. The way had already been carved during the pilgrim march, the day before.

"Pete! How about a ghost story later on?" Brad asked as he kicked the head away from a buttercup.

"Yeah, maybe. First things first though, okay?" Peter replied masterfully. "And Brad…"

"Yeah?"

"Don't call me, Pete."

In no time they were there, the mighty male hunting ground. Blocks of white on shades of greens and yellows, like a summery pattern on a giant's patchwork quilt.

At that moment a figure stepped out from an extremely large bell tent, presumably the main tent, the food tent and meeting point. Its guidelines were being used as makeshift washing lines, sweatshirts and socks blowing in the soft-scented air, tickling the daisy heads below.

"Jesus. They must've called the cops. Come on; let's get the hell out of here. And we ain't never seen them bloody tents, got it?"

Silently they headed back to their own campsite, nervous and a little afraid of what their scoutmaster might do if the police were to show up. The afternoon dragged on by, the boys sitting, talking in whispers among themselves. The sun shone warmly against a pale blue sky, gently travelling its east-to-west course. Peter cleared his throat, pulling out a piece of chewing gum, unwrapping it and placing it in his mouth with a tooty fruity chew.

"Listen up, I've been thinking, yeah, and..." He paused, waiting for Davier to leave the food tent. Then once he thought it safe to carry on, he did so. "...I don't think them pigs were after us, see? I mean, if they were, they'd be here by now, right? So let's go back later and check it out. What dya say?"

The boys stared at one another, each pondering over his words, although deep down inside, Peter knew there was only one right answer, and it would be the answer he wanted to hear. Reluctantly, all the boys agreed. It was well known that once Peter had made up his mind about something, eventually, be it sooner or later, he would always get his own way. And this was no exception.

The sun disappeared behind a fast-swelling rain cloud, growing darker by the minute. Suddenly the air grew much colder. A strong wind whipped up, twisting easily across the campsite. "Shit! Looks like rain, come on." They followed Peter into the food tent, in through its canvas flaps and out of the wind. They seated themselves, getting comfortable for the duration.

"How about a story now, then?"

"Yeah, all right, just give me a minute to think."

At that moment, Davier re-entered the tent. He looked different, not so greatly the whole world would've noticed, but he did appear different. He stared aimlessly toward the boys, that familiar glint in his eyes all gone.

"Shit. What's up with 'im?" John mumbled.

"Why don't you ask 'im?"

The group sat in virtual silence, Davier a stranger before them. He was no longer that good old, Edward Davier. No longer the tower of strength, the mountain, the father figure. No longer was he the great scout leader of which they'd all looked up to. Something was wrong. Something more than the worry of three missing children. This wasn't worry, this was blatant disregard. His eyes told a sad story. He looked pale and broken, looked as if he'd given up on life and was no longer prepared to bother. The leader was gone, replaced by a pathetic excuse for a human being.

After a good five minutes of nothing but silence, he turned and left once more. The boys waited until he was out of ear shot before verbally questioning their, once great leader's strange manner.

"He's lost it. Loco, friggin' loco," Darren chuckled, shaking his head slightly.

"It's not funny, prick," Peter cut in. He stood up and paced across to the serving table, propping himself up against it. He was speechless, for the first time in sixteen, nearly seventeen years of age, he was at a lose for words. He raised a hand to his chin and proceeded to rub it thoughtfully, as if it was his source of inspiration. "Come on, let's get out of here."

Outside, a cool wind brushed their faces. The sky was wet and gray, clouds full, ready to burst a summer downpour. The group waded out across the field, blades of green-like waves on a stormy sea, momentarily laying flat then rising, stretching for the heavens above.

Just then two figures came into view, heads bobbing over ridges of stormy, ocean green. Two immensely beautiful figures. Two girls, their hair riding high in the oncoming storm, cut in toward the all-male group until they were on them.

"Hi," Peter said nervously, a sudden recognition of one of the girls, her long blond locks flowing out, honey and gold behind her. Only this time she was wearing clothes, this time she wasn't under a shower cascade.

"Have you seen an old lady? She's quite fat with long salt and pepper hair, tied back in a sort of bun."

The boys looked at each other with a certain false innocence before replying. "No. No, we ain't seen nobody. Why?"

Slowly, a few at a time, more girls came cutting through the grass toward them until there were nine in all.

"Don't I recognize you?" Peter blushed while he waited for an answer. Sure she did, he kept telling himself.

"No, I don't think so," she denied. "I know I'm famous, but this is ridiculous."

Feeling uneasy, he turned his head briefly to look at his friends, almost as if silently pleading for help.

"Famous! I don't know about famous, infamous more like, you little pervert," she swore. "You're one of those peeping toms, the kind that climbs onto shower room roofs for cheap thrills."

"What? What did you say?" he growled convincingly enough. "Who the hell dya think you are then? You don't even know me, do ya? And here you are coming down on me like shit bricks for no reason. Hell, I ain't gotta listen to this bull anyway." He turned sharply, preparing to walk away.

"No, wait," the blond said softly. "Look, if it wasn't you then it wasn't you. It's just that we had some prowlers trying to get free peeps at us in the showers, that's all."

Peter smiled triumphantly at his companions before swinging himself around once more. "Oh, it's okay." He introduced himself and his group, trying his best to change the subject.

"My name's Sandy," the blond beamed, returning conversation.

"This is Lisa, Maria, Suzanne, Caron, Amanda. This is Jane, over there's Linda and last but not least, this is Sarah."

"Who's the ole gal, then?" Peter asked curiously.

They seated themselves among thick beds of buttercups and daisies, and Sandy explained the goings on of late.

"Well, this morning when we woke up, our matron was gone, two other girls as well. Anyway, we waited a couple of hours, then I went up to the farmhouse and called the police. They were here this morning."

A whisper carried on male tongues before fading without too many noticeable smiles. "Shit! Wow, that's weird. We had some boys go AWOL last night. Where are the pigs now?"

The girls moved in, their full attentions drawn to the topic of conversation. "The pigs, as you so nicely put it, are in the forest, I think."

It was suggested and agreed upon that they should take a stroll across the fields and see if they couldn't find out a little more. Suzanne walked behind, tugging lightly on Sandy's arm.

"Sandy," she said under her breath. "It was him, wasn't it? You know, the peeper, right?"

Sandy giggled, her cheeks a scarlet glow. "Umm, but he's cute, don't you think?"

The short walk gave both groups, male and female, perfect opportunities to get to know one another better, and it wasn't long before they stood before a mighty, age-old forest. Thick canopies of greens and browns swayed in the breeze above their heads. Beneath traipsing feet lichens grew, brackens and ragweeds fighting in twisted tangles, stretching high, reaching for light. Just then a voice sounded behind them, wiring its way through the greenery.

"Leave this to me," Peter said bravely, stepping forwards. "Hello, sir," he began. "I, um, I'm looking for the chief."

The policeman laughed, his cheeks rosier than an August sunset. "Well, I'm in charge here but as you can see, I'm no Indian chief." A half-hearted chuckle travelled within the group. "Now what seems to be the problem here, boy?" His voice sounded suddenly different, harsh, aggressive even.

Peter hesitated before going on. "Well, we're looking for somebody."

The policeman glared into the group, eyes tearing into them like torch beams in the night. He appeared angry, unjustly angry. "This is on a need to know basis and you don't need to know. Now run along before somebody comes looking for you."

"Yeah, well, see ya around, I guess."

The boys rushed toward open space, their young spirits bruised and uncertain. A slight drizzle dampened their brows, cool and fresh, clouds thickening, a dusty gray over head.

"Listen, girls, there ain't much we can do here, know what I mean? And we ain't gonna do nothin', so why don't you follow us back to our pad. It's okay, you're safe with us."

Hesitantly they agreed, following closely behind. On arrival at the campsite, a chill, stark reality steamed toward them. White canvas, poles and guide ropes against a dreary darken gray. Rain drops began to fall, swelling in size. Emptiness, loneliness and dismal gloom surrounded them, closing in around them like moving walls. A stale odor drifted silently across the land, tingling their nostrils, turning courage into nervous unease.

"Mr. Davier, you here?" John called out. There came no reply. "Oh well, let's wait in the food tent." He led the way, marching in out of the rapidly worsening weather.

Sandy twitched her pretty, freckled nose. "What's that terrible smell?"

Jason paced slowly around the tent's interior, raising his nose into the air and breathing in deeply. "Umm, fine bouquet, well bodied. Spring sixty-seven, I do believe. Definitely North Slope. Ah, it's Davier's old socks."

He burst into fits of laughter, rolling around like a courtyard jester, frolicking in the full glory of his own stupidity. Peter set about explaining for the benefit of his female company who Edward Davier was, as well as telling them about their missing three comrades, all gone, just vanished into the night. The rain fell in sheets outside, pounding down on the tent, gushing down its sides in torrents. A wind whistled over the campsite, shaking the makeshift building without mercy.

"That policeman was real weird," Linda complained and shivered. "He looked so strange and what did he mean by, before somebody comes looking for you?"

Peter smiled, feeling a story coming on. He was a great storyteller and in the past had never failed to terrify his male companions—even to the point of giving some of them nightmares. He possessed an imagination matched by no other as well as a certain way of using it to his best advantage. The boys in the group loved his tales of doom and of dread, and it was without doubt those tales told around the campfire and in darkened tents would be remembered with great fondness until their dying days.

Edward Davier on the other hand, had always found them to be quite disturbing. He had in the past brushed them aside, taking them with a pinch of salt. But still he had questioned himself. He knew Peter was a wizard at storytelling, storytelling based purely on death, and death in the most obscured manner possible. Death at the hands of axe wielding maniacs, death at the hands of blood thirsty creatures from the deepest pits of hell. Always death. The boy lived for it, loved it, bathed in it. He was obsessed by it and how could it possibly be healthy? In time he would probably find something else to amuse people with. After all, a child needs imagination, without imagination, what would a child be? As long as these fantasies remained fantasies, as playful bouts of imagination, as a gift used solely for the purpose of entertainment, Edward felt no need for deep concern.

On the other hand, it was quite possible that Peter possessed psychopathic tendencies, that one day he just might turn into one of those creatures from his imagination. One day he might well turn imagination into vicious reality, and with dire consequences.

"Forest demons," Peter blurted out. "That's what it was, Linda. Forest demons."

Linda flicked her sandy blond-haired head, somewhat startled by such a remark. "Excuse me?"

The co-ed group moved together, a magic in the air, a story preparing its entrance.

"It's only what I've heard. The story goes something like this." He slipped an arm around Sandy's slim waist, awaiting a response. Slowly her azure blue eyes rose, a smile of affection appearing on her pale face. The corners of her well-filled lips twittered upward ever so slightly then a hand, soft and supple slipped into his. She tossed back her long blond mane, resting her head against his shoulders with a contented sigh.

"A thousand years ago there were many tribes living in this area. It's said they lived in peace, they lived off the land. They grew crops and hunted wild game in the surrounding forests. Anyway, one morning a young boy left the village in search of wild strawberries, a large wicker basket in hand. His head was full of child-like dreams and the sun shone warmly on 'im."

Peter had the group enthralled, no amount of rain or thunder could drag their minds away. The scene was set, the master was at work.

"After a while he found his bounty, an area full of wild strawberries. He knelt down, picking handfuls at a time. Never before had he seen so many in one spot. For every one he placed in the basket, he placed five in his mouth and of course, he soon became quite full. Now, being just a child, no more than ten or eleven, he soon became curious and headed off into the forest, leaving his basket behind. Something pulled him, call it curiosity or call it fate, but something showed him the way and soon, he was quite lost. Now, feeling very alone and afraid, he pushed on blindly through the trees until coming to a huge, rocky plain. At that point he felt something, something dark and sinister. Invisible eyes cut into him from all sides and he froze in fear. For three days and three nights he was lost and alone and although he never knew how he made it back to the village, he found himself back home. The villagers ran to his aid, helping him into a hut. They tried to get him to talk, but he was speechless, his eyes all but jumping out of their sockets. His mother tried everything, but all to no avail."

"What's this got to do with the policeman?" Linda asked joyfully.

Peter brushed a hand through his hair, mildly irritated. "I'm getting there, okay? Jesus."

Once again the group settled themselves, tuts and stares of disapproval making their way to Linda's stare.

"In time the boy did manage to speak, uttering strange words at first and then, full sentences. He spoke of death and of the evil of the forest demons. The villagers, now naturally concerned, headed off out into the forest in search of the devilish, huge, rocky plain. They, too, felt the eyes of death on them, but seeing as they were a peaceful people and had only ever come across other peaceful peoples, they knew nothing of fear."

"Can I just say something?" Linda interrupted once more. "It's just that if the tribes were peaceful and never knew of fear, how come the boy frightened them enough to get them to go out and find this plain thing?"

A chorus of jeers and angry comments met her words, and she was made to promise that her mouth would remain closed until the end of the tale. Realizing she was alone, that her friends were not about to side with her, she reluctantly did just that.

"The sun began to lower in the sky, night time stepping forward. Something moved, something from deep in the forest moved toward them. At that point they met fear square on, and with that fear they felt something they'd never felt before— anger and rage.

A tribesman jumped out of the tribal gathering, lunging himself at the creature, half-man, half-beast. He killed it with his bare hands, tearing its heart out and casting it aside. The tribesmen now realized that that night would be a battle to the death as yet another creature screamed toward them only to be slain and thrown, gushing blood to the earth. It's said that just before the sun vanished behind the horizon, a mountain of bodies had grown and the tribesmen had to climb that mountain of bodies in order to place another body onto its bloody, torn pinnacle."

Peter studied the gathering. Seventeen pairs of eyes, bright and intense, stared back at him. Stars stood out in the near darkness. A streak of lightning crossed the sky, adding to his final assault. He had them just where he wanted them. Even Linda sat in silence, her mind drifting into a crazy world of fantasy. He lowered his voice, each word slowly pounding out cold steel.

"Then darkness, the hell of night had come, only the full moon as their light. Suddenly there came an almighty scream, the crack of trees falling away. The body mountain shook, each creature coming back to life. The forest demons took their revenge.

"Out of the forest grew a monster more hideous than a hundred nightmares. It was Tyrua, Lord of all forest demons. He raised his mighty army, tearing each tribesman limb from limb. It was a blood bath and by morning, the rocky plain was painted red. There was a tall oak tree, the tallest oak tree you might ever see, its thick solid trunk growing through a massive boulder. The only remains of the battle the night before, each branch growing through a dripping, blood-soaked head. A head for each tribesman killed in battle."

Groans left gaping mouths, the boys seizing their chances to comfort the nearest female.

"Now to this very day, so I've heard, those heads still hang. The blood never stops flowing and the forest demons still search for a victim to slay. The plain, thick with the rotten, although never congealing blood of the dead, is still used by the forest demons whenever a kill is made, and the policeman. Well, the policeman is just another unfortunate soul who has seen the plain of the forest demons."

Suddenly he let out an ear piercing scream, falling forward and out of Sandy's grip. Into the group he plunged, bringing pounding heartbeats to near standstills. Once the group had calmed themselves down, short bursts of laughter filled the air.

"I wonder where Davier is?" Mike said half-heartedly.

Darren winked at Sarah who sat to his left, convinced that she was his. "Who cares, I couldn't give a damn where he is."

"I do," Peter jumped in. "'Cause I'm bloody starving. And there ain't no way I'm cooking for you lot." He paused, thinking of his stomach, hearing it rumble inside. "Tell ya what, if he ain't back in twenty minutes, it's a free-for-all in the food box."

A fork of lightning flashed, lighting up the whole tent as it tore across a hateful sky, hitting the earth like a bullet. A clash of thunder roared, echoed. The initial boom sounding more like that of a bomb going off. Sandy flung her arms around Peter's neck, holding him tightly as yet another thunder clash roared in the heavens, screaming fury, the wrath of hell.

"Why is it that you sound so common when you talk to people, yet not when you tell stories? When you tell stories, you always sound so affluent," she commented, nibbling on his left ear lobe.

"Don't know" he replied cheekily. "Ain't never thought about it before. Guess it's just me, the second me, if ya get my drift."

Brad sat snuggled up next to Suzanne, a bright smile on his face, a song erupting for Sandy's benefit. "Maybe it's because I'm a Londoner that I love London town. Get it? He's a Londoner."

"Okay, I get the message, Brad," she smirked somewhat

The Maze   59

sarcastically. "Don't you have a radio or something? It would be nice if we had some music to take our minds off the weather."

Mike stood up, smiling at Caron who was sitting on one of Davier's discarded jackets. Could this be his lucky break? The weather so bad, so frightening to a teenage princess? Surely she'd need a little comfort soon.

"I got one in my tent, won't be a jiffy." He unzipped the canvas door flaps and charged out into the rain, his shoes squelching in the mud.

"Now tell me," Sandy playfully asked, "were you or were you not one of the peeping toms on the shower room roof?"

Peter took a moment to think things through, feeling the eyes of his fellow scout friends burning a laser hole in his forehead. "Well," he replied with a certain innocence. "You gotta promise me one thing though, right?" He flicked his head back, staring deeply into her azure blue eyes, placing his hands firmly in between his legs for protection. "You gotta promise me that you ain't gonna get me in the meat and veggies, okay?"

"Tell me, Peter."

"Promise me?"

"Okay."

"Right then, I was one of 'em. There, I've said it. Satisfied?" He fell from her grip, down into the gabble of male chorus. "But you promised. You promised, you did."

Conversations started up and ended, fun tales of past memories.

"Can't you tell another story?" Amanda asked politely.

"I know, why don't you tell one, Jamie?"

"Okay, okay. It was one late September night," he began, his stony voice lowering to a gruff bark. "Two lovers were driving down a lonely lane, the rain pouring, windshield wipers slapping back and forth. They had but ten more miles to go until they'd be home. Just then the car ground to a halt, the gas gauge showed empty. Well, they sat there wondering what to do next." He twisted his head sharply, narrowing his eyes, sending shivers down young spines. "I know, I'll go find a gas station, the boyfriend said, getting out of the car. And so it was done, the girl locking all four doors behind him. She waited there alone, her boyfriend disappearing down the lane and out of view."

Lisa slipped an arm around David, nuzzling him with her cheek.

"Suddenly she heard a noise," Jamie went on. "There. She saw something, something moving behind the hedge. A man staring out from the bushes with a gray, wet face." Jamie paused for effect for one long moment, scanning the young gathering.

"Well, who was it?" Maria asked excitedly, an arm resting on Jason's shoulder.

"I don't know," he replied. "She never told me." The whole group sighed.

"Boring," one said.

"That could've been good," said another, "if there'd been a different ending."

"Where's Mike with that radio? He's been gone bloody ages. I guess I better go find out what the dickhead's up to," Brad groaned, reaching for a white plastic bag and placing it neatly over his head. "I'll see if I can't find some matches for the stove, too, while I'm out there." He left, the pounding rain pinging on his white plastic bag rain cap.

"You wanna match?" Peter sniggered quietly to break the silence. "Your face, my ass."

Suddenly Sandy froze, a muffled scream coming from outside.

"Don't worry. It's only that prick pissing about out there. Pack it in, Brad. Stupid ass. Grow up."

His yell was half-extinguished under the next hellbound thunder clap. Just then a hand pulled the canvas door flaps apart, a policeman pushed himself half-way in. His beady eyes studied the group like Sherlock Holmes searching for clues. His lips were straight and tight, his clothes soaking wet, water dripping from the tip of his rather large, bulbous nose.

"I've got something for you," he said loudly. "Have you lost it?"

"Lost what, sir?" Peter asked politely, standing up and moving across to him.

"This!" the policeman shouted at the top of his voice as he pulled a carving knife out from behind his back, his eyes burn-

The Maze

61

ing like molten lava pools. He raised his hands high into the air, plunging the blade deep into Peter's head. There was a crunch as blade hit bone; blood spraying everywhere, Peter's lifeless body falling, slumped to the ground.

The mad man kicked the unrecognizable corpse into the air, lunging the blade at anything that moved. There was no exit, no way out as screaming, blood-stained bodies crawled for the entrance, each being hacked down as they tried to pass, the eyes of a rabid dog looming down on them. The blade swung this way, then that, slicing and carving its way through the carnage. The man spun around, still holding the knife, and stomped through the flaps, standing outside, the rain diluting the blood on his face. He raised the knife one more time before plunging it deep into his own heart. His arms fell loosely to his sides. He stood still a second, staggered and fell solidly to the ground, the puddles turning red. The thunder raged one more time and the storm was done.

Chapter 4
Andrew's Secret

Andrew slowly opened his eyes, his mind in an unholy daze. Could he just be in the midst of a terrible dream? He could hear a voice, soft and gentle, warm and caressing. The words: "Andrew? Andrew, can you hear me?" slowly became reality as he awoke from a long, deep sleep. A nurse was standing over him, the blurry blue and white of her uniform barely recognizable against the constant, almost drunken swirl of everything about her. Her warm and friendly gaze, not that Andrew in his state was able to focus on it, brushed over his badly battered body and deep down inside, she came close to shedding a tear for the boy before her.

He found himself lying in a steel-framed hospital bed. He ached, ached without end and yet, for some strange reason, the pain in his left leg intensified and then stopped dead just short of the knee. Dim memories entered his confused head then faded before definite pictures could form. Around and around and around and... He eventually remembered his young friend, Eric, then later still, his mother. Suddenly his head exploded, stomach sank, cruel thoughts torturing his agonized brain.

"Mom, Mom where are you?" he groaned within the nightmare of his dejected bewilderment. His eyes flowed and overflowed, tears cascading down his bruised cheeks. "Mom, what happened? Where's Dad?"

The nurse hurried off to fetch the doctor who marched over, looking long and hard at the broken soul before him. Andrew, a soul that at one time had the will to live, at one time had a life of fun and happiness. Now this sad, lost and pathetic creature, destroyed by an unknown past, torn to the ground, was reduced to no more than a frightened, nervous wreck. The nurse held his arm as the doctor sedated him.

"He's delirious, nurse. He doesn't know a thing, he'll sleep now."

With that, Andrew drifted back into the world of sleep. He entered into a semi-conscious state and drifted back into darkness again many times during the next several weeks. His comatose state lasted for three weeks and two days, only for him to wake up to a biting agony tearing through him without remorse.

"Nurse! Nurse, help me!" he cried out and within moments, the nurse was by his side.

"It's all right, Andrew. The doctor's coming," she whispered, a certain warmth in her voice. She stroked his damp, cold forehead, softly brushing a finger reassuringly down his cheek.

The doctor arrived, prodding him lightly in the upper and lower abdomen. He gave him painkillers then waited before leaning over him and saying in a soft voice, "Andrew, Andrew, can you hear me?"

Andrew painfully nodded his head. "Yeah, I hear you," he mumbled with considerable effort.

The doctor paused a moment before going on. "Andrew, how are you feeling? Are you in a lot of pain?"

"I ache," he croaked, throat dry and parched. "Some parts of me really burn, like I'm on fire."

The doctor stopped dead in his tracks. Maybe it was too soon to tell him the awful truth. "I have some tapes and a Walkman in my office. I thought I might put them by your bed and when you're feeling a little better, you can just tell the nurse and she'll hand them to you. Don't try reaching for them yourself. I want you to move as little as possible. You just rest now, and remember what I said about not moving." With that he strolled away, leaving the nurse to tend to her, still very sick patient as he once again fell into a sleepy world.

He slept almost constantly for the next four days before waking up on the morning of the fifth to see the doctor standing over him.

"Good morning, Andrew. How are you feeling today?"

Andrew smiled weakly, his body less painful, yet still something deep down inside worried him, tugged at his nerves without end, without mercy.

"I feel a little better today, thanks, doc, but my head is killing me and I just can't move. Don't seem to have the strength anymore."

The doctor breathed in loudly through his nose, gliding his tongue awkwardly across his lower lip then pulled the covers up around Andrew's shoulders.

"Andrew, now that you're feeling a little better, I think it's time for us to have a little chat." He paused, searching for the right words.

"I'm ready, doc, don't keep me in suspense, okay?"

The doctor cleared his throat, a strained expression on his Asian features.

"All right then." He paused thoughtfully, determined the course of his words and began. "You've been here under my supervision for just over four weeks now during which time you've made an excellent recovery."

His dark, glimmering eyes were soft and caressing, temporarily easing the fear in Andrew's heart like the lapping waves of a turning tide. "Andrew, I'm afraid you've lost your leg at the left knee."

Andrew inhaled deeply, unable to speak or even register those last devastating words. They charged through his mind time and time again, throbbing just as much as the bandaged stump.

"Oh boy," he managed to spit out, after quite some time, tears mounting his long black lashes. "Well, if it don't rain, it pours."

The dark, peaceful eyes of the doctor gazed down caringly on a figure tormented by words of dread. A youth with a once-hopeful future in mind, a future that had suddenly, aided by just one sentence, been totally destroyed.

How should he now explain to such a sad young soul of not only the loss of his family, but also to alert him to the constant dangers of the outside world?

"My mom, is she really dead?" Andrew asked quietly, his whisper barely audible.

The doctor had accepted, a long time ago, that part of his job was to tell of bereavement, but on this particular occasion it was not only that but more. "Yes, she is, son."

Andrew closed his tear-laden, blood-shot eyes, dragging a firm hand across his cheeks that were now sore and stained by a near constant, salty flow. He thought of how suddenly life could change, how one minute life could be a curious challenge, the next, a living hell.

"That's not all I'm afraid," the doctor went on. "Many things have changed during the past four weeks." He seated himself on the bed, a large, dark-skinned hand resting on his patient's right arm. "Andrew, I know this must be difficult for you to take in, but please try. Next week you'll be moved to a safe house on the other side of town where you'll be able to recover fully. When you're better, you'll be moved out into the country. Everything'll be fine, I promise you."

"What are you talking about?" he asked solemnly. "What happened to me?"

The doctor scrunched up his face, searching in desperation for words of applicability. He stuttered, throwing out a jumble of words until finally getting it right.

"It, um. Well, it's not what happened to you. It's just what happened. You see, some very strange things have been going on of late. Time's are changing, Andrew. The Second Coming, many believe. Andrew, do you believe in God? In life after death?"

"Yeah, I guess. Why?"

"Because in the good book, it tells of how God will one day intervene in human affairs, end the existing world order and open a new age. I'm not really a Christian. I do believe in something, I guess you could call it God." Andrew listened, although as whether he really heard anything … well, that was a different matter. "Thousands of people have disappeared without a trace, hundreds have died in strange accidents, been killed for no reason."

He grew quiet, looking down at his knees as if praying for inspiration.

"Andrew," he began once more. "Andrew, I really wish I could explain things better to you. I'm just a doctor; it's all I ever wanted to be." Tear drops glistened a lonely dance behind his chestnut eyes, welling up inside. He gently stood up and left the room.

Andrew laid in his bed, somehow the doctor's words making sense. He shuddered at the thought of his leg. How was he supposed to get from place to place? A desperate despair washed over him, a feeling of wanting to get up out of his bed and yet at the same time, feeling afraid to try. His mind ticked over, the cogs of time on re-runs. Those early school days. A boy who had no end of friends. A boy who at the tender age of ten had taken home the Silver Seal, a silver-engraved cup of which was awarded to the boy or girl with the highest amount of merits for one term. He'd taken it six times in all, a record never beaten. The last school dance, Jennifer Ayre, his date for the evening. Jennifer, so tall and athletic yet so petite and adorable. Every boy at his school had envied him that evening, had looked on goggle-eyed as Andrew and his dream date, everybody's dream date, had danced the night away. His part-time job at Reagan's Clothes. He was a great salesperson; his boss had even invited him to dinner with his family.

Then there was Bournemouth, that changing face. Fond memories of past visits. The last visit, how cold that feeling was within his heart, a holiday gone wrong.

The doctor's words, how they played on his mind. If there were a God, a creator, then why would he destroy it all? Andrew had been to church as a child, not that many times, he admitted, but he had been. The question of God had never really risen. It wasn't a topic of conversation for him. He'd heard the warnings, who hadn't?

In the past, he'd come across old men, old bible bashers, old tellers of doom and damnation. Those types who hang around on street corners holding a banner with such sentences as, 'REPENT FOR THE DAY HAS COME', or, 'THE SECOND COMING IS UPON YOU'.

Yes, he'd heard it all before. Those people with nothing more to do than frighten others.

Just then the nurse strolled in, swinging the door open with a gentle push. Blue and white, the uniform. No longer a drunken swirling blur, she was quite beautiful, not Andrew's type, but quite beautiful. Her skin was a pale creamy-white, lips a glossy red, eyes a dazzling blue. She wasn't young. Well, not that young, although she had the figure of a teenager. In her small, short-nailed hand, she held a tatty old brown envelope.

"Hello, Andrew!" she beamed. "And how are you today? All right, are you?"

"Yes thanks," he replied.

"Well, I think we can take the drip out of your arm today, then you can have a bite to eat later on. You look much rosier today." She smiled, tapping the envelope in the palm of her left hand. "Here, I think you'll find this is for you. I'll be back at five-thirty." With that she turned and left the room, closing the door quietly behind her.

Andrew held the envelope lightly in his right hand. It was dirty and dog-eared, and had been used before. The address had been scribbled out and the word, Andrew, written in large black print over it. Curiously, he opened it up, taking out a scrap of paper and reading it.

> *Dear Andrew,*
>
> *How are you? I hope you are feeling better now, it's been a long time. I don't really know what to say except that you are my friend.*
> *Eric*

Under his name he had written, in capital letters, the word: SORRY

Once again the door swung open, Eric breezing into the room. He strolled up to the bed, a bright smile on his face. "Hi, Andy. How are you?"

Andrew watched him as he reached for a stool and seated himself. Eric, yes he remembered Eric, that youngster, no more than thirteen or fourteen years of age, that youngster who he'd rescued and taken back to The Sunshine Guest House. How clear in his mind it all was now.

He looked different this time around, looked clean and tidy. His hair was short, not as short as Andrew's was, but short. It was soft, a slightly curly drab brown. His eyes were alive, a glimmering shade of hazel. His nose was neat and small and his cheekbones, high and well-pronounced. His mouth was neatly shaped, except for a slight scar on the left side of his upper lip. He wasn't a large boy; neither tall nor well built but he was Eric.

"So, when are you getting out of here?"

Andrew toyed with the letter, folding its edges over until forming an aerodynamic shape. "I'm off to a safe house or something next week," he replied, raising and launching his paper creation, letting it glide from his fingertips and lift off into the air. "Dunno what the hell that is, but there you go. Just wish I knew what was going on around here, I mean... Well, what *is* going on around here? I just don't understand."

"Nothing to understand," Eric said without apparent concern. "The important thing is that you're safe. Look, there's no point trying to understand, just accept what's happened."

"It's the house," Andrew commented.

"What?"

"The house, Eric. Don't tell me you've forgotten the house? It's the house, you gotta go there, promise me you will."

The two friends sat talking, Andrew's head filling with information, a new kind of menace in the outside world.

"D'ya believe in God?" Andrew asked hopefully. "In life after death?"

"Yeah, in a way. Yeah, why?"

"Cause I heard somebody say this is the Second Coming, that God's returned."

Eric laughed, a look of astonishment on his face. "Who gave you that idea?"

"My doctor."

"It's got nothing to do with God, Andrew. It's got to do

with something evil. Your doc's an idiot if he thinks that. God wouldn't destroy like this. This is something totally different, believe me."

Andrew gazed at his young friend. How different he was today. A world apart from that sobbing, frightened child curled up in a human ball. Now he, that child that was, was so full of himself, so in control, so hardened to reality.

"I live in a great safe house, Andrew. Maybe you can move in there. Why not ask the doc?"

Andrew moved himself a touch, easing his pillow up with an obvious amount of pain. "Eric," he began. "Go to the house for me. You do remember it, don't you? Go there, okay? Go inside, it's real important Eric, you must go."

His words were ignored. "Great safe house, Andrew. Just ask the doc. It'd be great, we could be like brothers."

Just then the door opened up, the doctor stepping inside. "I'm sorry, Eric, but Andrew really must get some rest now. You can come back soon, if Mr. Thomson doesn't object."

Eric and Andrew said their goodbyes, Eric promising to come back soon. He left, walking down the dreary, gray-walled corridor escorted by the doctor. They soon reached the entrance to be greeted by Mr. Thomson who was standing just inside the main door. He patted Eric lightly although firmly on the shoulder. Then he led him out to the car, a heavily scratched, white Cortina, two rather large guards on either side.

"Be careful, sir," one of them said in a friendly manner as both Mr. Thomson and Eric climbed into the car and drove off.

Andrew waited in his bed, the clock on the hospital white wall reading, five twenty-eight; it would soon be time to eat. He gazed around the room, a cabinet in the far right-hand corner, complete with drawers and three shelves full of surgical instruments and dressing materials. Next to it, on the wall, an eye chart. To his near right sat a mobile monitoring unit and to his near left, an intravenous drip he was connected to, for the time being, at least. A central control unit for monitoring heart rhythm and blood pressure stood silently by, a large white, locked wardrobe, a small sliding bed table and two chairs, one of which Eric had moved. That was about it. It was much the same as any hospital room, really. Mental description—dreary.

He thought back to his first encounter with Eric, so weak and so helpless, a lost puppy dog. It was strange. That boy curled up, all alone and afraid. But he was no longer a little boy. He was just a blur of gray. The house behind him, the dusty street. He remembered helping Eric up, remembered him sitting in his room back at The Sunshine Guest House. He remembered his sad story, the fear and uncertainty it had brought. He remembered meeting his mother on the stairway, going into her room. He remembered opening it and charging in as he heard her scream, remembered it all, those images so vivid in his mind.

He gazed rested on the doorway. Something stood there, something that made Andrew's stomach queasy. Was it Eric ? it had to be Eric. But that were true, then why was there a clouded blur of gray where he thought Eric should be?

He jumped as the door to his room opened. The nurse stood watching. The hands on the clock now read five forty-six. She was late, sixteen minutes late to be exact. But then, he had all the time in the world. She smiled warmly, a white plastic tray in hand. Upon it, a plate and a bowl, both covered by metal lids.

"Well, Andrew, quite a surprise meeting Eric, wasn't it?"

"Kind of," he answered, still trying to find a face and body in the blur.

She placed the tray on a chair then raised the head of the bed, helping Andrew get comfortable. "All right then, let's get this nasty drip out, shall we?" Her smile erupted, exploded from her well-boned face, spreading a warmth about the room.

Within moments the drip was out, a bandage on the pin-like hole where it had been. Reaching for the small sliding table, she placed the tray on it and wheeled it to the bed. The lower level went under the top, out of sight, the upper held the table and tray at just the right height for Andrew to eat.

"Well, you can begin when you're ready. I'll be back later with a nice cup of tea, would you like that?" Andrew thanked her and watched as she left the room.

Eric entered his mind once more. The letter, he'd read. He could even see it laying on the tiled floor, a sleeping, paper airplane. Eric appeared in the room. He pulled up a chair and started a conversation.

Andrew felt cold, suddenly ice cold. Where was the real Eric, that young boy, that friend? A dreary, formless grayish blur sat in the chair. Just then the door opened again, the doctor stepping inside as he did before.

"I'm sorry, Eric, but Andrew really must get some rest now. You can come back soon, if Mr. Thomson doesn't object." The blur left the room, escorted by the doctor.

Andrew sighed deeply at the replay of earlier events, the door closed, the doctor and the blur, both out of sight. Hadn't the doctor said those same things moments before? Hadn't he already ushered Eric out of the room.

He prepared himself to eat, lifting both metal lids and moving them aside. His first course was a piping hot soup, diced carrots and potatoes floating in a thick spicy broth. On the plate was a meal of boiled potatoes, green peas and steamed fish. It smelled good, really good. He picked up the spoon and tucked it into his soup, the taste just as good as the aroma, its thickness filling his hungry belly.

Just then he heard a noise, something close, something breathing heavily. He lifted his eyes from the bowl. The spoon fell from his gently shaking, right hand, falling to the bed covers. The blur was back. It sat watching him from the chair. Andrew couldn't move, invisible eyes staring back at him, cutting into him like hot knives through butter.

"It's the medication, it's not real," he whispered to himself. "It's the medication, it's not real. Just the medication, it's not real..."

The blur moved, spouting fits of laughter. Thick beads of perspiration popped out on Andrew's brow as the laughter becoming louder. Louder, louder, screaming all around him, twisting, turning, rolling waves of hate.

"It's the medication, it's not real," he chanted. "The medication, it's not ..."

The room began to turn, spinning about him. Voices entered his head, screaming all the time. "Great safe house, Andrew. Just ask the doc! Just ask the doc! Great safe house, Andrew. Just ask the doc! Safe house. Just ask the doc..."

"No, it's the medication, it's not real..."

Eric and Mr. Thomson arrived at the safe house, home at last. They climbed out of the car and marched briskly inside, sitting themselves at a rectangular, smoked glass coffee table. Mrs. Thomson entered the lounge with a healthy hello. She'd just baked a large tray of vanilla-iced fairy cakes, Eric's favorite.

"So, Eric, how was Andrew?"

Eric didn't reply straight away. Instead, he let the day trickle through his mind. That morning, the waking up after a restless night. The drive through the remnants of a once-highly populated seaside town. Five minutes to scribble a short note and leave it with his nurse. The reunion, finally an end to his wait. The chance to sit and talk, to talk about everything and yet, nothing. Just to talk. Visiting time over, time to say goodbye. What a day, a day that Eric had been waiting for since Andrew's brush with death at The Sunshine Guest House.

"He's okay, I guess. He's lost a leg."

Mrs Thomson sniffed sadly, not that she knew Andrew personally. "Yes, I know. He's a brave boy."

Eric sat in silence for a long time before heading to the kitchen. He took three, still slightly warm fairy cakes, then left for his room. They tasted great, light and fluffy, just the way his mother had baked them in times gone by. Once they were eaten, cake crumbs brushed away with the swish of a hand, he rested his head on his pillow, tears welling up in his eyes. Everything had been too much for him to take in. He cried himself to sleep.

At the hospital, Andrew opened two tear-stained eyes, finding himself strapped to the bed. The doctor, plus three nurses, including his personal nurse, stood over him, his food all over the floor.

"It's all right, Andrew. Everything's all right now. You had a seizure, but it's all right now."

He glanced from the restriction of at least three straps, one around his chest, one around his waist to hold his arms and hands at bay, one around his thighs and quite possibly, one around his ankle, he couldn't tell. "It wasn't, wasn't a seizure. It wasn't, it wasn't, it..." Once again he had to be sedated, a slur of incoherent words leaving his spittle-smeared lips. "It wa… No, see..."

Suddenly he was fully awake. He tried to say something, to tell them he was fine, to tell them he could be released. Silently, he screamed, "Listen to me! Let me go now!"

His eyes were wide and staring. The face above him, that friendly, Asiatic doctor with the comforting gaze. The nurse with the well-boned face and the figure of a teenager and the other two nurses. Their faces moved in unfocused swirls, reflections on glassy water. Then something else. "Help me! Get away!"

But it was no use, the blur was on him.

"He'll be fine, now. You can unstrap him, he'll sleep like a baby until morning."

"No! No, I'm not fine. Listen to me!" His silent pleas went unnoticed.

The nurses loosened the straps, letting them fall away before calling the doctor out of the room.

"Come back, don't leave me here. Please, don't leave me here!"

He was alone, the straps gone but still, he was unable to move. The blur moved about him like a vulture over sun-soaked desert sands. Faces, faces danced before him. Faces obscure and distorted. Faces he recognized. Jennifer Ayre, his mother and father, his friends and family. Tears streamed uncontrollably down his cheeks.

"Get off! Get off! Help, get off! Help!"

There was another face emerging, dark and evil, the other faces dissolving into the blur. Eyes, burning red, tore down hungrily on him, a mouth wide open, dripping blood. Suddenly it fell, teeth bright and shining. Eric screamed in silence, feeling them sink into his face. His own blood sprayed from open wounds, splashing against the walls and bedclothes. The pain was unbearable, a living nightmare without end. He could feel his body rise into the air, spinning around and then falling with a squelch to the tiled floor. Finally, his exhausted body lay limp and broken, his heart torn from his chest. His soul dragged off to the dark side of the maze.

Chapter 5

Deadly Holiday

Danny Walters lived with his mother and father on Bournemouth's East Cliff. He'd gone on a touring holiday through Europe, staying with friends of which he had met on previous occasions in Bournemouth. He had bought himself a ticket that enabled him to travel around Europe for anything up to one month. His mother had driven him to Harwich from where he would take the ferry across the rolling blue to Holland, Hoek van Holland.

Danny was a nineteen-year-old, soft-hearted youth. His hair was a dark brown, almost black and it fell in shoulder length curls. His eyes were a deep sea blue in between flashes of green. His nose, neat and pronounced. His cheekbones were high and his lips well-proportioned. His nickname was Jippo, and it didn't bother him one little bit. It was his mother who first used the name Jippo.

Danny bore the look of a traveller. He had that glint in his eyes and that, 'let me roam', style about him. One might say he possessed a mystical look. It certainly worked for the girls— they adored him. His skin was dark. Not too dark, if one can ever be too dark, just dark and his body, although not overly muscular, was well-defined.

Appearances were important to Danny and he wouldn't be

seen dead without his scruffy black, leather jacket. It was part of him, a permanent fixture. It helped to make him the Danny the girls adored so, a rebel with a cause. He'd been a troublesome child. Not spoiled, not spoiled at all.

His parents had always believed in teaching him the values of life. Nothing comes free, hell, when does it? It was just that he had a rebellious streak running clear through him. His father had been just the same as a youngster. Without a doubt, Mr. Walters had at one time been just the same. He was a Londoner, East End born and bred, from Dagenham to be exact. Yes, the man, too, had had a rebellious streak running clear through him. It had died down with age and Justin Walters knew Danny's streak would also die down with age. Of course, it would, he told himself convincingly.

Danny had been in serious trouble twice before leaving school. Once for hitting Mr. Rempstone, the English teacher. He'd asked for it, Danny had boasted afterwards. But after his three-week suspension, his parents thought he would settle down. But it never came. After only one term he was in trouble again. This time for pushing a boy against a roller black board and staple gunning him by his trousers and T-shirt to it. And, the girls adored him for it. Mean, tough and ready for anything, but, oh how they had been reading Danny wrong. It was all a fake demeanor, that tough man image of his. It was all just a show for his mates … and it worked. Once the ball had started to roll, he had found it harder and harder to stop it.

Mind you, he was a loving son, and although he easily found trouble outside the home, who didn't in those growing years?, he was never too bad inside it. He was never rude or disrespectful toward his parents. Never swore or raised his voice. He was a good boy at home and helped out with all the daily chores, washing up, peeling potatoes, vacuuming, dusting, helping his father work on the car, the list was endless. He was a good boy at heart, a soft-hearted youth. He was, and always would be, their little Jippo.

"Now don't forget to phone me from Oslo, and say hello to Thomas," his mother reminded him. "And make sure you come back in one piece!"

What a mother, he mused. He kissed her lightly on the cheek, said goodbye then headed off into the terminal, leaving her to drive back to Bournemouth.

It wasn't long before he was dragging his heels along the gangway and onto a spacious ship, its gleaming white hull shimmering with lively undulations on the sparkling, cool salty waves on which it sat. His rucksack, last years' Christmas present from his parents, rested heavily on his back, his guitar case in hand. His great passion, after females of course, was playing the guitar. For him the guitar held certain magical powers. After a hard day, he always knew that back in his room he'd find that heavily-stickered music maker. It was for him, a tool of relaxation. He wasn't a guitar wizard, wasn't even exceptionally good. He just liked to twang away in his own little world. He knew a few good tunes, enough to entertain family and friends, even at times, entertain a variety of females. Strange, how one passion could entertain the other.

He found himself a luggage compartment, placed his belongings on a large rack then left, searching out the nearest bar. He'd spent the past three months working in a fish and chip fast food restaurant in the center of town, slogging himself to death behind a deep fat fryer. He had had to put up with his friends coming in, sun-tanned and full of life, ordering large portions of Greasy Joe's fish and chips after a long day of kicking around in the summer sun, of playing football out on the golden yellow sands of the beach or chatting up pretty girls down in the Pleasure Gardens. He had had to put up with spoiled children crying when not getting what they wanted, or ordering and then changing their minds just as the last wrapper was about to go on. Then there was the old ladies he had to put up with who came in complaining about something all day long—if it wasn't too hot, then it was just too damn cold. Complaining about the amount of topless girls sunning themselves in full view of ordinary, decent people.

At night he'd come home, come home to that tool of relaxation. His head would buzz complaints. In his sleep he'd dream complaints and the next morning he'd hear complaints again. Thank heavens for that guitar, that musical sanity saver.

The worst thing, quite positively the worst thing of all, was having to stay late to mop the floors and seeing his friends passing by on the other side of the window on their way to a nightspot or bar for a beer and a girl for the night.

It was his dad who'd helped Danny get the job. It was one of his old school friends who owned the shop. The boss, George Mason was one hell of a boss and Danny got on very well with him. The first month had been rather difficult, though. There'd just been so much to learn. Danny had only worked weekends and the odd evening as he still had school to attend. The second and last month had been full time. Two months of seemingly eternal, back-breaking sweat and toil, although much easier than the first, the training period.

Mr. Mason had given his young employee a hundred-fifty dollar bonus when he left, as well as an assurance of future work. But this, this was what he'd been working for. This, the not knowing what might happen next. The strange sensation of feeling the earth roll beneath his feet, free on a shimmer of blue. It was this that made the struggle all worthwhile.

He climbed the green carpeted, slab stairway, observing a large and easily readable map on the clear white wall. At the top of the next stairway, as the plan had predicted, he found a large bar area complete with a circular dance floor in the center. He strolled in and sat down, sinking comfortably into the green velour, semicircular settee. The bar began to fill, people wandering in search of a place to rest and relax.

Voices filled with cheerful, exploding holiday spirit filled the air. Several groups gathered along the dark mahogany bar surface. A smartly dressed man stood behind it, black trousers, white shirt and black bow tie. He smiled politely, handing out his experience on the best and, probably most expensive, drinks to order. A family of four rambled noisily in, seating themselves at a table nearby. A blue plastic, old ice cream container sandwich box was handed around, the two children tucking into a cheese and pickle delight.

Danny watched the little boy curiously. He was young, no more than ten years of age. A puny lad with fly away, light brown hair, a long thin face and an extremely large gap between his front teeth. He wore thick-rimmed bifocals, making his eyes appear as if he were looking through a goldfish bowl. He gazed around the room, half a sandwich in his mouth, a cross between an alien, a hamster and two goldfish bowls.

The little girl, presumably his older sister wasn't so strange to look at. In years to come she would probably become something quite special.

Their parents both wore glasses and both seemed alien-like. The father was nearly bald and there was no doubt he was the boy's father. The mother was the typical stuffy school-teacher.

A middle-aged man wearing black jeans, shirt and shoes, plus a silver sequinned waist coat and top hat stood behind the DJ stand sifting through a pile of 'Greatest Hits' albums. Just then, a young lady breezed in, beautiful, long blond hair flowing over her mature shoulders in a golden stream and her eyes shone a crystal blue against her soft, pale skin.

She strolled up to the bar, standing a short while, waiting to be served. She was wearing tight denim blue jeans, pink sandals and a baggy pink and white jacket. Her legs were long, heavenly, and her bottom was small and tight under the edge of her jacket.

Danny let his gaze dance toward her, captivated by her entrance. His heart skipped a beat. The barman had noticed her. He was busy serving an elderly gentleman, but he had noticed her. Swiftly taking the money from the elderly gentleman, he moved down the bar to where she sat. Danny looked on as she ordered a drink, the barman magnetized. A few obvious chat-up lines were pushed her way, which she ignored, taking her drink, laying her money down and looking around for somewhere to sit. The DJ had noticed her as well, brows raised in appreciation as she crossed the floor and seated herself. The elderly gentleman at the bar watched her every step of the way, his eyes darting toward the mirrored wall behind the bottles rack.

The young woman held a glass of rum and coke in her dainty, right hand, taking a sip as her eyes travelled the room. He'd done it, Danny mused, he'd caught her attention. She took one more sip, her glance meeting his. He smiled, almost wanting to jump up and run across to her, closing the distance between them. He wanted to tell her just how beautiful she was, just how in lust he had fallen. The moment was intense, he was spell bound. An electric current flowed between them and he barely had the courage to stand up or make up his mind to invite her over. He found himself whispering angrily, mumbling under his breath.

Do something, damn it! At that moment a decision was made. Not by him, but by the young woman who held him enthralled. His heartbeat thundered in his chest, spiriting its way through his body, pounding vibrations all the way up to his ears. He felt uneasy, his nerves taunt as that beautiful creature wound her way toward him.

"Hello. Do you mind if I sit myself down here?"

"No. No, hell no. Sit, sit down." She seated herself, setting her glass on his table.

Danny smiled boyishly, feeling suddenly stupid, feeling like a flustered little boy. The palms of his hands grew cold and sweaty, and he could feel the elderly gentleman's eyes staring at him from the mirrored wall.

"So, what, um... My name's Danny, Danny Walters." He held out a sweaty right hand, hurriedly wiping it on his jeans before she reached out to take his.

"Danny, that's a nice name. I'm Johanna. I hope you don't mind if I sit here. It's just that these trips are just so boring when you're alone."

"No, no, of course not. It's nice to have some company."

They sat quietly as moments of silence … seconds raged by. It had never been like this before for Danny. Sure he had had his fair share of girls, who hadn't? His first real kiss, a Frenchy, had taken place under a table during a history lesson at the grand old age of eleven. His first sexual experience had taken place in the girl's bathroom at the age of eleven and three quarters. He and Sharon Williams had gone off to find out the difference between a girl and a boy. Man, did he get in trouble for that one. He had had full sex by the age of thirteen, with a sixteen-year-old STS student from Norway and had nearly gotten a young French girl pregnant by the age of fifteen and a half. Hell, he was a man of the world, a beast, a sex machine. Then why, just why did he feel so weak in the presence of this girl who sat across from him?

"You ain't English, are you?" he struggled to say, determined to begin a half-decent conversation.

She beamed radiantly, her warmth avalanching over him. "No, no, I'm Swedish. Well, half-Swedish anyway. My mother's from England, from Southampton. Do you know Southampton?"

"Yeah, yeah sure I do. It's not far from where I live in Bournemouth. Well, about forty miles, I guess."

Finally, Danny could feel himself loosening up, feel his nerves calming, the dragons inside him fading away. The young Swede before him had found the key to his heart. The Northern beauty, the Viking maiden from the snowy reaches, the ice princess, the blond goddess. Yes, that beautiful creature had opened the door and let herself in.

"You must think me really forward coming over like this," Johanna said softly, her voice as warm and refreshing as the summer sun.

"Ah hell, I woulda come over to you sooner or later anyhow." He rummaged deep in his jeans, rear left pocket, pulling out a twenty dollar bill. "Fancy a drink, Johanna? I mean, after that one, okay?"

She raised an eyebrow responsively as he pushed to his feet and a reply came without thought. "Yes, thank you. A rum and coke, please."

He turned and headed for the bar, returning after a good ten minutes with two pints of bitter, a double rum and coke, a cherry brandy and two packets of dry roasted peanuts on a black and red, circular tray.

"Here we go, I got something else too. Save us going up for a while, okay?"

She thanked him happily, downing her rum and coke in one swallow before reaching for the cherry brandy.

"See the old fogey over there?" he asked her.

"Old fogey?"

"Oh right. Yeah, that old man."

"Yes."

"Well, he gave me a real strange look when I was up at the bar. He's watching us in the mirrors behind the bar. Bet he's some sort a nonce." Johanna didn't say anything, a confused expression on her face. "You okay?"

"Yes. Well, no. No, what's a nonce?"

Danny laughed, opening up the packet of peanuts and handing them to his ice princess. "Pervert, Johanna. You know, like a dirty old man." The pair giggled, both sneaking a glimpse of the elderly gentleman at the bar.

The ferry began to move, riding up and down on swooning waves of white-iced, crystal blue water as it headed out to sea.

"Well, just seven hours to go and, Continent here we come," Danny said excitedly, raising his beer tankard to his thirsty lips with a slurp.

"Have you never been abroad before?"

From that point on, Danny and Johanna found a lot to talk about, everything from where her father lived in a little town near Gothenburg, to where she went to school. Danny told her his life story, told her of his three hard months in fish and chip hell, told her just how much he was looking forward to meeting Thomas, a language student who he had befriended two years earlier in Bournemouth's Pleasure Gardens. He told her of his school days, his holidays, and his friends, ex-girlfriends, family... And it wasn't long before their glasses stood empty again.

"Would you like another?" Johanna asked cheekily, not waiting for a reply. She rose and breezed off toward the bar.

Danny felt a little tingle deep down inside as he watched the sway of her hips when she walked away, a warmth that generated from everything this pretty young blond bombshell did or said. Something about her made him feel alive, made him feel fresh and clean, made him hungry for more. She was different, not like those girls downtown with their dirty talk and their childish stupidity. No, this girl was definitely different, definitely had a style all of her own, was definitely in a class way above all others.

Before his thoughts advanced to things he shouldn't be thinking about, she was back with a pint of lager, a double whiskey for him and a double brandy for herself.

"Here, now where were we? Danny, hello. Anybody in there?"

Danny jumped at the sound of her voice bringing him sharply back to the present, his mind a thousand miles away on a dreamy cloud of love, or was it just lust?

"Oh yeah, right. Sorry about that, I was off in space there for a while." He thanked her whole-heartedly, picking up the whiskey and tossing it down his throat.

As a rule, he hated whiskey. Ever since that fateful evening back home in Bournemouth, a good four months previously. A cool Saturday evening that found him sitting in the Pleasure Gardens with a couple of friends and a rather large group of Italian students. The whiskey that was drunk that night was enough to sink a battleship and the morning after, well, what could one say except, never again.

That special moment, that special girl was here. For her, he felt he could do anything. He shuddered, the golden brown liquid burning his throat as it wound its way down and warmed his belly. He tried not to cough, lunging for his pint of lager and swinging back a good two thirds in a desperate bid to dispel the taste.

"Wow," he croaked somewhat dramatically before joining Johanna in cheerful laugher.

"I wish I had my camera with me, I never knew that a face could change like that with just one drink."

Danny grimaced, dragging the back of his right hand across his mouth. "I take it you like a drink."

She raised her glass, downing the last few drops of her cherry brandy. "Well, I just wanted to get a little tipsy really, it could be my last chance for quite some time. My father won't let me drink. If he ever found out, I think he'd strangle me. To tell you the truth, I'm only seventeen, so it isn't exactly legal." She giggled to herself, her head slightly numbed by the effect of one too many. "Ah, but what the hell. James Dean was a rebel too, only his hair wasn't as long as mine."

Danny sniggered, shaking his head ever so slightly. He displayed a look of surprise at her sense of humor. She really was something else, something quite special. Something unique, exciting and sensually different. She was fun to talk to, fun to be with. She possessed a certain charm and a way of saying the funniest of things, of unexpected things. Her English was almost perfect and yet, still that accent shone through. She didn't cut words in the same way as one of the native tongue might. Instead, each word was defined, and well-pronounced, her voice true and clear.

Danny reached into the inside pocket of his black, leather jacket, pulling out a half-empty packet of Silk Cut cigarettes. "D'ya want one?" he asked kindly as he held out the crumbled pack.

"No, thank you, I don't smoke," she softly replied. "I did try one at a party once. I was with a friend called Malin and she gave me one. I was only about ten years old and I thought it would be tough to try it. It wasn't. I was so ill my father had to come and pick me up. I don't know if I was really ill. Maybe it was just guilt. Anyway, I told him I just had a bad stomach ache. My mother smokes, but only outside. My father hates cigarettes."

Danny gazed down at the pack of cigarettes he held loosely in his right hand. He thought for a second and then squeezed. "Hell, who needs cancer anyway." He cleared his throat, dropping the squished pack to the table. "I'm only a party smoker anyhow."

He watched with secretly loving eyes, a little unsure of her intentions. He had his own intentions. After all, he was no more than a red-blooded young man. She reached for her double brandy, casting it back in two mouthfuls and sighed contentedly.

Danny tossed back the last of his lager, not that he was a lager drinker, before suggesting a stroll up on deck. She brushed a creamy pale hand through her thick honey mane and stood up, leading him out into the corridor and up a flight of steps. A wire-glassed steel door stood before them and they pushed it open, passing through to a breath of fresh salty air.

The afternoon sun felt warm against their faces, a breeze so gentle, lifting strands of their hair toward the sky above. They seated themselves on a faded red plastic, three-seater bench.

Eyes cut out across a shimmering, sun–spangled silver-blue England, little more than a dark line floating in the distance.

Johanna leaned her head against Danny's moderately muscular, left shoulder, resting her intoxicated brain as the world slowly revolved around her. A large ship passed by against the horizon, its mighty bulk cutting through the waves toward the land of hope and glory. For Johanna it was, for her it was home away from home. For her it was the land of fun, of meeting exciting people, of drinking cheaply, of living without the strains of life back home. It was a place to escape when her northern world pushed too hard. For Danny it was just an island in the rain, a land of nothing but hope, a land of mass unemployment.

"Are you all right?" Danny asked genuinely.

Her eyes lifted in a friendly gaze and she planted a firm kiss on his cheek before smiling brightly. "You're very sweet, Danny, do you know that?"

Steadily she got to her feet, casting loose glances out across the waters of the English Channel. Danny sat in silence, his head in a heavenly turmoil. She had kissed him, had actually kissed him. Not a real one, granted, but she'd kissed him all the same. That was the point of no return, lust, if that's what it had ever been, had evolved into love.

"Why don't we go down to my cabin?"

A surprised twinkle grew in Danny's eyes. "A cabin?" he asked. "You have a cabin, a room? You have a hide out, a place for us to lie down?"

She nodded.

His appearance now took on a rather strange expression, cupping one hand to his face, fingers across the bridge of his nose, thumb under his chin, eyes at hock. "A cabin! Fantastic." He jumped up like a child with a new toy. "Yes, let's go."

Johanna took him by the hand, dragging him back inside then leading him down the flight of steps. Then another, and one more. He soon found himself in a long, pink wallpapered corridor.

"Ninety-one, ninety-two, ninety-three, four, five. Ah, ninety-six, here it is." She took out a key from her front right jeans pocket, unlocked the door and swung it open. Then she stepped inside, not forgetting to put the key back safely.

On entering, Danny closed and locked it behind him. Crossing the navy blue carpet, he seated himself on the hard, almost hospital-like bed. His mind filled with wild thoughts of the sexy young thing before him. Resting on his elbows, he gazed admiringly at his catch of the day. Plenty of fish swam in the ocean of life—isn't that a fact?—but he'd just landed the catch of a lifetime. A catch above all others, and tomorrow that catch might be gone, tomorrow that catch might be out there in that vast ocean of life once again for someone else to reel in.

His prize catch elegantly eased her way toward him, until she was on him. He wrapped his arms about her, embracing her, pressing his lips firmly against hers. She kicked off her pink sandals as his hand gently eased down, slipping under her baggy pink and white sweater. Upward his hand travelled toward fist-sized breasts of pure silk. Playfully, his inquisitive fingers caressed soft pink, rose bud nipples. They were hard and jutted, screaming her sexuality.

A smile crossed her face. She felt secure, so safe with her tall, dark and handsome stranger. Her body tingled in the closeness of the one she was fast falling in love with. She lifted her arms, allowing him to raise her sweater over her head.

Danny's hand eased its way down, dancing light circles across her neat, taut stomach until reaching, and unzipping, her tight denim blue jeans. They came away without resistance and passed over her long, slender, well-tanned legs, eventually being cast aside. Her skin was soft, smooth to the touch. Curious fingers, explorers in a brave new world, gently hovered in twisting motions, lowering to stroke her inner thigh. A warm, sticky dampness began to soak through her skimpy white panties, enhancing his lustful virility. Lovingly, she undid his jeans, releasing his large, fully erect masculinity. Like a fish out of water, he struggled to free himself of his clothing. His black leather jacket was cumbersome and difficult to tear off in the heat of the moment. He pulled a white T-shirt over his head, a gift from an ex-girlfriend, the fabric getting caught for a split second on the gold earring in his left ear. Johanna helped him with his dusty sneakers and black jeans, the cool air tingling his naked flesh.

They rolled over, touching, caressing each other. Skin on

skin, two hearts as one, young lovers entwined. Easily, hands and curious fingers searched out new frontiers. He inserted a finger deep inside her and she sighed her first orgasm. She was in ecstasy, her body, a writhing mass. Danny's love was so giving, so full of passion. His foreplay so light and supreme. He inserted his manhood with his left hand, stroking her breasts with the other as he rode up and down to her moans of sexual joy. A loud sigh whispered through her lips as he came and he fell, holding her close like he'd never held anyone before.

Just then somebody knocked loudly on the cabin door. "Fifteen minutes to docking."

Danny smiled, kissing Johanna warmly. "Typical," he groaned, rolling off the bed and dressing himself once more.

Voices sounded out in the long, pink wallpapered corridor, the seven-hour Channel crossing drawing to a close. Once they'd dressed, they left arm in arm. Their clothes felt damp and uncomfortable against their warm bodies.

"I shall meet you upstairs, okay?" Johanna whispered, biting affectionately on his left ear lobe. "I better just take the key back to the reception desk." She pecked his cheek then ran on ahead, disappearing up the stairway.

Danny strolled along the corridor, his head full of fine thoughts. How lucky he felt to have met such a wonderful girl, and how sad he felt at the thought of having to say goodbye to her when they reached the mainland.

Mainland, Continent, he was but minutes away from seeing a country other than his own. A tingle of excitement danced playfully down his sweaty spine. He felt alive, more alive than he'd ever felt before. He was a pearl in the shell of life, a wandering soul on an adventure in far off lands.

He climbed the stairway and found his way to a growing crowd of people, all anxiously waiting for the ferry to dock.

"All right?" Johanna called out, poking him in the ribs.

He jumped and turned sharply, grabbing her, pulling her in close, his strong arms enveloping her alluring petite frame. He brushed his well-looked after fingers through her hair. "Come on, let's get our luggage."

Their hands met, clasping tightly as they headed off to collect their belongings. Once they were done, they stood, still holding each other. The crowd began to intensify as time passed and after what seemed like a lifetime of waiting, the ferry docked and the doors opened.

A vast landmass stretched out before them through small, dustless windows. Container lorries and trucks being filled and emptied littered the dockside. Tall steel-framed cranes rose into the sky, reaching like mechanical giants, arms outstretched, pointing wayward.

Danny picked up his backpack, pulling it onto his shoulders. Picking up his guitar case, he helped Johanna with her belongings before going with the flow down the gangway. Not that many people, Johanna thought to herself, remembering previous treks to the Continent. She had taken the ferry many times before. In fact, she'd travelled to and from England in almost every way possible. Her first journey from Sweden, six years ago, at the age of eleven, had been by airplane. Her mother had just married an Englishman after a rather nasty divorce with her first husband, Leif Andreasson. Joanna's mother met her English dreamboat while on holiday in Cyprus.

Johanna's father was a great father. Although he'd worried himself half to death when his daughter had first been invited over to stay with her mother and stepfather in England. He'd telephoned his ex-wife in England five or six times in one week just to make sure somebody would be there at Heathrow to meet her. Over the years his grip had loosened and in later years, the ferry and the train, had for Johanna, been the most fun. Her father had always booked and paid for the tickets and, if he had a little excess money to spend, he'd pay that little extra so she'd have the added benefit of a sleeping compartment on the ferry or train.

So many people, Danny thought to himself. Before that journey, he'd never been outside of Great Britain. His summer holidays were, as a rule, spent down in Saint Austell, Cornwall with his Aunt Sylvia and Uncle Roy. Two weeks each year, sometimes three, were spent there. Uncle Roy was his mother's brother and he owned a huge house with a swimming pool and guesthouse. There had never been any need for the Walters family to holiday elsewhere and before Danny's journey abroad, it had never even been considered.

They soon reached the customs point. Nothing to declare and passports checked, they pushed on toward, hopefully, awaiting trains.

"Rest here for a while, Danny, put it all down for now."

"Yeah, okay boss. Whatever you say."

"Where are you going now?" Johanna asked nervously, praying for a right answer.

He fumbled in his backpack; unzipping a side pocket and producing a tatty, corner curled timetable. "Um... Well, let's see." He paused, searching for the right train. "Ah ha, here it is. The D237 to Denmark. Can't you take it with me?"

Johanna beamed like a Cheshire cat, throwing her arms about him. "Well, seeing as I shall take that one, you might as well tag along with me, okay?"

Danny breathed a sigh of relief. If he'd have to say goodbye, then at least it could wait a while longer. He picked up his pack and guitar case, and followed her across to a railway information clerk.

Danny's life had suddenly become very complicated. He'd worked so hard for this break, so hard for the chance to see a small corner of the world before returning to Bournemouth in search of a real job. Greasy Joe's was a fine part-time job. At times, it was even fun, but as a full-time job, as a bread earner and a way of life, well that was a different story. This break, this breath of fresh air had been planned long ago. Three months of serving fish and chips … job experience, one might have called it, stood behind him.

He had been looking forward so much to meeting Thomas in Oslo. Nothing had really been planned with Thomas as such, although Danny did have his address and telephone number. They had written and verbal contact and Thomas had become somewhat like a pen friend. Danny had planned on going to Oslo long ago. It was to be a surprise.

He'd just phone Thomas and say, "Hi. I thought we might meet."

"When did you say?"

"Oh, in about ten minutes."

It was a dream plan that still stood, or did it?

Now he felt trapped. It wasn't really a bad feeling. After all, he was in love. But now he felt forced into a corner, he had a decision to make. It crossed his mind that Johanna might already have a boyfriend back home in Sweden. That, in her eyes, he might just be a passing ship in the night. If that were the case, then it would solve a problem, or would it?

"Excuse me, sir," Johanna said politely. "Can you tell me where I might find the D237 to Denmark?"

The railway information clerk, a very large West Indian with an equally large smile pointed to a train. She thanked him kindly, leading the way toward it, she and her new-found lover boarding and finding themselves a vacant compartment. The compartment was frightfully untidy and it stank of stale cigarette smoke. Several empty beer cans lay scattered above their heads on the wire mesh case rack. They sat in virtual silence until eight fifty-nine when the train slowly began to roll and set off along its shiny, silver tracks. The sky began to darken as evening set in, illuminating fluffy gray clouds. The trees changed in shades, shining out against a heavenly glow. Buildings stood tall, reaching for new heights, proud reminders of man's creation.

Johanna gazed down at Danny's guitar case. "Why don't you play something?" she asked enthusiastically.

He reached over and opened the scruffy, Union Jack stickered guitar case, taking out a clean, although equally stickered guitar. He easily tuned it before strumming out a tune, each note ringing clearly around the compartment interior.

"Okay, I'll play and you can tell me who it is, okay?"

"Okay."

She recognized the introduction. It was a song she'd really liked at one time in her life. She probably had it at home somewhere in her vast record, cassette and CD collection. The words started, each one bringing the title of the song and name of the artist closer to the tip of her tongue.

"I was dreaming of the past/and my heart was beating fast
I began to lose control/I began to lose control."

She searched through the stacks of musical information in her head. The words clicked inside, but still she wasn't certain.

"I didn't mean to hurt you/I'm sorry I made you cry
I didn't mean to hurt you/I'm just a jealous guy."

Jealous Guy, she had it. The song was called Jealous Guy. She did have the record at home and yes; it was a song she'd really liked at one time in her life. Danny smiled as he sang. It was one of his favorites too.

"Ferry," Johanna called out. "Something Ferry."

The song carried on through the next two verses and chorus, but the artist's first name would not come to her.

"Well, who was it?" Danny asked happily. He put the guitar down and brushed a hand through his hair.

"Ferry something. Ferry... Brian, Brian Ferry, is it Brian Ferry?"

"Great, well done!"

Once again a tune came forth. He had a little trouble with it, it just didn't sound quite right. After running a few licks, it was perfect and the guessing game went on. He played long into the night, tune after tune after tune until eventually they gave up the game and cheerfully fell asleep, huddling close for warmth as the train moved on, hauling its human cargo through the Dutch countryside, into Germany and onward toward Denmark.

Morning came, fresh and alive after slaying the dragon of night, to the click-idi-click of pumping wheels on tracks of steel. Danny sluggishly woke up, peering around the compartment through sleep-dusted eyes, until they came to rest on Johanna, her head resting on his knee. She looked relaxed, totally at ease. He wondered what she might be thinking of within that sleepy world of hers. She was his sleeping beauty and deep in his heart, he hoped that he was her prince.

He glanced down at his watch, adding one extra hour to set English time so the hands read 11:16 am. Houses and parks, forests and fields rushed by the window only to disappear and be replaced by more of the same. The sun shone warmly through the window, reflecting on a huge lake. Such a wonderful sight, he'd never experienced anything like it before. The train appeared to be sliding across a mass of green and blue lake on either side of the tracks.

"Hey, Johanna! Come on, luv. It's getting a bit late now."

A golden capped head unwillingly moved, two sleepy blue spots shining out through the haystack on his knees.

"Okay, I'm awake." She yawned loudly, looking up into the eyes of her prince, and deep inside she hoped that she was his princess, a rosy smile stretching from ear to ear. "Wow, you look good enough to eat."

That cheerful, sleepy expression soon faded out. Her next look, one of deep concern.

"Danny!" she said somewhat impulsively. "Are you planning on just walking away and forgetting about me when we come to Copenhagen? I need to know if you are, that's all."

He rubbed the corners of his sleep-dusted eyes, digging away at dry flakes before taking her hand as she attempted to sit up. A sign hurled past the window; the word 'Kobenhaven' (Copenhagen) boldly printed in white on blue. A city grew out of cornfields and barley, swelling in size and height until like moving storm clouds, it was on them.

"Yeah, well I've been thinking about that and..... Now you're gonna buzz off to Gothenburg, right? Well, I thought... Maybe, well, I might just, well, you know!"

Johanna flung her loving arms about him. "Say it, Danny, say it!" She made little circles in his hair with the tip of her index finger, playfully nibbling on his right shoulder.

Danny kept a straight face, turning his head easily to gaze out through the window, the station in full view. He knew for sure he could drag things out for at least another five minutes, giving himself enough time to decide for sure, give her time to sweat a little.

"Well, here we are. Time to leave, don't you think?"

She grabbed him around the waist, swinging her legs up onto the dusty, threadbare, faded royal blue couch and tickled him furiously. Tight lips curled into a childish grin as laughter broke out, ringing around the compartment.

"Okay! Okay, yes, now pack it in!" He grabbed her and pulled her in close, holding her and pressing his lips passion-

The Maze 95

ately against hers.

"You're incredible," she commented as they both calmed themselves down. They sat holding hands, happy and content, cheek to cheek until finally the train came to a halt.

People hustled and bustled along platforms, searching out their next trains like clockwork mice, going about their daily routines. Bankers and businessmen, shop workers and general holidaymakers, all pushing on toward chosen destinations.

"Come on then," Danny said energetically, thrusting himself nimbly to his feet. "We can get some breakfast soon, I hope." Luggage in hand they left the train and waded through a mass, oncoming invasion. Like a swarm of bees, the human flood pushed by. "When's the next train?" Danny asked, pulling his guitar case in out of the marching legs.

"Um, it's the 462 on line two. Line two is over there, but we have almost forty minutes until it comes in. Come on, let's get something to eat."

To their left stood a small café and they headed toward it. Just then a strange thought flooded Danny's mind. The crowds, the people, yes, the people all appeared to be moving in one direction. Nobody appeared to be talking; nobody appeared to be smiling. He brushed his mild concerns aside, feeling his stomach cry out for nourishment.

On entering the café, Danny placed his belongings next to a vacant table. His backpack was heavy and it felt good not having to carry it around. With Johanna's belongings beside his, together they crossed the black and white tiled floor to the counter. A strong coffee aroma curled into the air, twisting warm and refreshing.

"Don't have much, do they?" Danny whispered as the young counter assistant appeared.

"Vad skal det vare?" *What would you like?* Danny blushed without understanding and he cleared his throat foolishly before speaking once more.

"You speak English?"

"Yes sir, I do," she politely replied. She had a very nice accent. It was much stronger than Johanna's, but then Johanna had spent an awful lot of time in England.

"Cup of coffee, please and... Give me a filled sarnie. D'ya have cheese?" he said pointing to a large tray of fresh filled rolls. "What you having, Johanna?"

"Oh, I'll just take a coffee."

He rummaged in his black leather jacket inside pocket, pulling out a brown leather wallet. Then he drew out a reasonably thick wad of Norwegian one hundred crown bills.

"Can you take this, I don't have Danish?" Again he felt stupid. He blushed feeling the blood rush over his face. Johanna took out a Danish note with a somewhat comical smile.

"It's okay Danny, I've got it." She paid up and thanked the counter assistant, then moved across to a coffee maker on a small circular table in the corner of the room.

"What about the sarnies?" Danny asked worriedly.

"Don't worry, she'll bring them over."

"Ah, ha." He watched as she poured the coffee, a look of disgust on his face.

"Milk and sugar?"

"Yeah, yeah please." They seated themselves at the table and she gave him a cup. He stared down at it without a word, eyes cutting deep into its darkness.

"Danny, are you okay?" His stare rose up to meet her uncertain frown and for a split second, she thought she'd done something to annoy him.

"This ain't coffee. What happened to real coffee, like powder coffee? Jesus, they can't even make coffee here."

"How very British," Johanna chuckled sarcastically. "I say, how very British." She took a sip as if to prove to him it was in fact drinkable, that it wasn't liquid poison. "There, you see. It's very nice, really. Besides, this is Europe, so you can forget that old powder junk."

"Is this the crap you drink here, then?" Johanna didn't reply, her eyes said enough.

A tall blond waitress came across with a well-filled cheese roll on a white paper plate. It looked great, thin strips of yellow on a crispy salad bed with tomato slices. He thanked her gratefully and tucked into the first bite to eat since the odd dry roasted peanut back on the ferry from England. Each bite graced his taste buds, a crispy salad crunch, soft, strong tasting cheese and fresh white crusty bread. Heaven.

"Sure you're not hungry?"

"No, I'm fine, Danny."

She sipped her coffee, enjoying its fine flavor, thoughts filling her pretty head. Meeting her father, meeting her friends. Her father wouldn't mind Danny staying a night or so, he was a very understanding man. Her friends would most certainly be happy to see a new face around town. She was to start school, her last year, again in just over two weeks, so he'd have plenty of time to spend with her, and still get to go to Oslo to meet Thomas.

"Whatcha thinking about?"

She jumped slightly, very nearly spilling her coffee. "Oh, nothing really." She reached across the table, placing her right hand over his left, massaging it with the flat of her thumb.

"What's your dad gonna make of me, then? Reckon it'll be okay with him?"

"Yes, Danny, don't worry about it."

Once they had rested, Danny sipping his way through the strongest cup of coffee he'd ever tasted, they stood up, picked up their belongings and left. The platform outside was a lot less congested now, the rush hour over. Again that strange feeling flooded his mind. Strange, a rush hour at 11:30 am. It made no sense to him at all. He glanced at his watch. 11:52 am; and it would soon be time to leave Copenhagen. They crossed over the railway line via the overpass and boarded the 462 to Gothenburg, finding themselves a compartment to relax in. The couches were a soft red velvet and were very comfortable. Patiently, they waited to get going.

"Can you take this, I don't have Danish?" Johanna giggled. She poked him jokingly in the ribs. "You're funny, Dan."

"What, what's so funny? What've I done now?" He looked somewhat annoyed, his face very tense and she felt bad vibrations.

"I'm sorry, Danny, what's the matter?" He shrugged his shoulders and chewed over a reply in his mouth.

Johanna waited, knowing full well he had something to

say. She'd learned a lot about the young man, even though she'd known him but twenty-four hours.

"I don't know," he began. "Something just ain't right here."

"What do you mean?"

"Well, when we got here, there were people everywhere, right?"

"Right."

"Like it was rush hour."

"Umm."

"But it was only eleven-thirty. Why was that?" He paused a moment, a new thought entering his head. "And what about the train we came in on? I think we were the only ones on it. Did you notice that?"

Johanna smiled comfortingly. "Relax Danny, you worry too much."

She positioned herself in such a way her head rested lightly on his knee. She was totally at ease and it showed. A shine emerged beneath her long dark lashes and slim, neat eyebrows. Her beautifully proportioned, slightly freckled nose swept gently to soft pink, pouting lips. Her hair flashed gold and honey in the light, slipping luxuriously away from a glassy clear scalp like pollen in the wind.

How could he ever bear to be parted from this temptation from the gods? How could he ever consider being anywhere else than at her glorious side? He took her hand, holding it lovingly, not tightly, just enough for her body warmth to penetrate his skin. Slowly she closed her eyes, canopies over a sun-soaked sea until eventually she fell asleep.

Within five minutes the glass-windowed, steel tube set off, slowly picking up speed. Danny gazed out from his comfortable seat, his head in a heavenly muddle, the only sound being that of wheels tearing along miles of winding track. He thought back to his mother at home in Bournemouth. She'd been the typical mother all the way from Bournemouth to Harwich, had said the things that all mothers say to their children when it's time to spread their wings and fly off to distant perches. She'd told him to have a good time, but not too good. No fighting, getting

The Maze 99

drunk, forgetting to write, forgetting to shower every day... Mothers.

He thought back to his first ever ferry journey, the wonderful girl he'd met. She really was wonderful, wonderful in every way possible. Surely even his mother would think so. He thought back to the very large, West Indian railway information clerk with the equally large grin back in Holland. The train journey and the rush hour crowd in Copenhagen.

All of a sudden, he felt cold, very cold. There was something wrong, something amiss. It was so quiet and peaceful, maybe too quiet and peaceful. Gazing out through the window, he was met by emptiness. There were no people wandering distant streets. The odd car passed by on a parallel road, yet so it appeared, all were heading in the same direction. South.

Johanna fidgeted bringing her head up toward his stomach, distracting him from his line of thought. Secure in his comfort zone, he closed his eyes and joined her in the depths of sleep, his uncertainties held at bay.

Countryside rushed by, a fast fading sun rippling on rivers and lakes, the train rattling on until arriving at the ferry in Helsingor. It boarded, sailed across to Helsingborg, left the ferry and carried on, pushing its way northwards through the Swedish countryside.

Johanna was the first to wake. She stretched her weary eyelids and swept a small, petite hand across her well-boned face. Sitting up, she lifted Danny's arm to take a peek at his watch. 3:05 pm. She gazed out through the window in amazement, it could have been mid-evening. There was no sun, nothing but near darkness. The odd car passed by at five to ten minute intervals, although all were heading in the same direction. Never before on any of her previous journeys from England by train had she looked out onto such an empty, desolate road. As a rule it was packed with motorists and noisy lorries keen to unload their heavy hauls. As the train pulled in at Gothenburg Central Station, nothing but grim silence presented itself.

"Come on, Danny, wake up! We're here."

Danny slowly opened his eyes. "Wow, guess I must've dozed off. Blimey, ain't much life out there. So ... this is Gothenburg." He stood up, pulled his backpack on, picked up his guitar case then helped Johanna with her items.

Leaving the train, they set off, slowly traipsing along the platform until reaching a set of stone seats. The seat felt cold and damp as they rested themselves, placing their belongings on the dark tarmac. The train stood silently on its rails like a sleeping ghost from a distant, forgotten past. The air was bitter cold, cutting into them like icicle daggers.

"I'm afraid, Danny. This is really strange. Where's my father?"

Danny rubbed her shoulders comfortingly. "Don't worry, sweetheart, he'll be here." Somehow he doubted those last reassuring words. Something was very, very wrong here. He'd noticed it long ago.

Johanna fumbled in her pocket, pulling out money for a lockbox. "Let's put everything into a safety box, then I can ring my father."

"Yeah, okay."

Once again everything was picked up and they trundled off toward a stack of orange, red and blue safety boxes. She slipped in the coin, twisting the key. Opening the door, she waited as Danny forced their belongings inside. With a sharp slam, it was shut. The key free of the lock and safe in her pocket, they set off toward the main building.

"We can get something to eat now, if a shop is open."

"Why shouldn't it be?" Moving through the wide, automatic doors, they stopped sharp. "Shit, that's why."

Inside, long wooden benches stood lonely against stone floor slabs. The shop that once sold cigarettes, soft drinks, newspapers and quick snacks was closed, totally void of life.

"Danny, what's happening?" Johanna whispered, her tone growing ever fearful. She held herself close to the one she loved, somewhat like a baby holding a comfort toy.

A mixture of adult fear and child-like curiosity dragged her and in turn, dragged him onward along a dank corridor and out through the exit. The sensation continued pulling at them, taking them down through the underpass and into a mass shopping complex. On entering, they drew to a stop, standing rigid, staring unblinkingly in disbelief. Shop fronts spewed out of gaping holes, jagged, shattered sheets of glass scattered all around. Display cases hung open like forgotten, nameless gravestones, no more than empty skeletons, lifeless and decayed. Loose wires and electrical cables hung from flaky ceilings and half-demolished walls, hung viciously, torn by a nightmare past.

"Jesus! What the fu… Shit! There's an explanation for this, Johanna. Trust me, it's gonna be fine." His heart sank, fear taking him by the shoulders, a battle to stay strong. Strong for his sake. Strong for Johanna's. Just to stay strong.

He took Johanna by the hand and led her through the debris, turning cautiously to the left at a four-point turn and carried on worriedly past the broken shell of a building. At one time it had been a fast food restaurant. Now it was a twisted, tangled wreck, a table, chair and snaking metal counter wasteland. They passed out through the main doors, out onto the street outside. The scene that lay before them was that of devastation. Cars cast on their sides, thrown into lampposts, hanging out of shop front windows, resting awkwardly on pavements like discarded toys in a child's playpen. A breeze travelled along each ghost town street, lifting broken objects and old newspapers high into a stale, rotten air, an air of hatred and unpredictability.

Just then, in the distance something came into view, a figure slowly moving toward them.

"Oh shit!" Danny managed to utter, his trembling body struggling to speak. The figure edged its way toward them. A man wearing a large black hat and a long dark trench coat. In one hand he held a menacing, serrated edge meat cleaver. In the other, a head. Thick crimson flows poured from the savagely torn neck, running down the man's arm and dripping stomach, churning strands from his elbow. He held the decapitated head high, a trophy of war, by its thick curly hair.

Danny turned frantically, searching for a car still upright.

"Come on, quick! Get in that car over there!" he yelled, charging over to a wine-red Saab 9000 and pulling hard on the passenger door. "Johanna, move it!"

Johanna froze, her mouth agape, body unable to move. Fear took her, closed in around her, hands of the dead holding her terrified frame motionless to the spot. The snarling, demented human form came prowling toward her, foaming at the mouth, a rabid creature of the deepest, darkest bowels of hell. She could see the crazed psychopath, knew it was almost on her, could see the head hanging from blood-soaked fingers. She tried to turn, tried to run but her legs refused to work.

Danny screamed in sheer frustration. He rushed back to her, dragging her away and forcing her into the car, then darted around to the driver's side, yanking on the door. "Johanna, open this fucking door! It's locked, for Christ's sakes, open it!"

Johanna didn't move, her eyes fixed, held captive by her antagonized brain. She wanted to move, more than anything, she really did want to move. She wanted to reach over and unlock the door, wanted to badly but she couldn't. Something was holding her back.

Danny picked up a broken paving slab, smashing the driver side front window, glass splinters spraying the car's interior. He lifted the door handle and climbed in, searching for a set of keys. "Damn it!" he growled, tearing at the dashboard.

Suddenly there was a loud thump on the car roof, the head rolling down over the dusty windshield then stopping, caught by a wiper blade, blood smearing across the hood of the car. The head was that of a young girl, one eye staring at them through the window. The other was missing; replaced by a thick, gray slime seeping out of an empty eye socket. A huge split oozed a river of red in the side of her battered face, running like a lava flow down her open cheeks.

Johanna closed her eyes, her terrified screams echoing Danny's fears. He slammed the car in gear and sped off up the street smashing the crazed, demonic man to the ground like an egg. In blind panic, Danny raced away, a man possessed, tears streaming from his already damp, blood shot eyes. He took a sharp left, feeling the back wheels spin and slide as tires screamed toward a bus depot littered with the remnants of a dead city.

He swerved to the right, following a one-way system, the road stretching away into the distance past buildings that quite easily could have been from the Blitz.

Feeling safer, he slowed down and pulled up at a T-junction, turning and taking Johanna by the shoulders. He held her tenderly, pulling her in close, holding the sobbing wreck, weak and distraught girl in his caring arms. The flats of his thumbs slid gently across her tear-stained cheeks.

"Come on, darling," he murmured softly, holding back his own salty tidal flow. She whimpered like a baby, nuzzling up to him. "Calm down, love. I dunno what's going on around here, but I'm gonna be with you. I love you, Johanna, I love you." He kissed her softly, the taste of her crystal tears salty against his tongue, as her frightened, watery gaze met his.

"I love you, too!"

The bottom had just fallen out of Danny's life. He felt helpless, useless, unable to heal the pain in Johanna's heart. Her world was gone, had just vanished like the setting of the sun as evening draws to a close. And he loved her more than words could tell. The past hour loomed over him like hungry black panthers and he just didn't know what to do.

"We gotta get to your place right away. Now you just try and direct me."

Suddenly, Johanna's mouth dropped, shaky hands rising to her face. "Look!"

A hand, bloody and torn, shot through the smashed driver seat window, grabbing Danny about the throat. His head was yanked back, each dirty fingernail sinking into his flesh. He yelled out in sheer agony, reaching desperately for a sliver of glass that had wedged itself between the driver's seat and the gearshift.

Almost there, his fingers touching the razor sharpness of the glass, his fingers inched forward until it was within his grip. Pressure around his neck tightened, squeezing tighter, nails digging, tearing, ripping, squeezing tighter all the time. Somewhere in the distance he could hear screaming. It was Johanna cowering terrified by his side. At last a trembling rush hit his shaking body, the sliver of glass sliced across an anonymous wrist. He sliced deeper, feeling the sliver sink through pumping veins and sinew. Blood gushed into the air, falling showers of red. The whole car rocked, someone or something on the roof hitting it with a sharp instrument, each thunder crack blow denting the metal top.

Danny raised the sliver once more, letting it come down deep into gristle and bone. The arm fell back, the hand loosening its deathly grip around his throat. Then it disappeared out through the window.

Frantically, Danny tried to re-start the car, as a hole appeared above his head, an axe tearing down through the roof. The engine ticked over, faded and ticked over once more before revving up and mounting the pavement and trundling off down the street. An axe man fell backward, tumbling to the tarmac below.

Johanna gathered herself, forcing herself back into reality. "Turn here and go straight on," she sobbed, wiping her wet eyes with her fingers. He turned and headed out of the city along a barren road.

The sky swelled above them, massive, angry black rain clouds sweeping in from nowhere. The journey seemed without end as Johanna directed him toward a highway. There wasn't a car in sight, not a sign of life. A deathly calm surrounded them, closing them in, nearly suffocating them.

The highway cut through rocky grasslands and conifer forests, through countryside alien to Danny's eyes. After a time it broke in two and as instructed, Danny swung to the right before stopping at a T-junction.

"Turn left now, and go straight ahead."

It wasn't long before a small town unfolded. He took a left turn at a crossroads and then one more until finally arriving at a rather large parking lot in front of a building.

"This is where I live," she explained, pointing to a window of a long row of apartments lined and stacked before them. "We just follow the path and turn right. It's number thirteen, bottom floor."

Danny took a quick glance around from the comparative safety of the car before swinging the door open and running swiftly around to the passenger side. Yanking open the door, he helped Johanna out, half carrying her along the path to the entrance of the building. Once inside Johanna fumbled in her jeans, front left pocket for the front door keys. The door open, they stepped inside.

A chill dampness hit them, cutting through their fearful bones with a hateful vengeance. Johanna escorted Danny into an average-sized living room with two windows and a glass door leading outside to a small patio. A long teak dining table sat at the far end of the room, a green domed, pendant lamp hanging above it. A large wall unit stood to one side of the room, complete with glass-doored cabinets and two fair-sized bookshelves. On the same side of the room a television, a DVD player, and a magnificent stereo system lined the wall along with an a large quantity of ornaments.

A fine four-seater, gray velvet settee occupied the near end of the room. In front of it sat a smoked glass table with a neat stack of five or so, cork coffee coasters, an old TV guide and a couple of pens. To its right, a tall, green-leafed rubber plant sprang out of a large container.

Pictures framed with teak beading hung from white wallpaper. Pictures of sweet memories. Johanna as a baby in her mother's loving arms, pictures of her dressed in white on conformation day. Enlarged student photos, the prettiest girl in the group. A bright bouquet, blues and reds, yellows and whites held in her young hands.

Johanna seated herself with a long and deep, nervous sigh. Danny knelt between her tight blue-jeaned legs, resting his tired head on her left knee. He followed a crystal tear as it wound its way down her cheek, the sight of his beloved Johanna, a broken, scared witless soul, too much for him to bear. She leaned forward, clasping him around the neck, her tears mingling with tender fingernail scars, stinging his wounds. They could only assume the worst, holding each other tightly until gathering enough strength to let go.

"It's gonna work out, babe, don't cry anymore. Please don't cry anymore." She put on a brave face, sniffing loudly. "I'll work this out, Johanna. Believe me, I will."

Slowly she pulled herself to unsteady feet, moving her boyfriend with doubtful hands to a new comfortable position. She brushed long strands of honey and gold away from her face, and left the room, leaving Danny to sit helplessly alone, a tired, worried, solitary figure surrounded by pain and confusion. How could anybody leave England with such high expectations, meet the girl of a lifetime and yet at the same time, be forced into such horrific terror in such a short amount of time?

Just then Johanna re-entered the room, two bathrobes in hand, one, a blue striped on wine red of her father's for Danny and the other, a soft shade of pink, her own.

"I've put the water on, so we can take a shower and the only food I can find are a few cans of stuff." She sobbed uncontrollably, sitting down once more. "If only I knew where my father is. God, I hope he's okay."

Danny swept her up lightly, laying her down on the settee, resting her head on a soft gray, scatter cushion. She yawned, eyes red and tender. Slowly they closed and she fell into a deep sleep. The room was so silent, they were able to rest, neither knowing quite what to do next. Sleep was one luxury Danny refused to indulge in at the moment, his head far too preoccupied by more important matters. Survival, his highest priority.

Once sure Johanna was asleep, he stood and left the room, walking softly out into the wooden-floored hallway. Quietly, he opened the first door he came to. He turned the fake brass door handle and stepped into a spacious bedroom. It was most definitely that of Johanna's father.

A stylish black-framed waterbed with matching cabinets and rustic red duvet took up most of the room space. As Danny scanned the room, a thick silver cross on a chunky chain caught his attention. It had been neatly placed on a scrap of white paper next to the built-in wardrobe on the cream-colored carpet. Moving in for a closer inspection, he lifted the chain and cross, our Lord, Jesus Christ hanging silently for the sins of all mankind.

Picking up the scrap of paper, he turned it over to reveal a picture, a frighteningly strange picture and even more strange, the figures drawn around it. He studied them, wondering what they could possibly mean, the very sight of them sending an icy chill down his spine. The main picture was of an eye, a wall of crocodile-like scales overhead and a totally non-understandable sequence of figures, possibly letters, beneath them.

Stranger still was the picture next to it. It was of a beast, a powerful-looking beast, half–man, half-reptile. In one huge hand it held a crossbow, in the other, a star.

He folded the scrap of paper, tapping it thoughtfully against the palm of his right hand, glancing down to see yet another piece of paper. Upon it was a set of more pictures. The first was of a boy holding his laughing head, standing in a hallway that didn't appear to end, doors reaching into infinity like an Ansel Adams photograph.

Faces appeared on each door, faces of hatred and of pain. Each slightly different, although each bearing a resemblance. A pattern, a series of lines, all met at a center point, all of which grew from ninety-degree angles.

The last picture, the most grotesque of them all, was a human-like creature resting on powerful forearms, dragging behind its much weaker back legs. It had a long neck and a human-like face, two mighty horns on its ugly head and two extremely long, thin, sharp fangs protruding from its lower jaw. Yet another piece of paper, not a scrap of any old paper, but a clean sheet of neatly written, lined paper lay nearby. He picked it up and tried to read it, although nothing made any sense to him. A sheet of words, words that although were alien to him, were different than the words on the first and second scraps of paper. He tucked it away with the first scrap then left to investigate further.

In the next room, the kitchen looked pretty much like every kitchen should. It was complete with all the latest gadgets, all the furnishings in a smooth pine finish. A split level cooking surface, a kitchen table, four matching chairs took up the rest of the space. A mug with the name, 'JOHANNA' written on it, hung above a finely engraved, glass-doored cabinet, right next to the mug with, 'PAPA' and a big heart. Magnetic fruit and vegetables clung to the surface of the white refrigerator door, almost the same as the ones back home in his mother's kitchen.

His weary mind drifted back to that memory-filled place, the place where sweet smelling, delicious meals were cooked by his loving mother. The place where he would often go in the middle of the night for a cool glass of milk and a midnight feast. He began to wonder just what she might be doing at that very moment all those miles away. Making a nice cup of tea, maybe cooking a meal for her husband or more than likely, she was cleaning. She was very house-proud, always striving to keep the house spotless.

His stomach roared a mighty lion "feed me" roar. "Damn, but I'm starving," he whispered to himself.

Opening a cupboard, he pulled out a can. Reading the label, he didn't really understanding what it said, although the picture told him enough. It was a tin of baked beans. "Beans, bruna böner," he mumbled before thinking back to the paper he'd found in the bedroom. "Swedish, great." He pulled out the paper and compared it to the words, 'Bruna böner'.

It was written in Swedish. Johanna's father must have written it, he reasoned. And if it was in Swedish, then Johanna could read it. Maybe, just maybe the paper held the answer to the pictures. He placed them safely back inside the inner left hand pocket of his black, leather jacket. In a set of drawers to the left of the stainless steel sink, he searched for a can opener, plus two spoons, then filled two glasses with water.

Just then Johanna called out his name. Placing the can, can opener, spoons and glasses of water on a serving tray, he headed back to the living room. Johanna looked pale and withdrawn, thick beads of perspiration collecting on her brow. He placed their meal on the smoked glass table, moving quickly to her side, taking her damp, sticky hand in his.

"You okay?"

She shook her head. "I had a dream." Danny listened as she told her story. "I was in some kind of building. A-a building, a dungeon of some kind. I was alone and freezing cold. Then I wasn't alone anymore. There was a man with me, but he was more like a reflection on running water. He was dressed in black and really angry. His eyes were black and his beard was black, all black, and..." She reached out, pulling Danny in close. "Oh, Danny. It was horrible! He was laughing at me, said something about a place. I can't remember the name though. He raised his fist to hit me. Then another man came and pushed the first one away. He smiled and said he wouldn't hurt me. Said that we'd meet in a distant land. That I was chosen, that I'd find him. Then they both disappeared."

She paused for a moment, looking up through a tearful gaze into her boyfriend's loving eyes. "Stay with me, Danny. Don't ever leave me!"

He pulled her to her feet, holding her in his strong arms, and kissed her dry, red lips. "I ain't gonna leave you. Never, okay? Never, I swear," he said warmly. "Come on, I got us something to eat. I know it ain't much, but never mind. The other two cans out there we can have for breakfast maybe."

Placing the two glasses of water on the table, he opened the can of baked beans, then spooned them out on a large white plate. He seated himself next to Johanna, handed her a spoon and dug in. Cold baked beans were nervously eaten. Slowly, slowly, very, very slowly. Each bite was chewed and savored, knowing there would be no more that day.

Their evening meal gone, washed down with a tall glass of water, Danny pulled out the sheet of paper. "I found this," he said softly. "Found it in your dad's room, or at least I think it was his room. D'ya understand it?"

She reached for it and read it slowly, translating as she went. "In the darkness I hid, waiting for the birth of mankind. Under the stones and hammers of destruction, the fire and blood of all things comes to be. He who has held the hand of death and has understood it to be a good and trusting friend, has nothing to fear from the one with power supreme. Let them follow me down to..." Suddenly she stopped, a shiver screaming up and down her spine before fading away with an icy rush.

"What is it, what's the matter?"

"Kadorelus! Kadorelus, that's what he said!"

"Who?"

"The man in the dream. That's what he said. Kadorelus."

"Okay, doll. Keep reading."

"Let them follow me to Kadorelus, let them feel the wonder of my father. For he is all great and blessed are they who fall to his feet. For forty days you resisted my father whilst in the desert, yet for forty days my father offered you gifts above all others. You, who could not turn the stone into bread, even though you hungered. Where is your God? You were taken to the highest mountain and you were offered things far greater than your God could ever hope to offer. You chose to serve him. You chose death. For you knew that your God was too weak to save you from the cross. Now my father rises once more, mighty and triumphant. My Lord's time has come. Kadorelus has hungered too long. Now my father's kingdom has risen."

Again she paused, stuttered without forming words at all. "I don't know what this says, it's not really in Swedish."

"Not really?"

"Well, no. No, it's a combination of Swedish and something else. I can't read it."

"Was it your father who wrote it, is it his handwriting?"

"No, no it isn't." She read on a little further, the jumble of words fading out and giving way to words of relative understanding once more.

"It says here something about a Hazzari. That he shall never find Shazaan because he or she is dead. Then it says something about a Pezzarius. I guess these are names. That's it, that's all it says."

The room had long begun to darken, a near blackness surrounding them as thoughts of despair passed through minds so young with frightening unease. Desperate fears, the aching of knowing the hurt and pain of the day was in the same lifetime as the carefree world of yesterday. Yesterday, two youngsters lived different lives. Both happy go lucky, looking forward to bright and wholesome futures. The day, lost, confused, afraid of life and all that it might bring. Danny moved across to the light switch.

"Wait, Danny. Maybe it's better if nobody knows we're here. We can close the bathroom door, and put the light on there."

She picked up the bathrobes and led him out of the room. They undressed themselves, turned on the water and stepped into a soothing crystal clear waterfall. Each drop felt like heaven, refreshing them, the day's horrors and pains temporarily flowing away. Hands stroked and caressed shoulders, bruised

The Maze 111

and battered after a day of trying to survive in a strange new world.

After fifteen minutes, two clean and much healthier looking faces climbed out into cool, fresh air. Danny painfully reached for a towel, each muscle in his body aching. He placed it loosely across Johanna's shoulders, gradually sliding it around her slender neck before dragging it in a smooth motion down the arch of her back.

Her skin felt soft and clean, warm and enticing. He worked his way down her thighs and lower legs before turning her around and scrunch-drying the honey strands of her hair. Both hands circled her slim waist, fingers tracing the line between her neat, taut belly and the sensual pleasure he knew was waiting.

She was a picture of beauty, her intense sadness and deep fears momentarily locked away behind a radiant elegance that quite simply demanded attention. He helped her on with her bathrobe, letting her slip silently away into her bedroom. Once he dried himself, he wrapped his body tightly in the bathrobe she'd given him, then he, too, left.

Checking each room in turn, he secured the windows and doors in a bid to stay safe. The last room, Johanna's, was small but very pleasant, a white wooden, single bed situated in the far corner of the room, alongside a cabinet with a large, oval shaped mirror on it. A few posters were scattered across rose cream wallpaper and flowered curtains, which had been tightly drawn.

He approached her, removing his robe before flicking off the bedside lamp and climbing in beside her. Johanna rested her head on his shoulder, feeling secure with the one she loved. She snuggled against him, dragging her well-manicured, red lacquered nails lightly through a small amount of curly black hair on his reasonably muscular chest.

"Danny," she said faintly, "what are we going to do? I mean, tomorrow, what are we going to do?"

He lay quietly, thinking of something soothing to say, just some simple words that might help to chase a few of her dragons away. "Look, all I know is that we need to rest. Tomorrow's tomorrow, we'll fix it then. I've checked all the windows, checked everything. Trust me, we're safe, just hold me."

His head rushed with wild horses, nagging pounding at his tattered nerves. Hatred, fear and the not knowing just what might happen next tugged at his already battered courage. Soon, they both slipped slowly into sleep, fearful of what the night might bring.

Chapter 6

Eric and the Mystery

Eric gradually rolled over in bed, waking up to a new day. The night had been a long one, the longest ever, full of tears and mass uncertainties. Andrew's words had plagued him relentlessly, tearing at him without mercy, thundering back, dark and sinister with each attempt to forget. What was so important about the house? It was a house, just a house. Nothing but a dirty, run down house. How could it possibly be held responsible for the wave of changing times? It made no sense. Could it really hold such a deep secret? Could it really be the key to hell on earth?

He climbed out from under the bed covers, a cool morning air nipping at his bones, icy fingers reaching in and dragging the night away. He pulled on his jeans then wrapped an old red, cotton shirt around him, buttoning it up. A dull gray peeked in through the black, cell-like barred windows, dark clouds looming overhead. A silence filled his ears, an unearthly, haunting silence. A silence so still and so empty that it almost screamed its silence for all to hear.

Once he'd properly dressed, he left his room and descended a stairway laid with a white and green patterned on orange carpet. He entered the kitchen, glancing around the sizeable, equally warm room. It was very well furnished and well-kept. Nothing looked out of place, almost as if everything had been built and designed solely for the Thomson family kitchen. Anything moved, anything added or anything taken away would surely hurt the room beyond repair. The room was divided by a flower engraved, wooden arch. On the side Eric entered, stood a beautiful old oak dining table, six Hefty chairs and an oak dresser with smoked-glass doors. Through its two lattice windows, sets of crystal glasses sparkled. Four shelves held four different sets of glassware. At the far end of the room, a dazzlingly clean bay window with seating space for six looked out onto a small but well-maintained garden and patio.

Through the flower-engraved wooden arch and down two steps, the kitchen really began. A split-level stove complete with copper canopy sat against one wall. Fake marble work surfaces, a large double sink with copper cookware lined the bone white walls. The kitchen had all the modern conveniences. Engraved cabinets, a built-in fridge, a microwave and dishwasher. Mr. and Mrs. Thomson were most definitely not short of money and their spotlessly clean kitchen could quite easily have been a show room in, 'Kitchen & Bathroom World', the kitchen designed by professionals, for professionals. He could see it now.

He glided across to the bread bin, taking out three slices of thick white bread, then placed them in the toaster. They singed under the heat, changing shade-by-shade until they were nicely browned, just the way he liked them. Once done, he covered each slice with a thick layer of butter and strawberry jam. Strawberry jam, like so many other strawberry jams. Strawberry jam, bought by the jar at the corner shop. One that tasted good, but was nowhere near as good as homemade strawberry jam. Certainly not like the strawberry jam his grandmother used to make. One with thick strawberry chunks and strawberry tang.

His mind drifted back to that fateful day in his own mother's kitchen. A vengeful shiver rose and curled the length of his spine. Suddenly he felt alone, so very, very alone. Suddenly it hit him. Words ran around in his head. New words, empty words. Deathly words. Words that made no sense, new words in the language of mankind. The two most common of words, 'Norm's and 'Crazies', had to be the most common of all. Nobody knew why a person became a crazy. Nobody knew why many thousands didn't.

Of course, there were also the 'Goners'. Just another word on another tongue. Goners, the ones, who just vanished, never to be seen or heard of again. This was a fast growing number, a number that at one time didn't really count. But now, now that number was increasing by the day and the word, 'Goners' was fast becoming the latest and most important new word. Where did the Goners go? Why did they go? The questions were just too many to know where to begin asking.

Six prisons in the country had faced riots, most of the prisoners escaping, the rest, killed in the turmoil. Thieves, swindlers, junkies, hooligans, rapists and murderers, all had escaped leaving their dead behind. The troublesome slum estates, so well known for their violent outburst, were quiet and still, empty. Religious folk, on the other hand, had in a lot of cases, risen up and become Crazies, turning into lawless killers intent on death and the will to destroy. The world was falling apart, the wheels of time catching up, the human race on the verge of extinction.

Eric raised the first slice of toast to his mouth, tasting that sweet crunch between his teeth. Andrew's words, like the boxer's punch, ran through his head time and time again. He felt afraid, confused, stomach twisted by nerves. A feeling of wanting to run away, far away. Away to some place safe, to some place out of harms' reach, away from the pain and hardship of a world without understanding. Away to a quiet, peaceful place where people lived normal lives and did normal things. He wanted to be away with it all, just away. Yet another feeling showed itself. A curiosity, a burning desire to find out the truth, to prove himself wrong. To prove to himself there was something in that old house, be it yes or no.

Once he had eaten, his belly full, he walked back up the stairway to his room, closing the door behind him then locked it tightly. A fleeting gaze of his pale green eyes drifted out through the window, so quiet and lonely. Nobody walked the empty street outside, no life at all. Not even a bird crossing the sky in search of an insect meal. Just … nothing. The odd car rested, discarded across the road, like sleeping, mechanical monsters. The whole scene reminded him somewhat of a childhood nightmare, a nightmare that found him alone, isolated in a dead world, a world scarred by war and disease. A world lost of all life except for his own.

After a few more moments, he opened the window, pushing at the bars. One appeared to be quite loose. He looked around the room searching for an inventive idea. With a little persuasion, the whole frame could probably be wriggled enough for the steadying pins to be pulled free of the brickwork. The only real problem would be setting them back once more.

He walked quickly to the rather tacky looking, oak-veneered wardrobe, taking out a clothes hanger, then set about the task of breaking the brickwork away from the steel pins, loosening the bars up enough so that with one last push the barred grid came away.

He stopped a few seconds to sift things through his mind then climbed through the space, carefully swinging himself around, clothes hanger clamped tightly between teeth. Taking a firm grip on the black metal drainpipe with one hand, he struggled with the other to replace the grid, haphazardly forcing it back into place. Then taking the hanger from his mouth he squeezed it into the space where the steel pin at the center point had been. Once in place and looking reasonably convincing, he edged his way down the drainpipe until reaching ground level. After a quick glance around, lightly scanning his surroundings, he darted off down the street. A cool breeze blew through his hair, cutting into his cotton shirt like a knife through fast melting butter, chilling his fast beating heart. His mouth felt dry, a strange feeling deep inside, an aching throb pumping through his veins.

On reaching The Sunshine Guest House, he stopped, gaining his breath and bending over, rested shaky hands on his knees. His frightened head throbbed, fear swelling up inside.

"Don't chicken out now," he whispered tight-lipped under his breath. The hands on his watch ticked on. The time read 7:15 AM. It was still quite early. His parents would be getting up soon, getting up and thinking about that little boy upstairs. He inhaled loudly, then exhaled through the nose before charging off as fast as he could across the street and up the alley on the other side. A large whitewashed house stood on his left. It looked ordinary enough, an every day, run of the mill, rundown house. It wasn't really that different than any of the others, except for the fact it was so dilapidated. But then again, every street had its fare share of decaying, empty buildings. It was just a sign of the times.

A green damp crept up the front wall and the front door swung on one rusty hinge. As for the garden, it was more like a jungle, weeds growing around weeds, struggling to survive on the stony ground.

Cautiously he headed up the rugged path, climbing the step and entering the building. The house was cold, wooden floors wet and rotted. The stairs creaked, soft footsteps edging their way up to the top floor. He checked each room in turn, finding nothing but broken relics of the past. His parents had told him never to go out unless accompanied by an adult. He knew only too well the dangers of going out alone, and yet there he was exploring in the filth and degradation of a house that looked as if it had never been lived in, not in this lifetime at least.

Half wanting to leave, half wanting to complete the task at hand, he brushed his fingers firmly through his hair. He pushed away from a wooden door frame, a woodworm infested hive of activity, then headed for the next room.

On entering, something touched him. The deepest, darkest, coldest feeling, a feeling of not being alone. The hairs on his agitated neck rose sharply to attention, his heart beat like that of a steaming train under his goose bumped flesh. An odor, not of rotten wood nor of damp, fusty walls, hung in the air. This odor was different, burning his young nostrils. This smell was alive; alive and breathing, sending its hatred about the room on stagnant air.

This was the house, he told himself. Andrew was right and this was the room. He stood staring into the dampness wondering what to do next. He'd found the house, had indeed found the room. But what was to be done next? How could this room, this dirty, damp, run down excuse for a room be held responsible for the way of life in the outside world? All this, all too much for a boy so young to put into perspective. Raising a hand to his mouth, he glided an index finger lightly across his lower lip. Time passed by slowly but surely, minutes of his tender life passing before him.

Just then he heard a noise. His heart jumped up to meet his dry throat as he recognized the sound of footsteps treading on damp wooden floors. With no time to think, he slipped behind the rotted, half-hanging, half-leaning door. The sound came closer. Closer, closer, closer all the time, with each step thudding along the corridor. A man of roughly forty-five years of age and of rather slim build, trod into the room. The side of his head dripped a crimson flow from a deep gash just above his right ear. In his left hand, he carried a silver spoon. Then split seconds later, three boys entered, arms hanging loosely at their sides, heads hung low.

Eric froze, a chill wind whipping up from nowhere, dust and old leaves that had probably blown in from the small, smashed window were lifting, rising into the air in swirling plumes before settling once more. The four pathetic looking creatures headed toward the far wall, silently moving forward. And then, and then, and then... nothing.

Eric stared unblinkingly. He gazed up at the moldy ceiling, gazed down at the dusty wooden floors and let his head slowly follow his eyes to the far wall. He saw nothing, absolutely nothing. The four figures had gone, had quite simply vanished without a trace. A look of bewilderment crossed his pale, ghostly face. Still nothing.

His brain tried to picture the man and three boys, picture them as he'd seen them standing there moving toward the far wall. Gathering up what little courage he still possessed deep down in his horrified frame, he slowly padded forward, eyes fixed, unable to move, lost within the past thirty seconds.

It was just a wall, just a plain, ordinary wall. Just a wall, that's all and nothing more. He just had to convince himself. Nervously he raised a hand, holding it out to the wall, fingers disappearing through its mass.

"Huh? I don't... What the...?" He gulped loudly, jerking his

The Maze 119

hand back sharply. In front of his disbelieving eyes he waved them, shook them, wiggled them, touched them, and examined them. They hadn't changed. No, they were still the same old fingers, the same old flesh and blood, skin and bone fingers. They were still his fingers and yet, yet for a minute space in time he'd temporarily lost them.

Suddenly he took a deep breath, forcing his head down and charging straight forward. He tumbled to the ground on the other side. In fact, he wasn't sure what he'd landed on, as he found himself in a huge space. A dull glow lay in the distance like candlelight in a misty window on a late winter's eve. He climbed to unsteady feet and headed toward it. Taking a quick glance around, he could see nothing but the glow. It was as if he was on solid ground and yet on closer inspection, bending down to investigate closer, pushing his hands down through the darkness, he could find nothing. The glow grew larger as he neared it, his head full of empty silence. No thoughts rattled through his curious brain. Amazingly, he felt no fears or inhibitions of any kind, just a strange feeling winding, twisting, turning butterflies deep down inside.

Finally arriving at the glow, he found himself looking down from a rocky cliff face onto a motionless valley below. Embedded into the rocks, long flaming torches burned, lighting the area with a dull orange ray. At the bottom, possibly three hundred feet down, he could see people sitting lifelessly on giant granite slabs. No one appeared to be moving, didn't appear to be talking. They were sitting in total silence, surrounded by rocky shafts of granite, except for a small, narrow lane leading wayward and winding out of sight. It was almost as if the valley was floating in space. The valley itself let off a dull glow, lighting the meandering lane away and yet nothing, but nothing surrounded the valley. Nothing but total darkness. No sky, no land, just darkness.

After composing himself, Eric steadily eased himself over the edge, climbing down ledge by ledge, stopping at each one to scan his surroundings. It took a long time before he reached the bottom. In his way of thinking, it felt like forever, but in time, he was on flat ground. An old man sat on a granite slab just to the left of him and he edged cautiously toward him. People were everywhere. Maybe these were Goners. He seated himself next to the old man, smiling timidly before speaking.

"Hello," he greeted softly.

The old man didn't reply. An old man, surely someone's father or grandfather, an old man just sitting on a granite slab as if he were at the bus stop just waiting for a bus into town. His hair was long and gray, his beard thick and matted. The old man's flaky dry, left hand caught Eric's attention. He stared at it, puzzled by it. Somebody moved a little further away and he looked up to see who it might be. A young to middle-aged male, too difficult to tell in the dim light, was perched on a rather uncomfortable looking flat boulder, who rocked slightly before keeling over onto the granite earth below. Eric jumped to agile feet, bounding over the fragile figure, pulling him up and helping him back onto his boulder.

"You okay?" Still there came no reply.

There it was again, that mark on the left hand. The same mark on the old man's left hand. The mark was some kind of a tattoo. An eye. Above it lay a thick band of scales and below it, a set of letters he'd never seen before, each letter stamped into the flesh.

Suddenly fear raised itself, hurtling down on him. A loud, deep scream echoed the valley walls. A scream that originated from the alley winding into the rocks that lay somewhere beyond the valley. The scream was followed by mighty thuds as footsteps sounding like war drums, gradually grew closer. Fleeing hastily from the boulder, Eric proceeded to climb shafts of granite rock, so sharp and steep, his arms reaching high, his fingers gripping tightly, pulling himself upward to safety out of reach of whatever it was down inside.

Just then a dark shape crossed his vision. Something big, slightly human, as big as a horse, walking on all fours, its neck held high in the air, red eyes glowing hateful lava pools. Two extremely long, thin, sharp fangs protruded from an open mouth, dripping in blood. Two mighty horns grew out of its head and a spear-like tail grew out of its backside. Its forearms appeared to be much stronger than its back legs as it dragged itself along, its tail lying heavily behind.

Eric stared back fearfully, his body nervous and shaking, beads of sweat relentlessly forming on his brow. The creature moved in toward the seemingly unconcerned gathering, their minds apparently blind to the danger and potential gruesome ends that might await them. Time seemed eternal—the calm before the storm.

Eric tried to climb higher, fear holding him at bay. He struggled, frozen to the spot, a raging war with his inner most feelings, unable to do anything but stare down from his, hopefully, safe ledge. His heartbeat sounded loud in his ears, sending a torrent of uncontrollable spasms throughout his system, his breath, the raging wind.

Suddenly a gong sounded, each rock shuddering under the strain. The gathering jumped to their feet, rushing over to, and scrambling in vain toward the rocky ledges. The devil creature raised itself on its hind legs, waving its huge horned head high into the air. A hell raising scream burst through its razor-sharp, tooth-encrusted, cavernous mouth. It lowered itself once more, staring at the rocks, staring at the people who were frantically forcing themselves up toward safety, pushing each other back down in blind panic. The creature studied them a short while, its head turning easily from side to side, almost as if deep down inside, it was laughing at them, laughing at how, in their confusion and fear, none of them could escape.

All of a sudden, the beast lunged forward, its own screams extinguishing the terrorizing screams of struggling, human meals. A thick, long, red tongue shot out of its mouth, wrapping around a desperate woman's slim waist. It raised her high into murderous air, yanking her down to the rocks below, her skull shattering on impact. It licked thick blood trails from solid granite before taking up the body and swallowing it whole.

Not content with one meal, the creature thirsted for more. This time its victim was an old man. The creature bit into his head, holding it to the ground with its mighty front, taloned claws. Then jerking its powerful neck back, the old man's head was ripped from his body. A quick flick of the creature's menacing jaws sent it flying high into the air, blood gushing from the savagely torn neck, spraying down in a shower of red rain. It caught the head in its mouth, swallowing it whole. Then raising its arms, it screamed triumphantly before taking up the remaining blood-soaked torso, its saber fangs piercing it, blood, thick and red, oozing to the ground. Slowly it turned, clawing its way along, swishing its massive spiked tail behind it, before disappearing around the corner and out of view down the gray-walled alley.

As soon as it was out of sight, the remaining people slowly climbed back down to the valley floor, heading for their rocky perches, sitting themselves in silence. Desperate fears were replaced by expressions of emptiness. Eric's stomach rolled, heaved. He spewed, choking a second on his own vomit. He raised the back of his hand to his lips turned pale from nausea, wiping away thick strands of spittle and vomit, eyes streaming tears for what he'd just witnessed.

Again the rocky valley shuddered, another sound heading toward them. He carried on, forcing himself up as fast as possible until he was no more than fifteen or so feet from the top. His head buzzed, fear for his own safety reducing as he gained height. Those sad, lifeless souls beneath him, haunted him as he worked his way to the top. How meaningless expressions had changed to terror at the sight of such an awful creature. It seemed they'd stood no chance of survival, trapped in a strange world, live food for an evil creature of death.

Gradually, very gradually, people began to move toward the center of the valley, forming a large mass as a giant wooden cart pulled by another creature, half-man, half-reptile, arrived. There were several baskets resting on the cart, each full to the brim with loaves of bread. The gathering milled around the small wagon, each person taking a loaf before moving away and sitting down to eat.

Eric hurriedly climbed the last few feet, hauling himself onto flat land that couldn't be seen. Walking through the darkness, he estimated the distance and the direction of the glow in the hope of entering his own world. His fears were gone, no more than distant memories somewhere in the back of his mind. The darkness, or whatever lived in the darkness, had eased it away.

The Maze 123

Suddenly darkness turned to day as he tumbled back in the dusty room. A slight warmth filled him, the knowing he'd at least escaped the unnatural world left behind. Somehow, it felt more like a bad dream, more like a horrible nightmare than reality. Somehow, it felt as if he'd just fallen asleep and had just then woken up in a bitter, ice cold sweat.

He stood a while deep in thought, trying to understand what he'd just experienced. Andrew had been right all along. In that hospital, that young soul torn from a life worth living, weak and confused on that cold, slab-like hospital bed. He had been right, had been talking sense. He had been right all along about the house.

Finally, Eric left the room, traipsing along the corridor and descending the stairway, making his way through the main door. Cool air freshened him, clearing his cobwebbed head. He hastily strolled out into the alley, remembering the stark reality of his own world. Glancing down at his watch, his eyes widened, as he noted the time. 07:35. He tapped his fingers on the glass face. It was still working, still ticking on as it had done since it had been bought for him that Christmas two years ago. Two years to a time when the only things on his mind were Suzie Perkins and finding ways to avoid mathematics with Mr. Bonehead Benson.

But how could it be, he thought to himself, how could it be possible that just ten minutes had passed? How could it be possible when so much had happened? It should have taken a good ten minutes just to get into the house, find the room and leave again.

He ran up the alley and out onto the street, salty tears drying in the breeze. The faster he ran the more his head buzzed with the world left behind, the terrible things inside it. Maybe it was all just a bad dream after all, maybe just a horrible nightmare. Maybe he had just fallen asleep in that damp, old room, maybe he had just woken up from a deep sleep after a nightmare. Maybe he was still dreaming.

Yes, that had to be it. Soon he'd wake up in his own bed, in his own home, with his own life. He'd wake up before all this happened, a long time before the pain and the uncertainty. Before the nightmare became reality, if that was really what it was.

Before, to a time when people followed sidewalks lined with shop fronts and walked down pathways toasted by a warming sun. Before, to a time when shoppers and tourists alike searched for a good bargain down town. Before—before all this crazy stuff began. If this was all one bad dream, one horrible nightmare, he just wished it would end.

A chilling breeze stalked each lifeless street, resting an invisible second on a lonely porch or bow of a tree before rushing on again. He reached home, crossing the small garden then looked up. Now he was faced with another problem, the problem of getting back in his room. The old black drainpipe looked a great deal safer coming down that it did going up. He forced an arm into the air, pulling his body up the pipe aided by his short, but powerful legs until his fingers touched the windowsill. The grid was removed without too much difficulty and at last he was back in the comfort of his bedroom. It had taken only ten minutes, he saw, taking another peek at his watch. He threw himself on the bed with a loud sigh.

He gazed about the room, searching out all those familiar objects around him. He liked the Star Wars figures—Darth Vader in a motionless battle to the death with Luke Skywalker. R2D2 and C3PO stared back at him from under a pink tasselled lampshade, along with a sandman and a hammerhead. Princess Leia, Hans Solo and the faithful Chewbacca with a broken hand, no doubt bitten off by the last child to stay in the room, stood silently by.

Upon the bookshelf were some more models, a Tyrannosaurus Rex crossing a mahogany desert accompanied by a Triceratops, a Diplodocus and a tail-chewed Protoceratops. What a strange band of travellers, he thought.

All these things he'd found in the room when he first moved in and he'd left them where they were. All these things seemed to calm him, soften his heartbeat, and soothe his tattered soul. After much thought he rolled off the bed, swinging his feet around. Then he stood up, crossed the floor, unlocked the door and threw it open, cautiously peering out the doorway before walking down to the kitchen. Upon entering he noticed Mrs. Thomson cooking herself a hearty breakfast. A sweet, inviting waft of toast and honey, of bacon and fried eggs and of mushrooms and baked beans curled toward him. A large pot of tea rested patiently on the table. Fumes burst comfortingly from the spout, those blends of India's finest tea filling the lavish room.

Mrs. Thomson swung easily around, poking her head through the flower engraved, wooden arch. "Well, don't just stand there, you can't let all this good food go to waste, surely. There's Cornflakes in the cupboard, if you want them instead. Otherwise you can have a nice fry up. There's plenty here, so come on, come and sit yourself down."

Mrs. Thomson was a rather attractive looking lady, not yet completing her second year of marriage. Love was young and fresh. Mr. Thomson always received a good morning kiss and a happy-go-lucky gaze. Everything for them was new, everything a wonderful adventure. Not like couples who have spent years together. Mrs. Thomson was tall, thin, had long dark hair and her skin was soft and clear. She was helpful, motherly, everything in fact that a perfect wife should be. She had worked as a hairdresser before meeting the man of her dreams. She had been a good hairdresser too, and the job had paid her bills, had kept her afloat. Then along came her knight in shining armor to take her away from all that nasty bleach and shampoo, and that's the end of the story really. From hairdresser to proud and loving wife. What a lucky man Mr. Thomson was, he thought.

Eric thanked her for her kindness, seated himself at the table and helped himself to a slice of toast from a rather large center plate.

"Did you sleep well?" she asked, turning the bacon as it hissed and crackled contentedly within its dark, metal skillet.

"Yes, thanks, Mrs. Thomson," he replied. "I slept just fine."

His mind flowed and overflowed, the urge to say something, to get things off his chest, just to say what he so badly wanted to say. Oh, say he'd been out of the house, that he'd made the discovery of a lifetime. Words gathered on his tongue, almost leaping for the chance to escape before being swallowed once more.

"Didn't you come down earlier, Eric? It's just that I

thought I heard somebody."

Eric paused a moment, just long enough to find an adequate reply. "Umm. Umm, yes I did. Yes, I was hungry so I took a sandwich."

Mrs. Thomas laughed. "Oh Eric, you sound as if you're in trouble. You're not, of course, you're not. I was just asking, that's all."

Once he'd eaten, Eric thanked her once more then returned to his room. Locking the door firmly behind him, he reached for a pen and a note pad, both of which were on the floor next to the bed and jotted down a few notes. He wrote:

> *Life on the other side.*
>
> *I went to the house today, the one Andrew spoke about.*
>
> *I found a room and a wall that leads to somewhere else. On the other side there is another world. Nobody's going to believe me, but I'm going to write it down anyway. I saw people with a strange tattoo and a giant valley. I saw a monster kill them. I saw a creature feed them. I saw something that I can't explain. I saw a new world. And I didn't like it either.*
>
> *Finishing off here.*
>
> *The date is the 4th of August 1998*

He lay back on the bed, rolling the pen between his fingers, his mind ticking over like the cogs of a Grandfather clock. No matter how he ran things through in his head, nothing made any sense. Even if he could make it back, what then? That lane, where did it lead to? How could it have led anywhere? There was nothing but black, empty space on either side of the valley of death. The creature of death then? Where had it come from? Was there another world out there, hidden within the darkness? Maybe a world that even he hadn't seen?

Just then someone knocked on the door.

"Eric, can I come in?"

He stood up, placing the pen and note pad back under the bed, marching over to unlock the door. It was Mr. Thomson. He looked sad, his usual cheerful smile replaced by a look of deep concern. He paced slowly into the room, leading Eric back to the bed, seating himself with a weary sigh.

"Eric," he uttered. "Sit next to me. I'm afraid I have some bad news to tell."

Eric never said a word. He seated himself and waited nervously as Mr. Thomson struggled to say what had to be said. He bit worriedly on his upper lip as he searched deep down inside for the right words, every muscle in his well-boned face showing his inner most feelings.

"Eric," he began. "Eric, Andrew's dead. I'm sorry, I'm so sorry." He paused, realizing what he'd said, realizing that after all the soul searching, only the plain facts had come forth. How terrible to have to be the bearer of such bad tidings in such bad times. The boy before him, his only true friend was gone. Gone from this world. His mother was gone, his father and now, now Andrew was gone as well.

"He was killed, Eric. By what I don't know, not even the hospital staff know. He was just killed." He took Eric by the shoulders and pulled him in close, wrapping his powerful arms tenderly about him. "Go ahead, Eric, you can cry. It's all right to cry."

Eric pulled himself away, a lonesome tear riding on a lash of black. He found himself all of a sudden unable to cry. He stared blankly toward the wall, eyes picking out objects on it. He stared intently at two oil paintings, one of a little girl, the other a little boy. Scanning the wall, his gaze came to rest on a china boxer dog on a stack of Natural History encyclopedias and a map of Great Britain as it looked five hundred years ago. He tried to cry, tried to cry for Andrew. He tried to cry for all the bad in the world, to cry, for God's sakes, just to cry, for all the evil in the world. But he couldn't, he just couldn't.

Mr. Thomson slowly raised himself and crossed the floor to the door, turned once to gaze back, opened it and then left, closing it gently behind him. He trod silently down the stairs to his equally concerned wife.

"How did he take it?"

"I don't know. I mean, he never said a word. I tried to hold him, but he didn't want me to. He didn't cry, but he was pretty damn close to it."

The whole house mourned Andrew's death while Eric sat alone in his room trying his best to blot it out like a bad dream. Downstairs, Mr. and Mrs. Thomson, unaware of Eric's discovery, unaware of his plans, sat in silence, holding each other with comforting hands and arms. Pain and death, nothing really new. The news, what little there was, told of nothing else. People dead; people disappearing, people going crazy. But this was different; this was a young boy, a young boy who had touched their hearts. A young boy who in a short space of time had become family, almost a son to them.

Eric dozed and woke up many times during the following few hours. He had tossed and turned, churning things over in his head. Why? Why? Why? Andrew, the young man who had done so much to help a defenseless boy. A young man who had picked him up when he was down, had acted as both mother and father for a short time. A young man who had been through so much, only to die in a hospital bed, only to be murdered in cold blood. Where was the justice? Where was the right in that?

Eventually he fell asleep again, a deep, undisturbed sleep. Mrs. Thomson didn't wake him for dinner. Instead, she took up a plate of cheese sandwiches and a small glass of milk, leaving them on the side table. The day passed, night closing in on the earth. It was late when Eric finally woke up with a weary yawn. He rubbed his eyes and flicked on the bedside lamp. He smiled on seeing a midnight feast at his side. The digital clock flashed red, 00:00.

"Damn," he mumbled as he reached for and bit into a cheese sandwich. "Bloody power's been off." He gazed down at his wrist, the time read 2:06.

Something clicked deep down inside, an adventure raising its head. He thought back to Mr. Thomson's sad words, thought back to his last time with Andrew, that brave young man cut down in his prime. But he no longer felt sad, no longer felt the pain of such bad news. Instead, he felt an inner strength, a warmth unknown and a power without equal. He stretched and raised his arms high in the air with a quiet groan. A sudden com-

The Maze 129

pulsion to be alone overcame him. Not just for now but indefinitely. Mr. and Mrs. Thomson were good people; there was no denying that. He liked them, he liked them a lot. But he had made up his mind.

He rolled off the bed and pushed to his feet, opened a dresser drawer and took out a fresh pair of socks and underwear, stuffing them into a plastic bag he found in the back of the closet. Reaching for a pen and note pad from under the bed, he began to write once more.

> *Dear Mr. and Mrs. Thomson,*
>
> *I went out this morning, went to a house Andrew told me about. I found something there. No point in telling you because I doubt you would believe me anyway. Thank you for everything you've done for me. I shall miss you both very much. Look after yourselves and take care.*
>
> *Love,*
> *Eric*

He placed the note on the bed and reached for the glass of milk. All that remained to do was finish his supper and leave.

Chapter 7

The Voyage Home

Danny rolled his head steadily from one side to the other. He'd tried to sleep but found it to be a near impossibility. Johanna was restless, too. He lay watching the ceiling as it gradually changed shade from black to a shady pale. As daylight arrived he sat up, brushing fingers through his hair before crawling out from under the warmth of the blanket. The night had been a very quiet one, a little too quiet, he thought to himself.

"Morning, Johanna," he greeted softly, walking over to the curtains and drawing them open to let the light in. "Another day, another story to tell."

Reluctantly, Johanna dragged herself from the warmth of her bed; wrapping her bathrobe tightly around her naked, goose bumped body. Danny crossed the floor toward her, kissing her gently. "Best we try'n get back to England today, doll. We gotta get our hands on a good car, gotta be loads out there anyhow, what dya say?" he mumbled through a wide yawn. "Leave our gear at the station. No point risking it." He bent down, picking up his T-shirt and pulled it over his head.

"You go into the living room when you're ready, Danny. I'll wash up and put some clothes on while you wait." She collected a clean towel from the rather cheap looking, white wardrobe.

Once ready, Danny left the room and strolled off into the living room, trying his best to iron out the pieces. He quickly took a good glance around before walking lightly over to the stereo system. It was an absolutely splendid system, he noticed, one of the nicest he'd ever seen. It rested patiently in its mahogany cabinet behind smoked glass doors, just waiting for the chance to come to life in a musical embrace. Two tall CD racks stood to one side, a large tape case plus a black, metal tape rack crammed with at least fifty or so tapes. Whether the vast music collection belonged to Johanna or to her father didn't really matter. Danny was in 'hits' heaven. His eyes danced from CD to tape, curious fingers reaching for and taking out his favorite songs. From rock n' roll to pop and soul—60's, 70's, 80's and 90's—disco and funk and blues and... It was all there, a history of music through the ages. He pressed the power button then took a CD from the black, metal rack and opened it up. Pressing open, he placed the CD on its plastic tray, pressed close and hit the play button.

Within a few seconds a soft tune floated about the room. His mind lifted from his unrest, the music temporarily soothing and caressing his pain into distant, deep and dusty corners. Turning, he noticed a glass-encased cabinet full of bottles of alcohol. Rum, brandy, gin and vodka to name but a few. On closer inspection, he spied a bottle of Newcastle Brown Ale behind an old bottle of West Indian dark rum. He took it out and opened it, raising it to his lips with a thirsty gulp. It felt good, more than good. It felt like liquid gold rushing to kiss his stomach. Apart from the sound of Jim Morrison singing out one of his oldies, all that could be heard was the rush of water as Johanna took her shower. A smile crossed his face, a slight smirk, really. If only the situation could have been different. If only the pain and the fear could have been part of some wild, although soon to end, nightmare, then that moment would indeed be a treasured moment. Moving over to the couch, he seated himself, his bottom sinking into its tremendous softness.

It wasn't long before Johanna entered, her hair damp and clinging to her perfectly rounded shoulders. The waft of her perfume filled his nostrils and he studied her lovingly. Magnificent, absolutely magnificent. A gift from the almighty God especially for him. She was beautiful, everything about her was beautiful. The way in which her soft pink sweater hung neatly about her sexually petite frame, the way in which her tight blue jeans sat against her creamy pale skin and the way in which her white sneakers protected those dainty little feet against the outside world.

"You look gorgeous," he remarked sincerely as she seated herself at his left side.

"I see you found your way to the drinks cupboard."

"I'm sorry, I should've asked."

She giggled, taking the bottle and sipping from it. "It's okay. This is a good song, Danny, one of my father's all time favorites."

All of a sudden, she looked very sad, her eyes closing, long lashes lying softly against her skin. Playing that particular record was in real bad taste, Danny thought to himself, but then, what was he to do? He placed a reassuring hand on her upper arm, feeling her body warmth penetrate his skin.

Suddenly a loud roar erupted somewhere outside. The roar sounded like that of a car screaming along at exceptional speed, getting louder, louder, heading in their direction.

"Hey, listen, do you hear that?" He froze, as the vehicle tore toward them. In a flash he dived over Johanna, throwing both her and himself across the room as the car came hurtling through the front wall.

"Johanna!" he yelled, feeling his body forcefully bouncing across the floor. A shower of glass and brickwork rained down on him, pounding against his back as he cowered, head in hands. He lay low, too afraid to move until the room was still once more. Slowly he raised himself to unsteady knees, debris falling from his battered frame. His head thumped, a trickle of red dancing down his right cheek.

"Johanna? Johanna, you okay? Johanna, answer me! You okay? Where are you?"

As the dust settled, coating everything in an off-white film, he could just make out a figure slouched over the car's steering wheel, a head hanging somewhat awkwardly through the smashed windshield. In the far corner of the room something moved, a grubby pink shape shakily rising to hands and knees.

"Danny, over here!"

Johanna dragged to her feet and climbed a mountain of rubble, grasping Danny, holding him tightly, feeling a gentle hand glide softly across her cheek.

"Come on, let's get the hell outta here."

He led the way out of the smashed room, glancing over his left shoulder just once toward the wrecked car. Nothing had escaped the impact, the room now little more than an angry, open hole. The four seater, gray velvet settee was now just a sleeping, splintered bulk at the wrong end of the room. That once, oh so beautiful, old teak dining table now spewed out through the remnants of a glass door. The cabinets and stereo system were now gone, buried in time, as were all the photos and memorabilia of years gone by.

They left the apartment and headed off for the car. Once inside, Danny tried to start it up, the engine ticking over only to fade out once more.

"Damn it!" he growled through tight fiery lips, turning his head to face Johanna. "Come on, let's..." He paused; staring in disbelief at her long flowing, honey mane and fresh, clean clothing. His head lowered to his own jeans. They were also clean, spotless. "What the..." Fearfully, he lifted his confused gaze toward the long row of apartments they'd just left. "No car, where's the bloody car?"

"We're in it, Danny, what's the matter with you? You look as if you've seen a ghost."

"I think I just have."

"Excuse me?"

"Nothing." She took his hand, squeezing it lightly. His face looked pale and distraught. "Come on, best we get us another set of wheels." Johanna climbed out and followed him down the road, not quite understanding his bewilderment.

Silence hovered on every corner and pathway like a secret just waiting to be revealed. There were no birds flying against those swells of graying clouds, no people wandering along by the T-junction that led into town. Nothing. There was nothing at all.

"This is the police station," Johanna commented as they

passed a large, dreary gray building. "And that place over there is called Kungsmässan. It's a place with lots of shops in it."

"Big deal." In the distance Danny saw his prize, an old ocean blue Volvo parked by the side of the road, its right front wheel perched awkwardly on the curb edge like a spoiled child with nothing better to do. Its driver side door was slightly ajar.

"Look, Danny, a car. There, see it?"

Danny turned sharply, a glare of irritation crossing his face. "I know, I know. What am I, blind?" he snapped as he stormed off toward it. The car, a type 244 DL model 1979, had its front, driver side door propped open by some kind of object. As they neared it, they stopped.

His thoughts rushed haphazardly through his mind before worriedly stepping foward, leaving Johanna behind. A frightful stench filled his nostrils. He raised a hand over his mouth and nose to block it out, pushing the car door open wide.

"Jesus," he gasped, his voice muffled by his hand. "Stay back there. Shit, don't come any closer!"

He knew all too well the corpse had to be pulled clear of the car, had to be pushed out and onto the pavement. His stomach rolled and he swallowed deeply, his body not wanting to move. Stale, dry blood clots covered a gray, stone cold face, a face missing its eyes. Two gaping dark holes fell downward into pits of grayish black. One hand of the rapidly decaying body gripped the steering wheel as if even in death, it wasn't about to give up. He could feel Johanna's fearful gaze driving into his back—icy steeled daggers—and he knew exactly what had to be done. Once he had composed himself, he forced himself forward, grabbing at the corpse's thin blue striped cotton shirt and yanking it back. The decaying body rocked once before falling from the driver's seat.

Again Danny's stomach rolled as he stared into the car to see a hand, its hardened fingers clutching at the wheel. Kicking the body away first, he reached for it, wrenching it away and casting it out across the road. Deep down inside he could feel his stomach muscles tightening into solid knots, his face turning a pale shade of green. He raised his right hand, wiping vomit from his mouth, before he climbed into the car.

Johanna still stood nervously a few feet behind the car. He could plainly see her in the cracked rear view mirror. He cranked the front windows down and sighed heavily, more heavily than a ten ton boulder.

"Okay, Johanna. Come on over and get in."

He gazed down at the ignition, the key safely embedded in its groove. Johanna hesitantly padded forward, climbing in. She cast her sights in the direction of the body lying in the middle of the street like a discarded rag doll at the bottom of the toy chest. Then she turned, head facing straight on and sniffed loudly.

Danny sat in silence, his lips twitching as if he wanted to free the pain and the fear inside him, yet words rose and died before being allowed to enter the outside world. Johanna wanted to speak for him, wanted to reach out with open arms, wanted to say something, anything. Whatever he wanted to hear. She so much wanted to take his pain away, so much wanted to strike it down and cast it into the fiery depths of hell below. But there he sat lost for words, lost and alone with his pain and there was nothing, but nothing she could do to help him.

"I-I wa..." He paused, choking on wasted syllables, the body a broken lifeless form, minus one hand only feet away. "I really wanted to put that poor bastard someplace. What the hell kind of burial's that, anyway?" His fist fell down hard on the steering wheel, projecting the anger and fear he felt. "I couldn't do it, Johanna, just couldn't do it. What's happening to us?" Tidal waves of mental as well as physical torment washed over him, mighty desperate walls of confusion rising up with lashing, hateful tongues.

"At least it was real."

"What do you mean?"

"Ah, I don't know." His eyes, thick and swollen, were blurred by a million tears. Even Johanna's gentle touch couldn't ease his pain.

"I'm sorry, Dan," she softly said, holding back her own salty flow. "I'm sorry, I really am." She tried her best to fake a smile, feeling helpless as he reached for the key and turned it, the car revving up. He pushed his foot down harshly on the accelerator and stormed away.

"Where to?" he snapped. "Where do I go now?"

"Turn right."

Brakes screeched, a T-junction rushing to meet them, on past a derelict train station. At a set of dysfunctional traffic lights, he made a left turn then on again through the remnants of a small, desolate town. The road ahead stretched out before them, a dreary gray line heading into the distance. Housing estates rushed by, then farmland and in time, he slowed down to a normal pace. Sheets of greens and yellows fell away in all directions, the odd farmhouse, gas station and church jumping up like pictures in a pop-up book.

"Feels good to be on the road," Johanna said loudly against the rush of wind rushing through the open windows.

"Anything feels better than being stuck back there. Where we going anyway?"

"We turn off soon, I'll tell you when."

A sign moved in to greet them and they took a gentle, sloping turn to the left, a wide and empty highway opening up in their path.

"This is it, the road we need. We can cover a lot of ground now, Dan."

"Oh yeah. Look, listen Johanna, I know, well, um..." He waited, feeling the urge to speak, but not quite knowing what to say. A whirlpool of thoughts swirled wild horses in his head. Questions that just couldn't be answered, answers that just couldn't be questioned. The car back at Johanna's. He had seen it; of course, he had seen it. He wasn't stupid. He'd felt the earth move as it crashed though the wall. Had felt glass and brickwork rain down on him. He'd felt the cool sting of blood. He had, he knew that he had. Then why, why, why had there been no sign of a car from the outside? The body in the old blue Volvo, that poor wasted life left to rot without even a decent funeral. Nothing made any sense, reality and illusion becoming lost in a rolling gray.

"I know it doesn't make any sense but... Well, I'm sure there was a car back at your place. I mean, I'm sure a car crashed into... Ah, what the hell." He waited once more, staring on ahead, eyes picking out the odd discarded vehicle, scattered mechanical wrecks. "I'm sorry I snapped at you back there, I shouldn't have."

Johanna smiled, rolling up her side window, then edged herself toward him and placed a reassuring hand on his knee. "It's all right, Danny, I understand."

Rock faces lined the highway, petering out at intervals to reveal spacious fields and forestlands.

"Where are we going anyway?"

"South," came her reply. "Helsingborg, if we can."

Danny laughed, tears and fears banished for a false five minutes. "You got a great accent."

Johanna thought for a while before returning conversation. "Try and say this, okay?"

"Okay."

"Sjuksköterska."

"Shoo-shirti-ska," he mumbled confidently. "What's it mean, anyhow?"

"It means nurse. That's all, nurse."

For the first time since leaving the once beautiful little town of Kungsbacka, the pair found themselves laughing. For the first time, the thick ice on the lake of unease was broken, even if in time it would surely freeze over once more.

"Say something else. Something important I can use."

"Well, let me think." She tossed a series of sentences in her head, coming up with probably the most obvious.

"Jag älskar dig," she beamed. "Jag älskar dig, jag älskar dig, jag älskar dig."

"Yeah, me too. What's that then?"

She dug her well-manicured fingernails lightly into his leg with a certain playfulness. "I love you, of course. It means, I love you."

The hours passed as they made the most of their undeserved prison sentences. The highway charged on ahead, reaching for and caressing a distant horizon like a giant gray arm aimlessly pointing the way. Danny glanced down at the gas gauge, noticing the needle was dancing dangerously near red.

"Ah no, we're almost out of gas," he said somewhat worriedly. "What to do?"

The Maze

Johanna peered out through her side window, the gloominess of her world just waiting as if preparing to pounce. "First things first," she said softly. "I'm freezing. Can't you close your window now?"

"No, not yet. The very thought of being locked up where that poor, dead bastard was ain't that appealing to me, see."

"Okay. There's a turnoff soon, should be coming up on your right. Ängelholm is just two more miles."

Sure enough, an exit broke out just where she said it would and off they drove into another ghost town. The scenery changed, houses and offices climbing up out of mighty expanses of fields and forestland. Within a short while they located a gas station and pulled up by a pump. The parking lot stood empty, no other cars except a burned out shell just fifty or so feet on the other side of the street. There were no people and no attendant.

"Okay, well I guess I just help myself, huh?" Danny sighed heavily, looking around to observe his surroundings. It appeared to be quite safe from within the confines of the old blue Volvo, somewhat graveyard-like out there. Nothing moved, not even a breeze. "I won't be but a second, I hope." He opened the door and climbed out, reaching for the pump.

The air stank, closing in around him thick and heavy, icy cold and yet sickly warm at the same time. He watched the gallons roll by until the car's tank was full. Once he replaced the cap, he climbed back inside and prepared to take off.

"It's only about twenty-five miles to Helsingborg from here. There's a port, so I hope we can take a ferry to Denmark from there," Johanna commented helpfully.

"No problem. You direct and I'll get this piece a shit as far as we gotta go." He smiled warmly, leaning over and planting a neat kiss on her brow, then put the car into gear and set off. "Shoo-shirti-ska. Ja-alska-da," he said perkily with a youthful wink of the eye

Somehow he felt better, felt stronger, safer, in the knowing that the pain and horror of the past twenty-four hours was miles away, far behind him. What lay ahead of him, he didn't want to think about. It could wait.

He cleared his mind, for the time being at least, he didn't

need thoughts of worry. A warmth suddenly filled his bones. Whether it was the thought of leaving Sweden or the thought of seeing Denmark once more, he didn't really know. One step closer to home, that's where he was heading. One step closer to normality, to familiar, loving faces. Home. Oh yes, home, sweet home. His original dreams were miles away, far off in a distant memory. Far off in a time when worry and fear was never a concern. Far off in a time before his journey to Holland, before his hours of hard slog at Greasy Joe's, before his holiday plans had been given the chance to hatch. Before, yes, before. Before a time without worry and fear, without pain and heartache. There had been such a time, there really had. Those school days, sneaking off for a quick cigarette behind the bicycle sheds to name one. Going down to the local youth club and meeting the guys. Sitting in the back room, homework completed for another day, a good film just about to begin. Comfortable, resting with a bottle of Coke and a bag of popcorn, knowing his mother was out in the kitchen preparing a meal and his father was in the garage working on the car.

Danny was a dreamer. As a youngster, he'd re-enacted scenes from his favorite action films, had almost become those super heroes. He'd been a 'Doctor Who' fan, had happily wasted hours in front of the television set watching the Daleks and the cybermen. Doctor Who was afraid of nothing. Not that time traveller with his Tardis, stunning assistant and long scarf. Afraid of nothing and no one. He was a hero, a traveller on a journey through time and space. Danny, as a youngster, had played the roll of Doctor Who a great many times and even though his Doctor Who days had passed him, happy memories that they were, he couldn't help but wonder how his old time hero would have coped with the situation in hand. In the emptiness of the world around him, Danny too, felt like a time traveller. The times were changing and the old blue Volvo, his very own police box, time Tardis, was the key to his own world.

Once they arrived at Helsingborg, Johanna directed him to the pier. A few people wandered the dock, all heading in the same direction toward a large ferry. Only two men weren't moving with the rest of the crowd. Two men in their early twen-

The Maze   141

ties, Danny guessed. One of them appeared to be praying. He was resting on one knee, his face hidden by grime encrusted, cupped hands. The other was sitting in total silence, his feet hanging out over the dock edge. He looked thoughtless, eyes staring out across a seething mass of gray.

"Okay, let's go." Danny coughed, opening the door and stepping out into the cool, salty air. They followed the small group onto the ferry, filtering up its narrow gangway and into a spacious lounge area.

Johanna gazed about the room. "Strange," she whispered. "This is a long distance ferry, not like the one from Harwich to Hoek Van Holland. Not an ordinary ferry."

Danny took her by the hand and led her to a vacant settee. "So what? We'll get to England faster this way."

"No, you don't understand, Danny. From the outside, this was just a small ferry, the type that goes from here to Denmark. And from the inside it's huge."

"Paranoia."

"Excuse me?"

"Well, I mean, it's a bit like the Tardis. Little on the outside and huge on the inside."

Johanna looked confused, her eyebrows twittering like wind blown canopies over pools of deep blue. "Danny, what are you talking about?"

"Ah, nothing."

After several minutes the ferry set off, bobbing lifelessly about on a salty darkness. Seven or eight men, a small silent group of women and the odd child, all below the age of ten, sat in the center of the circular dance floor. Their eyes appeared to be glazed and their faces were expressionless. An old man rested in the near, right hand corner. He fidgeted on his orange, foam filled stool. Suddenly Danny noticed something, something he'd seen before. There, there stamped on the man's left hand. A pattern, the same pattern as he'd seen on the scrap of paper in Johanna's father's bedroom. An eye, scales above and figures below. The memories came rushing back in blazes of fury, hungry and vengeful, screaming as if to kill. The car in the wall, the bricks and the dust, the man with the axe on the roof.

Danny closed his eyes tightly, rubbing them with dirty fingers. Easily his mind started to wander. His mother, his father, what were they going through? Maybe home sweet home would be just as alien as the rest of Europe.

His life passed swiftly before him, his childhood suddenly becoming as clear as day. The time many years ago when his mother had taken him to the zoo. They'd become separated in the crowds and his mother had almost been driven frantic with worry. She had searched all over, only to find him watching the penguins being fed. He remembered the security of being back home. How great the feeling of knowing that everything was okay. Be it a hot meal, clean clothes, a guiding hand or a place of safety, everything was okay. Back home in that pleasant little seaside town in the south of England. The place where he'd grown up, the place he'd learned to love, just as much as the family, the house on the East Cliffs with that spectacular view.

On a sunny day, the Isle of White could be clearly seen from his bedroom window, shimmering in the distance like a dancing white angel on the blue. Now, now that was all gone, gone, but for the memories. The laughter and the fun of Bournemouth with its Pleasure Gardens and golden shore line. He felt sure these things would never grace his sights again.

The ferry pushed on, cutting through an angry, swooning, murky gray. He sat in silence, Johanna fast falling asleep. Carefully, he placed a reassuring arm around her, letting her nuzzle into his black leather jacket and, by now quite grubby, white T-shirt. The hands of the fancy wall clock above the splendid old oak bar, moved aimlessly about their face, seconds ticking by, rolling into minutes. A curiosity burned inside him, the urge to find some answers, to find some food. Pushing to his feet, making sure not to disturb his sleeping beauty, he left the lounge area and headed to the top deck to see what he could find. Nothing but a deep, empty silence filled his ears, nothing that is, except the continual drone of the engines.

Climbing the main stairway, he forced the main door open. All around him, as far as the eye could see, nothing but a mighty darken swell angrily presented itself. Towering, ferocious waves buffeted the giant red and white hull. Roiling thick clouds filled the sky above, crossing the heavens like chariots thundering in from hell.

He stepped back inside and descended the stairway once more, leaving the wind and the waves to rage on alone. Back in the lounge area nothing had changed. Johanna still lay curled in a human ball, hands clasping at her knees. The group in the center of the circular dance floor looked somewhat like waxwork dummies. The old man fidgeted on his orange, foam-filled stool and the hands on the fancy clock above the bar with the brass hand and foot rails, still carried on about their face. Nothing had changed, nothing at all.

"Johanna," he whispered softly. "Hey, wake up." She rolled her pretty head, gazing up into the face of the one she loved. "Listen, I've just been up on deck. We're miles away from anywhere. I don't reckon we're going to Denmark, that's for sure."

Johanna smiled affectionately, raising a soft, gentle hand to his cheek, gliding a finger lightly across it. "I shouldn't worry too much, Danny. Maybe it does go straight to Harwich. What's the word you used? Oh yes, paranoid." She closed her eyes once more and faded into the land of sleep.

Unable to join her, Danny left once more. Hunger screamed at him like a raging lion. He needed food, and he needed it fast. A large and easily understandable map of the ferry sat neatly on a mint green wall by the luggage compartment. According to it, the café was located on the second floor, and he soon found it. A rather large L-shaped room with views onto the ocean. Tables and chairs sat against cream white walls and serving area where glass cabinets boasted a variety of cream cakes, tarts, sandwiches and crispy rolls near a drink machine with an assortment of sodas nearby. The only thing missing were people.

The door was unlocked and he marched in, walking up to the counter and waiting a short while.

"What the hell am I doing?" he growled under his breath. Nobody was coming, of course nobody was coming. Why the hell should they be? He reached over, grabbing at two cheese rolls. A few cans of soda from the drink machine and a medium-sized, wicker basket full of tasty snacks would be enough to satisfy the roar of his angry stomach. Arms full, he left once more. Back in the lounge, he seated himself, nudging Johanna lightly.

"Hey, Johanna. Come on, I got us a little something to eat."

"Great," she yawned excitedly, lunging for a roll. Quickly unwrapping it, she tore into it almost as if she'd never seen food before. Her eyes lit up, teeth tearing and chewing vigorously. Her thankful gaze rushed to meet his, her mouth full almost to capacity, making her look somewhat like a long-maned, golden hamster.

"Where did you get this?"

"Up at the café. Loads of stuff up there to eat. And well... Well, ain't as if nobody's gonna go up and buy anything, right? You wanna can of Coke?"

"My hero. Thank you." She took the can, popped the cap and raised it to her lips, taking a thirsty slurp. The bubbles tickled her tongue, refreshing a dry, parched throat. "Wow, I needed that."

Once full, stomach contented, her expression changed. Look," she whispered. "Just look. Nobody, not the first person has even moved. What's the matter with them?"

"Damned if I know. Come on, I got an idea."

She grabbed a chocolate bar from the basket, before following Danny out of the lounge, up the main stairway and out through the main door. Stretched out before them, far upon the horizon, lay a block of land, surrounded by a shield of gray, rising above the waves and crashing down like a wall in a prison compound.

"Look, there." Johanna gulped, a near gale force wind blowing in her face, and not hesitating to at least try to steal her words away. "Land."

She glanced down at her watch, the wind lashing her hair like miniature whips in her face. "We've been on this floating hell hole for twelve hours now." She paused to catch her breath, eyes staring unblinkingly toward the hands on the dial as they began to travel wildly about their face. "Danny, this doesn't make sense." She pushed her wrist forward, letting him look at her watch and noted his confusion.

"What the?" The hands whipped wildly back and forth, moving insanely without finding a safe haven, a place to rest. "Stay here Johanna, just stay here. I'll fix this." He kissed her strongly, pressing his lips firmly against hers before turning and battling through the raging wind to a flight of white, steel steps. Once at the top he pulled the large steel door open and stepped into the control room. A man stood ahead of him, a man in a uniform.

"Excuse me, sir? Sir?" A reply never came. Body tense, nervous, confused and angry, Danny lunged forwards. "Look, it's time for some answers."

Suddenly the uniformed man jumped, head swinging around to face him, his eyes burning like little fires in a witch's cavern. His mouth hung wide open, dripping saliva trails from his bloodied lips.

"Holy… Ah, shit," Danny managed to utter.

Slowly he edged himself back toward the large steel door. Once there, he paused a terrified second, fought to find an inner strength and finally forced the door open, almost tumbling down the stairway. How he made it back to Johanna, he didn't know, but through the nightmare, she came to be at his side.

"Quick, let's get back inside."

He yanked her through the main door, hauling her down the main stairway and into the lounge. Then he threw himself on the settee, dragging her down with him. His face was pale and ghost-like, his body shaking uncontrollably.

"Danny! Danny, what's the matter? What happened in there?" she asked softly, trying her best to calm him down. "What is it, Danny?"

"It was horrible!"

"What was horrible?"

"The man in the control room. Scared the shit out of me, he did. Bloody hell, bloody horrible. A freak, friggin' freak. Damn, Johanna, we're in trouble." He held her tightly; beads of sweat charging down his traumatized face. "What's happening, Johanna? I can't take it much longer. It's doing me in, I tell ya. It's doing me in."

Suddenly the ferry jolted, bottles and glasses falling from dusty bar surfaces and smashing to the ground. People tumbled helplessly across the strip wooden dance floor, chairs and tables sliding into the far wall.

Danny crawled across the floor, reaching for and grabbing Johanna, as the very earth beneath their feet began to roll. An ear-piercing screech tore through the ferry's interior, everybody and everything sliding to one side as the water level rose, forcing portholes to burst in sprays of glass under the pressure. Icy waves gushed through small, circular holes, filling the lounge with the gray waters of the deep.

"Hold onto me!" Danny yelled, pulling himself up and holding on for dear life to the foot rails around the bottom of the bar. He forced himself—and her, clinging to his trouser leg, around its side against the lounge door. Still the water level rose, passengers falling away, sinking to the bottom, not screaming for help, not trying to swim for their very existences. Just slipping away into the icy depths, sliding to their deaths.

Again the ferry's huge bulk shook wildly, throwing both Danny and Johanna backward. Her grip loosened, felt herself slip, just managing to grab his foot.

"Johanna, hold on! For Christ's sakes, hold on!" he screamed, tightening his grip on the rail. A roar as loud, if not louder, than that of thunder tore through dishevelled corridors, water gushing in all around. The ferry moved again, breaking into the water, the sheer pressure forcing them apart. "Johanna!"

Her grip loosened one last time, then she was gone. Seconds later he, too, fell, twisting and turning, rolling uncontrollably down into the waves, hurled into a swirling abyss.

Darkness surrounded them, icy cold, murky water enveloped them. Johanna felt herself being pushed upward from the mass swell of bluish gray water. She found herself screaming in silence, gasping for air, swimming upward until bobbing through towers of waves. She clung for dear life to a reasonably large piece of wooden board floating boisterously among the wreckage. Something splashed in the waves just ahead of her, a head bobbing about.

"Danny! Danny!" she spluttered, swimming over to him.

"It's okay, I'm all right," he choked a reply, pillars of seawater raining down on him. They pushed forward, riding on the crest of each skyward reaching wave. Tired and exhausted, they met, splashing and kicking, holding each other up against all odds. Waves avalanched down on them, raining down like liquid skyscrapers. "You're alive, thank God."

Land lay only a mile or so away. Obviously, the ferry had struck some kind of obstruction, a sand bank or low tide rock face. They swam toward the waiting shoreline, helped on by the surging water. Bodies weak beyond belief, they reached for and clung to an orange life buoy that floated nearby. Eventually, hurtling waves rolled at the crest and plumes of white sprayed forth, saturating the sand ahead. Their feet touched land and they fell near lifeless to the sandy shore. Daylight faded, night time set in. Both too exhausted to move, they lay, waves rushing ferociously against their still bodies.

Morning came, thick clouds of steel gray, hovered overhead. Danny opened his eyes, scraping sand grains away with his fingers. His body was sore and half-numb with cold. Johanna lay face down to his left. Crawling across to her, he raised her head and turned her over. Her face was icy cold and pale, but she wasn't dead.

"Johanna," he croaked. "Johanna! You okay?"

"Morning, Dan. How about a...?" She paused, groaned, forcing herself into an upright position somewhat awkwardly. "How did we get here?"

Danny pulled her gently to her feet, propped her against his side and staggered up the beach.

"The ferry," he moaned painfully. "It sank."

A lonesome tear wound its way down his tender skin, a silent prayer for the ones who had slipped away to their deaths out there in the icy swell of the night before. He stopped to gaze out to sea, to momentarily picture things as he had remembered them.

"Wait up! No wreckage, no bodies, but..."

Dumbfounded, he raised a shaky hand to his face. How stupid it all sounded. His clothes were suddenly clean and dry, no longer thick with damp, cold sand. There was no sign of a sunken ferry out there.

Johanna smiled, a crystal star shine in her eyes. "What ferry?" she asked gaily. She, too, looked fresh and clean, her hair, soft and golden, flowing back in a lightly salted breeze.

Danny didn't reply, his mind lost somewhere in the depths of an unbearable turmoil. He helped her off the beach, up a set of stone steps and onto a lonely promenade, recognizing this place. The pier with its amusement arcade and theater. Sandy cliffs rose up and away from the beach huts and ice cream stands.

"Bournemouth!" he said with great surprise. "This is Bournemouth!"

They moved on, a cool, somewhat welcoming drizzle pattering against them, dampening their faces. Just then Johanna stopped, turning a weary head out toward the far end of the pier, to the theater and café.

"This is Bournemouth, I remember now. My mother brought me here once."

Danny sighed heavily. "Didn't I just say that?"

"No."

"Yes I did. What are you, deaf?"

"The ferry, I remember now. There was a ferry, we were on it. Where is it?" She stared worriedly into his eyes, his sad returning gaze half-blinding her.

"I don't know, but it's not bloody well out there, is it?"

"You don't have to swear, Danny!"

Her mind clouded over, every cavity in her confused brain screaming for answers, nothing making any sense. There was no order to things; nothing seemed real any longer. "I remember a car, Danny. Back home, I remember now!"

Danny tutted loudly, a certain anger escaping him. "Bit late now, don't ya think? Look, forget it. Just follow me."

Slowly they made their way through the Pleasure Gardens, leaving the hungry and vengeful sea behind them. Nothing but empty silence filled their heads—a lonely, eerie silence—almost that of death itself.

The Gardens looked about the same as they always had, minus the familiar chatter of holidaymakers laden with picnic baskets, towels, bathing suits and sun screen. Each tree stood ridged against the darkened sky, thick tangles of dandelions, bind weed and stinging nettles growing wildly about the crazy golf course, spreading an ugly mass of neglect. No flowers bloomed in the hedgerows, no pigeons scratched the grass. Almost as if the town had been forgotten by mankind, left to Mother Nature to do with as she pleased.

On reaching the far end, they moved through the underpass and into the Square. Shivers, icy and cold, ran with a frenzy down their spines, tearing at nerve endings with destructive power. Cars lay all around, left on curb edges, smashed into shop front windows and doorways. Buildings stood broken beyond repair. Brickwork, glass, rubble piles, memories of Gothenburg rushing back.

Danny shuddered, remembering Bournemouth as he'd left it, as he'd always known it to be, as he'd always longed for it to stay. He fell to his knees, sobbing into his cupped hands in despair. His worst nightmare had come true. All the wishing, all the praying, all the hoping that Bournemouth might bring warmth and safety, all that was gone.

His family, the ones he'd left behind less than one week ago, those who he loved, who he'd promised to write to, promised to come home to. But he was home, home to a Bournemouth that was totally alien to him. His friends and family. Yes, this was their town, the town which had nurtured them and had comforted them. The town that had known most of them since birth. Now, now the very thought of going and finding them was enough to make him feel decidedly sick. How could it be possible that in less than one week a whole way of life could just vanish?

If he was to find them, if he was to go home to that house on the East Cliffs with the spectacular view. If he was to climb the three stone steps to the main door, turn the brass doorknob and step inside, what then was to greet him? It was all too much for him. He knew going home was not the answer.

Pulling himself together, he raised himself and took Johanna's hand, squeezing it comfortingly. They moved briskly away from the town center, followed a lonely hill lined with empty, derelict shop fronts. A narrow side road lay to their left and they headed along it.

"Come on, let's rest here," Danny suggested softly, walking toward a rather run down building at the other end of a cracked, asphalt driveway. The building had at one time most likely been a guesthouse or hotel, a large grubby sign hanging above the doorframe alluded to that fact.

Danny tried to read it, barely picking out the word, 'THE', and two letters, 'S', something 'I'. The rest had been lost in the grime of everything about it. He peered in through a dirty window, just making out a dining room, complete with a dusty center table, several tatty old chairs and an old teak dresser with only one door. Through the next window he could see into a small room, empty except for a pile of potato sacks and scrunched up newspapers.

"Come on, doll. Let's take a look round the back," he said softly, almost whispering. He glanced cautiously over his left shoulder before helping her down the narrow side passage and around to the rear side of the building. On the other side of the building, a thick, dense jungle of brambles and stinging nettles grew wildly into the stale air. A fresh track had been beaten into them leading to a small, smashed window. Slowly, they edged their way toward it, peeking through the opening into a rather damp, cold room. "Okay, be real quiet, okay?"

He raised his right leg, pulling himself through to the other side. A quick glance around the room's interior, eyes scanning each danky corner, he turned, helping Johanna through, guiding her feet over the faded green window sill and onto the damp, wood planked floor inside. Once safe inside, he tugged lightly on her soft pink sweater, then headed for the rotted doorframe and into the hallway.

Suddenly he tripped, landing with a painful thud to the floor. Johanna tumbled on top of him, a tangle of arms and legs. Tin cans rattled along the hallway, clanging like rusty bells on the damp wooden floors.

"Shit! A trip wire!" The house came to life, footsteps sounding above their heads.

"Danny!" Johanna screamed on seeing a figure charge

down the stairway wielding a sharp knife. The figure, a young male, dived on Danny as he struggled to his feet. Danny twisted his attacker's arm back, violently tearing the knife away from his teenage hands.

"Okay, okay. You're breakin' my friggin' arm!" the youngster yelled, face red and screwed up in pain.

The attacker-come-victim found himself being forced into the air and then thrown with considerable force to floor. Cautiously, Danny loosened his grip, releasing the streetwise youngster, standing up and stepping slowly away. Johanna came to his left side as the youngster climbed to his feet.

"Okay, kid, what's the big idea? You could've killed me. Stupid little snot, I oughta kick your cheeky ass!"

"Danny, calm down. He's just a child."

The youngster stepped back, slouching against a mildew coated wall. His eyes landed firstly on Johanna, working their way from top to toe, then hopped to Danny. Somebody's brother, somebody's son, that grubby cheeked youngster standing before them, Danny thought. He stared back, the anger within him gradually fading into friendly smile.

"Look, I didn't mean to rough you up, kid, but what the hell are you doing here?"

"I live here. You broke into my house," he replied calmly, body relaxing. "I'm sorry about the knife. I didn't know who you were."

Danny glanced at Johanna. All of a sudden he felt a little stupid. Imagine, fighting a youngster who was only trying to protect his own property. "We can go if you like. We thought the place was empty, that's all."

The boy never replied straight away. He bent down, picking up his knife, tucking it neatly into the back left pocket of his filthy blue jeans before crossing the hallway floor and climbing the first two steps of the carpetless stairway.

Danny and Johanna waited uncertainly as he stopped, paused a moment before turning to face them, a certain twinkle in his eyes. His skin and clothes were dirty beyond belief, stained by severe lack of attention. His hair was greasy, hanging in solid strands about his face.

"You can both come up, if you want," he said kindly, sniffing loudly then proceeding to climb.

"I ain't sure," Danny whispered. He looked doubtful, could this be a trap?

"Come on!" Johanna barked decisively, taking him by the hand and following the youngster up to the next floor. They followed him into a small room. In the middle of the room an old man lay on his back under a pile of old potato sacks.

The young boy sat down on a thick plank of wood resting on two orange beer crates. "Sorry there ain't no place to sit, but the floor ain't too bad."

Danny and Johanna sat among the dust making themselves comfortable. "My name is Johanna and this is my boyfriend, Danny."

The boy smiled brightly and cleared his throat. "Yeah and I'm Eric. You're normal, ain't ya? I mean, like me, right?"

Just then the potato sack pile began to move, the old man waking up and poking his head out into the world.

"Morning, Harry," Eric greeted softly. "These are some friends of mine. Johanna and Danny."

Danny couldn't help but notice a certain pride echo in his words. Johanna glanced at the old man, her sights locking onto him, unable to pull away or to even move. A chill travelled the length of her spine. The old man, eyes so soft and gentle hair, beard, gray and long, had a face she recognized, a face she had seen in a dream back home in Sweden. A face that had spoken to her, warning her of bad tidings, saving her from a certain nightmare. The old man smiled and greeted them politely.

"Eric, you say your name is," Danny said tentatively, not noticing the nervous unease on his girlfriend's face.

"Yeah, and this is my best friend, Harry."

Eric began to tell his life story. How he had run away from a safe house after the death of Andrew. How he'd met Harry, his only true friend in the whole world and the three new names which so aptly described the people of Bournemouth—Norms, Crazies and Goners.

"Harry's my everything now," he explained. "My mother, father … everything!"

Johanna ran a worried finger over the palm of Danny's hand. Now he sensed her unease, could feel those strange vibrations pulling at his bones. Eric went on, explaining some of the strange goings on of late, although nothing really made any sense at all.

"Is that it?" Danny asked curiously. "I mean, well, there must be something missing. Something that just might tie this shit together."

Eric just smiled, Danny awaiting impatiently for a reply. He swung his gaze toward Harry and lowered it to the floor. "No," he finally answered. "No, that's all I know."

Harry grunted loudly, eyelids hanging in folds over his tired, gray-speckled, green eyes. Slowly they closed once more and he fell asleep.

Quietly Eric pushed to his feet, beckoning his two new-found friends out of the room, down the corridor and into another equally shabby, damp and discarded room.

"Close the door," he whispered as he lowered his body to the grimy wooden floors. "How did you get here?" he asked, almost demanded.

Danny tossed the question over in his head. Indeed it was a simple question, a simple question that deserved a simple answer. But no matter how he tried, he just couldn't find one.

"It's a long story," was all that he could say.

"Your girlfriend's very secretive, isn't she?"

"I guess. Look, you obviously have something to say, so why not get on with it."

"I will, I will. Don't rush me," Eric snapped back. "Before I say anything, you must tell me something."

"And what might that be?"

Eric paused, waited a heartbeat before he answered. He had so many questions he wanted answered, so many questions charging around inside his head like a meteor shower out of orbit. He, too, had noticed something, some strange connection between Harry and Johanna. Was it possible they knew each other, that Harry knew more than he was letting on?

Harry wasn't a straightforward kind of person, that much Eric knew for sure. Yet, Eric held back, sure he was and why not? He knew there was something he felt sure Johanna knew nothing of. Nevertheless, it disturbed him. He narrowed his eyes, staring at her in a strange way, eyes cutting into her like knives through fast melting butter.

"What's between you and Harry? Do you know him?" he asked suddenly.

Johanna shuddered. She felt trapped, like a cat in a corner with no way out, except through the mad dog's paws. The hairs on her slender, soft neck rose to attention, a shiver of ice running the length of her spine.

"Yeah," Danny commented. "Yeah, I noticed something, too. What was that all about?"

"I don't know what it is," she nervously, almost fearfully, replied. "Really I don't. I just got this strange feeling, that's all."

Eric wasn't really satisfied, although intuition told him his secret would be safe with them. It was almost as if he knew these two, as if they were all a part of some mighty plan, that their meeting was destined to be.

"I don't know why I bother pretending really," Eric admitted all of a sudden. "I mean, well Harry's not stupid. Probably not even asleep." He paused, driving an index finger through the grime on the floor, a wafer thin trench, like a snake forming a swirl on some alien wasteland. "There's something else, see. Well, I know he's my friend, Harry is and... There's just something else. He's strange, really strange. I mean, one minute he's like me and you and the next, then he's not. Sounds stupid, doesn't it?"

Danny shook his head thoughtfully, nothing surprised him any longer. "No. No, go on."

"Well sometimes he's just..."

Just then Harry called out. "Eric, Eric! Where are you?"

Eric jumped to nimble feet and briskly marched toward the door. "Wait here, okay? I told you he probably wasn't asleep."

On entering Harry's room, he stopped dead in his tracks, staring at his aging friend with a burning worry inside. The old man's body shook, veins pulsating briefly in his face.

"You told her!" he screeched under an angry breath. "You told her, didn't you? I trusted you, I trusted you and you told her!"

Eric looked on, a dumbfounded look on his young face, feeling confused and somewhat afraid. Never before had he seen Harry in such a way. It was a fact Harry often said strange things, that he often mumbled under his breath. He was strange, always had been, or had been for at least as long as Eric had known him, it was just his way. Eric had done everything for him.

He had gone out alone, breaking into shops for food to fill the old man's hungry belly. Had brought it back, had fought at times like a maniac possessed to make it back home in one piece. He had made the old man's breakfasts, dinners and teas, not an easy task without running water, electricity or gas. He'd only given, had never taken, had looked upon Harry as a father figure and most of all, Eric had put up with his strange behavior.

"What's the matter with you? Why don't you understand?" Harry went on. He groaned loudly, eased himself from the makeshift bed before staggering across to his young friend. "Stay with her, Eric, she's the one. I've had my time; it's all over for me."

Suddenly, he was grabbing at his chest, letting out a pained screech and fell to the potato sacks below. His face was pale and ghost-like, a crystal tear forming in the corner of each eye. "I'm sorry I shouted, I shouldn't have done that."

Worried now, Eric crouched down and leaned over him, raising his head. "Harry! Harry, what's wrong? What are you talking about?" His friend closed his fast dying eyes, his loving, although distinctly pained smile gradually fading out. "Harry! Harry!" he yelled. "Don't you go dying on me, don't you dare!"

Salty flows cascaded down his dirty young cheeks as he rested Harry's head neatly on an old sack. He stood respectfully to attention, stepped away and breathed in loudly through his nose. It was all over, the great man was gone.

Harry's sudden death brought on an emptiness, the end of an era. Once again Eric felt alone, no longer strong, now he was lost. Slowly, head hung low, he left the room and headed sadly to the others.

"He's dead!" he sobbed upon entering.

Danny bit harshly on his upper lip, not good in such situations like this. "Can I go in and see 'im?"

Eric's eyes glistened like stardust over green-blue seas. "Yeah, doesn't really matter what you do now, does it?"

Eric's body fell heavily to the floor, where he leaned back against the wall, brushing a hand through his hair. Johanna sat opposite him against the far wall. She was silent, deadly silent. Her mouth formed a straight line, her face quite emotionless.

Danny left the room and entered Harry's resting place, the emptiness hitting him like a bolt of lightning across a midnight sky. The same old dusty wooden floors, the same old potato sacks and scrunched up newspaper strewn across the floor.

"Jesus! Where's Harry?" he mumbled, leaving hastily.

As he raced down the corridor, his heart beating faster than a drummer in a rock band, the darkest shiver danced across his grave. Frightened, he rushed to the room, eyes wide, body trembling. Eric shot out of the room Danny had just left, charging after him, almost bowling him over. Danny caught him in his strong arms.

"What's the matter? What is it?" he asked Eric.

Eric uttered something, could have been anything, just an avalanche of frightened words, spun on the balls of his feet to swiftly return to the room where Johanna waited. On entering, they both stopped dead in their tracks. Johanna sat on the floor, her body shaking, almost shining, a ray of light escaping her body.

"What the..."

Danny stepped toward her, leaving Eric to stand alone. Hesitantly, Danny moved across to her, reaching out and touching her. A shrill scream escaped his parted lips. His body burned intensely. He felt himself rise and fly back, crashing into the wall with a mind-numbing thud.

Eric edged his way across the room. Too frightened to look directly at Johanna, he looked at Danny instead.

After a short while Johanna returned to normal. She fell to the floor, exhausted, gasping for air.

Slowly, very, very slowly, Danny lifted his dazed head, his fingers dancing lightly across a rather large bump on his forehead.

The Maze   157

"Johanna! Are you all right?" he called, easing his way toward her.

"I'm fine, Danny, just fine. In fact, I feel fantastic. Eric, you didn't tell me everything. The house, for example."

Danny straightened in amazement. "What the hell are you going on about? Eric?" He looked over his shoulder at Eric as if praying for a slice of sanity. "What the hell's she talking about?"

"No, I didn't but Harry thought that I..." He paused, thinking over what she'd just said. Now he, too, found himself searching for an answer. "The house! How d'ya know about it?" It was the question of the day, the question of a lifetime—an impossible question to answer.

"Eric, trust me. Harry wasn't crazy, Harry was a dream. A living dream, you're safe now."

Danny rushed across to her, wrapping his powerful, devoted arms about her. "Thank God, you're okay."

He didn't understand and he didn't expect to understand. Something had just happened, something far beyond his understanding. But Johanna was alive and that was all that counted. Eric moved in toward them, seated himself and in the silence about them, he rested his strangely optimistic head.

Chapter 8

World's Apart, The Maze

Once busy streets, now lifeless and decaying, were falling into the ever-hungry jaws of history. A town, once so popular as a seaside resort, now was little more than a sleeping concrete and steel monster. Bournemouth. That place by the sea with its bars and its cafés, its shopping centers and its miles of golden coastline. Bournemouth, now little more than a desolate town in a desolate county. A desolate county in a desolate country, a desolate country, part of a desolate continent. Where was it all supposed to end?

Danny sat holding Johanna, his eyes tired, wanting to close, to leave the world behind. He found himself lost, bewildered by all he'd been through, dumbfounded by his girlfriend's strange manner. Thoughts mingled with memories, shuffling around in his head, almost to the point of giving up. He systematically pictured them, trying to fit them into place. All to no avail. When would it all end, the pain and the hardship? What had happened to the love of his life? Where was Harry's body? Did he really ever exist, or could he have been some crazy figment of the imagination? A living vision maybe, caught in time, waiting for someone or something? Nothing made any sense. Nothing fitted together, the pieces of the jigsaw puzzle lost in a nightmare world.

He gazed down at Johanna, watching her lovingly as she slowly closed her eyes and fell asleep. She looked totally drained. He, too, felt the need to sleep. The journey to England had been a long and extremely tiring one, had paid its toll, and had robbed him of the courage and the strength to go on. The whole journey played on his mind. The morning before, he was waking up in Sweden, waking up within the warmth and comfort of Johanna's bed. The car ride to Helsingborg. The ferry, the captain, the waking up on the beach. Looking out across swells of angry waves to see nothing. No sign of a ship wreck, no sign of any other bodies floating around in the water. Nothing, nothing at all. Like the universe itself. Like sitting and wondering what might lie beyond the stars in the heavens above. What there might be in the next solar system. Where does it all end? He, too, could find no end, no answers to the questions that needed to be asked.

Eric sat resting on his elbows. He too wanted to sleep, but he just couldn't. He tried to make sense of all that had happened, tried to understand how it could be possible for Johanna to know about the house. He stood up and left the room, leaving to take one last look at Harry's body. He just wanted to be close to the man who had saved him from insanity. The man who had given him a reason to live, a reason for standing up and fighting to survive against the odds. Eric didn't feel sad to the point of tears. Maybe he didn't even feel sad. In fact, it was quite possible that he felt almost happy. Harry had been a fine man. He was very old, very quiet and deeply secretive, never getting too close to anyone. He had loved his life. Be it for better or for worse, he had lived his life. He was now most definitely with his maker.

On entering the room, Eric came to a complete stop. Harry's body was gone. He stared thought provokingly toward the potato sacks, to their grayish brown, lifeless forms. Suddenly a warmth came over him, a soothing, caressing warmth, a warmth from deep inside him. His head filled with sweet music, soft words echoing in his brain.

"Eric, Eric!" He jumped, although not for anything less than pure joy. "Eric, Eric! Hear my words! Eric, don't see me as dead, for I was never alive. Eric, listen to me now. Know now that Johanna is as much a part of me as she is your friend. Where she takes you, I take you. Where she says to go, I go with you."

Slowly the voice faded out, the warmth easing away. Strangely enough, the strength within stayed within. He felt no fear, no uncertainty or pain. He felt strong, felt alive, he felt … invincible.

His stomach rumbled, screaming out for nutrition. His next thought only to erase those hunger pains. He headed back to the corridor, then descended the stairway. The kitchen looked more like a fallout bunker than a kitchen. All the cupboards were still in place, a dusty sink and draining board, too. The cooking range was gone, as was the fridge and freezer. The spaces where they had been were nothing more than gaping, empty cobweb-filled mouths. It wouldn't have mattered if they were there since there was no electricity in the building, no heating either. He opened up a cupboard door, taking out a couple of cans of baked beans and half a loaf of sliced white bread that rested within a red and white wrap. Reaching for a can opener and three spoons, he climbed the stairway once more, thinking to himself that it wasn't much of a feast.

Just then, for a split second, his nerves turned to ice, as Johanna began screaming at the top of her voice. "Danny!" she yelled. "Danny, Danny!"

When he reached her, he knelt down at her side, placing a weary hand on her shoulder. "Okay love, I'm here!"

She gazed around the room, eyes dancing across the dust coated floor like two honey hunting bumblebees. "Harry's not dead," she whispered. "Harry's Hazzari, key holder to the Maze."

Danny smiled meekly, with a rather nonchalant shake of the head then gazed up toward the flaky ceiling that had once been white but now turned a yellowish-gray. Just at that moment Eric popped his curious head into the room.

"What did you say?"

"She's had a dream," Danny commented. "Says Harry's not dead, or something. She'll be okay."

"He's not," Eric replied as he strolled in and placed the poor excuse for a meal on an old beer crate. "Johanna. What's going on?"

"Take us to the house, Eric," she begged. "Have you been there before?"

"Sure I have. In and out. Yeah, I been there, but I ain't too sure about going back again."

Danny sighed heavily, an agitated look crossing his face. He reached for a can and the can opener, opening up a saucy, baked bean feast. "What? Am I not here?"

Eric never replied. He took the last can and handed it over to Johanna with a positively sunny smile. "Eat as much as you want, I'll take what's left."

Danny was confused, confused beyond belief. Something had happened, something he never thought possible. It was quite apparent Johanna had some kind of connection with the dead. In some strange, strange way she appeared to know more about Harry as a dead man than she did when he was alive.

He took a spoon and began to eat. The beans tasted okay, not the best meal in the world. How could they be? Nice, now and again, but not all the time. He was already tired of them. Baked beans, not 'bruna böner'. Baked beans or bruna böner— what the hell did it matter, it was food.

Once all three had eaten, Eric jumped to his feet. "Well, I guess that's it. You ready, Johanna?"

The three of them left the room, stamping along the corridor and down the carpetless stairway into the room Johanna and Danny had first entered. Eric was the first to climb through the smashed window, to climb out into the dreariness of yet another uncertain day. Then Johanna climbed out, followed last, but not least, by Danny. Precariously, they walked along the freshly beaten track that led into a dense jungle of brambles and stinging nettles, until coming to a moss covered, stony wall.

"Here we are. Now once we're over this wall, we need to hurry. I'll get you there Johanna, just follow me."

Over the wall they went and then it was time for them to run like the wind across an empty road and into the Lower Gardens. Out at the other side, along a maze of roads and lanes, they ran. Eventually they came to an alley and there they stopped to gain their breaths.

"Was that really necessary, all that running? I'm beat," Danny gasped.

"Not far now." Eric walked them the rest of the way, although his eyes scanned every square inch like an eagle searching a fine rabbit meal. They soon arrived at a shabby old white washed building and marched up the pathway toward it.

"This is it, Johanna. Feel anything?"

"No."

They edged their way up a flight of damp steps and into a small room.

"This is the one," he smiled with a rather noticeable unease. "Guess you already know that though, Johanna, huh?"

She looked anxiously toward Danny, then Eric and lastly toward the damp and fusty floor. "No, not really. All I know is that Harry is Hazzari and that you, Eric, know how to enter the Maze."

Eric cleared his throat awkwardly before reaching into the left side pocket of his grubby blue jeans and pulling out his knife. He held it a short while, let his right index finger dance across its rosewood handle. It wasn't large or particularly impressive, not a Bowie or a stiletto, nor was it a razor sharp dagger or a serrated edged cleaver. It was just an ordinary knife. More like a fruit knife, a fruit knife he'd found in a darkened corner of the kitchen in that run down place he called home.

"Right, watch this!" He cast the knife toward the far wall. It clinked as it hit on the moldy brickwork before falling tip-tap to the floor. "What the...? It should've gone through." He took a few slow and tentative steps to where it lay, hesitated and picked it back up. Reaching out to touch the wall, his fingers gradually dancing in the air, he slowly came to touch its surface, then slipped away out of sight. "Ah, here it is."

A distant fear played on his lips, his tongue worriedly pushing against his lower teeth. Danny just stared, words not even being given the chance to rise and flow. His mouth dropped open and his eyes widened, his frown showing the deeply etched lines of countless uncertainties.

"I really don't wanna go through again, Johanna. You ain't been in there, it's hell."

Johanna raised a hand, soft and gentle fingers fluttering across his cheek. "Don't be afraid, Eric. Be strong, you must show me the way."

Still, Danny said nothing, nothing at least that could be heard. Again he'd seen the impossible. He'd just seen a hand disappear through a solid mass. Had seen it withdrawn unscathed—unmarked. The impossible, he had seen the impossible. How many impossibilities must come to be before something appears possible?

"Danny, you hold Johanna's hand. Johanna, hold mine, before I change my mind."

Suddenly he charged forward, pulling them both through with him into the darkness. All three landed, none the worse for wear, surrounded by nothing but the black of night. The glow lay in the distance like a welcoming candle in the innkeeper's window, although at that point neither Danny nor Johanna had noticed it. It didn't really give off light. It was just there. There was nothing before it, nothing behind it. Nothing except the glow.

"What the...?" Danny whispered. He was spellbound, totally transfixed. "Where the...? What the...? But...?" He stared about himself, reaching down at his feet, feeling nothing below them. "There ain't nothing under my feet! There ain't nothing under my feet!"

A fearful cry for help might well have been justified at that point. It probably would have happened, too, had it not been for something in the distance. The glow had caught his attention, had caused his panic to cower away in the face of curiosity.

"What the... What's that?"

Eric picked himself up with a weary sigh. "That's where we're going."

All of a sudden that fear was back. A terrified scream parted his lips, the fear of finding himself in another world was nothing compared to the fear clawing at his insides now.

"No, get away from me! Get off, get off!" Danny's desperate fingers pulled violently at his shoulder length, dark brown hair. "Ah, get off, get away! Help someone!"

Johanna turned sharply. She grabbed him, shaking him like a rag doll. "Danny, Danny! Come on, it's nothing." She slapped him harshly across his left cheek with the flat of her hand and slowly, very slowly, he calmed himself back down.

"My God. Damn … my God," he panted. "I was covered in spiders! I swear!" He raised his still somewhat shaky right hand to his pale spittle-smeared lips and wiped the moisture away, inhaling deeply, and held his breath a split second then exhaled. "I saw them, felt them. You gotta believe me. True as day, you gotta believe me!"

"I believe you, Danny, I believe you think you saw them. It's all right now, it's all right." She took him by the hand and followed Eric off into the impending darkness. "Trust me. It wasn't real."

When they finally arrived at the glow, they peered over the edge. Their gaze descended down, down into the bowels of a giant rocky valley.

"Who are those people?" Johanna asked in puzzlement.

"I don't know," Eric replied. "They won't know we're here though, that I can tell you. I've been down there and not one of them knew I was there." He jumped down onto a reasonably wide, although precarious-looking ledge.

"No, Eric, come back," Danny called sharply, a deep fear for his young friend's safety.

Eric didn't listen; he knew what had to be done. From the first ledge he seated himself, letting his legs ride up over the edge. Then using his hands as steadying points he let himself slip down to the next.

"Shit," Danny exclaimed. "Come on, Johanna, he's gonna get himself killed down there."

Carefully they followed Eric down to the floor of the cave, their fingers reaching and gripping at each possible crack and cranny, ledge by ledge. Eric pushed on, stealthily guiding himself down until reaching the bottom. He stared back at his friends from the comparative safety of a huge boulder, his two best and only friends gradually working their way down no more than ten or so feet above him.

A young lady sat lifelessly on the rough, stony earth to his left, her back resting against the rough boulder, and he headed easily to where she sat. At one time she had probably been an incredibly attractive teenager. Her face was well-boned and her body, although terribly undernourished, was petite and graceful. Her hair was long, a tangled, dirty blonde and her big wide eyes were chestnut pools of color. Her clothes were torn and shabby, her jeans ripped at both knees and ex-white T-shirt, filthy beyond belief. She wore no shoes and the second, third and fourth toe on her right foot were missing, three savagely torn stumps encrusted in dried blood. Sadly, her beauty had long since faded and even though it was apparent she had at one time been very beautiful, her beauty was now lost behind a dusty, sunken gray.

Eric rested himself by her side and he tried in vain to attract her attention. "Hello," he said softly. "I, um... Can you hear me?" There came no reply, not even the remotest acknowledgement of his presence. "Hey! Come on, talk to me."

Still, she stared straight ahead. A tattoo on her dirty left hand caught his attention, a strange tattoo embedded deep into the flesh. It was the same tattoo he'd seen before. A tattoo he'd seen imprinted on the left hand of that fragile figure, the old man of his last visit. He stood, arms akimbo and couldn't help but think there was something Johanna could do to help these broken souls. He trusted her. He didn't know her, but he trusted her. And he knew if anyone could do something to help them, then she was without a doubt, the one to do it.

Johanna stopped, her neat little frame resting on a ledge no more than a foot or so above ground level. She looked worried, as though something was wrong.

"Danny, stay here. Don't go any farther," she cautioned. "Eric! Come on, quickly, climb as fast as you can."

"What's up? Come on down."

"Eric, just listen to me. Hurry up."

"Yeah, yeah, I'm coming."

Just then he heard a shuffling sound, something moving in behind him and he turned sharply to see what it might be. A person, a young boy of no more than ten years of age, edged his way from the alley that lead into the rocks.

"Eric, don't muck about. Come on, get back up here,"

Danny ordered masterfully.

Eric proceeded across to the giant jagged boulder, reaching up and preparing to climb. "What's the panic? It's just a kid."

"Move it!"

Together, they scrambled up as fast as they possibly could until finally reaching the last ledge. As Danny pulled himself up and over onto the flat, although non-apparent, firm ground, he reached for Johanna's hand. Once she was safe, he helped Eric the last bit of the way. Peering down they could see the boy, his eyes wide, burning, staring up at them. A smile spread on his round, grubby face, breaking out into fits of laughter. A face so young, so full of childish playfulness.

"See, there's nothing to get hysterical about," Eric remarked. "We could've learned something from that kid."

"I don't think so," Johanna replied with a nervous sigh. She felt something inside. Something warm, warmer than before, something friendly telling her to retreat, something telling her to leave that place without delay.

Suddenly the boy's appearance changed. His eyes began to bulge, to pulsate, the veins in his neck pushing hard against his skin. The laughter became louder, nearly unbearable, echoing the valley walls. Blood trickled from his purple, swollen lips. He raised his hands to his face, his fingernails clawing at his flesh, sinking deep. A swift crack filled the foul air, bone cracked from bone, his head held high. Thick oceans of blood gushed into a seemingly non-ending flow, cascading from the torn, fleshy neck. His body, totally bathed in red, still pulsated with life. His eyes spun in their sockets, his tongue flickered in and out of a screaming mouth.

"Come on, let's get the hell out of here," Danny gasped, his heart thumping like a steaming train on eternal tracks. They charged off into the surrounding darkness until, with a flash of brightness, they fell back into the room. Back into the shabby room in the white-washed building. Back to their own world, the light stinging their unaccustomed eyes.

Cautiously, Danny lifted his head, his eyes, small and pin-like, staring around into the dampness of the room. He glanced back, first to check on Johanna and Eric, and then to the wall, a

The Maze 167

cold unearthly shudder travelling his spine. He raised himself to his knees, shook his head lightly, as if trying to wake up from a terrible dream, and then stood up.

"What the hell was that?" He turned, helping Eric to his feet then tugged Johanna up. "Was that a dream?"

"No, Danny. No, it wasn't."

"No, a frigging nightmare, more like," he hissed back. "Look, Johanna. What the hell just happened back there? Was it real?"

Cautiously, Eric stepped in toward his male companion, remembering Danny's temper on their very first encounter. "Danny, look, just take it easy. I mean, don't be mad at us, all right? We saw it, too." He paused and let a fearful gaze touch Johanna, a cocktail of nerve-wracking fear and desperate curiosity building up inside. "Johanna, how did you know? I mean, it hadn't even happened."

Johanna wiped a crystal tear from her long black lashes with a fingertip, searching her tormented brain for an answer. "I don't know. I wish I did, but I just don't."

"Jesus, I'm getting pissed off with this. I'm outta here!"

"Danny, wait!"

But it was too late. Forcefully, he rushed from the room, Johanna and Eric catching sight of him as he bounded down the stairway, reaching for the open door.

Suddenly, an earth-shattering roar echoed about them, an almost transparent figure standing in the doorway. Transparent except for the slight image of a creature, the veins and organs visible for split seconds like reflections on running water.

Danny jumped back, falling into Eric's shaky arms, a breath as cold as iced steel hitting him squarely in the face. A slight impression of a mouth, teeth gleaming flashes of visibility. He closed his petrified eyes tightly, fearing his end. Waiting, seconds like hours, holding his arms back and feeling both Eric and Johanna behind him. A deathly purr filled his ears, a hateful rush of stale air, of heavy breathing, hitting him square on, pressing closer, closer, closer all the time, dampening his brow. His body trembled like Jell-O on a plate.

"Come on, screw you," he growled under his broken breath. "Come on, come on then."

A frightened murmur paved the way for things to come. That fear, the fear of impending death giving way to a last attempt at dying with a little dignity and pride. Suddenly Danny was screaming, his tight white-knuckled fists rising into the air. Nineteen years of life gathered together, thoughts of friends and family, happy memories of days gone by. If he were now to die, if he, Eric and his ice princess were now to lose their life forces, then he would die trying to protect them. "Screw you," he screamed once more. His eyes sprang open, ready now to face his maker.

He stopped, the scream cut like a radio on/off switch. Those once fearful, angry, desperate, ready-to-die eyes widened and fell in all directions. The information hitting his brain told him he was still alive, that those seconds of certain death were gone. That death was gone, that it had charged off and left him behind. He stood away from Johanna and Eric, still not sure how death could have spared him. There was nothing there.

"It's gone," he mumbled, thick rolling beads of perspiration mounting the ice of his skin. "But, but it's gone. How can...?" Slowly he swung himself around to face his companions, his tongue working its way around the inside of his mouth with confused unease.

Johanna was relaxed, a broad smile on her face. "Yes, it's gone," she said evenly. "Gone back to where it came from."

Eric flung his arms around her, kissing her squarely on the cheek. "Oh, Harry!" he beamed excitedly.

Danny said nothing; he didn't really know what to say. He cleared his throat and stepped forward.

"No!" Johanna pleaded, but it was too late. She took Eric by the hand and ran outside.

All three stopped dead in their tracks, eyes dusting the distance, thankful to be alive, smiles turning to devastation and heartbreak. Ahead stretched a vast desert. A range of mountains rising into a fiery sky far off toward a deep blood red horizon. Behind them, where the shabby, white-washed building had been just moments before, a seemingly eternal ocean of wind blown dunes rolled away into the distance.

"Oh God, dear God. What've I done?" Danny fell to his

trembling knees, his tormented, tearful gaze rising to meet a cloudless azure blue sky. "Why? Damn it, why?" His face was red, eaten by waves of destructive despair.

Johanna touched him lightly on the forehead. "Dan, come on. We can do this, it's all right. All we can do now is find the end." She helped him gently to his feet, her warm tender smile momentarily chasing his demons away. "Come on, trust me. We can do this." A soft silky white hand pattered down, touching his. She looked reassuringly toward Eric, then set off into the blazing inferno.

"The end, Johanna, what's the end?" Eric needed answers. His young, curious mind called out like a puppy on a rain-drenched street.

Johanna thought for a short while, her flesh stinging in the scorching heat. "We're in the Maze, this is it. Don't ask me to explain it, I can't." She let go of Danny's hand and lifted an arm to her forehead, a vain attempt at protecting herself from the raging sun.

Danny wanted so much to say something. Like Eric, he too, felt the dire need for answers. He knew his young friend had a burning desire to ask all he could; and he knew that sooner or later he probably would. Danny, however, just couldn't.

Why had she been chosen for such a task? She was just a teenager, not more than a mere child. Just a young Swede, a tender soul made to bear the brunt of the world. What made her so special? Hazzari, this man Harry, this man from her dreams. This man who had died in order to give her an unknown power. Who was he? *What* was he?

Questions, so many questions bubbling, burning in the endless heat. Now he, Danny, that once strong and confident youngster, found himself in a different situation than before. No longer was he the brave young hero, the type we read about in stories of old. No longer the knight in shining armor who would ride out into the valley of death and slay the fire-breathing dragon. No longer was he the courageous warrior who would come back victorious with the pretty maiden safe in his comforting arms. No longer was he the man of the moment, the strength in the backbone, the light in the dark. Now Johanna was the backbone, the light. She was the power, the guide through this strange new world. She was the hero and he felt lost and alone.

Eric staggered to a stand still, his body exhausted to the point of collapse. "It's no good," he groaned, throat dry and tender. "It's just not ending."

He gazed back painfully at the range of mountains before slowly trudging off once more. As they forced their weary selves on, feet sinking like falling stones into the soft sand hungry for human flesh, he noted something in the distance. A huge castle-like structure stood dark and cold against the surrounding heat. Four skyward pointing angle towers, a solid curtain wall and well-protected inner wall. A keep, a portcullis and drawbridge. A main hall and huge courtyard, a battlemented parapet and castle gate. And... and water, there was water … everywhere, more water than he could ever imagine possible. He adjusted and readjusted his sights, eyes strained and squinted, almost blinded by the severity of the heat steaming down on him.

"Dan, look. Over there." Beautiful words like refreshment and shade filled his head. A place to rest, to take refuge from the desert sting. "Danny! Johanna!" He turned to face them. "Danny? Where are you? Johanna?"

There came no reply. Eric found himself alone. Completely alone, lost in the angry wilderness about him. A broken soul, he fell to the dry, sandy earth, the sun bright and molten, glaring down on him with hateful vengeance. "God, what have I done?" His eyes swelled like silver pools, overflowed with tears and cascaded downward to sting his tender cheeks. "Give me back my friends! Harry, help me, please!"

Just then he heard a voice, the familiar voice of Danny. He staggered to his feet, looking around only to find a vast emptiness. "Danny? Where are you?"

"I don't know," came the reply. "I'm in a cave somewhere. I was just walking with you and… And-and then I was here. Is Johanna with you?"

Eric gazed around in all directions before aiming his voice where he thought Danny would be. "No, no, she ain't. There's a building not far away. Like a castle. I need water." He awaited Danny's reply.

The Maze 171

"Okay, but put something down on the ground to mark where you are and come back here at..." He stared at the dial on his watch." Listen, set your watch for half-past four. Be back at half-past five, all right? No, make that half-past six." Eric took off his shoes, placing them to point upward like gravestones in the sand.

"Okay, Dan, be safe." His throat pulsated, a raging fire inside. "Please let me find water," he groaned under his tired breath.

Chapter 9
Captive in Time

Johanna woke gradually, rubbing her eyes with a tired yawn. A dream, she had had a dream, the strangest one ever. A sleepy groan parted her thirsty lips and she sat up quickly.

A dream. It wasn't a dream, not a dream at all. Where was she, where were her two friends? Surely it had all been a dream, how could it not have been? But wait, where was she? A confused, somewhat frightful stare cut into a gloomy darkness. Faintly she could just make out a large wooden door ahead of her. Damp, black walls surrounded her, a low stony ceiling like a midnight storm rose above her. Thoughts darted to Danny and Eric somewhere out there in the hell of a burning wilderness.

This was most definitely not a dream, not a dream at all. This was real, this was happening. She tried desperately to think back to when she was with her friends. One moment she was awake in a vast, seemingly non-ending desert. The next, she was waking up in a cold, damp and danky cell-like room.

Just then she heard the heavy thud of footsteps and a jingle of keys, then the door swung open with a loud, ear splitting creak. A short, although exceptionally well-built, man stepped inside. He was in his early to mid-thirties and wore a long red and black tunic with a neat cross of gold stitched decoratively on it. He was also wearing shiny black shoes with large gold buckles and a small black cap made of what looked like fox or wolf hide. He held out a lantern, its weak ray just touching each darkened corner of a dirty cell. How had she gotten here? How had she gone from the sting of desert heat to the bitter cool of a cell?

Johanna froze, the hate within this man's glare cutting into her like two streaks of lightning at the end of a violent storm. He never said a word, just moved closer, his long eerie shadow closing in on her. All of a sudden an immensely large and aggressive, dusty right hand was about her slender pink neck. That hand, so strong and powerful, she found herself totally incapable of fighting off. She was lifted into the air before being thrown over a solid bulk of a shoulder and carried out into a long damp corridor.

She screamed out mixed anger and defenseless fear, only to receive a swift smack across the face for her futile efforts. She tried to wish him away, that mountain of muscle in much the same way as she had the creature in the house, but this time there was just no strength left in her terrified frame.

In less than a minute they arrived at a large, open door. Slowly he turned his ugly head toward her, an icy grin on his beardless face, a breath so foul, she could feel her stomach heave.

"You're hurting me!" she screamed, scrunching up her face like a discarded newspaper. He paid no attention to her tearful pleas, barely taking note of her desperate cries. Instead he just carried her into a large, gloomy room full of medieval torture devises. Again she tried to resist. Again she tried her hardest. With a painful thud she was cast down on an extremely uncomfortable, iron rack. Holding her down with his right knee, he tied her arms and legs to each of the four corners. A small wheel was turned, raising her a good foot into the air. He turned and headed toward the far end of the room to where a little old man sat watching from a wooden stool.

Cold beads of sweat trickled down her tense face as he rose from his resting-place and came hobbling in her direction. He lifted and lowered a long thin whiplike stick in his frail, filthy, right hand, his eyes burning into her flesh as he closed in on her.

"Well, my dear," he cackled in a menacing tone, gliding his long fingers across her soft pink sweater and trembling chest. "Are you going to co-operate?"

He reached for another wheel, one a little larger wheel than the first, turning it sharply, the ropes about her wrists and ankles tightening until she felt sure she would split open at any moment. A finger moved, sliding up inside her sweater like a cold, dead object, circled her navel two or three times then danced toward her firm neat breasts. "If you tell me everything, if you confess, then I will be kind. If not, you will tomorrow, be sure of that." He grinned, a wide black and decaying toothy grin, his pin-like eyes studying the fear on her face.

Once again the wheel was turned and he stepped back, rubbing his hands together with a certain satisfaction. He pulled something on a cord from under his tunic and placed it in full view. It was a small pebble with a hole in it, a hagstone, a safe guard against evil spirits.

"You will confess, my dear, you will confess."

"What have I done?" Tears streamed down her pretty face, tidal flows of fluid salt.

"In this year, sixteen-hundred and sixty-six, you are accused of being bewitched. Sentenced by witch finder, General Mathew Hopkins, acting under Cromwell. You are accused of meeting on Leigh Common, near Yetminster, at the Mizmaze, a site for pagan rituals. You are accused of using a mament, a familiar witch's toy, a stuffed rag doll. You are accused of being a witch. You *are* a witch! You will be tried as a witch and you will die as a witch!" He watched her closely, awaiting a response.

"I don't know what you're talking about," she gasped as the ropes tightened, cutting into the soft flesh of her wrists and ankles. "Honestly I don't. I'm not from your time, let me go."

The little old man wrinkled his long, narrow nose up like a sun-baked raisin and sniffed loudly, pondering over her last remark. He scratched at his goat-like beard, let his tongue slither along his lower lip, then moved slowly away without releasing her from his sights.

"A witch," he whispered. "You are a witch, you will see."

His companion, the short muscular man, now hovered about like a cat on hot rocks. He, too, sniffed loudly, then spat the contents of that sniff on the cobbled floor. He, too, gradually moved forward, as the little old man turned away and moved to sit on his wooden stool once again. The ropes were untied and the rack was lowered onto its four sturdy legs, Johanna being pushed into a sitting position. Her hands were tied behind her back, a large black sack viciously forced over her head. She sobbed, lost and confused as he threw her up and over his right shoulder, his mighty deltoid muscle pounding into her rib cage.

In time she was able to hear voices. The sack was removed and she was dropped painfully to the ground. She found herself resting in a huge cobbled square. A roaring river wound its way under a small stone bridge and on through a picturesque little town. People stood at the river's edge, all anxiously waiting for something to happen. Two young children sat cross-legged a few feet away to her left. They were playing some sort of game with several small, stone balls. A large black dog sniffed at them as it passed and one of the children scared it away with a swift tap on the snout.

Just then the gathering parted, a young lady of no more than twenty years of age was dragged by two hefty men to the river's edge. Her hands and feet were tied together and a thick, long rope was tied about her slim waist. She fought in vain to escape and she pleaded tearfully for her life all to no avail. The gathering jeered as she neared them and some even spat at her. Once near the river's edge, one of the men crossed over the bridge and stood on the other bank. One end of the rope about her waist was thrown across to him, the other held by the first. The gathering silenced and the young lady was given the opportunity to confess her sins. Then away she fell, out into the swooning gray waters. The ropes tightened, the men on either side of the river's edge taking the strain. Like a rag doll she bobbed about, up and down without breath. Up and down, up and down, up and then down one last time. Then she was gone, lost in the depths of a raging dark river.

The man that had attended Johanna smiled easily, gazing down on his twenty-first century victim. "You could be there in the morning if Grindle gets his way." Johanna turned her head, her eyes red and puffy beyond the ability to see clearly. "Best you confess."

Again the large black sack was forced over her head and she was lifted up and onto his mighty shoulder, the sound of people's chatter fading away. It wasn't long before she was back on the rack, tied down and preparing herself for more interrogation, which soon arrived in the form of Grindle. In one scrawny hand, he held a red-hot poker, and something that resembled an athame, a black handled knife used for drawing magic ritual circles, in the other. Unlike an athame, this tool was razor sharp and its blade edge glistened against a dull torch light glow.

"Well my dear, did you enjoy yourself?" He turned sharply to face the other guard, eyes narrowing, dark and evil. "Leave us," he growled. The guard left without a word, hurriedly moving toward the still open door and disappearing.

Once alone with his victim, Grindle spoke. "Sixteen-hundred and sixty-six," he sniggered coldly. "This isn't sixteen-hundred and sixty-six. I know who you are. You are Hazzari's abomination and a pitiful one at that. You think you can save this world? Let's see you save yourself first. Hmmm?"

He lowered the poker just inches above her ghostly white face, its scorching heat penetrating her shaking frame. "The Maze hasn't even begun and already you are under my control. Soon my master will be all powerful and Hazzari will just be a forgotten name." He lifted her soft pink sweater with the tip of the athame, the ice of its point touching her naked flesh. Slowly it rode up across her navel, over her upper abdomen before resting a second against her left breast. Johanna held her body taut, pulling back from the blade, feeling its coldness cutting through her.

"Harry," she moaned. "Harry, help me!"

Suddenly the athame moved, rose up into the air, sliced through her shirt like a typhoon through a paddy field. The shirt fell to her sides, ripped clean down its center. Grindle grinned wildly, a hungry beast of prey. She could feel his eyes lustfully scouring her body, feel them digging grooves deep into her flesh. The red-hot poker hovered, hungry to scar her for life and the athame rested, held tightly in a dirty hand.

"If only you knew the power of the great one, if only you knew what can be done."

A mighty boom of laughter escaped his narrow, parted lips, the laughter of a man possessed. The red hot poker hovered above her. Hovered, hot and hungry, ready to strike. It moved, ever so slowly, lowering all the time. A wave of heat passed through her, the poker lifting to and coming down on her chest. She screamed out in sheer agony, feeling its fiery touch and its light drag over her right breast, down to her neat stomach. The pain grew more intense than she could bear. She clenched her fists until they ached, her body trembling as never before. Her mind blurred, her sight grew fuzzy, unconsciousness taking her and throwing her into the realms of darkness.

Meanwhile, Eric staggered through the heat of a raging inferno, his mind playing cruel tricks on him. With a throat, dry and sore, too weak to walk anymore, he crawled until arriving at the gates of a mighty castle. Its massive bulk stood out against a rolling ocean of yellow, the outer walls providing shade from the relentless sun. Through the gates he fell, a broken murmur, a call for help barely escaping his swollen lips.

Suddenly he found himself in near darkness. Breeze tossed lanterns dangled precariously from tall posts at the edges of a narrow, cobbled street, giving off a slight glow. He could hear voices, people singing and the piercing chime of a bell.

"Time, boys," a man called loudly, his gruff voice wiring away from a building nearby. Footsteps sounded behind him; and he turn to see who it might be.

"Well, well, well. And what've we got here then? Bit young to be out this late, aren't you?" A tall, bearded policeman looked gently down on him. "Where's your mother?"

Eric sat in silence, unable to reply. Instead he just stared into the eyes of the man who spoke. The man's face was bright and alive, the little of it he could see under a thick, wiry jungle of fast graying beard. He was quite tall, and rather fat, too. Had he been dressed in a shaggy white-edged, red suit and had he been holding a large sack with bulging presents, he would well have fitted in at the local super store Christmas grotto. He bore helpful eyes, eyes that shone a caring concern. The deep drawn lines about those helpful eyes told a story, the story of a man devoted to his job, devoted to helping his fellow man.

"I don't know, sir," Eric faltered. "Where am I?"

The policeman laughed, a deep throated, black velvet tone from deep inside, if only he would say, "ho, ho, ho! Merry Christmas boys and girls," he'd be a perfect Santa Claus.

"This is London, boy!" He helped Eric up to his feet. "1778, in the year of our Lord. Come on, let's take you down to the station." He chuckled, sounding more like Father Christmas by the second, and placed a large firm hand reassuringly on Eric's shoulder. "Where am I?" he chuckled once more.

Eric didn't know what to say. He was spellbound. How was he to explain he wasn't the average, everyday youngster with a family and a life in London 1778? How was he to explain he just happened to be there, that he'd just come from the scorching hell of a desert? He had passed through a time warp, caught in the Maze and was just passing through. How would an eighteenth century officer of the law take that? Within a short space of time Eric found himself standing at the foot of a flight of stone steps.

"Another homeless kid, Sarge," a policeman even more taller than the first, said clearly to them when they entered the building. The sergeant sat behind a long wooden counter. Strange, Eric thought, him being extraordinarily tall. Even sitting, his chest and shoulders rose high above the counter surface. Stranger still, was his eyes and thick wiry jungle of salt and pepper beard. He was an exact copy of the first policeman. He even spoke in the same manner, a deep black velvet tone.

"Okay, put him in a cell, fourteen's the best bet. I'll speak to him in the morning."

He sifted through a large pile of papers, humming some old tune as he did so. "Ah, ha." He raised a paper, twisting his upper lip with a certain thoughtful twitch of the nose. "Male, twelve years of age." He looked across at Eric, letting the fingers of his left hand twiddle lightly at his beard. "Missing since last Tuesday. Goes by the name of Tom Dickens. Are you Tom Dickens, boy?"

The Maze 179

Eric didn't reply. The tall bearded policeman lead him down three stone steps and into a long corridor, then fumbling for a set of keys in his black trouser, left front pocket, he opened up cell number fourteen and let him enter.

"The sarge'll fix you tomorrow, young Tom Dickens," he said kindly. "We get a lot of your type in here. You're from the workhouse, no doubt. Now you just get some rest and..." He paused, squinting into the far corner of the small, dim cell. "Murphy Doyle! You leave this boy alone, you hear me? Or I'll fix you come morning." He turned, patted Eric lightly on the back of the head. "Don't you worry about 'im, he's harmless enough. He's just in to sober up. Murphy almost lives here, ain't that right, Murphy?" He left, locking the iron-barred door behind him.

Eric seated himself in one corner, not quite knowing what to think. It was cold, very cold, a dampness chilling his young bones. Strange, the heat of the desert still burned inside him. Murphy Doyle sat crouched in his corner like the pathetic waste of a life he was. Almost unreal, ghost-like behind a thick beard. His eyes were narrow and blood shot, barely able to stay focused on the boy just a few feet away. His hands shook uncontrollably and an alcoholic stench surrounded him. He was a mess.

"Hello," Eric said softly, although oddly enough not fearfully. "Um... nice to meet you."

Murphy grunted loudly, cleared his throat as if he had never cleared it before, spitting noisily on the cobbled ground.

"Hurmph," he growled. "I d'wanna sh'cell wi'yo! Nee'jing!"

Eric pondered over a jumble of disjointed syllables, running them through his head in an attempt at understanding them. "I don't want to share a cell with you, either. I need a drink, or a gin," he whispered under his breath.

A conversation with this sad waste of a deadbeat, human life wasn't going to lead anywhere, that was a fact. The night was to be a long one, Eric knew that all too well. He wasn't afraid, didn't feel as if he was in any real danger. Besides, Murphy Doyle couldn't stand up, could barely sit up and that was with the help of a thick black wall behind him.

It was far too cold to sleep and even if it wasn't sleepy, Eric doubted that he could. Instead he let his thoughts drift back to life on Barrymoor Avenue. Life with his mother and father, oh how he missed them. That wretched little crossbreed with the annoying yap, yap, yap. George "Gorgon" Adams and his wife, Annie "Fanny" Adams. Made for each other, they were, those two whiners. Always complaining about something, always keeping on about something. Nasty little people.

Surprisingly, now all Eric wanted was to be told off by them, wanted to be whined at. He wanted more than anything to sit on the fence, the dreaded Adams family fence, wanted to make that wretched little crossbreed yap on and on and…

Just then something moved and Eric turned sharply to see what it might be. In the corner, a shape in the corner shifted. Something scratching; and it wasn't deadbeat Murphy Doyle. There it was on the ground, some shape that was small and dark. Eric jumped as a rat scurried across the dirty cobbled ground.

"Wow!" His heart jumped into his mouth only to be swallowed once more. "Disgusting!"

The dead beat paid no attention, obviously pretty much used to seeing such things. Mind you, he was little more than a rat himself. All of a sudden the rat vanished. Gone, had just disappeared into thin air, vanished without a trace.

Eric stared in disbelief at the space where it had been just seconds before. Murphy did, too, although the dull expression on his dirty, weather-worn face didn't change in the slightest. Murphy might not have thought it odd, but Eric certainly did.

Cautiously, he raised his body, crawling over and reaching into thin air. Slowly, as if sliding into an invisible pocket, his hands disappeared out of sight. Nothing. There was nothing there. Nothing but space—thick, dark space. Hurriedly, he forced a hand around, estimating the width of the portal.

Drawing his hand back and inspecting it a short while, he asked himself if going through would be to his advantage. A quick glance around the cell, the drunk in the corner, the damp and the dismal gloom closing in about him, he made up his mind.

"Here goes nothing," he whispered uncertainly as he climbed through. He found himself in a long cave-like chamber, standing above a deep black hole in the rocky earth below. He was floating, just floating. Just then he heard the jingle of keys somewhere in the distance.

"Come on, Tom Dickens, time to go home." Gradually, like whispers in the wind, the words drifted away, echoing slightly in his head. "Murphy! Where is he? What've you done?" There came a loud thud and far off scream. Then the hole was gone.

The chamber stretched on into the distance. Stalactites in countless shapes, sizes and colors loomed down from an impressive, pink rock roof. Beautiful twists, stalagmites shot downward like giant frozen jelly arms. On occasion, stalactite and stalagmite met with colorful embrace. After thousands of years in waiting, finally, lovers entwined.

Biting harshly on his lower lip, he sighed heavily, fear and curiosity as one. Never before had he seen anything so wonderful, so alien to his own world. Never so beautiful, never so breath-taking, and never so bold and awe-inspiring.

Eric set off, following a rough trail. In time the chamber narrowed, the jagged ceiling lowering at great speed. Then he passed through a seemingly non-ending tunnel. A deep foreboding silence filled his head, a feeling of being in some magical place, some place only heard of in fairytales and yet at the same time, some place positively nerve-wracking.

On one side, a rock face stretched to a damp pinkish red. The other filtered away into what at one time had probably been a twisting river. The rocks in this particular area showed the familiar signs of water erosion. The whole scene reminded him somewhat of a graveyard forest. Everything was dead, frozen in its secretive past.

Those mighty, prehistoric trees of a time long since gone, now decorated stalactites and joining stalagmites. The river that perhaps once flowed into a deep swooning gray, now became a river of rock. A scene from a land of prehistory. Millions of years past, those giant reptiles lost, gone forever. The fearsome Daspletosaurus waiting, all eight and a half feet of him. Waiting, hidden by the dense forest at the water's edge, those heartless eyes searching out a meal while a pteranodon soars over head, his massive skin wings lifting him high into the trade winds. A young male styracosaurus comes into view, a horned battle tank. Daspletosaurus pounces, razor sharp teeth sinking like stones into thick scaly flesh. Screams fill the air, a horn reaches its mark. Indeed, this place was a place for enhancing the imaginative mind. This strange place, this strange world he found himself in.

Just then he heard a noise, a stone rolling down from above him and landing at his feet. He stopped, noticing a narrow ledge about six feet up. Again a stone fell and then another and yet one more. A dark shape moved, something far above him. A head bobbed behind a rock. Strange voices filled the air, his nerves turning to icy fear as he charged off along the tunnel, down a seemingly endless passageway.

There were no stalactites, no stalagmites. No dead river. Suddenly he felt himself fly backward, the dusty earth becoming his roof. Unwittingly he had stepped into a thick rope noose. It clamped tightly about the ankle of his left foot, hauling him up into the air until he found himself hanging upside down, swinging gently from side to side.

The air turned electric, voices sounding from every rock and cranny. Strange beings scurried along the ledge, winding their way down. Their bold heads were so large they appeared too heavy for such puny bodies.

Eric swung, caught like a fly in the spider's web, as they gathered below him, chattering to each other in a language that sounded more like high-pitched static clicks than words. They pushed one another playfully, jumping up and down, their large global, yellow eyes shining out against their bluish gray skins. They didn't appear to be dangerous but then looks can deceive. They looked more like alien, child clowns, their peculiar activities making no sense to him at all. The cheerful excitement, the hustle and bustle of these comical creatures soon ended. Heads jittered like fish bowls in a gray skin room as if listening for something only they could hear.

In a flash they scurried away, climbing back up the rocks

The Maze 183

and disappearing. Eric curled his back, pulling himself up using stiff fingers to push himself higher. A loud roar echoed through the tunnel walls, a long drawn out thud of footsteps scraping toward his terrified frame. Icicles formed deep down inside him as a huge shadow appeared on granite slabs.

He shrank inside himself as he spied a creature, a mass bulk of solid flesh and heaving muscle. Closer, closer, closer it moved to where he swayed in the air continually. It passed below, unaware a potential meal twisted gently like the bait on a fisherman's line only a few feet above him.

At last it was gone, out of sight, dragging itself along the tunnel. Eric thought back, unable to do anything other than dangle like socks on a breeze-chased washing line. He remembered his first journey into the Maze, remembered the lifeless faces in the valley of death, an arena of hell. The creature, the very same creature had just passed underneath him. Remembered the way in which it had moved in on its human prey. Waiting, watching, taking them in jaws of steel, tearing them limb from limb.

"Jesus," he mumbled, sweat rolling thick beads against a damp, cold brow.

A gong sounded in the distance, followed by the agonized screams of the creature's victims. He felt helpless, unable to do anything whatsoever to prevent this horror, this atrocity. He could imagine faces of pure terror. Men, women and children desperately fighting to escape such unworthy ends, struggling to preserve their very being, the right to live, to see another day. He was helpless and there was absolutely nothing he could do to help his fellow man at the end of the tunnel.

The gong sounded again, the creature dragging itself, its stomach now full of human remains, heading back toward him. Thick fleshy strands dripped crimson droplets from its mighty, tooth-encrusted mouth. In one claw it held a viciously dismembered body, a limb caught, hanging from one upward pointing fang.

Eric closed his eyes tightly, praying to God above that he wouldn't be noticed, wouldn't, too, become a victim. On opening them again, a sigh of relief escaping through his tightened lips, he noticed the goldfish bowl headed beings peering noisily over the ledge. Vigorously, they waved their small, three-fingered hands high in the air. Then down to the tunnel floor they climbed. Slowly he could feel himself being lowered until he found himself amongst a fast growing group. Like crazed jesters, they danced a crazy dance around him. Up and down, up and down, like excited drunken sprites.

Within mere seconds they lowered him to the dry earth, dragging him away, and lifting him up the rocky tunnel wall to the ledge. He was just able to take a quick glimpse down before being moved into another tunnel. The roof above him was much lower than the first and at intervals of maybe two to three feet; a lighted torch had been pushed into an accommodating crack or cranny. The tunnel soon ended, opening into a rather large chamber.

"Hey, where are you taking me?" Eric cried out in a fear-stained voice, his back thumping against the dry, stony earth. They didn't reply, or not at least as far as he knew. Strange sounds spouted from many mouths, sounds that could have quite possibly been words, but then who except they themselves could know the answer to them?

He thought about trying to break free, about trying to escape. There were a good many of them, at least forty. They were little though, no more than two feet tall compared to his five foot frame. The idea of a forceful break and a quick dash back into the tunnel had crossed his mind. And, it might well have worked, except for one little thing—fear. What a horrible word. Fear of what might be out there waiting for him.

His mind buzzed, his head whirling like a spinning top out of control, and his body ached and burned. Flashes of desert and Seventeenth Century London shot through him, a tear of confusion winding its way down his cheek.

The goldfish bowl headed beings pushed on with their human cargo toward one of seven narrow openings. Inside one of them, the one he found himself being hauled down, the cave walls were alive with hundreds of tiny fires, like twinkling stars in a cloudless night sky. The narrow opening soon filtered out into another very large chamber. At least three hundred feet from one starlit rock face to the other. There, the beings released him, letting him rest a short while on the soft sandy earth. He watched them suspiciously as they charged about in a fast accelerating jumble. Around and around they jumped, skipping and dancing with noticeable excitement. His ears filled with extra sounds, hundreds of beings suddenly trundling through the narrow opening and into the sandy chamber. They all appeared to be smiling, gathering in around him, closing in with curious faces. Tiny rubbery fingers reached forward, brushing through his hair, tugging lightly on his clothing.

The crowd moved apart, forming a blue-gray lined pathway as yet another being came into view. This being was much taller than the others standing a good foot above them, although it was obvious that he, she or it, was of the same species. The taller being moved in, eyes large and global, staring out with bulb-like swells. The back of a long, fine nailed hand rode up against Eric's cheek, then clasped softly at his left shoulder.

A series of clicks rose into the air and all of a sudden the pathway broke, the crowd pushing forward. A forceful break was out of the question, if it had ever been possible at all. His fear reached new heights, when the beings lifted him, kicking and screaming, then hurriedly crossed the chamber floor to a large, wooden trap door.

"Get off! Get the hell off!" It was useless, there was no escape. Then he was cast into a hole . Down, down, he fell, screaming all the time as he tumbled into darkness.

A feeling inside him told him that he wasn't alone. Gradually his eyes became accustomed to the dimness about him, shapes shifted slightly in front of him. Sad, with their heads hung low, humans rested in silence.

"Where am I?" he asked nervously, his head still pounding from the fall. "Please tell me."

He raised himself, holding his back near the base of his spine, a sharp stinging pain ripping through it. Then he stepped cautiously forward. He could make out at least fifteen people, although there could have been a great many more or less. One of the group slowly moved and Eric turned painfully to see who it might be.

"Don't be afraid. Come on and sit here. I think you'll need

the advice." A young man took Eric's hand, feeling it, studying it. "You're new, I thought as much."

"What d'ya mean, new?"

"Doesn't matter," the man went on. "Listen, when your time comes, avoid all far corners." He sounded as if he was genuinely trying to help, although his words only served to confuse Eric that much more. "The chain breaks sometimes, but as a rule, stay clear of all wide, open spaces."

Eric wrinkled his forehead not understanding and cleared his throat worriedly before speaking. "What are you talking about?"

"You're here for a reason, don't you get it? You're part of the game now. Look, all you gotta do is to survive. You make it through; you go on to the next level. You'll catch on." Somewhere above them a crowd cheered in high pitched, static clicks. "What's your name?"

"Eric. Eric Wilson."

The crowd silenced. A grinding sound splintered the air, the sound of metal against metal. A single loud voice echoed against an ear-piercing creak.

"Okay, Eric Wilson, stay alive."

Suddenly the back wall began to move, gliding noisily toward Eric's shaky frame, dust rising in thick clouds of suffocating gray. They found themselves being forced along a low, narrow tunnel. Several groups of humans fell into them from deep, dark, moving side chambers.

"This is it, Eric Wilson. Remember what I said."

The wall ground forward, slowly, slowly, a screeching grind until they found themselves in a large, sandy arena surrounded by a massive silent gathering. The beings sat far above Eric and his fellow captives on floating, circular stands. Before each being stood medium-sized screens, a flick of a switch to change the channel to suit each world game level. A large dome-shaped dial would enable each spectator to move a personal camera angle just enough to catch that special moment when a captive would die. Each being held a handful of credits and waited patiently for the chance to fill a small-computerized box, a chance to place a bet on an unlucky loser.

The Maze   187

Just then, the dry, sandy arena vibrated beneath them. The ground moved slowly up and then lightly back down, something encircling them from below. The beings rushed for their screens, tuning into their world game levels and placing bets with great excitement.

Eric watched his fellow man, sure they could lead him to freedom. Eyes studied the ground, waited, prayed, listened and prayed again. Whatever was down there was homing in on them. Its large sweeping circles lessened, the sand rippling split seconds in a fast diminishing spiral before lowering once more. Suddenly it was time. A huge, horned, half-man, half-lizard creature threw itself into the air, free now of wherever it had come from, a menacing scaly grayish-green, arrow-tipped tail, thrashed from side to side. Eric dived across the arena, as a head as large as an elephant and ten times as ugly, lunged toward him. It clasped a middle-aged woman, its razor sharp, dagger-like teeth sinking into her soft flesh. With a single bite the corpse, bloody and torn was cut in two.

There was a thick row of nails embedded in the end wall, each one being a good twelve inches in length, and he bounded toward them, climbing as fast as he could. On reaching the top he stopped a second to rest. The crowd roared, loud clicks and whistles of encouragement, loud clicks and whistles of failure. Little bluish-gray, three-fingered hands reached forward, preparing to change the channel. Below them, the creature, its head held high in the air, scoured the arena for a potential victim. It was huge, at least fourteen feet in height with a tail that added an extra six feet. Its hind legs were solid and chunky, it forearms much smaller, little more than two razor sharp claws. The scene was one of devastation. Limbs torn and bloodied lay scattered like soft drink cans after a day on the beach. Nothing but death, a repulsive , grisly nightmare.

Just then the wall rocked slightly, the creature homing in on the last human. Closer, closer it came, moving in all the time. The wall rocked again then back it went, sending Eric to the other side. Still the creature neared, like a flesh and bone battle tank closing in. Its glazed gray eyes were small; half hidden by several layers of thickly wrinkled skin flaps. It was blind, Eric thought, it had to be blind.

Again the wall moved. This time in an upright position. Eric closed his eyes tightly, too afraid to scream, too weak to fight off the creature only a few feet away. He prayed to God for forgiveness and behind tear-filled eyelids, he awaited a ghastly end. What a terrible, terrible end. Time passed him by and still he was alive. The feeling of being alone reached him. Gradually, he opened his eyes, touched daylight, the wall back in position, the creature of hell locked away in the arena. He was free, he had made it. He had survived game one of level one. He breathed a deep sigh of relief, wiping thick beads of perspiration from his dirty face.

"Close one," he mumbled to himself reassuringly. "Nuts, that was close."

Something caught his attention, his eyes dusting across the sandy floor that stretched away at least a hundred feet to another wall. The sand below him appeared to be moving. Not moving in wisps as if being blown along by a warm desert breeze. This was different.

He knelt down, fingers gliding lightly over its surface. The ground appeared to be falling away. Falling down. A desperate scream escaped him, his body sinking at an exceptional speed. He caught hold of something, something solid and thin, a bar of some kind. He kept his eyes tightly closed as a golden yellow rush rained down around him. He tried to breathe, coughing and spluttering all the time, grains of sand entering his mouth.

From the jaws of death he had escaped only to find death rushing up to meet him once more. Sand no longer rained about him, but now a tremendous heat reached up and singed his flesh. On opening his eyes, he found himself hanging from a vast iron grid, suspended by a circle of granite rock. Far, far below, maybe twelve hundred feet or so, a glow of red bubbled under a vapor cloud.

The world passed him by. The world as he knew it, his world. His world before all this came about. There was Suzie Perkins, the girl of his dreams. The only girl to steal his heart, and she didn't even know it. Those school days, days of security and of innocent fun. Weekends. Waking up late, eating breakfast in the kitchen. His grandmother's homemade strawberry jam. The drip, drip, drip of the old metallic tap with the faulty valve. Days of lying under a bright blue sky out in the back garden. Days, all those days gone by. All those days, all those wondrous, glorious days rushed back to greet him as if to bid him farewell.

Johanna and Danny, his only remaining friends, even they were gone. This was it, the power to go on now drained out of him. His hold loosened, fingers sweating ice, slipping inch by inch.

"Harry! Harry, don't leave me this way!"

His grip gone now, he fell, twisting and screaming. Down, down, down, the glow hungry and alive, rushing up to welcome him to the land of eternal sleep.

Suddenly his fall was broken by two thick ropes tied to the rocky volcano walls. Still he lived, still death had spared him. From one thick rope he dangled momentarily before pulling himself up slightly and stepping onto the lower one.

The heat below burned like death itself and as he painstakingly hauled himself toward the long ledge, he knew that death might still take him at any time. Tears rolled down his face, sweat stinging his eyes, each forceful reach feeling like his last. Finally he was there, had made it to the ledge, and he hauled himself up until he was on it. Solid rock lay beneath his feet like a refreshing orange drink after a hundred meter dash. He found himself with three options. There was a narrow, somewhat uninviting, rocky tunnel leading into the rocks, a set of stone steps leading to yet another ledge or a rather dangerous looking climb upwards. None seemed exceptionally welcoming, although he opted for the cave. Worriedly he entered, silence screaming at him, so loud that it was almost deafening.

Then there was a shape on the ground. A body, limp and exhausted, close to death on the gravely earth.

"Hey. Hey you. You okay?" he whispered gently as he bent down, rolling the body over. "Danny!" His eyes lit up, two fires of pure joy. "Danny, it's me! Eric!"

Danny groaned, his skin pale and ghost-like. He was bleeding slightly from a tiny split in his bottom lip, but he was alive.

"Eric, is it you? Is it really you?" he barely whispered. "Thank God, you made it this far. Are there anymore?"

Eric helped him to unsteady feet, placing a reassuring arm around his waist. "Let's talk later. We need to rest first."

Together they staggered along, both propping each other up, both tired and worn out, in desperate need of rest. Finally, unable to go any farther, they both fell to the ground.

"I'm surprised you made it this far," Danny struggled to say. "This is only level one."

Eric didn't reply, he was already asleep.

Chapter 10

Time Zone, Future To Home

Johanna slowly came around, finding herself back in the gloomy darkness of her cell. An icy quiet painfully enveloped her, a numb throb riding her sore chest and belly. She could feel the tight pull of ropes about her wrists and ankles, her legs astride. Ahead of her she could just make out the door, damp and black, blurred by the lack of light about her. Her mind, frightened and confused, wandered each lonely chamber of her past. Thoughts of her own time, events far gone by. Thoughts of Eric and of Danny, the two most important people in her young life. Thoughts of Harry, the man who in death had left something more than mere memories behind. The man who had left something strangely warming, like the waiting out of a long and snowy winter, knowing spring will soon be on its way, soothing, caressing, melting the chill of a frozen heart.

Just then she heard a noise, her mind falling back into the realms of reality with a sudden jolt. Footsteps tapped toward her cell and then stopped. She heard the jingle of keys, the creak of the door as it swung open. A beam of light trickled into the cell, as Grindle stood in the doorway. He hovered a short while, staring toward the frail figure ahead of him before moving in on his prey.

"So, savior. Your road has reached its end, I see. How does

it feel?" His eyes, evil pins of night, scoured her, following each and every well-defined curve of her body. He grinned and let his tongue wash his lips.

"Strange. You don't look like a savior to me. You look like a little girl fearing for her life. You look pathetic, a weak and foolish child. So young, such a pity." A flash of silver passed by her face, then lowered to her stomach, the bitter cold steel blade caressing her skin. "What savior is she who cannot save herself?"

Consumed by fear, she found herself powerless to do anything other than stare straight ahead. Long thin fingers slipped between her legs, the other reaching for the zipper of her jeans.

All of a sudden the cell lit up for a long moment, a sweet sound meandered from dark, danky corner to dark, danky corner. Grindle released his grip, cowering away, slipping back into the darkness like a scolded dog before hurriedly leaving once more. A warmth entered Johanna's tired, aching body, the same sensation as drinking a hot cup of coffee after a long stroll in the snow of a Swedish winter.

Somebody, something, spoke, softly whispering her name. A voice from within, soft and gentle, caressed her inner soul. She jumped, flesh tingling. Her eyes fell to greet the deep, festering gash in her chest as it slowly faded away. Her shirt moved, strands of wool, like fingers reaching toward each other, stitch for stitch until no sign of a rip remained.

"Fear not my child. Fear not, for I am with you." The ropes that held her at bay, loosened, her wrists and ankles set free. "Quickly, my child, be on your way. Find your exit now, for only now can I help you. Go child, go, go, go..."

As the voice came, it faded just as quickly, whispering, the words "go, go, go" disappearing, riding into the light as it slowly faded out.

"Harry! Hazzari, don't leave me," she pleaded as she jumbled everything over in her head.

Calming herself, she exited the cell and without hesitation, walked silently into a torch-lit corridor. Both directions looked as dismal and as gloomy as the other, although somehow a decision appeared to have already been made. Through an orangish-

The Maze 193

gray light she passed, a dampness stinging her skin. Thick beads of perspiration collected on her brow, as the corridor ended in a vast network of tunnels, running this way and that. She wasn't lost, wasn't walking a pathway to destruction. She knew exactly where she was going. She didn't know why, but she did know an escape waited just around the next corner.

At last light wound its way in her direction, a flight of at least fifty stone steps, a welcoming sight. Half-running, half-jumping two steps at a time, she climbed them, the maze of tunnels left behind. She scanned her surroundings, pleasantly surprised at what she saw. Ahead of her stood a large white cottage with a freshly thatched roof. Five large windows, three up and two down with flower boxes crammed full of marigolds and pansies. Fields of varying yellows and greens tumbled away in all directions, tall oak trees swaying thick foliage in a soft, scented breeze. Birds on the wing flew across a pale blue, cloudless sky, swooping down on unsuspecting insects.

She took a quick glance over her shoulder, only to find more fields, the stone steps were gone, vanished without a trace. A soothing sun caressed her tense, although strangely enough, spotlessly clean body, the warmth softly relaxing her A curling waft played on her senses, whisking on the breeze, tickling her pretty nose, a soft gusting of fresh cut grass on the air. She breathed in loudly before exhaling, relishing in the wonder of just being.

A sound echoed behind her and she turned sharply to see what it might be. Two Labradors bounded through a buttercup and daisy-spangled field, bowling her over with paws and friendly tongues.

"Hello, me dear," a voice boomed in a deep English, country accent. "Don't you go worryin' 'bout them there dogs. They won't 'arm ya none. Just wanna bit a fun, that's all." A farmer ambled to where she sat, two dead common pheasants in one hand, a hunting rifle in the other.

Johanna dragged herself to her feet, stroking the dog's big black heads as they calmed themselves down. They panted, eyes a bottomless hazel brown, twinkling like naked flames on darkened windowsills.

"Hello, sir," she greeted politely, returning conversation. "Isn't it a wonderful day?"

The farmer smiled, calling his dogs back to his side. His cheeks shone redder than roses under an August sunset, a smile so wide it almost reached from ear to ear.

"'Tiz that, me dear. Grand ole weather." He scratched the end of his large rounded nose, gazing out at a forest of green. A light breeze tossed his fast thinning, silver-streaked hair to one side.

"I'm afraid I'm a little lost, sir." She gazed skyward as a magpie flew overhead, calling for her mate.

"Come on into the 'ouse, me dear. There's some nice lemonade you can 'ave, if ya like, then maybe we can get ya back on track."

Johanna was only too pleased to follow, and it wasn't long before she found herself sitting on a comfortable chair, a cool glass of lemonade in hand. How refreshing it was, like the first rains on the sun scorched earth. The giver of life, the quencher of parched throats, the washing away of Grindle gloom.

"So, me dear, where be you headin' for?" the farmer asked helpfully, as he filled a small briar pipe with tobacco and lit it up.

Johanna thought for a short while, watching fluffy plumes of curling white rising high into the air, twisting around themselves and dancing in time on shafts of light beaming in through the window before dispersing.

"Well, sir," she replied hesitantly. "I don't really know where I am."

He laughed aloud, a deep thunderous boom, his stomach rippling as he rocked in his chair. "D'ya ear that, Sabre!" he said heartily, patting one of the dogs firmly on the head. "This is Bodmin, is this. Cornwall, me dear. Where you from then?"

"Sweden, sir, I'm from Sweden. I, um, I'm on holiday you see, here with my mother. On a farm some place near by."

The farmer gazed up at the oak beamed, nicotine tarnished, white artexted ceiling. He breathed in deeply and exhaled, scattering plumes of smoke in all directions.

"Sweden, ya say," he mused. "Come by boat, did ya?"

The Maze 195

Johanna felt very tense all of a sudden, an uneasy haze coming on her. "Airplane, sir, we came by airplane." She studied his thoughtful expression, slightly perplexed by it.

"Airplane, ya say! Well, well. Airplane from Sweden. Rather you than me what with them there Jerries blowin' up the show."

An icy cold took hold of Johanna, a sleeping dragon waking up, something dark and sinister crossing her grave. "Jerry's?" she asked.

"Jerries, me dear, or 'ave ya forgotten there's a war on?"

A distinctively worrying smile crossed her lips and she cleared her throat meekly before gazing around the kitchen's interior. Her glassy eyes drifted to a dog-eared calendar tacked on the white papered wall near the lattice window. 1944, she thought to herself. Oh my God, it's June 5th, 1944.

"Oh, yes sir, but when you live in such a beautiful part of the world, it's almost possible to forget." He pushed a large glass jug of homemade lemonade across the heavily dented, old oak table. "Help yerself, me dear. Sweden, well, I be... Cold there, is it?"

"In the winter, yes. Very cold."

"Strange language though, eh."

They both chatted and laughed long into the afternoon, all topics of conversation rearing up and passing with tobacco wafts, including the progress of the war. Johanna had been taught of the confrontations between England and Germany in her history classes at school. She remembered certain dates, had read about Hitler, that foul little man from Austria. The little man with a tiny, useless black caterpillar under his nose. The fascist with a dream of evil doings, a vision of world dominance.

Something happened in June of 1944, something important, now what on earth was it? Think, think now, she told herself. What was it that happened in June of 1944? If only history had been interesting for her, she would know this. Yes, she knew a little about the war, both the first and second World War. However, being born more than forty years after the war, those history lessons back home had meant very little to her.

Now though, being around it, living in England, being in the year 1944, she could feel the horror of it all.

History was no longer history, history was today. It crossed her mind that maybe, just maybe, this wasn't England in 1944. Perhaps this was just another world within the Maze. The farmer with his briar pipe and rosy red smile, maybe he was just a figment of the imagination. Yes, yes it was possible, of course it was. The Maze and everything inside it could quite easily be part of some giant, crazy nightmare. The lemonade, cool and refreshing, was that just imagination, too? The sunbeams dancing through the lattice window, imagination also? What about the wonderful countryside and the waft of freshly cut grass? Imagination?

Yes, maybe that's what it was. What all of it was. Just imagination. But still the very thought of being in England in 1944, be it imagination or reality, gave her a whole new perspective.

The sun gradually began to lower in the heavens, illuminating the odd cloud with an orange candyfloss tinge.

"It's getting late, sir. I really must be on my way."

The farmer smiled cheerfully, standing up and reaching into a large old oak cupboard. He took out a quarter loaf of brown bread and a small chunk of cheese.

"Well, me dear, this should keep ya goin' for a time." He seemed so friendly, never once losing that, 'everything will be all right', twinkle in his eyes, or that broad and inviting smile on his large round face. He helped her up and out of her chair, pointing through the lattice window toward a farmhouse far off in the distance. "But stay under cover of the trees, or follow the hedge rows, eh. Just in case, best be safe, see."

"Thank you for everything, sir."

"That's all right, me dear. You just follow this field now. Ole Mrs Beal's, I reckon that's where you be stayin'."

She thanked him once more then left the large white cottage with the freshly thatched roof, setting off across a magnificent patchwork of greens and intermingling yellows. The sun hung low against a waiting horizon, its warmth still penetrating her body. So light and care free, for the time being at least, she sighed and inhaled, breathing in the freshness of country air.

The yap, yap of the dogs barking a farewell in canine chorus was left behind her now at the cottage. As the sun disappeared behind its last painted cloud, she sat down, making herself comfortable in the shrubbery of a thick hedge. Taking a small piece of bread from the quarter loaf, crumbs falling silently to the grassy earth, she began to eat.

Fresh bread, um, fresh bread and fresh cheese. She was in heaven. Just then she noticed a movement in the grass. Then another, and one more. It wasn't long before the ground was a hive of activity, little mice scurrying around her feet, nibbling at the wasted crumbs. Sparrows, blackbirds, bluetits and robins appeared from nowhere, perching precariously on the branches about her.

"This can't be real," she mumbled curiously, handing a piece of bread to one of the birds who took it and ate it without fear of her presence. The shrubbery moved, a white rabbit popping its head out of a large, dark hole.

Just like the children's story, 'Alice in Wonderland', she found herself thinking. That was an untrue story, a fairytale. Yet this, this was actually happening. This was real. She tossed things over in her mind, wondering what to do next. The white rabbit waved at her, beckoning her to come to the hole. Instinct told her that going on, going through was the best, indeed, the only way. Yet, Bodmin had been the first real comfort since entering the Maze.

Gazing around her, her eyes cut into the peace and tranquillity of the England of 1944. Before she could change her mind, she pushed to her feet, strolled across to the hole and climbed inside. The rabbit bounded on ahead of her. Once inside, the hole appeared much narrower, closing in around her like a black, plastic dustbin bag.

She squeezed on, forcing herself along its muddy clay walls. Light shone in from the far end, growing brighter with every forceful haul. In the distance, she could barely make out a high barbed wire fence, a small hut behind it.

Suddenly the earth moved, her body sinking, slipping down through the blackness. In twists and turns, she fell, until with a loud thud, she landed. The sound of playful chatter filled her ears as she slowly opened her eyes, sitting up, a stunned expression crossing her features. Before her stood a long table draped in fine white lace. At its head sat a lady, a queen or a princess, most definitely a lady of royalty. Her hair was a bright orange, in stark contrast to her clothing of reds and blues, greens and yellows. Diamonds hung from her ears, sapphires and gold about her slender neck. To her left sat the white rabbit, a glass of port wine in hand. To her right, a large and very drunken, nine of diamonds playing card. The card laughed time and time again at the rabbit's childish jokes. It wasn't long until their attentions turned to Johanna, who was sitting in a crumpled pile beneath a gaping hole.

"Well, just look at that mess. Look at that mess, well, well, well," the royal lady remarked sharply. "I say. Well, well, well. What a mess, what a terrible mess. Well, well, well, I say."

Meanwhile, the rabbit and the drunken nine of diamonds playing card had begun to argue. The card had grown tired of the rabbit's jokes.

"Laugh, d'ya hear? Laugh, go on, laugh. That one was funny!" the rabbit screamed at the top of his voice as he jumped onto the table. An oval shaped, diamond encrusted ashtray fell to the ground, jewels scattering across the floor like multi-colored streamers at a summer parade. The card picked up a wine bottle, ready to strike.

"I'm fed up. Fed up, you stupid, bloody rabbit. Every day, every bloody day. Jokes, I hate your stupid bloody jokes." He lunged forward, catching his opponent's head with the end of the bottle, smashing it, sending splinters of green flying through the air. A thick trail of blood oozed from a deep gash in the rabbit's left cheek, a steady pitter-patter to the tablecloth below.

The royal lady was far too interested in Johanna to worry about her two friends on the table, each armed with a broken bottle.

"Took you once, I'll take you again. Took you once, I'll take you again," the card sang provokingly at the top of his voice in a rather childish manner. The royal lady laughed, gliding a long, thin finger across the tabletop.

"Little girl, little girl, lovely little girl. Why don't you come and sit with me? Little girl, little girl, lovely little girl. Why don't you come and sit with me?"

Johanna didn't move. She could see the card staggering around the rabbit. Could hear his childish song.

"Took you once, I'll take you again. Took you once, I'll take you again..." But all the time she found herself locked onto the royal lady. Their eyes met and now, like hands entwining, she was caught.

"Took you once, I'll take you again. Took you once, I'll take you again..."

"Little girl, little girl, lovely little girl. Why don't you come and sit with me? Little girl, little girl, lovely little girl. Why don't you come and sit with me?"

Johanna wanted to get up, wanted to leave, to be far away from this terrible place. She wanted to be free of those staring, glaring, ice-cold blue eyes and that moaning, droning, almost psychopathic chant. Yet those staring, glaring, ice cold blue eyes cut into her, almost reaching into her very soul and that chant, that moaning, droning, almost psychopathic chant, held her like invisible weights about her terrified shoulders. The playing card hurled his bottle through the air, just missing his rival. With that, the rabbit took his chance. He stabbed at the card time and time again.

"Little girl, little girl, lovely little girl. Why don't you come and sit with me? Little girl, little girl, lovely little girl. Why don't you come and sit with me?"

Suddenly the card split open, a river of red gushing out, the sheer pressure forcing Johanna up against the far wall. She struggled against the flow, clawing her way up through the hole in the ceiling. Behind her all the time she could hear:

"Little girl, little girl, lovely little girl. Why don't you come and sit with me? Little girl, little girl, lovely little girl. Why don't you come and sit with me?"

At last she was back in the main tunnel, and blew out a sharp sigh of relief. The chanting faded, replaced by a deep, dark silence. Her only sound was her own heart beat, pounding like wild horses in her mouth. The tunnel was so narrow, so restrictive, so tight, it almost suffocated her, closing in against her.

She paused, tired and out of breath as she neared the end, nerves taut and on edge. On reaching the end she climbed out, exhausted and frightened, unaware of her present surroundings.

A hot and hateful sun streamed down on her, scorching her skin relentlessly. She gazed down momentarily at her clothing, only to find the blood and grime of her past world, gone. She was clean, unscathed, not a single mark or sign of her fairytale nightmare. Looking back toward the tunnel, she could see nothing. It had also disappeared. She found herself in a shallow, sandy pit, and slowly she gained her strength, climbing up and peering over the edge.

A soldier marched past only a few feet away, a rifle hoisted against his shoulder. Further away, men, women and children sat in a dusty yard, a high barbed wire fence holding them at bay. A lookout post stood proudly in each of the four corners, guards gazing down masterfully on their captives. The hole she had passed through lay at the edge of a mighty compound, a prison camp of some kind. She watched in silence, hidden by the cover of the pit. A khaki uniformed soldier marched over to an old man, handing him a spade and pointing to the dry, dusty earth. The old man, weak and obviously terribly undernourished, struggled to his feet, taking the spade and digging. Beads of perspiration dripped from his gray, gaunt face. The soldier stood over him, his arm now resting on the butt of his gun, until he had grown tired of waiting.

"Come on, dig, man!" he yelled. "Dig, d'ya hear!"

An old lady hobbled across. Barely able to walk, she fell at his feet, raising her hands in the air, tears streaming down her heavily wrinkled face.

"No! Please, kind sir, have mercy," she begged.

The soldier laughed aloud, kicking her to the ground before aiming his rifle at the old man's head. Johanna closed her eyes, a shot ringing out through the air, the old man's head exploding on impact with the bullet. The blood soaked body toppled lifelessly into the freshly dug hole. The butt of the rifle came fast, swinging into the old lady's face, sinking deep into her fragile skull. Johanna froze as the soldier raised his rifle one more time, firing at anything that moved. The air filled with screams and gunfire, until nothing within range remained—just blood bathed

The Maze 201

bodies left in the sun.

The soldier smiled, looking down at his handy work, before he headed for a small wooden hut in the near distance. Within a short while he was back, accompanied by three other soldiers, each laden with armfuls of black, plastic bags. She watched in sheer terror, too afraid to look away or even to lie low in the pit as they produced long, razor sharp sword-like knives and proceeded to cut the bodies up into several more manageable pieces. Once done, each piece was placed in a bag and carried away.

Johanna lay still until the soldiers had disappeared, tears of terror; tears of rage pouring down her pretty face. But what was she to do next, where was she to go? The choices were in fact, quite simple. The only answer being, to go on. The porthole that had brought her to this evil, wretched place was gone. There was no way back to Bodmin, no way back to safety, only the need to carry on. The camp stood in silence, the heat of the sun scorching a wasteland below it, and a waft of food being cooked rose high into the air.

She lay face down in the pit until darkness set in before deciding which way to go next. The best idea appeared to be to crawl around the perimeter of the compound and to what might lie on the other side. She kept watch, counting the seconds in between each massive sweep of the search light in her direction. A good fifteen seconds would keep her in the shadows before light would shine on her again. As the beamed passed she jumped up, scurrying along on her hands and knees to the near corner, ducking down low as the beam passed overhead. It took roughly twelve seconds to cover that distance, less than half as far as she would have to go on her next run. Gaining her breath and counting down to the last second, she bounded off once more. The penetrating beam slowly turned its full circle, a glowing monster creeping up behind her. Finding nowhere to hide, she lay down as low as possible against the dry, rough earth. A guard silhouetted in the search light ray had noticed the movement, had seen something fall to the ground.

Concentrating the beam onto the area, picking out a figure in the dust, he shouted loudly. Suddenly lights shone all around, a siren whistled through the night air. Guards charged in all directions before heading out to where she lay, aiming their guns at her through thick wire mesh.

"Don't shoot," she mumbled, face low to the ground.

Footsteps sounded behind her, a guard pulling her viciously to her feet. He dragged her in through a large steel gate and into a small wooden hut, not the same small wooden hut as she had seen the first soldier enter into. She was shoved to the floor in front of another soldier sitting at a rather untidy desk. Sheets of paper littered its surface. The guard stood behind her, his gun at ease.

The soldier wrote some notes on a piece of filing paper before glancing up, his eyes a cat's eye green, brushing her up and down. He wasn't a particularly large man, but he was a strong looking man. Not a soldier, but powerful nevertheless. He was wearing a desert sand colored jacket and trousers, although the trousers couldn't be seen behind the desk, plus a matching peaked cap with a black band. Upon his jacket were seven or eight medals, gold stars from red, green and blue ribbons.

"Name!" he barked sternly, tapping his pen on the desktop.

"Johanna, sir!"

The soldier wrote this down before going on. He took on a deeply concerned expression, gazing awkwardly across the hut. The pen twisted in a soft, unarmy-like hand and was let to roll from his well-manicured fingers, down to his paper work jungle.

"How did you get this close to the compound? You're not part of this block." He stood up, moved away from his chair and paced slowly across to a small, dusty window. "Damn it!" he growled coldly, exaggerating his words. "Nothin' but zones from here to sector three, and you just happen to find your way here. How did you get here? Answer me!"

"I don't know, sir. Really, I don't."

He turned sharply and marched toward the door. "Well, it's not important. You made it here so you're staying." He reached for the handle, swinging the door open wide then stared across to the guard. "You know where to take her. Tag her and set her in." He left, slamming the door shut behind him.

The guard moved forward then reached into the left, inside

pocket of his jacket, taking out a thin plastic rod with a black, metallic cap. He held the tube lightly, turning the cap in a counter-clockwise direction.

"Close your eyes. Stand still." he ordered. She did as commanded, not wanting to waken the hate in his deep sea blue eyes. A sharp pain caught her neck, stinging intensively a split second or so before fading out. A sensation crept through her bones, a strange numbing sensation. She opened her fast tiring eyes, trying to fix them on his unfriendly face, his returning glare one of total disgust. The hut moved about her, turning all the time. Around and around and... Then darkness.

On coming to, Johanna found herself in yet another small hut, although she wasn't alone. Her head pounded with the feeling of a massive hangover, on a more suiting occasion for her it would have been a sign of a good night out.

Thirty or so bodies lay scattered across a grimy, wood board floor. They were thin, frighteningly thin, nearly naked in the dim light. It soon grew quite cold, the heat of the day and the cool of the evening, now the bitter ice of night. Weak and tired she fell asleep, nervous for what the morning might bring.

The night passed quietly, if not comfortably, until once again a new day began. She awoke to the creak of a small wooden door being thrown open. Guards swarmed in, grabbing her and her fellow captives. They were pulled to their feet and dragged outside into fresh morning air. The prisoners formed long, tidy rows, other prisoners stumbling in and joining them from a good twenty other small huts scattered loosely about the compound. So many faces, sad and pathetic faces. Faces of despair, agonized in their animal-like captivity.

Next to her stood a tall but worn looking man she guessed to be about forty-five years of age. His clothes were torn and dirty, probably never been washed. His eyes were the brightest cornflower blue, even if miserably sunken into a dull, gaunt face. He bore a large scar down the near side of his left cheek and his chin was lightly whiskered, dashes of gray on soft brown.

"Hello," she whispered.

He smiled meekly, staring straight ahead. "Don't say a

word, damn it. See that tower? You wanna get us all shot?"

Johanna gazed out at a tall wood and steel framed tower of about forty feet in height. She noticed two guards at the very top. A soldier, the very same soldier she had encountered in the hut the night before, was standing in between them, hands resting on the wooden safety barrier.

As they all stood motionless in the dusty yard, prisoners fell time and time again, only to be forced back up again by the many guards standing about them. Their bellies were extended , full of food, smiles on their healthy faces. The sun shone warmly, slowly rising high into the sky, penetrating the weary crowd. Johanna's legs felt like bursting, each and every muscle screaming for the chance to relax. The hours pushed on by, the day turning from a mild cool to a scorching hell.

Just then the soldier at the top of the tower raised his right hand and the prisoners began slowly falling out of line to find shady corners to rest. The tall man who had stood next to Johanna throughout those long, arduous hours of painful standing, tapped her lightly on the shoulder, pointing to a large tree stump under a makeshift shelter. The shelter was composed of four upright wooden poles and a galvanized tin sheet.

Once they had reached it and settled themselves down in the dust about them, he rubbed his stubbly chin thoughtfully.

"My name's Rutter, Frank Rutter. You must be the new one who caused the disturbance last night."

Johanna smiled. Less than smiled, she faked a smile. "Yes, yes sir." She cleared her throat. "I guess that was me. My name is Johanna. It's nice to meet you, Mr Rutter."

Rutter smirked, gazing into a scorching, almost sanity melting sun, momentarily lost within a reminiscent gaze. "Just Rutter'll do. They all call me Rutter around here, just plain old Rutter."

He scratched his name in the sandy earth with the tip of his right index finger, let his tongue dance a second across his sunsplit lower lip, and then went on. "Well, Johanna, you're in here for good, so listen up. Life's no ball game in this place. I'm in charge of our group, and I'll tell you now. Tough it. Endure it, that's all you can do. See this scar on my cheek? That's what you get for disobeying commands. If you work hard in the fields, you'll get good food and sometimes, even tobacco. If you don't smoke, you can exchange it with McNally." He pointed to another prisoner sitting a little further away talking to an old lady. "He's our local filter, been here the longest, been here about four years, not many go over five. Anyway, he can get you sweets in exchange for it if you like, but this you bloody well keep quiet. If it ever got out, there'd be hell to pay." He smiled bravely and sighed." I only want to help. The first few weeks can be a real bitch, so the sooner you get used to it, the sooner you'll get on with living. There's no way out, not unless it's in a black bag. This is it, we work for the master race now."

Johanna felt a distinct unease at his last statement. If this was a prison camp, then who were the master race?

"It's absolutely crazy," he went on despairingly. "Thought Hitler was insane, but not like this. We could only read of his madness in old history books. Now even that's all gone. You know, sometimes I wonder if there might be civilizations out there some place. People who've escaped the ravages of time, people who were never deported and tagged." He paused once more, unaware of her innocence.

"One moment, Mr, um, Rutter. You might think me mad right now, but I'm not. I'm confused. I mean, who is the master race? And the tag, what's it for?" She sat awaiting a reply, a reply that never came. "Rutter, look at me. Look at my clothes. These jeans, my watch, look at my watch." She stopped to think a short while, a sudden click in her worried head. History books, Hitler in old history books. "What happened to Earth? What is this?"

Rutter stared at her, just sat and stared, his eyes cutting into her blankly. "Earth..." he replied. "What happened to Earth? This isn't Earth." Johanna froze, ridged icicles touching her spine as he spoke. "This is Second Earth, Sector Two. What kind of talk is this? What are you?"

What was she to say? Like trying to convince him water isn't wet, that fire isn't hot, or that ice isn't cold.

"Rutter, trust me. Just trust me; I'm here to help you. Believe me, I am. But I need some answers first."

He looked lost, a million miles away—about as far as she

might well be from home—slowly drifting to far off shores before floating back once more.

"Okay, maybe... Look, I... Well, I don't know, you could be one of them." The other prisoners began to move, standing up and trudging away. "Come on," he coughed. "It's time to go."

Guided by a small group of armed guards, they soon set off out through a large steel gate, not the same gate as she had first entered through, and into a field of fresh green cabbages. The climate was suddenly cool and damp, raindrops falling from a cloudy dismal sky. She turned her pretty head, the sun streaming down relentlessly only a hundred or so feet away.

"Okay, listen up," Rutter said softly as the group dispersed to go about their daily chores. "Stay with me. All you have to do is take the cabbages as I dig them up and put them in the barrow over there. When it's full, McNally'll come and take it away, leaving you a new one, okay?"

With that, he marched off across the field, picking up a spade and digging into the earth. Thoughts of the old man digging his own grave filled her mind. The old lady, probably his wife, all the pleading in the world hadn't prevented their deaths. This place, this whole place was evil. Pure evil. This place was a new world, a world of pain and death, and she was part of it.

She started to work, the first day of, quite possibly, many more to come. Sure enough, as the first barrow was filled, McNally came across and took it away, leaving another in its place. This carried on through the drizzle of the afternoon, each droplet a cool, refreshing bead of life.

Eventually a guard shouted for them to finish. Immediately, they formed a long line and headed back toward the compound. The cool, refreshing drizzle petered out, the dreary rainy cabbage fields left behind. Back in the compound, the sun stood high in a hateful blue, pointing to the fact that it was only midday. And yet, in the field only a short walk away, it was almost dark.

"That's what they call Second England," Rutter whispered as a guard marched passed. "Cabbages and rain."

Johanna and Rutter crossed the compound with their fellow

The Maze

207

captives, seating themselves at several long rows of knot ridden, wooden benches. Bowls of rice, nuts and a few half-cooked cabbage leaves were passed along each line.

"Eat it slowly," Rutter advised helpfully as he scooped a few grains of rice in his mouth. "Learn to taste it, it's all you get until morning."

Johanna watched as he chewed, using dirty fingers as eating utensils. He raised small amounts to his lips, chewing slowly before swallowing. She followed his lead, doing exactly the same until her bowl stood empty. Conversations broke out, the odd smile crossing the odd, weather-beaten face. "Well, that was your first day. So, what did you think?"

"Not a lot."

She brushed a hand through her hair, picking at a thick knot. Slowly she eased it apart until it rested evenly against her honey mane.

"Is this what you do every day? I mean, every day of your life?" She was curious. Questions, questions, questions: So many questions. She just needed to know.

"Not every day, no. My group work goes wherever they tell us to. England's best. The rain forests are tough; just so damn many snakes and insects. Not a whole group make it back without somebody getting hurt, or worse still..."

"Rutter, you have such a lovely accent. So English." Rutter smirked, eyes flickering a split second. "No, but really. I mean, just like in the movies. The English gentleman, like on TV." Rutter's semi-cheerfulness faded at that point, a look of irritation, almost anger coming over him.

"Come with me." Finding a reasonably comfortable place to rest, he turned to face her. "Take that again."

"What do you mean, take that again?"

"You've seen movies, seen TV?"

She laughed childishly. "Of course, who hasn't?"

He sat in silence a short while, deep in thought, occasionally eliciting the odd sigh and nervous grunt.

"Me." He raised the back of his thick-fingered hand to his left eye, wiping away a lonesome, crystal tear. "TV's were banned years ago, at least fifty years after the last cinema showing. Let me see now, it was a few years before I was born. Must have been." He paused, casting his eyes down at her clothing. Her sneakers, clean and unscathed. Jeans, tight, clean and blue. Her pink shirt, soft and unsoiled.

"What is it, Rutter?"

He fidgeted, biting harshly on his lower lip, a look of total confusion on his weather worn face. "Okay, you tell me who you are and I'll tell you what you want to know."

Johanna knew what she had to say. Saying it on the other hand, she knew would be a problem. "Well, where should I begin? Um, okay. I'm from Earth, the real Earth. I was born in 1991, am half-Swedish and half-English—"

Rutter cut in. He was tense, sweating cold beads, fighting for words. "It can't be. This is 2135!"

"Please Rutter, let me finish. I was caught in a maze, a labyrinth if you like. I'm lost in time and I think I know who your master race is."

Rutter listened carefully before telling his story. "It was back in 2117. I was working with a small band of renegades up on the North front. We were one of the last groups; the others had been caught and systematically killed within the first five years of the Battle of Recard. The war was over freedom rights, we just wanted to be able to do the things our forefathers had been able to do. Simple things like living our own lives. The governments as far back as 2092 had begun to ban everything from dance floors to drinking halls. Of course, there were those who tried to fight the laws. They were rounded up and shot well before my time.

"Now I was born in 2099. My father was killed in action just weeks before my birth. By the time I was fifteen I had learned to survive in no man's land, my mother and I, as well as a small group of soldiers. I was sixteen when she was killed, God rest her soul. She was killed in cold blood by the Government crack squads. I soon got involved with an underground movement who were convinced the governments of the world were not to blame for the atrocities against mankind. They were convinced the governments had been overthrown and replaced by an alien nation. We found the proof but it was too late and they were too strong, their plan was in full swing and we were powerless to do anything about it. In the following thirteen years they not only destroyed country by country, but also built a whole new planet, using ideas of man's own way. They created their own idea of paradise, hot, cold, rainy, dry, all in walking distance of itself. Some say that as far back as 2124 people were being deported to Second Earth. As for Earth, I don't know, maybe it exists no more. Or maybe it's just an alien playground nowadays. We're here to harvest, to give them vegetables in the damp fields of England, fruits and nuts in the rain forest jungles... Whatever they want, we get it."

Johanna took it all in, frightened at the thought of knowing the future, the hell that it held. Still one thing puzzled her, biting at her, tearing inside, pushing the urge to ask. "What is a tag?"

He sighed heavily and cleared his throat, paused and raised a hand to his stubbly chin. "You've been tagged, that's for sure."

"Yes, last night."

"Well, if you feel the side of your neck, you'll feel something like a small bump, a bump that grows." He cocked his head to one side, showing her the shape on his neck, a shape that at one time had been little more than a bump like hers.

"Jesus," she whispered nervously. "My God, now I know exactly who your master race is." The shape was so small, it was almost invisible without close inspection. A shape, a tattoo. An eye, a wall of crocodile scales overhead and a strange sequence of letters below. "I've seen it before, seen it somewhere else. Not on the neck, but on the hand. Bigger, much bigger, but what does it mean?"

Rutter searched the lonely corridors of his tormented mind for the right words, staring out across the fast darkening compound. "Well..." he began hesitantly." We can harvest fruits and vegetable. Rice in the paddy fields, wheat, Maize, corn ... things like that. But there's no....." He paused, the apple falling from the tree to the ground with a thud. He was stuck, fighting to throw words from his tongue, all to no avail.

"There's no meat, is there?" she cut in, fearing his reply. "We're on the menu and that tattoo is some kind of sell-by date, right?"

He didn't reply, he didn't have to, she could see the answer on his features. His face was pale, full of fear. Johanna felt sick, felt the sudden urge to heave, to be free of that fear and that anger inside her. No, Rutter didn't need to reply, the truth clearly written, engraved into every pitiful figure within the compound.

The two of them sat a while, both miles away in their own distant worlds. Hundreds of years apart, sitting side by desperate side, both agonizing over mankind's demise. Finally, Rutter broke the silence.

"Come on, let's hit the sack." They stood up, heading for that familiar hut, entering and laying down to sleep.

"Don't worry, Rutter, we're going to fix this," she whispered, closing her tired eyes.

Uneasily she rolled over on the hard wooden floor, trying to sleep. She was exhausted, of course, she was exhausted, tired beyond belief, but sleep wouldn't come her way. Something prevented her eyelids from dropping, forced them to remain in their daytime positions just a little longer. It was almost as if something was about to happen and she was to be a part of it. She mentally prepared herself, although she still jumped deep down inside when that something happened. A voice, a voice so soft and gentle, sung a chorus in her head, her body warm and tingling.

"Johanna, Johanna, you are so far away. Come back, you must come back. Come back through the Maze, come back to me..."

The voice faded out, warmth gone. Suddenly she knew the answer, knew where to find her only chance for freedom. Her escape filled her mind, a map of the Maze, a porthole near its center. Fear left her with a strength reborn. She was ready and eager to move on, to fight and to see another day.

Morning came with great speed, the sound of guards rushing in, waking them abruptly with sticks and boots. Her second day began in much the same way as her first. Exactly the same way as it had done since the birth of Second Earth. They were pushed and kicked violently outside before being forced into rows in the cool of the morning. For some reason several of the prisoners appeared to bear smiles, a shining star holding up through the pain. A young boy of no more than five or six years of age moved forward, stepping away from the group.

"Merry Christmas, it's Christmas Eve. Merry Christmas!"

A guard darted in on him, the bloodthirsty hawk so powerful and mighty, swooping in for the kill. The boy never stood a chance. He was taken by his tangled, greasy brown hair and dragged harshly to the ground.

"You fools are prisoners, you've left your old world behind. You serve no earthly traditions. This is Second Earth. You live only to satisfy the master race, only to appease the new order. There is no Christmas here. No Easter, no birthdays, no weekends or holidays. You live to serve, that's all." With that he aimed his gun at the boy's head. "We must all obey orders," he went on. "If we don't obey orders, then we must be punished!" With a steady pull of the trigger, the gun went off. The boy's head exploded, a spray of blood and bone, his body falling, slumped, bathed in red to the sandy earth. Rows of prisoners stood in horror, in silent fear for their own lives.

"Bastards! Evil bastards!" Rutter growled under his breath, the hate within him almost ready to burst out in a blaze of suicidal glory. A lonely tear meandered across his colorless right cheek and he sniffed, holding his breath a split second before breathing again.

The guard coughed loudly, handed his gun to another guard who was standing nearby, then spat on the bloodied remains of the young boy.

"Your punishment, to stand an extra hour."

He walked away, the soldier at the top of the tower staring down at them. The first thirty or so minutes passed reasonably fast, but as the sun rose in the heavens above, toasting their flesh, it soon became quite unbearable. They stood in silence, hour after pulsating, agonizing, and heartbreaking hour. Each hour was like a lifetime, each lifetime passing only for another to begin. Prisoners fell time and time again, the guards kicking them and beating them back to their feet. If ever there was such a place as hell, then this was it. After what felt like an eternity, a blistering, baking millennium, the soldier raised his hand, the sign for the sun-scorched gathering to disperse.

"Merry Christmas," Rutter said softly as he wiped pools of

sweat from his strawberry red forehead. "Some bloody Christmas."

The two walked slowly to their usual spot, resting themselves under the shelter of galvanized tin, not the best resting place in the world, but one of the only. "Some life, and this is paradise."

He stared helplessly out across to Waxman, another member of his group, his head hung low as he slowly paced over to the corpse.

"Poor bastard, poor bloody bastard. He's got to go and bury his own son, poor bloody bugger."

Johanna didn't reply, her mind absorbed in the nightmare of what she had just witnessed. She gazed solemnly into the face of the man she had learned to call friend, studied him—his grief. The grief of a man broken by the winds of time, destroyed by his past, his present and the thought of his future.

"I need a cigarette," he whispered, his throat parched and dry. Taking a small tin from his dusty, slate gray trousers, he began to roll a neat, thin cigarette.

"In some strange way, I can't help but feel sorry for that guard. I mean... Well, let's face it, he has to obey orders, too. He'll get his comeuppance, just you mark my words. By God, he will." He paused, lighting up his cigarette, a feathery plume of blue-white dancing in the air, pirouetting ballerinas romancing invisible stages. "God'll strike the likes of him down, be sure of it." He inhaled deeply, held the smoke in his lungs a short while, then exhaled noisily. "That's better."

Just to the right of his filthy dirty, once shiny black left shoe, there was a long thin twig and he picked it up, tapping it lightly in the palm of his left hand. Again he was off in his own world, far, far away. Away from the pain and the hurt surrounding him.

Johanna wanted to speak, still having a good many questions to ask, although she knew all too well now was not the time. Instead she waited for him to return to the present and prayed his distant five minutes had brought a little joy. He grunted, clearing his throat exaggeratedly. He was back. He pushed the twig into the sandy ground, using it as a primitive clock.

The Maze   213

"It's night. See the stick? It must be four o'clock now. This is bad. It means we eat, sleep early then go off into the rain forests. You stick with me and keep yourself covered. It's a tough job. The toughest. You get bitten out there all over by bloody mosquitoes and there's no medicines either."

"My watch says a quarter to one."

"It's wrong, Johanna, trust me."

She smiled, suddenly quite brightly. She took the stick and cast it aside. "Don't you worry about me, Rutter, I'm not going out there tonight. You don't have to either if you don't want to."

"Don't talk daft, girl!"

"I'm not, I mean it. Maybe you should start trusting me." Rutter didn't reply, his mind back in that distant world he called his own. "I have two friends out there, Danny and Eric," she went on, knowing very well he wasn't listening, but spoke all the same. "They're in another world and they're waiting for me to return. I'm going, Rutter, I'm going tonight. I'd like you to come with me … if you want to, that is. Anything would be better than this, right?"

In time the sun began to lower in an ocean of blue, perching itself spectacularly against the horizon. Slowly the other prisoners began to move, climbing to their feet and heading toward the long wooden benches.

"Come on, Johanna. Let's get our places."

Standing up, they scuffed their feet across a fast cooling compound, finding their seats and sitting down. Bowls of food rested before them, bowls of rice soaked in slightly sour milk. They proceeded to eat, chewing slowly with each bite.

"This is disgusting."

"Eat it, Johanna. It's all you get until tomorrow."

"I can't. No way. I just can't."

"Then give it to me, I will."

Once bowls stood empty, excuses for meals gone, the group rose and headed off to their sleeping quarters. Johanna tugged Rutter lightly on the shoulder, she wasn't about to leave.

"Don't go, not just yet."

She picked up a small pebble from the ground, tossed it in the palm of her right hand a couple of times then threw it toward the base of a wooden hut. It tapped loudly before falling to its resting place.

"Damn it. What are you trying to do, get us shot?"

As the last of the group disappeared she tried again. She moved forward, picking up another stone.

"Look," she said softly, dropping it through the wooden frame.

Rutter shook his head, eyes wide and alert. He jumped up, pushing his hands in front of him. "My God, I don't believe it, my God. It's a miracle, a bloody miracle!" He was overcome with emotion, his hands momentarily out of sight. "What is it? What on earth is it?"

"Our only escape," she replied confidently. "Well, Rutter, are you coming with me tonight or not?"

With that said, she turned and walked away, heading for the dirty floor that had served as her bed since entering the hell of Second Earth. Rutter stood a short while, his head in a heavenly muddle before following her.

Once settled on grimy wood boards, he spoke, his words soft and gentle … sad and almost tearful. "I should've believed you. Should've... But I can't come with you, my dear. Did you think you could teach an old dog new tricks? This is my destiny. Doesn't matter that I hate it, it's my world. I can't come with you." He lay, gazing deep into space, deep into that world he'd created to ease his pain.

"But Rutter... Look... I… listen, I..."

She stopped, waited, giving her action a lot of thought, sighed heavily before raising a hand to the flowing ocean of golden waves in her hair, and stood up. Nothing but the rush of sleeping breaths filled her ears, the odd snore and broken groan. She bent down, kissing him lightly on the forehead, then raised herself and walked away. The wooden door creaked slightly as she pulled it open, although not enough to disturb prisoners or prison guards. Outside, the compound stood empty. Searchlights scanned the perimeter, illuminating flashes of insects as they darted around in sweeps of orangish-yellow. It wasn't long before she reached the porthole. She eased both hands around its opening, feeling her way to her next world.

The Maze   215

It was time to go, time to leave this terrible place behind, time to head off into the unknown, to travel ever onward toward the center of the Maze. She paused, a second or so of silent prayer for the ones left behind, the ones who would surely die on Second Earth in the year 2135. Then she climbed through. Darkness surrounded her, the feeling of passing through space.

"Johanna!" a voice shouted, a body hurtling through the portal after her, pushing her to the ground.

"You changed your mind, I knew you would." She held out a hand, letting him help her up. Her body wobbled, sinking slightly into a soft, straw-filled mountain.

"That hole will be gone soon, if it's not gone already. You made a good choice." She patted him wholeheartedly on the shoulder then sat down to rest under a star spangled, velvet black sky. "We can rest here, sleep a while. Forget about Second Earth, Rutter. You're free... *We're* free, Rutter. Free."

Her words comforted him like a mother's song, caressed him like the lapping waves of a turning tide. He closed his sleepy eyes with a loud, thankful sigh and prepared himself for the land of dreams.

Morning came to the chitter-chatter of birds overhead. A cool, refreshing breeze danced a tango over them, bringing them toward the world of daylight. Insects buzzed by, a sweet waft of freshly cut grass playing on the senses.

"Morning," Rutter mumbled. "What a dream, what a great dream I had." Slowly he opened his eyes and sat up. "Bloody hell!" He fell back, coughing loudly before trying again. He sat up, rubbed his disbelieving eyes, blinked, fell back once more. "Johanna! Bloody hell, either I'm crazy or..." He paused, sitting up one more time. "I'm crazy."

Johanna smiled gleefully, finding herself on a large golden yellow haystack. Green and yellow fields surrounded them, oceans of color rolling away in all directions. A large white-washed farmhouse with a freshly thatched roof stood in the distance.

"Wow! Wow, I did it. I did go the wrong way. It was that damn rabbit's fault. That's what Harry meant by, too far away. I was in the future," she said excitedly. Rutter looked on dumfounded. "How about a nice glass of lemonade, Rutter?"

"Yesterday, Johanna. Yesterday..." Rutter replied. "Yesterday I was a prisoner, a prisoner in fear of my life and today... Well today, I'm free. I'm sitting here like it's a lazy Sunday afternoon. Sitting here breathing fresh clean air, looking at fields. What's going on?"

He looked lost, not sad. His cheeks were a rosy red, shining out through the dirt on them. Johanna tried to make sense of her story.

"Okay, it's like this. You see, I've been here before. Here in this world, this time or whatever you want to call it."

"A bloody marvel, that's what I call it. A bloody marvel."

"Okay, I was in this bloody marvel," she grinned widely, strands of hair flickering like candles behind her. "With a farmer. I told him I was on holiday. Anyway, when I left, I found myself in some sort of fairytale, but it all got a bit out of hand. Then I crawled through a tunnel until finding Second Earth. The choice was to go back or to carry on."

Rutter listened; his mind focused a full one hundred percent.

"Well, I decided to carry on." She sat, waiting for a response. It never came, but then, did she really expect one? "I understand this is difficult for you, Rutter. I'd think it difficult too, if I were in your place. But it's okay now, we've made it." A broad smile crossed her face and she rolled down off the haystack, down into the breeze tickled green below. "Come on then," she said warmly as she strolled out across the field, flattening a track in the grass. Rutter followed close behind, not saying a word.

The field to their left, neatly boarded by a high green and yellow hedgerow, had recently been cut, fresh sweet smelling grass laying loosely over it. His mind flowed and overflowed with strange thoughts. Somehow he'd fallen into another world onto a haystack in the middle of a field of all places. He gazed at the haystack, its mass a golden-tangled monster. The grass surrounding it, waves of green rising to a crest, riding in the breeze. Taking fleeting glimpses behind him, he could clearly see a forest standing tall and proud under a sky of blue. How could he have fallen into a world so wonderful, so peaceful and free? How could he have left the hell and degradation of Second Earth behind? There was no hole in the sky. Just a few clouds floating, like vanilla candyfloss, but no hole. The more he fought to understand, the less he did.

"Johanna?" he asked softly. "Where… where are we?" His words were long and drawn, uncertain yet full of curiosity. "Where exactly are we? More to the point, how did you know we could escape? I mean, so many have tried before. So many have tried running for freedom whilst out in the fields, tried climbing fences. Nobody ever made it, we'd given up."

She stopped, nearing the farmhouse, kicking the top of a buttercup, then turned to face him. "Well," she started positively. "This is England. Cornwall. Bodmin, to be exact. The year is 1944, July or August at a guess." She thought back to that fateful day so long ago. The day she and her lover had met Eric and consequently, Harry. "And the reason I knew how to, and where to, escape is due to a man called Harry. Well, not Harry really, Hazzari actually. He is the key holder of the Maze. I met him in Bournemouth before all this started. He's my protector, I guess. Look, I don't really know enough to tell you everything, except that I thought he was dead and now I know he's not."

This didn't really help Rutter understand, but then not knowing had become part of his life.

Walking on, they soon reached the farmhouse. Two black Labradors bounded playfully toward them. Rutter jumped in fright, remembering the guard dogs on Second Earth, Sector Two. How at one time two dogs had been set on a young female prisoner who had tried to escape up and over the barbed wire fence. Her clothing had gotten entwined in the thick razor-sharp metal spikes, piercing her innocent flesh. He remembered her terrified screams as the two dogs pounced, sinking their teeth into her legs, tearing her down into jaws of devil steel. By the time the guards had arrived, beating them off, all that remained was a bloody, torn corpse. Savagely dismembered, flesh and bone stretched out, the sacrificial lamb. The friendly licks of the Labradors soon calmed him down, slaying his fears behind him.

The farmer stood in the doorway, a broad smile on his face. "Hello, young lady. I thought you'd forgotten me." He turned and strolled casually inside, fetching a cool jug of lemonade from the fridge and placing it on the table.

"Come on, then." Johanna smiled. "Let's go in."

The dogs faithfully followed at their heels, two large black shadows on strip wooden floors, the hallway leading to the kitchen and that mouth-watering homemade lemonade. Once in the kitchen she introduced her friend to the farmer, all three seating themselves at the old oak table.

"Sorry about the state of me," Rutter said quietly, gazing down at his trousers. His eyes grew wide, a look of total confusion crossing his features. In disbelief he stared. A pair of brown corduroy trousers, clean and tidy. A fresh white T-shirt, a brown corduroy jacket and a pair of shiny clean, brown shoes. His confused stare rose, lifted skyward then returned to meet Johanna's cheerful smile. "But um... Well, we've been out walking in the fields." He felt himself blush, an embarrassing warmth burning through him.

The farmer took out his small briar pipe from the inside pocket of his jacket. He held it neatly in his large, work-roughened right hand, held it lovingly as if it was his best friend. Then he reached for a medium-sized pouch of tobacco that rested together with a box of matches in the center of the table. His eyes were wide and alive, and Johanna clearly noted his joy at seeing her once more. He took out a sufficient amount of tangled golden brown tobacco, pushing it lightly into the pipe bowl with a contented sigh, and raised the pipe to his lips. There, it rested a short while before, with a sharp flash of light, a match gave that tangled golden brown a life of its own.

A smoke. Wow, a smoke. Rutter gleamed. Yes, a cigarette. He reached into his pocket, it was empty. Tried the next pocket, still empty. Then yes, victory. He drew out a small tin. It wasn't his tobacco, wasn't his tin. But it was a tin and it wasn't empty. Inside he found seven pre-rolled cigarettes... Heaven.

"And so 'ow d'ya know this lovely young thing?"

Rutter lit his cigarette, inhaling deeply. It tasted good. Better than good, it tasted fantastic. More than good, more than fan-

The Maze 219

tastic, it was his first cigarette in freedom for as long as he could remember.

"Oh, he's staying at the same house as my mother and myself. He's a very good friend of my mother's."

The conversation ended just there with Johanna gazing about the room. Her eyes dusted the calendar by the lattice window. 1944. Well, at least it was the same year. The date was September the second. She tried to think back to her last visit, to the date—what was it now?—she couldn't remember. The farmer pushed two tall glasses across the table, pointing toward the jug of lemonade.

"Help yerselves. Thirsty ole work out there, 'tiz that."

Conversations came and went, Johanna having to make up quite a lot as she went along. Rutter remained pretty silent throughout. He just nodded politely now and again, and at times he added the odd yes or no. His mind was far away. He was happy, glad to be free of the hell left behind. Pleased to be a part of this world so strange to him. He gazed around the kitchen, picking out objects of beauty, objects of a day far gone by.

At last it was time for them to leave that historical place. Johanna could have quite happily stayed all day, but she could plainly see the unease on Rutter's face. She said her goodbyes and Rutter said his.

"Shall you be coming this way again, me dear?"

"Oh yes, I'm certain I will." How bad it felt to lie to such a welcoming man, how down right bad it all felt. She smiled brightly then pushed her chair back and rose to her feet. "Thank you for the lemonade."

"Yes, thank you for everything," Rutter added.

Once outside, they were greeted by a fast cooling sun. Light, fluffy clouds floated by like cotton wool in candy land. A large forest stood like a 3-D motion picture at the top end of the field and they headed steadily toward it. It looked beautiful. It was beautiful. Greens and browns, yellows and rustic reds, all shades intermingling into one within the softest, most gentle breeze. Parasol upon parasol of thick foliage protected them from the fast retiring, although still warm, sun. Stepping over brackens and weaving around hawthorne bushes, they found themselves a place to rest at the base of a tall, thick pine tree. The tree stood in the vast splendor of the forest like a proud reminder to mankind that Mother Nature still ruled supreme, even if mankind was and indeed, still is, dedicated to death and destruction.

The tree had probably stood there for years. Years of growth, maturing from a tiny little seed into something mighty and strong. Surely that tree had seen times a changing, certainly could have told a story or two if only God had blessed it with a tongue. It had probably been a part of Mother Earth far longer than the eldest of men and women, and it would probably outlive the youngest. It's noble trunk provided an adequate backrest. A late summer breeze buffeted its top branches, rattling its needles relentlessly. Something moved a little further away, scurrying across a golden brown, pinecone floor.

"Look," Johanna said softly. "A..." She paused, trying to say something. "A sk...."

"A squirrel!" Rutter popped in.

"Yes, a skerl. That's difficult for me to say."

Rutter laughed, watching the squirrel as it foraged in the undergrowth for nuts and berries. "Yes, I suppose it is really. I've never really thought about a word being difficult to say." So she had difficulties saying the word, squirrel, he thought to himself. Big deal, no loss at all really. She could do everything else. What time traveller needs to say such words as squirrel anyway?

The squirrel soon bounded off, scaling a tree as if it was on level ground. Up, up and away, high into those parasol-like branches, hidden in its cover. It was gone.

"How do you know where to go next?"

"I don't," she replied casually, a starry twinkle in her eyes. This puzzled him somewhat. A time traveller without a map, what kind of time traveller would travel without a map? If that's what she was... She could well have been God to him. God, yes God. Well, maybe not. But then what did it matter? She was his savior.

They sat laughing and chatting of past experiences throughout the late afternoon and early evening, Rutter keen to

The Maze 221

gain as much information as he possibly could. Within the span of his lifetime he had done a good many things. He had lived a life of uncertainties and in later years, uncertainties and great fears. He had lived through wars that hadn't even begun until long after Johanna's life force had dried up into the realms of history. Now he was in his past, in history and he was desperate to learn all about it.

The sun began to lower in the sky, hiding itself indifferently behind the earth's curvature, heading for foreign lands. Darkness, and in time, coldness set in. And then the dire need of sleep. Rutter closed his eyes first, his stomach rumbling with hunger, although hunger was something he'd lived with for many years. Johanna sat in silence, hoping for a sign. It never came, not at least until she had fallen asleep.

Slowly she drifted into the land of dreams, thoughts whispering and rising like giant kites in the wind. The way things had been before all this, the way life had been back home. Those school days, her best friend, Malin. The journeys into Gothenburg, strolling along The Avenue. Sitting in one of the many street cafés, watching all the people passing by. Holidays in England, that distant island retreat across the rolling blue. Lying on golden sandy beaches soaking up the sun. Danny, the warmth and the love he'd offered her, the time he'd spent with her. The affection he'd willingly lavished on her in times of need, the joy and the protection.

In the end she had to sleep, just had to. Her eyes closed, canopies over sparkling oceans of crystal blue. Her eyelids quivered in the depths of a dream. It was Harry, Hazzari, key holder of the Maze. He was standing before her, a deep sadness on his ghostly face. He pointed to the dry earth, to a large stone, a large headstone. She moved toward it, reading the words engraved deep into its rough surface.

IN MEMORY OF
FRANKLYN RUTTER
BORN 2099
DIED 2136 IN CAPTIVITY
REST IN PEACE

"You can't take him with you; he must be left in Bodmin. You can't take him. He's not of this place and his time on this planet has yet to come. He'll die a free man if you carry on and defeat the Maze." The dream slowly faded out, Johanna crying in her sleep, mumbling through streams of tears.

"No, don't take him. Please don't take him. Let him come, let him follow me."

Morning came, darkness fast thinning out. A sun, warm and gentle rose up into the heavens above. A deep-throated groan escaped Rutter's dry, thirsty lips. A loud yawn and he was awake. He watched as Johanna fidgeted before opening her sleepy eyes.

"You slept bad last night, girl. Tossing and turning, mumbling something too."

She looked at him, a shiver treading her spine. "Just a dream..." she replied adamantly. She looked up, listening to the rustle of pine needles and sighed heavily. "Today we go on."

A vast green field spread out before her, Danny and Eric beside a winding stream. Watery plumes sprayed against the far bank, waves cascading over rocks and pebbles, a constant battle to reach the salty ocean tides. Then she was sitting with her two friends. Yes, and Rutter was there as well, his joyful laughter filling her heart with happiness non-ending. The four of them were sitting around a grand red and white checkered tablecloth, a huge picnic spread before them. A wonderful display of sandwiches, crisps, cakes and plenty to drink patiently awaited them. She gazed up at a pale blue sky. A swift darted overhead as she bit into a ham and crispy salad roll. She was laughing loudly, Eric trying his hardest to catch a large white butterfly, which was perched somewhat precariously on an anemone. As he grabbed at it, it flew through his hands and up into the air.

Once they had eaten, Eric produced a little red ball. Where the little red ball came from, she didn't know. It was just all of a sudden there. They played with the ball throughout the afternoon until they were all so worn out they had to sit down and take a drink. They sat talking of old school days and of fun memories, of days gone by. A large black cloud floated by overhead, blotting out the warmth of the sun and it soon became quite cold. Things were packed into a straw hamper and off they set across the field. Eric charged on ahead, pulling his shirt tightly around him.

Suddenly he fell back on the grass, a pained cry slashing the air. A strong wind blew up, leaves dancing a twisting swirl. She ran over to where he lay and helped him to his feet, worriedly reaching out a hand in front of her. She felt something, some kind of shield. Although it was invisible to the naked eye, she used her fingers to follow it around until finding herself back in the same spot. Tearful eyes gazed back at her friends as they beat against the shield, trying to attract the attentions of a family nearby. The circular shield began to move. Desperate hands came away, holding each other tightly. Around and around the shield turned. Around and around and...

The grass beneath their feet began to lower, revealing dark soil underneath. Screams filled their prison, their bodies sinking deeper, ever deeper into the earth. Heads disappeared, the descent becoming much faster. Light filtered in far up above them. In time, the stony earth petered out into thick gray shafts of granite rock and in seconds, a bright glow of red.

Danny fell to the ground first, closely followed by Eric and Rutter, all three gasping for air. Their skins began to dry out, flaking off to reveal raw flesh. Johanna screamed in silence, bones crumbling to dust before her. At last the cylindrical prison stopped as it entered a long dimly lit tunnel. She fell to the ground, the tunnel cooling until a damp freshness enveloped her terrified frame. The cylinder was gone.

"My God," she whispered to herself, sitting up.

Just then she could feel something, something soft, something warm and alive. She turned and looked down, jumping to her feet when she saw a body. A little further away, another huddled up in a little ball. After plucking up enough courage to investigate, she rolled the first body over.

"Danny!" she whispered, uncertain if she was still in the depths of a dream. Gradually, he opened his eyes, raising a shaky hand to his dry, thirsty lips. "Danny! Danny, thank God!"

"Johanna," he barely croaked. "How did you get here?"

She thought for a short while, not really having an answer

to such a question. She wasn't dreaming. No, she was awake, she had to be...

"It's not important, Dan. We're together now, that's all that matters."

"Eric, go check on Eric."

She eased herself up and moved across to the next crumpled figure, rolling it over and waking it up. A face, ghostly white and rather bruised, lifted slightly to greet her. A trickle of congealed blood rested on his right cheek. She noticed something a little further away and she moved in for closer inspection.

"Oh no, God, no!" Her cheeks reddened, tears mingling with dust. "Oh no. Harry, why?" A stone, a headstone to a lonely grave. Old and chipped, discarded, the man of whom she had once known as Rutter.

Suddenly the tunnel began to move, dust and rubble falling from its roof.

"Quick! Come on!" Johanna shouted, helping them up and dragging them off along the tunnel. The earth shook, beer barrel-sized craters appearing in the ground.

"Come on!" Eric screamed, feeling his body sinking, Danny grabbing him just in time. Off they stumbled, light shining in from the far end. On reaching that shining light, static clicks of joy filled their ears. They were back in the arena. A large global capsule lowered from the arena's center point until it was no more than a foot or so above the sandy earth. The bottom half of it was red and made of some kind of metal. The upper half was made of glass. A creature sat inside, a wide grin appearing on its goldfish bowl blue face. It raised its three-fingered left hand, spiralling an index finger two full turns before the capsule rose once more.

Two guards stood up from the crowd. They moved toward the edge of the floating circular stand, stepping onto a red disk. The disk moved, a large button-shaped lift lowering them to the sandy floor below. Each guard held a long pole shaft of which had a small, electronic current at the top end. Johanna and her two young companions, worn and tired, were forced into a large steel-framed cage. The guards studied them a short while, three gladiators, three victims, ready to fight again.

In time the crowds began to disperse. The guards locked the cage door tightly before they left. Danny held Johanna like a baby holding its mother. He stretched out a hand to Eric, who took it and held it, feeling its comfort.

"How'd ya find us?"

"I had a dream," she replied. "I was on a picnic... I had a dream then I found you. How has it been for the pair of you?"

Danny told his story as Eric slowly closed his eyes and fell into a deep sleep. They, too, soon found the need to sleep and in time, their eyes closed and they joined him in a dreamy world.

Chapter 11
Level Two

Plans had begun to further the games along. Only one had made it through level one, game one, the others killed by a creature in the arena. Only one other had made it through level one, game two. The others had fallen to their deaths into the fiery depths of a vast inferno or at the evil hands of that same creature in the arena. A survivor from the game before and a survivor from the last. Danny and Eric knew only too well, the worse was yet to come.

The arena began to fill once more. Strange voices filled the air, the beings seating themselves on their circular stands. The guards were back. They clicked and squeaked at each other, eyes wide and bright, staring in through the bars. They looked almost comical, dancing about excitedly, jibber-jabber leaving their wide mouths. One of them held a large black box and after much ado, took out its contents and pushed it through the bars. It fell to the ground like several lumps of cold, although thankfully, cooked meat. Obviously it was breakfast, time to eat before the day's fun and games.

Johanna picked up a small chunk and lifted it dubiously toward her mouth. She sniffed at it, toyed with it and then bit into it. It tasted like meat. What else should it taste of? she wondered. Tasted like slightly salted, not too well-cooked meat.

Danny and Eric watched her as she chewed. For them it was continuing hunger or what lay before them on the dusty earth.

"Food, yeah right," Danny growled under his breath. The war was on, the war between continuing hunger and the urge to throw up.

"Eat," Johanna ordered, in between bites.

"Yeah, but..."

"No buts."

Eric knelt down, picking up a small chunk. "Here goes nothing." He shook his head slowly from side to side with an uneasy sigh, held out his right hand, then opened his mouth before casting it in. He chewed hastily and reached for another chunk.

"Come on, Danny. Do it." Johanna's mind drifted back through the depths of time for a second. Back to the depths of a future time, a future time full of hate and pain. Back to the future, back to that place far, far away, where food was a luxury and mankind was a potential meal for a so-called master race.

Moments later, a desperately poor excuse for breakfast gone, the cage door opening up and the back bars crunching steadily forward, they found themselves being forced back into the arena.

"Shit! At least give us enough time to let this crap go down."

The crowd silenced as once again the red metallic and glass capsule lowered. The creature inside held a large and extremely sharp, curved dagger.

"The Dagger of Teorna," Johanna whispered.

Danny gazed at her in amazement. "You know what that thing is?"

She looked surprised. "No," she replied with equal amazement. "I don't even know why I said it. I'll tell you one thing though. We need it."

Eric paid little attention to her words. In the heat of the moment he let them pass through one ear and out the other. Top priority number one for him was his own safety. Top priority— survival. Besides, he had every confidence in her. For him, she was a little tiny piece of Harry, a little tiny piece of the man who he had learned to love and to trust. She was a little tiny piece of the man who had died and left a piece of himself behind. For him, Harry was Johanna. Harry and Johanna were one and the same.

The capsule began to rise, the crowd watching with great anticipation.

"This is it," Johanna said boldly. "Keep with me, I'll get us out." A strong vibration travelled through the ground, a huge door at the far end of the arena opened up with a loud creak. "Okay, let's go!" she shouted as she bolted off toward the space.

A sudden jolt, a pair of powerful, scaly hands rose up through the sandy earth. Eric dived out of their reach, nearly falling as the ground tremored again. Slowly, a huge granite slab rolled sideways, inch by inch across the space.

"Quick, move. Don't look back." Danny grabbed at his young friend before throwing himself to temporary safety. They had made it out of the arena.

Silence, eerie and empty, only a dreary gloom filled their ears. They appeared to be in a small valley. Pink and red shafts of jagged granite rock rose up above them like giddy, lava-spewing giants. Ahead of them, at least fifty feet up a rock face, was an entrance to a tiny cave. A narrow zigzagging bridge of stone led the way toward it.

Johanna seated herself on a pile of rubble, breathing deeply to regain her breath. She gazed thoughtfully at Eric, and Eric noted the worry in her eyes. She looked sad. Something burned deep down inside of her. She was tired, more than physically tired, she was mentally tired as well, drained, exhausted. She knew what had to be done. She knew the dagger, knew the power of the Dagger of Teorna, knew the large and extremely sharp, curved Dagger of Teorna was the one thing she needed more than anything else. She didn't know why she needed it, didn't know what she would do with it even if she were able to obtain it. All she knew was that she needed it as much as she needed the air she breathed. She knew it as surely as she knew of the heartbreak she was about to face. Something stung, cut deep into her very being. She knew only too well of the loss she was about to endure.

"That's where we must go."

"You realize we ain't got a chance in hell of getting that bloody dagger," Danny gasped as he rested his hands on his tired knees. "You think they can't see us? Hell, no, the bastards are out there betting on us. They got bloody cameras out there. Trust me, we're cooked."

Johanna knew the situation they found themselves in looked bad. The odds were against them, stacked a mountain high. She knew that, knew the outlook was grim. Again she looked at Eric. Eric, the boy, who became a man. The worn gaze on his face, the dimness within his once sparkling eyes. Like a stray puppy on a noisy pavement, ignored and forgotten by the passerby. The hell he'd been through. Danny and Eric were just so different, not just in age. Their way of thinking, their way of doing, both were different. A little like chalk and cheese.

Eric was a streetwise youngster. He had seen more in his life than most might in ten lifetimes. He was tough in his own way, but most importantly, he had faith. He believed in her, looked to her for guidance and trusted her every word.

Danny was older, in many ways more experienced. He wasn't really the tough guy type. His toughness was all part of an act, a wonderful, beautiful act.

Johanna had never been out after a man, had never wanted to meet the man who dreams and heroes are made of. She had only ever wanted to meet somebody who she felt good with. She felt good with Danny, loved him and more than anything, needed him.

The only thing that had ever hurt her was his lack of faith. Almost as if he resented her telling him what to do. After all, she had only been trying to help. She would have loved to have listened to him, would have loved to have done precisely as he had suggested. He was so negative, though. In his own world he might well have been the life and soul of every party. He might well have been every girl's dreamboat, but in the Maze, he became useless.

She gazed across at him, wondering where she might be without him. She possessed a strange power she couldn't explain to herself and anyone else for that matter. If she could have

The Maze   231

given this power to him, she gladly would have. But the fact still remained. She was a force to be reckoned with. Useless, she grumbled to herself. Rather harsh words really, especially when referring to Danny. He wasn't really useless. Danny was just Danny. Danny was the one who gave that power within her the life to fight on. He was the spark plug in the power machine.

Precious seconds passed, that feeling of loss greater than ever. If something was going to happen … something horrible, something terrible... If something was going to happen, then she just wished it would hurry up and be done with. She wanted to jump up, to hug them both, to hold them and say goodbye. But then who was she to say goodbye to? Something stirred above them, a rock falling, a solid raindrop at their feet.

"Shit! What was that?"

"Shhhhh, quiet," she whispered, gazing up in the direction of the disturbance. The time had come. Yes, she felt it, she felt it now. A deep and vengeful darkness crept up her spine, digging along, digging claws into her flesh. Yes, the time had come.

Suddenly their peace was broken.

"Get out of the way!" she screamed, as a huge creature, half-man, half-reptile fell as if from nowhere into their midst. Its body, human from the waist up, rested on two massive, muscular mint green scaly legs. A thick tail flicked from side to side.

The beast glared, eyes tight with primeval devilry. It held a large golden bow, an arrow already in place. Strapped to its battle tank back were six more golden arrows resting in a neat cigar-shaped, black leather quiver. The arrow was aimed, Eric feeling his nerves turn to jelly as he watched, the arrowhead no more than three feet away, staring him hungrily in the face.

"No. No please," he struggled to say.

A scream like thunder echoed the valley walls, Danny desperately fighting his fears, fighting to come to the rescue. The arrow was pulled back, resting hard against the bowstring and stabilizer. A loud whistle passed his ears.

"Eric!"

Suddenly he found himself flying through the air, a rugby tackle bringing Eric to the ground. The arrowhead cut sharply into the rocks about them, sinking with an almighty crack.

Golden sparks hurled in all directions, showering the stony earth in color cascades.

He looked up sharply, seeing the creature as it reached for another arrow.

"Danny, Danny! Eric, quick!"

Johanna's fearful cry meant nothing, like ripples on a shimmering lake. In the horror of the moment, they meant nothing. Danny pulled Eric to his knees and dragged him along. The eyes of that creature of dread spelled impending doom. Ice cold and evil.

They ran off toward the narrow zigzagging bridge of stone. Johanna was already halfway up it, clambering as fast as she possibly could.

Again an arrow hurled toward them, just missing Danny by mere inches. It hit the base of the bridge, stone splinters flying into the air. Up they climbed, the creature grabbing for a third arrow. Johanna reached the top and turned to help her friends, although deep down inside, she knew only too well one of them was destined to die. Seconds later, reaching out, she took Danny's hand. The arrow ripped into the bridge, it surely wouldn't take much more. Danny was up, he had made it.

"Eric, hurry up!" he pleaded, the fear within him causing his body to ache. A fourth arrow hit the bridge. It rocked, a large chunk of stone falling away. Then a fifth. Eric fell back, tumbling to the earth below. A sixth arrow fell, just missing him as he nimbly jumped to his feet and lunged toward the remnants of the bridge. With hands torn and bloody, he grappled to haul himself up.

A sudden ear-splitting scream tore through the air, causing Danny's mouth to drop open in horror. Somewhere behind him, could have been a million miles away, he could hear Johanna. They were seconds of hell as he waited, his eyes wide, almost bursting out of their sockets.

The seventh and last golden arrow embedded itself in the back of Eric's head. Blood, like thick lava streams flowed from the gaping wound, his head pinned to the rocks. His body shuddered slightly, ripples working their way down before escaping through his toes. Lifeless now, he was dead.

The Maze 233

Fractions of seconds passed by, or a thousand years. Trapped, eye to eye, facing the unholy enemy, they were lost in no man's land, held at bay, glued to the spot, unable to find the courage to move.

"Danny! Danny, for God's sake! Quick!"

He didn't move, couldn't. The creature in front of him, minus its deadly arrows, swung its mighty tail into the bridge. It crashed down like thunderclaps, tearing at the remaining stonework, tin soldiers on a make believe battlefield.

"Danny, hurry!"

Tears streamed uncontrollably down Johanna's face, the feeling of loss so great inside her. Danny fell back into the cave entrance, knowing the creature was out there and out there to stay. The bridge was gone, there was no way up.

"Ah, no, man, No, hell no." He fell to his knees, taking his head in cupped hands. "Hell, no. His fists, tight and clenched, touched skin. His fingers twisted around strands of his hair, pulling with sheer anger and fear. His friend was gone. "We can't just leave 'im there."

Suddenly Danny was up and on nimble feet.

"You bastard! Damn you!" He was out of control, consumed by rage. No longer was the fear inside him just a simple fear. Fear had turned to rage. Mindless, foolish rage. "Come on then, take me too!" He could hear the creature down there, could hear it as it tried in vain to reach them.

"There's nothing we can do, Danny. He's dead, can't you understand that? He's dead, damn you, dead!" He could feel her behind him, a fist landing heavily on his already bruised, left shoulder. "He's dead!"

Yes, he was dead, he finally admitted. Danny turned, taking her in his arms. His friend was dead, and now Johanna had faced her great loss. He was her friend, too. They moved on into the cave, feeling its dampness closing in around them.

"There was nothing we could've done, Dan. I'm sorry," she sobbed. Once safely inside they rested, seating themselves in a sad and crumpled pile.

"I can't believe it, just can't believe it. He's dead, Eric's dead."

His own fears, those terrible, terrible fears that in the past had returned time and time again to relentlessly hound him, were gone. Gone into the realms of darkness. His own anger, that sleeping, suicidal monster inside him, was gone. Gone off to hide behind another emotion. Heartbreak, pure unbridled heartbreak, had taken their places.

"He's dead, Johanna. Don't you see? He's dead. We're dead."

What could she say? What on earth could she possibly say to ease his pain? What could she possibly do to bring back that young soul cut down so young? She raised a finger to his dusty cheek, wiping away a salty cascade of moisture.

Eric was gone and now they were just two. Two young people lost in the Maze. Would it help if she were to tell him that she knew one would die? That if she could have chosen, she would have willingly chosen herself? That at least her beloved was still alive. No, these things wouldn't have helped.

"Danny? Danny, please be strong. I need you to be strong. Please Danny, be strong for me."

Gradually he calmed himself, trading the pain for the uncertainty of the future ahead. He pulled himself up and stood straight. "Come on then."

She took him by the hand, feeling a flood of icy sweat on it. Moving along the cave, the walls soon became much narrower. The rough, pink and red ceiling lowered at such a rate that in mere minutes, they were forced to crawl on their hands and knees.

"This is useless, Johanna. I'm almost stuck fast."

Useless, that word was back. Useless. Danny was *not* useless, she told herself yet again. Of all the things he was, useless wasn't one of them. He had proven that when trying to help Eric. He'd failed but failure didn't make him useless.

They pushed on, slowly, ever so slowly all the time, squeezing through a small gap in the rocks.

"I can hardly breathe," he ground out.

The gap soon widened, offering them a little more space to move in. It wasn't long before a light shone ahead of them, the static click chatter of the beings in the distance.

"We've made it. That was level two," he growled under his breath.

"No, Danny. We aren't on any level now. Be very quiet now, okay?"

On reaching the exit, they waited a short while to catch their breath. Ahead lay a long thick tube, painted red. Below, about forty feet or so, was the arena. A creature, huge and hairy, wandered about in search of a meal. It held its massive, shaggy head high, its narrow, cat-shaped eyes studying the bluish-gray crowd in the circular stand. Its arms and hands were gigantic, much larger than its lower body and legs. Each hand bore seven razor sharp claws and each fang in its wide-open mouth glistened crimson flashes.

"Come on, don't look down."

"What? You've got to be kidding me! You're telling me we're going across there. Ah, come on. What if we fall?"

He could clearly see the creature, the giant hairy creature, roaming about down below and the very thought of being down there with it sent icy chills along his spine.

"Look, they can't see us on camera. Just stay calm." Johanna straddled the tube, edging her way along it. "Trust me, just come on."

Silently, they eased themselves along, sliding toward the bubble they'd seen lowered into the arena earlier on. Their hands grabbed nervously at the tube, thick and strong, holding their weight. It didn't bend or bow under them, didn't move or rattle, to give their positions away.

Danny fought an inner fear, a fear Johanna apparently knew nothing of. He felt inadequate, felt weak, felt... He felt like a coward. A lifetime away from that carefree young man of smiles and good cheer. Now he, the youth once near manhood, was no more than a helpless childish fool following a mother figure in a world totally alien to him.

Weary of riding the serpent's tail, he searched for a space to call sanity. He could clearly see the crowd beneath him. He had a bird's eye view, could see them moving their dials and domes, could see them studying their computerized screens. He could see it all and, oh, how it terrified him.

Johanna had once again been right. They hadn't been spotted by one of the hundreds of pairs of globular eyes, had not become part of that blood bath the creatures had so badly wanted to see. His banner, his power and strength had seen him through yet again. Johanna was his everything. With death at his door, his darkest hours were lightened without end by the light of his life. How could she not possibly be his everything?

It wasn't long before she reached the bubble. She turned her honey-coated head to gaze back at him a second, her eyes glowing with loving sparkles.

"Stay there now, okay? Just stay there. You're safe." Sliding up against the bubble, she eased herself under it, holding on tightly, then lowered herself down to the footrest. "Don't fail me now, Harry," she mumbled through beads of icy sweat as she turned a large steel wheel.

Slowly it moved, a set of iron disks slipping apart like the serrated teeth of a large circular mouth. Once inside the bubble, she waited a second to gain her breath. The bubble itself appeared much larger from the inside than it did from the outside. It seemed to reach in all directions, as if not finding a place to rest. Mighty silver tunnels spewed out from its center point where she was and each tunnel appeared to move like ghostly shadows on muddy water.

"Damn it!" she growled, knowing that only one of them would lead her to her ultimate goal. Moving away from the hole, she could see the arena down below. "Right. Now what?"

She knew she had to think fast, had to think very fast. Danny was waiting, waiting out there like a worm on a hook. She knew he was safe, knew he wasn't about to be detected by beings or a creature. However, she also knew he didn't know he was safe.

One of these tunnels would lead her to the Dagger of Teorna and she had to find it, just had to. "Which one, Harry, which one?"

The tunnels all looked the same, an infinite number reaching translucent tentacles around her. So many tunnels, so many choices. Although somehow a decision had just been made. She marched off, nearing a glimmer of an entrance. A sudden wind whipped up, the tunnel flashing translucent swirls. Words filled her head. 'Stay away, stay away', they seemed to cry.

"So much for instinct," she sighed almost angrily. "Harry? Where are you?"

Maybe the next tunnel would lead her to the dagger. On entering, she found a giant hexagonal mirror. She could see herself, could see the lines of wear and tear on her pretty face. Her hair was a mess. Those long flowing honey locks she'd always treasured so dearly, the long flowing honey locks she had so shampooed, conditioned and brushed so diligently, now were hanging loosely like wasted straws after a children's birthday party. Something moved behind her and she turned sharply to see who or what it might be but saw nothing. Nothing but tunnels, nothing but silvery glimmers stretching away. She turned back to the mirror, catching a reflection behind her again. She turned once more and again, saw nothing. Casting a fleeting glimpse into the mirror one last time, she did see something after all. A reflection, a figure. It was Harry.

"Harry," she beamed. "Harry, oh thank you!" Harry smiled back brightly, a comforting hand touching her right shoulder.

Now more than one reflection. She could see Eric, could see Eric standing with a tall policeman. She could see Danny holding out his loving arms. The Dagger of Teorna. Yes, she could see the Dagger of Teorna, too. Could see her mother and father, her best friend, Malin. She could see the bluish-gray beings dancing around each other and could clearly see the arena with all its entrances and exits marked out before her. The ghostly reflections moved, gradually swaying in wide circles. Harry faded out. Her mother and father, her best friend, Malin evaporated like mist blown away in the wind. Slowly, slowly the reflections disappeared, until once again, she found herself alone.

All of a sudden she could see bodies. Piles of bodies. Arms and legs, bleeding and savagely torn. A grave. A headstone. Thick blood trails seeped around the words engraved into it. It was Rutter's headstone. She closed her eyes tightly, shaking her head in a useless attempt at escaping the heartbreak about her.

"No!" she screamed, raising clenched fist high into the air. Fear, mixed with anger, took her by the shoulders, sent her raging out of control. Then she was moving, charging forward, fists tight and solid, lunging out. There came a loud crack, then a deep searing pain. Slivers of glass fell away and a crimson cascade danced about her. She was bleeding and bleeding badly, the mirror before her gone. On turning she could see the Dagger of Teorna once more. All the other tunnels were gone and now she found herself in a large flat-floored dome. The dagger rested in all its glory. A curved silver blade and diamond encrusted, golden handle on a panel surrounded by thousands of buttons and switches.

Danny waited worriedly inside the thick red tube. The crowd beneath him cheered high pitched clicka-di-click choruses. The iron cage door opened up, fifteen or so figures falling out into the arena. The fur-ball waited, watched their every terrified move. A deep and gaping hole appeared in the ground, two young men tumbled in and out of sight. Seconds later it opened again, ruby red plumes reaching high in the air. The fur-ball swung itself around, huge arms were outstretched, catching a victim with fatal blows. Credits fell into boxes, fingers fell swiftly on domes, beings becoming decidedly richer or decidedly poorer, with each and every bet.

Just then Johanna reappeared. She climbed back out and onto the tube. The Dagger of Teorna clutched safely in her left hand, thick trails of blood tainting its gold and silver sheen.

"Follow me onto the next tube," she ordered. "Climb under the bubble, quick."

She clamped the dagger tight between her teeth and Danny followed without hesitation. His leg slid over the tube before coming to rest on the footrest. He righted himself and reached out, grasping for a secure grip. He hauled himself up and onto the other side. The tube stretched on toward a rocky cliff side just below another small spherical opening.

At last they were there, Johanna was first to reach and stand on solid ground. She held out a hand, helping Danny into the cave. In that cave opening, they rested, seating themselves on the rocky earth.

"Jesus, Johanna. You're bleeding like a stuck pig." He took her bloodied hand, noting a deep, open gash in her third finger

The Maze   239

and knuckle, so deep and open, the bone could clearly be seen.

"It's nothing," she replied. She raised her hand high above her head. Then taking the dagger in the other, she placed it on the bleeding tear. "Heal me."

Danny watched in astonishment, stared unblinkingly, his eyes wide, concentrating on the flow of red dripping from her once creamy white hand. Slowly, the flow lessened and seconds later, it stopped entirely. The gash closed up and the excess blood on both hand and earth faded out. He could see the gash, could see how it was and could see how it was vanishing into her skin.

"What the...? What the hell, Johanna?" He inhaled heavily, exhaled in much the same manner. His eyes grew wide, flicked wildly as if trying to escape such goings on. "What the hell are you?" he snapped without thought. "What the hell are you? This ain't normal. You ain't normal." His eyes, that glare, that anger inside him. Was he afraid? Was he afraid, angry and confused beyond compare? Or, did it really matter? "What the hell did you just do?"

"Danny, listen to me." She paused, unsure of what to say. The words were there, were gathered and ready to march. However, the force to move them on was far behind in some remote and distant corner of her brain. "Look..."

It took some time for her to use that army of syllables on her tongue, some time before they were ready to be lead toward victory. However, in time, she did.

"I'm me. I've always been me. Don't ask me to explain things to you, Danny. I can't. Can you just trust me a short while longer?"

"Mmm."

"Everything's going to be fine. I know it. Believe me, it's true." A deep sadness came on her and Danny noticed it directly.

"When I was away from you, when I was alone, well, when I was five hundred years in the past, even though I wasn't at all, I was to be tried as a witch. The year was 1666 and I was going to be killed. You were my strength, Danny. You still are."

She took his left hand and squeezed it gently, a sweet smile gracing her lips.

240 Gavin Hill

"You see, I need you. Without you, I'm nothing. I might as well just curl up and die. You're all that's real to me."

Danny smiled back, her words warming him, a lone crusader, the knight returning from slaying the fire-breathing dragon. Heading home to that fortress up high in the 'Sunny Mountains' to claim his princess, magnificent. He was still the champion of love. He was needed, he was somebody.

The tension was broken. For a moment, it was a thousand miles away. A moment of memories, of smiles past. They held each other tenderly like young lovers do and they let their young souls meet for fleeting glimpses of sanity. Nothing but the pounding of heartbeats filled their ears, nothing but the gentle caressing touch of fingers, skin on skin. Two, for moments became one.

Johanna flicked strands of honey cord away from her face. "You know none of this is real, don't you?"

"Not real? What d'ya mean, not real?"

She sniffed loudly, although not disgustingly, her eyes dusting each silvery pink crack and cranny. Her mind drifted back to Rutter, that man not yet born, with the heart of gold and the courage of steel. That man from the future, a prisoner in an alien world. Was he not real? He appeared to be real, appeared to be more than real. Maybe she had just wanted him to be real—she just didn't know.

"It's not real, Danny. None of this is real."

"Oh yeah, and what about Eric then?"

Words. What were words anyway? Words—just groups of blind letters placed together in specific formation. The smallest single meaningful unit of speech or writing. One, just one of the things which helped a man or woman become what they were today. Just words but Johanna couldn't find any. She couldn't find the words she so desperately needed.

The farmer back in Bodmin in 1944. He must have been real, just had to be. How could he not be? If he wasn't real, if he was just some crazy part of the imagination, if he, just like the Maze and everything within it wasn't real, then why, oh why was Eric dead?

She had to answer a question, a question without an answer, and how difficult it was. "That's the only thing I don't understand. But wait, tell me where we are? Look about and tell me what you see?"

He sighed heavily, what kind of game was this anyway? He knew, of course, he did. There was no answer, even knew that. She had just changed the subject, even though it seemed to be such a stupid thing to do. "I see rocks, we're in a cave. I see light coming in from over there. And you, well, you're avoiding my question."

"No, no I'm not," she replied softly. "I see no entrance. Look again."

He did, surprised to find that she was right. The tunnel stretched on in both directions seemingly without end. He stared, scratched his head, rubbed his chin and looked decidedly confused. "But... What now? Where's it gone then?"

"It's here. It hasn't gone, I can see it. The point is, which is real? I don't know, I really don't. I keep thinking I might wake up back on the ferry to Holland. Keep thinking we might both wake up in Gothenburg with my father. The thing is, neither of us know what is real." Slowly, she eased herself up and onto her tired, sore feet. "The Maze isn't real either. Or at least, I don't think it is. The only thing that's really important is that we come out of this in one piece. It's a game, this is a game. We're part of the game. It's mind over matter, Danny. A case of believing in the truth, of not believing in anything else."

That sounded good, she thought to herself, silently patting herself on the back. Sounded convincing. She didn't really know if talking, if trying to explain something she knew nothing about was better or worse than just keeping quiet. The most important thing was that he, her beloved Danny, feel just a little more at ease with the whole situation. She knew it hurt him, all the uncertainties, all the not knowing. She could plainly see the pain in his eyes. A chance to take some of that hurt and that pain away, to banish it to some distant horizon, was all she had ever wanted to do.

Chapter 12
The Continuation

They set off along the tunnel. It soon became much wider. Huge stalactites protruded from a rustic red roof, stalagmites reaching upwards like fangs of death. Red and orange beams of light shone at their tips. The temperature rose by slow degrees, damp and burning slightly, making the going much more difficult. A vapor mist closed in, rising, bellowing, engulfing them, swirling like breeze-whipped fog on a midnight moor.

Danny's legs felt weak, felt as if they would burst at any moment. He found himself in desperate need of rest. Struggling to keep up with Johanna, he stumbled all the time. Just then, an object shone in the far distance, something twisting and turning, getting larger, getting closer all the time.

"Danny," Johanna said loudly, although not worriedly. "Concentrate hard now, okay? Believe me, just imagine you're a thousand miles away. Think of home."

A scalding breeze blew into their faces, rushing about them, burning dry.

"Help, we're gonna die," he yelled as he forced both hands upward to shield his eyes. He began to choke, to gasp for air and it hit him then that death was only moments away. "I can't breathe."

The world swirled about him. Around and around and.... moving all the time. Burning hands touched his flesh, melting down to the bone. His legs gave way and he tumbled heavily to the scorching earth below.

Johanna bent down, resting at his side. "Concentrate!" she screamed. "Concentrate, God damn you!"

Her skin was cool, fresh to the touch. A second to think, she lifted the dagger, taking the ring finger of his right hand and drawing the blade firmly across it. It sank into his flesh, blood gushing from the open wound. A pained cry escaped through his parted lips. He raised his right hand, free of hers now, rising up speckled red to meet his left hand.

"Hey! What did you do that for?"

His head filled with silence, momentarily numb. His body no longer burned, those deathly, fiery swirls gone. The cave was damp. The walls were solid granite, like tombstones in a forgotten world.

"What the...?"

"I'm sorry, Dan. Look at your finger."

If looks could kill, then death would have come her way that very moment. His face echoed his disapproval, his expression much less than grateful. "What the hell should I see? I'm bleeding!"

"How did it look before I cut it?"

He raised his finger to his dry lips, tasting the salty sting of his own blood. He said nothing, shocked at the stupidity of her questioning.

"Try and imagine your finger as it was, before you cut it."

"I didn't cut it, Johanna. You did!"

"How did it look?"

"What are you now, Johanna, a shrink?"

"Danny, please. Just take it away from your mouth and imagine."

That was it. With his patience all dried up, he jumped to his feet with fury burning through him. "Screw you!" he yelled back, marching off.

Johanna didn't respond. She understood his ignorance, although his lack of trust and foul language, she most certainly did not. He marched on a little further, slowed his long strides down to a stroll then stopped completely, turning once more to face her. His eyes lifted from narrow slits of anger to his usual distant gaze. His finger still rested in his mouth, a slight blood trail dancing loosely on his solid, stubbly chin. Thoughtfully, he removed his finger as if examining it, trying to imagine it as it had been before the blade had sliced into it. His eyes grew wide in bewilderment. He was stunned, amazed at the sight of what was happening. Slowly each blood trail vanished. Like a video film in reverse, the open gash faded into the surrounding skin. By the time his hand was back to normal, Johanna was by his side.

"Good, Danny," she said helpfully. "See, you can do it." She took him by the hand and strolled on a while before stopping to find a place of rest. "Let's stay here for now, Dan. We need to keep our strength up."

Danny seated himself, staring long and hard at his finger, not wanting to imagine it any other way. He was speechless.

"I know this isn't easy for you, Dan." She made herself comfortable, resting her head against his right shoulder before going on. "When we were apart, you and I, I… well… I was in some pretty strange places. I was in a place called, 'Second Earth'. Forget your finger now, Dan. It's over. Anyway, Second Earth was real, I'm sure of it. Second Earth is what might happen if you and I don't find the Dark Fortress."

Danny cut in, abruptly interrupting her explanation. "You weren't gone long enough to be all over the universe. What, maybe ten, fifteen minutes?"

She went on. "It's not important. I met a man called Rutter who became my best friend. We were surrounded by death, forced to work for a master race and for a while there, I thought I would never get to return to you. The point is, I did. The point is that anything is possible if only we trust in ourselves."

A glistening tear mounted her lower eyelash, a sadness inside her seeping to the surface. "I took Rutter as far as I could, but he was real. Eric, too."

Danny had been listening carefully to her every word. Nothing really made any sense, nothing to write home about. He

The Maze 245

still didn't have the answers he so wanted to hear. Words like Rutter and Second Earth meant nothing to him. So she had been there and she had met him. One thing puzzled him and another intrigued him. What was the Dark Fortress? And who, or what, lived there?

Johanna had been to the future. Part of him wanted to know what was in store for mankind. Another part wanted to forget the whole thing, to pack up and go home. The last part of him, the doubting Thomas inside him, wanted to put everything on hold. Why believe without seeing with one's own eyes? He wasn't going to ask, just wasn't. No, he had made up his mind. The future—who cares? Who really needs to know? Important? Of course not. He sat quietly, letting things roll around in his head.

"What's the future? You've seen it, what's it like?" There, he'd said it. Stupid, stupid, stupid, he thought to himself. Well, at least he knew he was now to receive a good answer.

"It's bad, that's all. Real bad."

Was that it? Was that the answer to the question of the century? He sighed, sniggering slightly. "What's the matter?" she wanted to know.

"Nothing. Where's this Rutter bloke then?"

"He, um. He..." A second's pause like a thousand years washed over her. The future, a memory. Tomorrow, her past. "He's dead," she said solemnly. "You can't change reality, only the sub-conscious. He's dead and buried. I've seen his grave-stone."

Danny wrapped an arm about her, holding her close, his guideline to a better day. "The Dark Fortress. What's that then?"

"I don't know," she replied frankly. "Just a name I found in my head, really. I don't know where it came from. And, and I don't know what it is. We must find it though, come on."

Again they set off, words bursting to escape just moments ago, now spent. Danny's head felt slightly clearer, slightly more understanding to the task in hand. He didn't know why. After all, the only answers Johanna had given him were answers any old fool could have given. Nevertheless, he felt better for hearing a fool's answers. Somehow he felt good. This was it, the confrontation, the final conflict. Soon, he felt sure he'd meet a much higher force. Could be God, the maker of all things. Could be heaven, a fortress in the sky. Could be hell, indeed, it could be hell. So much had happened, so much confusion and mass destruction passing through in avalanches of that young mind. Ravaging, smashing, raping him of all he'd ever considered good and wholesome. His head felt clearer now, the cobwebs lifting, untangling his muddled brain. For the first time in a long time, he felt the will to fight, to stand up and to live.

The cave seemed to go on without end, stretching away in the distance, like being trapped within the gut of a monster snake. The cave veered from left to right, weaving into the giant, rocky walls before finding its path once more. Silence surrounded them. Silence, that is, except for the tip-tap of their own footsteps and the drip-drip-drip of water seeping in from above.

Danny pushed on just a few feet behind Johanna. Great, he felt great, felt all-powerful. As long as he could complete the puzzle, as long as he could come to terms with it all, he knew nothing could possibly bring him back down. To put the pieces together though, that was the problem. They didn't really fit. It didn't matter how he jumbled things over in his head, didn't matter how he tried to place them together, they just didn't fit.

The tunnel gradually sloped downwards, making the going much easier.

"Johanna, where are you?" he asked, suddenly finding himself alone. Johanna was gone, had disappeared without a trace. "Johanna! Hey, Johanna!" He gazed around in all directions, but there was nothing. She had just vanished.

Johanna turned sharply, seeing nothing but the tunnel meandering away from her. Worriedly, she scanned the area, hearing his frightened call.

"Johanna, where are you?"

Just then she caught a glimpse of a head. It was Danny's. "Danny, stop! Don't move!"

"Shit, Johanna. There's something on my bloody leg!"

She moved back, kneeling down. "Danny, listen to me now. Turn around and walk, just walk. Do it, do it now!"

Slowly his head turned in the rocky earth, his shoulders

The Maze   247

and within time, his waist reappearing until he was back on her level. "My leg! Ah, my leg!" he growled, his ankle already growing red and swollen.

"Concentrate, Dan."

"I thought I was, Christ's sakes."

Again they set off; Danny's head a hive of activity. He tried to dismiss the pain in his leg, but still it throbbed, a burning ache. What had he just done? He was sure the tunnel had begun to slope, sure he'd just walked along following the path straight ahead. He felt exhausted, every muscle in his body suddenly screaming for release.

"Hey, can't we stop a moment? I'm exhausted."

"We're getting close now, Dan. I can feel it. You rest here; I'll just go up ahead and take a quick look." She left him and trudged off.

"Ah, wait up, I'm coming."

The Cave began to widen at an exceptional rate. In the space of mere footsteps, the distance between the two walls had reached a good mile. Looking on ahead, it appeared to come to an end, fresh warm, caressing sunlight seeping in. The rocks below their feet gave way to gravel and further along, into soft yellow sand. A light breeze gently embraced them, their nostrils inhaling a soft, salty air. The rush of rolling waves brought memories of Bournemouth. Foaming ridges of blue washed over a golden shoreline. Sea gulls flew by overhead, dive-bombing the shimmering surface in search of a meal.

Danny marvelled at the sight before him. Yes, the cave was gone, they had made it. Was this now Bournemouth? Ah, surely not? No wait, maybe it was. Yes, yes it was. Bournemouth, glorious Bournemouth. Yes—there, the Pier and Pier Theater, the amusement arcade. Yes, yes it was Bournemouth. They were back, yes back in the wonderful seaside town of Bournemouth.

Johanna strolled on toward the water's edge. She looked beautiful. Her hair danced in lapping waves, riding out behind her like honey flares. He stopped, seeing her walk out across the rolling crests. Within time he too found himself walking out across the waves like our Lord Jesus Christ had done so many hundreds of years ago. He smiled boyishly, a child with a new toy. Unable to understand why he was not sinking into those watery depths, but then still he enjoyed the sensation below his tired feet.

"Johanna," he beamed. "This is great. This is bloody brilliant. My feet feel great." She turned her pretty head, tossing her honey flares like firework displays on July Fourth.

"Come on, it's not far now. Should all come to an end soon. Look, the tunnel's getting wider."

Getting wider, he thought to himself, *but isn't it gone?*

"Jesus," he whispered, concentrating harder all the time. Slowly, the wishy-washy sway of waves faded out, replaced by a drip-drip-drip, the sky becoming shafts of gray.

"Okay, we can rest here, Dan." She sat down, leaning squarely against a large pinkish-blue boulder. Danny rested at her feet and his faithful gaze rose to meet and embrace hers. Bodies relaxed in the near silence about them and in time, Danny found the doors of sleep opening up for him to pass through. Johanna didn't sleep. She wanted to sleep, dear God, how she wanted to sleep. Those doors to the world of sleep awaited her; indeed they beckoned her, but sleep... She just couldn't.

Suddenly, a figure loomed before her.

"Harry," she whispered, not wanting to waken her sleeping prince. "Thank goodness, you came. I knew you would in the end." The figure ahead of her blurred somewhat, drifting in and out of view. "Harry, Harry, don't do this to me." Danny fidgeted, hearing Johanna's voice somewhere in the murky distance. Colors formed in Johanna's head. Twists and twirls dancing and rolling, swaying and intermingling into flashes of molten gold. Days passed, lifetimes passed. Rutter as a youth. The death of his mother. His death and gravestone. The farmer in Bodmin, 1944. Cheerful and smiling in his kitchen, his two black Labradors at his side. Grindle back in 1666. The creation of all things. Stars and planets, milky ways and universes. Hundreds of images riding around, voices filling her ears. Children playing by a river's edge, picnics by the seaside. Rainy summer afternoons and snowy winters by a large open fire. Christmases gone by, both in England with her mother and in Sweden with her father,

The Maze   249

Christmases possibly to come. Birthdays and Easters, Mother's Day and Father's Day. Holidays and school days.

She jumped inside as the visions faded and reality took hold of her once more.

"Were you talking to someone? There's nobody here. Who were you talking to?"

"Harry," she replied nervously. "It was Harry."

"Harry?"

"Yes, Harry. He can't come any farther. This is it, we're here."

"Here? Where's here?"

"On the edge of the Maze, I guess. We must have made it through."

"Yeah, that's good, right?"

"I guess so."

The arena had begun to fill once more as level three started. Out of seventeen pawns in the first two games of level one, only four had survived, only three in level two. Now, just as Eric had attempted his first level, second and almost third, terrified victims were preparing themselves to meet their maker. Preparing to fight for their very lives, preparing to die, to meet their grizzly ends in the name of good fun.

All of a sudden the earth opened up, huge fountains of boiling lava spraying up and into the air, falling down like devil raindrops on the arena floor. Those who hadn't been felled within the first few moments of level three ran in vain toward a small opening in the far wall. The choice, to die in the arena or to clear a set of razor sharp spears that had been strategically placed in the ground just before the entrance.

Danny and Johanna waited, neither knowing what might happen next, neither knowing what might lie on the other side of the Maze. Light flooded in on them, particles of dust floating a gentle dance, riding on crystal beams of sun light like silver-winged horses riding an invisible plain.

"Danny, hold onto me. Hold me tight and close your eyes. This is it."

He did as she suggested, pulling himself in close, feeling her neat form, warm and comforting against his. The ground beneath their feet began to move, turning gentle under them. A wind whipped up, violent and angry, twisting and twirling, cutting about them. He held her firmly, too afraid to reopen his eyes, too afraid even to move.

Suddenly the earth was gone, slipping away into the depths of nothingness. Down they fell, plummeting through their own inner most fears. The wind raged, whistled past their ears. Their mouths were forced open under sheer pressure, a silent scream struggling to escape Danny's out stretched lips. Down, down, down...

Down through the thousand faces of the Maze, they tumbled. Gradually, their descent eased and they found themselves back on solid ground as if they had never been away from it. Gradually, they opened their eyes, nervously scanning their surroundings.

"Johanna," he faltered. "Where the..."

Nerves crunched, crawled inhumanely deep down inside in fear. Not just fear, but an intense pain, angels rejoicing the beauty, come-horror of this place. He felt afraid, yes, he felt afraid. Afraid and terrified, yet he felt happy, felt certain all the time.

All about them lay space. No sky, no earth, no walls, no trees, no life. Nothing but space and a feeling from inside him. A feeling, a strange feeling, a feeling of life and of death. A feeling of pure evil. A feeling of darkness and a feeling of light, a feeling unknown and yet known. Just a feeling.

"Shit, this is weird. Where are we?"

"This is where our worst fears lie. This is the beginning of all things and the end of all things. The land of all things bad. This is where creation begins, here in the 'never.' It's also where we can find Pezzarius."

Danny didn't reply straight away. Instead, he let that name, that equally strange name run through his head time and time again. It was a name he'd never heard before, although a name that somehow sounded familiar to him. In time, he found himself able to ask.

He turned around, lightly scanning the emptiness around him and scratched the top of his head thoughtfully before speaking. "Who?"

The Maze   251

"Pezzarius. The evil that lives within us, the one who causes mankind to do such wrongs on Earth."

Suddenly, she looked quite surprised, the realization of what she'd just said. Where such words were coming from, she didn't really know. They just seemed to spout from her lips, almost as if she was an authority in such matters. "Life on Earth is just a testing ground, just a beginning. Throughout time, evil has been at constant war with the forces of good. We all have our own names for such." She seated herself, not feeling the touch of earth beneath her small, rounded bottom. Danny followed her lead, resting beside her, hungry for the truth. "We all have names that we use. All over the world, language by language, they're different."

Danny listened intently, only the odd sound or indescribable feeling tearing him away. Sounds, so many sounds. Sounds from within and sounds from without. Sounds from nowhere and yet sounds from everywhere. Just sounds.

"We use the word, God. Protestants have a God, Catholics and Jews have a God. Indians, tribesmen in the jungles have gods. God is just seen in different ways, given different names. There is only one God and one Devil. The names don't really matter and this is where neither and yet, either dwell.

The pain in Danny's leg had returned. It intensified, chewing away at his flesh.

"Where'd the name, Pezz..." He stopped abruptly, something catching his eye. Something shining in the distance. Something growing, separating, a thousand lights a glow. "What's that?"

Johanna jumped to her feet, helping him up. The air was suddenly alive, huge balls of light crossing overhead before swooping down around them.

"Stand behind me," she said loudly. She raised the Dagger of Teorna high into the air, striking out at the fearsome balls. The blade edge swung angrily this way and that, a ball of light breaking up and flying in all directions into a million sparks. "Okay, run!" She took his hand and charged off, the lights suddenly gone.

Within seconds they found themselves standing before a

mighty fortress. Lanterns hung in each window. A long, high wall surrounded the massive building and there was an entrance right in front. Two large stone gargoyles stared down at them, their evil eyes like knives slicing through butter.

Danny's heart turned to ice as they stepped forward, passing through into a seemingly endless courtyard. Towering pillars of stone lined both sides of a long and wide pathway. Upon each pillar stood a statue. Creatures, half-man, half-beast. Each portrayed an evil force, built of man's own nightmares.

Danny wanted to speak, wanted to get things off his chest, wanted to break down and tell his beloved Johanna just how frightened and desperately lost he was in this world so alien to him. He felt the urge to express his true feelings. Only his foolish pride stood in the way. Words bubbled up inside, rose and marched to the tip of his tongue. There they waited equally lost, then rested before bolting and finding safety. As fearful as those words inside him were, he just swallowed them time and time again.

As they moved on in silence toward an immense metallic door, he felt the agonizing burn in his leg once more.

"Ah, my leg," he moaned. "It's killing me."

Johanna smiled kindly, gliding a finger back and touching his arm. "Concentrate," she recommended helpfully. "It's not real, it's your imagination, that's all."

He gazed down at the tear in his jeans, just below the knee. "That's my imagination?"

On reaching the metallic door, Johanna forcefully pushed it open, a loud creak shrieking its objection. She marched on in without apparent fear, and Danny could only follow. As they both entered, the door slammed shut with a thunderous clap.

"I think we're expected," he gulped, his throat tight with apprehension.

Johanna didn't reply, she knew what had to be done. A long corridor stretched out before them leading to a spiral staircase. "Danny, you can't come any further," she whispered sadly. "You must stay here."

He took her by the right hand, letting his fingers touch and caress it lovingly. "I'm coming with you."

"No, you are not!"

Her face screamed her pain. A salty crystal tear lifted and floated before sliding away. She wrapped her arms about him, a moment of warmth, of security before leaving. For the first time in a long time, she, too, felt lost and afraid. The young Johanna, expressions of loss and of great sadness adorning her features. Just as in Gothenburg, when innocence and schoolgirl uncertainties were all that she had. Then, before all this. Before her encounter with Hazzari, known now as Harry, key holder of the Maze.

Useless, she once thought. Danny wasn't useless and now she knew that more than ever. He was her spark plug, her giver of energy and her unstoppable strength. Her power plug came from him. He was her giver of life. And her spark plug, she was about to leave behind. Useless? Not, not her Danny.

"I must do this alone, Danny. It's the only way. Please, you must understand, it's the only way."

She held him tightly, so tightly, not wanting to let him go. Not wanting to leave the one who sparked her life behind, that giver of energy and of unstoppable strength. "You'll be safe here. I'll be back when it's all over, okay?" She cried into his solid shoulders.

"I'm scared, Johanna." There, he had said it. It was off his chest. "I'm really scared. Not what you need to hear, I guess."

The urge to break down rolled through him at a staggering rate, his true feelings finally dampening her shirt as tears slid down his cheeks.

"It's, it's just..." he sniffled. "I just wish we could leave all this shit, get back to what we had. I love you. You gotta believe that, I do."

Johanna pulled away, finding the power deep inside to go on. "I'll be back soon, Danny."

Their lips, damp and salty, touched one last time and she was gone. Helplessly, Danny stood watching as she headed off down the spiral staircase. She looked back just one last time before disappearing out of sight.

He fell to his knees, tunnelling dirty fingers through his shoulder length dark curls of hair. The pain in his leg intensified again, slowly burning. He seated himself on the top step of the spiral staircase and gazed at the rip in his jeans. He tore them just a little more, noticing the deepness of the wound underneath. His stomach turned somewhat on seeing it.

"No, it's not real," he growled. "Just my imagination."

The wound was only small, little more than a hole. Although as he studied it, he could clearly see it ooze, pulsating veins. An agonized screech left his tired frame, echoing about him. The wound turned steadily to a sickly green before his very eyes, spreading up his leg, the skin rippling before peeling away to reveal damp, seething flesh.

"No! Ah, God, no!"

He gritted his teeth, grasping at his leg, his whole body throbbing without control. A sound ripped through his head, voices screaming. Thousands of voices, deathly, child-like calls for help. He raised a shaky hand to his forehead, feeling the heat burn through into it.

"No, hell no! Ah, God, Harry, where the hell you are?"

A sudden crack tore through his broken frame. He choked, gasping for air, coughing and spluttering thick red globules.

Johanna stopped at the bottom of the staircase. It was an exceptionally long staircase; spiralling seven full turns before finally reaching a hallway. She could feel a presence about her, a presence that couldn't be defined. It was cold, evil, waiting as if to pounce. The hallway before her stretched on until disappearing into nothing, just disappearing into a vast empty space of nothingness.

Seven large wooden doors, three to the left and four to the right, were carved with a face of evil deep into the wood. She wanted to leave, wanted to turn and run away, wanted to return to the strength and power of her lover's arms. More than anything she wanted to return to her world, back to all the comforts it so readily offered.

She turned to take one last look at the staircase, the staircase that would lead her back to her beloved Danny. The staircase, was still there. Or was it? There should be a staircase. Yes, she saw it now. It was there. She had descended it, all seven full turns of it. She wasn't crazy. Yet when she looked again, she

The Maze   255

saw nothing. Behind her the hallway disappeared. Beyond it, nothing but darkness.

Suddenly, she could hear crying. The terrified screams of children calling in vain for their mothers. Old people praying for forgiveness. Each door started to rattle, ghostly shapes filling the foul smelling air. Distorted faces, bodies torn and bleeding. A figure in the distance staggered, falling toward her.

"Oh my God. Harry, help me," she uttered, holding the Dagger of Teorna tightly.

Only inches away stood the half-decomposed body of Eric. Insects crawled in and out of his stinking, rotten flesh. Those hard beetle-like bodies rattled up against each other, gnawing away at his internal organs. He raised a blood-soaked hand to his face, laughing all the time. An index finger crawling with maggots gradually drew across his cheek, his nose falling away, dropping to the ground.

Johanna shook her head fearfully. "No, no you're not real!" she yelled at the top of her voice.

She raised the dagger and prepared to strike out at the abomination before her. It stopped laughing, cowering back.

"No, Johanna, don't kill me. I'm your friend." Piece by piece the face began to change. Flesh returned, skin soft and pale until he was the same old Eric she had learned to love so much. "Don't hurt me, I love you," he whispered sadly. A tear lifted and danced a waltz down his cheek. She paused a moment, visualizing him as she'd last seen him. The way he'd looked before his horrific death. "Take my hand, Johanna. We can be together now, be as one. Please don't hurt me."

His voice was soft and gentle, his words playing on her badly battered mind. Thoughts ran through her tired head. Thoughts, memories of days gone by. Thoughts of days to come. She hesitated, remembered her first encounter with that child who had quickly became a man. Then he was on the ground, tin cans rattling about him. A youngster with a knife in his hand. That was her Eric, the Eric she'd left behind in the Maze. This Eric, this wasn't her Eric.

"No!" she screamed, swinging the dagger down and letting it sink deep into Eric, but not Eric's, throat. The blade struck flesh and bone, blood gushing from a gaping wound. Seconds passed, the fear inside her holding her motionless to the spot. The dagger was clear, loose in her right hand, blood dripping pitter-patter to the ground below.

The head rotated, eyes spinning in their sockets. Lips, large and bloated, chattering up and down. Gaining strength once more, she lunged again, sending the head spiralling through the air. The torso fell, twisting and turning until still.

"Bitch! You killed me, bitch! I'll get you, by the blood of Pezzarius, I'll get you!" Johanna lifted her hands to her ears as the creature screamed around her, echoing in her brain. "You bitch, you'll die, bitch! I'll get you!" Slowly she stepped forward, fast congealing blood sliding like lava flows onto her hand from the upward pointing knife. "Bitch! Gonna die, bitch! I spit on you, slag!"

"Oh, shut up!" Her fingers, damp and sticky, played along the diamond-encrusted handle.

"Bitch! Gonna die, bitch! I spit on you, you fuck!"

Suddenly the dagger moved, fell down with a surge of strength, coming down full force. There came a crunch, the blade disappearing, the head falling in two. Now she found herself in silence, the ghostly figures gone along with the bloody, torn body of her old friend.

"Harry," she sobbed fearfully. "I wish you were here, Harry." She stood a while, not quite knowing what to do next. There was, however, only one way to go, the choice was a single one. She just had to go on.

Seconds later the fear roiling inside her disappeared. Like the rejoicing of angels, it was gone. Gone, thankfully, all gone. Banished into the darkness that had surely created it. Then she was enveloped in a warmth, a warmth that eased her and caressed her with loving embraces. It felt like Hazzari. Could it be Hazzari? It felt like his power, his supreme power reviving her, giving her life where life was once gone.

She smiled meekly and set off along the corridor. She stopped, set off once more then stopped again. Something strange, something very, very strange was happening. She was alone, totally alone. She had to be alone, she thought as she

The Maze 257

glanced around her, there was no one or nothing else there with her. She looked sharply about in all directions once more, only to confirm the fact she was indeed alone. Although she felt she was being watched by something menacing with glaring invisible eyes, driving like knives into her flesh.

It wasn't Hazzari, she knew. The hairs on her soft pink neck rose steadily to attention, standing rigid.

"Show yourself!" she demanded.

She heard a sound. Only a slight, distant sound. The sound of a whistle of wind and a crack. Then that of fire burning wildly in a virgin forest, the ferocious, hungry flames forcing branches to crackle and fall away. Louder now, the sound came. Louder, louder all the time. It circled about her, around her, reaching out to grab at her. A wind whipped up behind her, an icy chill rushing in avalanches down her spine. She turned full circle once more, very, very slowly. Almost afraid of what she might see.

The time had come; it was time to meet the darkest of all forces. Time to meet Pezzarius, Lord of Eternal Night. King of Death and of Hell Fire. As she turned, a man stood before her. His long black hair rode away from his scalp like tentacles of night and his eyes bore nothing except evil and pure hatred. It was he, the same man she'd encountered in her lounge back home in Sweden. He, the first of the two figures in a dream with his long iced black beard and flowing hair. He, who had spoken of Kadorele. Kadorele, what was Kadorele anyway? she wondered, her mind racing to grasp it. She only wished she knew.

Without thinking, she raised the Dagger of Teorna, thrusting out. A squeaky scream escaped her. She fell back, the dagger flying through the air, Pezzarius reached out and caught it before it fell. He laughed with a frozen boom, dragging his left index finger along the dagger's razor edge.

"You did well, you came a long way," he snickered. "Fun, wasn't it? I thought Grindle would take care of you. Never mind, he paid for his mistakes. As shall you!" He thrust an arm out in the air, a devil heat burning from his fingers. With that thrust, pictures were forming in her head.

"Do you see what I see?"

"Stop it!" she screamed, closing her eyes tightly and slapping her hands forcefully over her ears. "Stop it! Stop it, do you hear! Stop it!"

Screams roared from deep inside her, as she watched Grindle paying for his failures, his body torn beyond recognition, tied to a long metal pole.

"Stop it!" Her pleas went unheeded. His pain echoed in her mind, as long needle-like lengths of solid steel pierced his flesh. She fell to her knees, curling her body tight into a human ball.

"He's dead. You see now the power I possess? Nothing can destroy me. Not even you, my dear Kadorele, not even you."

It was over. Grindle's agonizing death was done with. Kadorele? She was Kadorele! Now she knew.

"You took the Dagger of Teorna. Well done. Very well done indeed. You and that fool boyfriend. He slowed you down, made you weak."

Johanna struggled against his power, but there it was again. Another picture entering her head. The end of a nation, the people of Teorna plagued by death and disease. The little blue-gray beings of Teorna, their leader dead, their arena in ruins.

"Quite wonderful, don't you think?" Pezzarius went on, aided by the visions he himself had created. "You stole the dagger, Kadorele. You stole it, you destroyed the last of a once mighty civilization. You, Kadorele, yes, it was you!"

The scene swam across her vision. Scenes of decomposing bodies, of foul and decaying flesh. She shook her head vigorously, trying to fight it off. All to no avail.

"It was Hazzari who made you steal, Kadorele. He's evil, he tricked you. Join me, Kadorele, join me and I'll take you to places beyond all imagination. Be my queen and together we shall rule creation."

"Never!" she screamed.

His eyes widened, a smile of evil intent. Suddenly she was falling. Down, down, down through an impending darkness. Her screams echoed through the vast emptiness about her, light gushing in from below. She twisted and turned like an unwanted rag doll until landing with a painful thud onto a rocky island of no more than ten or so feet from its center point. The island appeared to be floating on a lava ocean, molten fountains shooting high into a burning air. A whistle of wind rushed by and there he was, Pezzarius, standing strong and menacing before her once more. He laughed masterfully, lifting the dagger and casting it out into an ocean of red.

"I gave you your chance, now it's my time. Prepare yourself, Kadorele, for your kingdom awaits you!" His eyes gleamed like pools of tar, of stars in a devil sky.

Gradually he moved forward, forcing her closer to the molten rock. She shook uncontrollably, thick beads of sweat rising and drenching her skin before drying into tiny salty beads. She edged her way back, her face full and overflowing with fear. Inch by inch, her body weak and broken.

"Destroy me? As if you thought you could. I offer you your empire. I offer you the kingdom of Kadorele, it's named after you in the blood of all who dare to defy you, my queen." Closer, closer he moved in on her, swamping her with his deathly presence. "Your death is imminent and then, our souls can unite. You shall see the wonders of our world, and together, we shall rule supreme. Glory in death, I offer you and pain is ours for eternity. Hell fire and damnation, I give you!"

Just then the air turned a strange color and eruptions barrelled in at a staggering rate, happening so fast it barely registered in her confused brain. Behind her the lava swoons temporarily parted, the Dagger of Teorna rising up out of the fiery abyss. She caught it in her right hand as if it was where it wanted to be—home. Her body felt suddenly cool and fresh, a hidden strength escaping the diamond encrusted handle and entering her body. Courage regained, she lunged forward, plunging the dagger deep into an icy steel heart.

A roar, louder than that of a hundred lions, filled the boiling air and Pezzarius fell back on the rocky earth. He clutched at the dagger, still embedded in his writhing flesh. No time to think, she cast herself upon him, thrusting it deeper all the time. Around it twisted, blood avalanching gushes of red, almost knocking her back. With one last effort, she sank in her hand and ripped his still beating heart out of his chest.

"Yes, Pezzarius, now it is your turn. Time to pay for your wrong doings!" she raged.

A heart pulsated, damp and alive in the palm of her hand. She felt almost sick, the most disgusting thing she'd ever had to do. Her stomach churned, the urge to vomit burning her throat. The heart fell from her hand, landing on the ground with a gelatinous thud. She didn't even know why she had torn it out. She just had, that's all. Something deep down inside her told her to. Something moved behind her and she turned sharply to see what it might be. A figure hovered only inches above the lava mass, a figure she recognized.

"Danny?" she whispered, a tear dampening her cheek.

"Not all pains are imagined, my love. Now I fill my place on high. Take the heart and bury it now on the outskirts of the dark fortress. Spill nothing; you must bury the evil done here today and save mankind." With that he was gone.

"Danny! No, Danny, come back!"

She closed her eyes tightly, feeling an icy swell rise up behind them. On opening them once more, she found herself at the bottom of the staircase. The rocky island floating on its lava ocean, the entrance to the kingdom of Kadorele, was gone, left behind at the doorway to hell. The heart pumped weakly on the dusty floor as she watched.

After a moments thought, seconds echoing a millennium of her own heartache, she bent down and picked it up. It felt warm and sticky in her right hand, pulsating with unearthly life. She proceeded to climb, each step like a mighty mountain. The staircase appeared to go on forever, turning seemingly without end, with its spiral course.

Finally reaching the top, she rested a while to catch her breath, her hand dripping with blood, leaving thick trails behind her.

Staring into the distance, at the opposite end of the long, gloomy corridor she could just make out a body slouched across the floor.

"Oh, my God!" she sniffed sadly, walking to where the body lay. On reaching the corpse, she stopped, giving a moment of silent prayer. Tears flowed off her lashes, dancing a silver

The Maze 261

stream down her cheeks, the sight before her so gruesome. Danny, her lover and best friend, lay in a pool of foul stinking blood, his body torn apart, bare bone breaking through chewed flesh.

She fell to her knees. "Why? God damn it, why?"

"Don't cry, my love," a voice softly surrounded her. She turned to face an image, a translucent, ghostly form.

"Danny," she sobbed, her voice breaking under the strain.

"You must finish your task, Johanna. The heart must be buried alone on the outskirts of the dark fortress walls. Move with haste, for time is short."

Slowly she rose to unsteady feet, casting an eye of contempt at the heart resting in her hand. "Oh, Danny, it wasn't you, but me who was supposed to die. You should have gone home to your own world." Her eyes stung, red and tender with the tears of past memories.

"Don't cry for me," Danny went on, his words like swaying waves on a vast, sun-danced ocean. "We all have tasks to fulfill. See me not as dead for I am not. See me as resting in sleep, for tomorrow I shall be. With the coming of morning, your memories shall be gone. Your pain has never been. Now, go my love, your task is not yet done." He faded away, leaving her to complete the task in hand.

She stood a while, a solitary figure oblivious to the importance of the task she must do. Loneliness crept in like a strangulating weed. Everything she'd ever needed to go on, just memories in a day gone by. Her love for Danny, so intense, so much stronger than she had ever felt at any other time in her young life. Now it was all over, a holiday romance turned sour by the Maze and the pain within it.

She tried to imagine how it might be once her task was completed. How might it be, knowing that Danny had never been part of her life? That she had never met that handsome, dark haired teenager from Bournemouth? Had never talked to him, never shared her bed with him, never fallen hopelessly in love with him? Life without ever knowing who Danny was. How would it feel?

Sorrowfully, she left that place, pulling open the heavy metallic door and stepping outside. Ahead of her, the courtyard stretched on until meeting the outer wall. The scene this time was totally different. The stone pillars were gone, replaced by blossoming cherry trees. A sweet gentle breeze danced lightly on soft spring air. She smiled, realizing now she'd been responsible for closing the gates to the kingdom of Kadorele, that she and she alone, had been responsible for destroying Pezzarius, for ending his reign of terror. She had brought life to a world with nothing but death. She had lost two friends, two dear, dear friends, but what a small price to pay for the future of all mankind. Yes, she had a task to complete and it wasn't done yet.

The sun shone warmly above her. Young and alive, burning with tender excitement. Birds flew by overhead, their song welcoming the glory of life.

On reaching the main wall, she passed through the iron gates. Turning, she found a suitable place to bury the heart. She knelt down, digging into the dry earth with her bare hands. A deep wide hole was cut and the heart, dripping wet, dropped into it. This was it, her task, her final challenge drawing to a close. The good, the bad, the mystery within. All this was behind her now. All this evil locked away in the kingdom of Kadorele and there for all time to stay. She had made it through. The heart laid still and dead in the darkness of its prison. Grains of black fell in about it and after a time, totally covered it. Her nightmare gone, task done, she closed her eyes with a heavy sigh.

"I love you, Danny," she whispered softly, knowing she'd never get to say it again. Suddenly her ears filled with the clicki-di-click of steel wheels on silver tracks. On opening her eyes, she found herself back on the D237 to Denmark.

Epilogue
What Goes Around...

Eric woke with a loud yawn, then rolled over to look at his clock. The time on the dial read 09:15. He clambered out of the warmth of his bed, thrusting the duvet away from himself. Then reaching for his slightly faded blue dressing gown, he wrapped it around his semi-conscious frame and shoved his feet into a pair of tatty, threadbare slippers. He left his room, opening the door with a creak and stepped out onto the landing. The sun felt warm on his back as it cast rays through the small, spotless window behind him. The radio sounded downstairs, some old favorite winging its way throughout the house. He descended the stairway, the boards moving slightly at each touch of a step. A sweet and enticing aroma of toast and his grandmother's home made strawberry jam tickled its way under the old oak door. He reached for the handle, gave it a twist and pushed it open.

"Hi, Mom."

A sudden screech escaped his lips, his fingers clasping at the door handle, his body hanging precariously in the air. The kitchen was gone. Nothing but blackness beneath him.

Lightning Source UK Ltd.
Milton Keynes UK
24 March 2010

151771UK00001B/3/P